HISTORY'S PASSION

STORIES OF SEX
BEFORE STONEWALL

edited by
Richard Labonté

A Division of Bold Strokes Books

2011

HISTORY'S PASSION: STORIES OF SEX BEFORE STONEWALL
© 2011 BY BOLD STROKES BOOKS. ALL RIGHTS RESERVED.
INTRODUCTION © 2011 BY RICHARD LABONTÉ.
"CAMP ALLEGHENY" © 2011 BY JEFF MANN.
"HEAVEN ON EARTH" © 2011 BY SIMON SHEPPARD.
"TENDER MERCIES" © 2011 BY DALE CHASE.
"THE VALLEY OF SALT" © 2011 BY DAVID HOLLY.

ISBN 13: 978-1-60282-576-5

THIS TRADE PAPERBACK ORIGINAL IS PUBLISHED BY
BOLD STROKES BOOKS, INC.
P.O. BOX 249
VALLEY FALLS, NY 12185

FIRST EDITION: NOVEMBER 2011

CREDITS
EDITORS: RICHARD LABONTÉ AND STACIA SEAMAN
PRODUCTION DESIGN: STACIA SEAMAN
COVER DESIGN BY SHERI (GRAPHICARTIST2020@HOTMAIL.COM)

For Asa
Thanks for our past, our present, our future: our history

CONTENTS

INTRODUCTION: SOME WRITERS (AND READERS) LIKE THEM LONG

When I first started to edit erotic anthologies, back in 1997, the norm was for shorter short stories—4,000 words was the upper limit that writers in the genre tended to turn in, and most submissions were between 2,000 and 3,000 words. That was back in the day when the glossy gay mags (*Blueboy*, *Mandate*, *Drummer*, *Numbers*, *In Touch*, *Honcho*, *Torso*...) defined erotic fiction, and for all of them (*Drummer* was an occasional exception), most stories climaxed at that upper limit of 3,000 words.

So, more from habit than desire, cocks in the fiction were long but the fiction itself was short.

Over the years, though, writers who were less porn-genre oriented drifted over from more mainstream queer fiction outlets—a market is a market, after all—and I was receiving longer short stories, right up to the 4,000-word limit of the calls for submission. And, often with hopeful apologies appended, I started to receive 5,000 words' worth of sex. And the stories (was I becoming a size queen?) were often more satisfying reads. No surprise—writers were claiming more space for stronger character development, more intricate plots, and, tangentially, less-rushed sex scenes.

So these days I'm open to work as long as 7,000 words; one recent anthology contained an irresistible story that exceeded 9,000. So satisfying...a read that lasted all night long!

Add that trend toward longer stories to wistful e-mails from several writers yearning for a place to send their longer-than-short-story, not-quite-novel-length prose...and this anthology was born.

❖

Most often, introductions to erotic anthologies focus on either the editor's connection to the collection's theme, the broad subject of eros itself, or the individual stories. Instead, I want to talk about the four contributors to *History's Passions*.

I won't dwell on their other work; that's what author bios are for. I want to write about how we met. Or, more honestly, "met."

Simon Sheppard is the only one of the contributors with whom I'm in-the-flesh (not that way!) acquainted; we know each other from my years in San Francisco, where I lived from 1987 to 2001, and where he lives. His stories have appeared in maybe 30 of the 40 books I've edited over the years—a SmutSmith submission to the inbox is always a good day. He's a pro: meets deadlines, writes cleanly, accepts most of my (few) edits with good grace, and argues a good case whenever I've been an editor with one of my two typing fingers up my ass.

Have I ever met Jeff Mann? Probably (I know, I know, a good editor would fact check something like this), perhaps at one of the legendary OutWrite literary conferences in San Francisco or Boston, or at one of the five Readers & Writers Queer Literary Conferences that A Different Light Bookstore (which I then managed) coordinated in SF in the late 1990s. Anyway, what I said about Simon goes for Jeff. His writing is an editor's wet dream—and that has nothing to do with the sex scenes.

I know I don't "know" Dale Chase and David Holly. They're more recent emission-submission acquaintances, sending quality short stories to most of my anthology calls, and as with Simon and Jeff, they are an editor's blessing. They write to theme, they take the erotic as a given, crafting succulent stories within the genre—and they suffer my focus on commas with good grace.

So when Bold Strokes gave me the go-ahead for this unusual anthology, I invited Simon, Jeff, Dale, and David to suggest story ideas, both because I knew they could write and because a couple of them were repeatedly stretching the word limit for more bite-size collections. They all responded with alacrity. No reading 100 lackluster stories to find a good twenty-five, no winnowing that good twenty-five to a final fifteen. What fun for me. And what fine reading for you.

My only stipulation: set your stories in the days before Stonewall. For Simon, that was Depression-era America and sex on the run; for Jeff, the Civil War, where soldiers were more than bunkmates; for Dale, California's old-timey Gold Rush, where desperate fortune-seekers found release with the camp "boy"; and for David, the very queer era of Sodom and Gomorrah—four worlds the authors never lived in, but which they researched with diligence. The result? Lots and lots of sex, to be sure, supplemented with an authenticity of settings that reminds us that queers are everywhere—and have been "everywhen."

Richard Labonté
Bowen Island, British Columbia

CAMP ALLEGHENY
JEFF MANN

For Kent, Highland County historian
For John, my favorite Yankee

My little Virginian, it's hard not to stare at him. He brings up the rear of the regiment before mine. His winter coat's a short one, so I can watch his compact ass—twin curves in gray trousers—moving right in front of me as we march east up the gusty Staunton/Parkersburg turnpike. Sometimes I'm so close I could reach out and grab him, pull him to me, drag him off the road and into the woods. I'm twice his size; it would be easy enough.

I don't, of course. Not only would he most certainly object—and my mother raised me to be a gentleman, never to give undeserved offense—but, more to the point, my comrades might hang me for a sodomite. I learned long ago to keep my desires for other men, my "unnatural vice," as the preachers would call it, a secret.

As it is, the remnants of our little army—the Army of the Northwest, an exaggerated title for the twelve hundred men we have left—well, we all have bigger issues at hand. After months stationed at Camp Bartow, all those men lost to illness, and then an artillery battle by the Greenbrier River in October, and then more sickness, today we burned the bridge, right under the Yanks' noses, and our colonel, Edward Johnson, is pulling us back to Camp Allegheny. There, it's hoped, we can hold the turnpike and protect the Valley of Virginia from Yankees massing in the traitorous western mountains. We've got to hold them back and keep them out, God help us, no matter how bitterly cold that

mountaintop camp might be. The Confederate States of America, our
new country, depends on us.

Still, my glance keeps fixing on the boy's rear, on the sway of his
small shoulders and his lean hips, movements somehow both graceful
and manly, and the way his shaggy auburn hair glimmers when the
sun breaks through gray cloud and gives more light to this bleak late
November of 1861. He showed up a week back, and I haven't been
able to keep my eyes off him ever since. His youth and good looks help
me forget death for a while, and my kin back in Georgia. I'm so afraid
one of these whizzing Yankee balls will catch me in the head during a
skirmish and I'll never make it home to see them again.

A few miles along the switchback turnpike as it climbs the forested
side of Allegheny Mountain, Colonel Johnson gives us a rest. The
regiments halt, fall out, sit on stumps or lean against tree trunks to take
some nourishment. Around us the gloomy and leafless forest stretches,
silent except for a woodpecker rapping in the distance. I look west,
where the mountains unroll like gray waves, ridge after ridge of them.
The enemy's out there, and, knowing them, pertinacious Yanks, they'll
soon follow and we'll have another fight on our hands.

Instead of keeping company with the other Virginians, my compact
little man goes off by himself, sits wearily beneath a pine tree, and
unpacks his lunch. We're both loners, I can tell; we have that much
in common, along with our duty to the Confederacy. I see my chance.
I'm fond of my fellow Georgians—we've already seen a lot of battle
together since we left our home state behind—but I can't resist getting
closer to this Virginian. Even if he's married or with a sweetheart at
home, at least I can sit by him, take in his looks, perhaps even his scent.
He's as pleasing to the eye as my mama's biscuits were to my tongue,
those biscuits I dream about every night while my belly rumbles.

"Looks like you've no more rations than I," say I, sitting down
a few feet from him in the amber mat of pine needles. He looks up,
startled, not used to company, I guess. Deep blue eyes with long
lashes, a boyish face with high cheekbones and a pug nose, full and
slightly pouty lips, and, about them, a closely trimmed beard, chestnut
brown, like the thick hair framing his face. He's sitting cross-legged,
unwrapping a napkin from a piece of moldy cornbread.

"Old bread's all I got too. Except—look here!" I say, unpacking my haversack. "There's this piece of ham some young ladies at the stage stop in Travelers' Repose gave me as we left town. Want some?"

My Virginian stares at the thick slice of ham I unwrap. He licks his lips and clears his throat. He coughs—camp cough, we call it, it's run all through the army, every morning in camp sounds like a damned consumptives' convention—and clears his throat again. "Yes, sir, please. That would be very, very kind of you."

With my Bowie knife, I cut the slab in half. Our fingers touch as I pass it to him. He sinks his teeth into the meat, tears off a piece, starts chewing, then, wide-eyed, looks up. "Oh, uh," he mumbles, mouth full. He chews harder, making a little space for speech. "I'm sorry, sir. Didn't even introduce myself. I'm Private Brendan Botkin. From Head Waters, here in Highland County, a few valleys east of us. I'm much beholden."

We shake hands. He's a small, lean man, but his grip's firm. His calluses scrape my palms.

"I'm Shep Sumter. The boys call me Big Shep. I'm a private too. From Georgia. You a farm boy?"

"Yes, sir, I am. How can you tell?"

"Good manners." I chuckle, tearing into my own ham. "The city-bred, they tend to hold themselves a little high. I grew up on a farm, though I've done a little school-teaching too."

Brendan nods. "Teaching? You must be well read, sir."

"Yep." We sit through a long silence while the sun shuffles off clouds, spattering light through the pine boughs above us, then goes pale again.

"Fixing to snow," I sigh. "How old are you, boy?"

"Twenty, sir. And you?"

"Thirty-five. I've only seen you in the ranks recently. Did you just join up?"

"Yes, sir. I wanted to join last summer, but there were crops to harvest, and my pa, he died a few years back, and my ma, she begged me to stay, stay to keep up the farm, and truth be told, I was afraid to join, afraid, you know, of not coming home, but I'm a man now, and a man has a duty, sir. But you know that, I suppose, being here already." The boy coughs and wipes his mouth with a handkerchief. "How long you been fighting?"

"Since the summer. Been with Colonel Johnson defending these western hills for months."

"Do you like our Virginia mountains, then?"

I take a last bite of ham, follow it with a swig of canteen water, and shake my head. "No, boy, sorry to say. Too steep, too cold. I miss Georgia. Flatlands, thick pines, warm days and nights, green cornfields, peach orchards, honeysuckle. Ever had a fried peach pie, boy?"

"No, sir." Brendan grins. "But it sounds like something I'll be dreaming about tonight."

"Like I dreamt of my mother's biscuits last night." I wipe my hands on my trousers. "Rations *have* been very scant of late."

There's a shout ahead, and down the line comes the order to pack up.

"You ever had Virginia buckwheat cakes and maple syrup?" Brendan shoulders his haversack and rifle. "If we make it to Monterey safe and if we're given time, I'll have my Aunt Doris fry us up some."

Another shout. We fall into line. Brendan looks back once. "Thank you very much for the ham, sir."

Before I can answer, he turns, moving forward, his precious rear end recommencing its graceful sway. I grip my gun, brush the hair out of my eyes, cock my kepi over my brow, and follow him, stumbling forward through thick mud that sucks at my boots. A few snowflakes scuttle along a gust. Above the naked trees, the clouds look curdled, a dirty cream, sure sign of snow. A long march yet we'll have till the mountain's crest is reached, and I fear it will be a bitter night. What I want's a fire at day's end, and soup beans in a pot, and quilts, and this boy in my bed, rubbing his pretty bare rear against me, but the God of War isn't likely to be so accommodating. Damned Yankees. If they hadn't come down here, I'd still be at home. Except then, I guess, I wouldn't be admiring the sway of Brendan's meaty butt, and that would be a pity.

❖

The shack's the smallest in camp. Set in a rolling field, it's built of wooden logs with a crumbly stone chimney, surrounded by larger huts of similar construction. It's just about the most pathetic excuse for a dwelling I've ever seen, but after today's exhausting climb up the mountainside, it's a welcome refuge, and a damned sight better than the flapping tents that some of the boys are housed in. I say a little prayer under my breath, first apologizing to God for doubting His generosity, then thanking Him for such unexpected luck. The cabin's so small it can only house two. Brendan and I are going to be cabin-mates.

Camp Allegheny, set smack-dab atop the mountain, allows amazing vistas. In summer, it would be a scenic wonder, this view out over the blue-gray Alleghenies to the west. In winter, however, it's hard to appreciate the view when the camp's extreme altitude allows such savage wind. It tore at us during the entire march, increasing in power as we ascended. Here, among the shabby cabins erected as winter quarters, it claws at the dead grass, slaps our faces, makes chimney smoke slant into our eyes, and soughs through tree boughs like the angry ghosts of young soldiers who have fallen too soon. Now it's twilight, and the cold grows deeper still. Brendan and I look out over the mountains, the simmer of a scarlet sunset fading, then duck inside.

The windowless space is no more than eight feet wide. There's a blackened and ashy hearth, a candle on the mantelpiece, a narrow bed on either side, two hardtack boxes to serve as chairs, and room beneath the beds to store our haversacks. We do so, then, collars curled up, head out to use the latrine ditches, "sinks," the men call them, and gather in some firewood.

Chilly as the surrounding woodlands are, I'm warm nonetheless, somewhere inside, thinking of sharing the cabin's tiny space with a boy so handsome. It was a matter of mathematics, really, the cabins reserved for Virginians filling up, then the Georgian cabins all full to the brim, and only one miserable hut left, room for only two. Lugging armfuls of wood warms me up further, and by the time we have a fire started, I'm almost comfortable.

"Keep this going, Virginian, and I'll see if there's food to be had." Fetching cup and plate from my pack, I step out onto the cabin's stoop. In between the rushing rack of clouds, the stars are very bright, with the arc of the Milky Way right over the camp. Some say you can read men's fates in the stars, and for a second I wish that were true, that I possessed such skill—wondering what will happen to me, to Brendan too, before war's shifting necessities let us leave this mountain. If we leave this mountain. God knows several of my Georgia compatriots never left Camp Bartow this past autumn. I helped bury Willy myself, a boy I used to play in the creek with when we were boys. Bad whooping cough; only lasted a week.

Despite the bitter weather, the boys are in high spirits. Laughter echoes here and there around the camp, and someone's even playing "Dixie" on a fiddle. Among the campfires, I search for my mess, the few men left from back home after months of battles and illness. Here they are: Jason, who could be my twin, with his barrel chest and big black beard almost as bushy as mine; lithe, clean-shaven Rastus, best hunter in my home county; and John, the tall, blue-eyed boy with strawberry-blond hair, the best cook in the bunch. I was infatuated with him before the war, before I grew weary of all the stories about his wife and daughter, all of which just reminded me of how lonely I am. To my delight, he's already got something simmering over the embers.

"Coffee!" I say, waving my tin cup.

"And cush, your favorite." John ladles me a plate. It's a messy hash of beef scraps and crumbled cornbread I've come to love. Steam's rising off it. As small a portion as it is, it smells wonderful after such a long march.

"Excellent brute," I say, patting his shoulder. "And, um, perhaps you could spare another helping…for my cabin-mate?"

John cocks a brow. "As long as your all's next meal is provided by *his* regiment. You know how little food we have."

"Done," I say. John, with a dubious crease of the brow, ladles out another sparse portion. I fill my tin to the brim with coffee, then, balancing plate and cup precariously, head back to the cabin, eager to impress my handsome cabin-mate with my fragrant haul.

"Behold!" I say, waving the plate beneath his noise. Brendan cheers. "Sit here," I say, patting my bed. He obeys. Side by side, we share food and drink.

Evening muster and inspection are halfhearted on everyone's part, even the officers', as clouds have thickened and a heavy snow is beginning to fall around our little army's rows of shivering soldiers. Soon Brendan and I are seated side by side atop the hardtack boxes, hugging ourselves and huddling about our cabin hearth, the small, priceless fire glowing there. Much of the wood's pine. It burns fast and hot, with lots of resinous sparks.

A rap on the door. When I answer, big-bearded Jason steps in, nods at Brendan, and slips me the pewter flask he'd borrowed from me earlier in the day. "Filled it up for you, friend. Applejack a little vixen down the hill gave me. These Virginia girls surely do 'preciate their defenders. And they're skilled distillers." He gives my hand a hard shake and is gone, back to the cabin he's sharing with John and Rastus.

"Care to?" I say, returning to the fire and offering Brendan the flask.

"I haven't had much experience with spirituous liquors, sir. My mother's always warned against them."

"It's wartime, boy. That suspends a few rules. And it's cold enough to freeze a gentleman's…nether parts off. Take a swig or two. It'll warm you up. And while we're at it…" Handing him the flask, I pull a blanket off my bed. "Looks like you don't have as many coverings as I do, and your coat—forgive the blunt observation—looks a bit threadbare, so here, borrow this." I cover his shoulders, then pull a second blanket around me before sitting back down. "Better?"

Brendan sighs, snuggling deep into the wool. "Oh, yes. Oh, yes. I'm thinking the Lord sent you to me, sir. Thanks so much. I'm surely glad to be sharing this cabin with a man so kind. My family would, would, they'd be glad to know…"

Brendan's face looks wet in the firelight. He wipes his glistening cheek with the back of his hand. The poor boy's crying. Something beneath my breastbone breaks. I want to comfort him, to pull him into my arms.

"I'm sorry, sir. It's just that I'm—"

"Young, scared, tired, and homesick. I know, Brendan. I'm not so young as you, but the rest, well, strong as I look, I feel all that much of the time." I nudge his shoulder with mine. He's pungent, much the same as I: unwashed male body and wet wool. On him, it's an appealing combination. I lean closer, breathing deep. "I like it when you call me 'sir,' because it bespeaks those fine country manners I admire, but you *can* call me Shep or Big Shep every now and then."

Brendan nods. "Yes, sir, Mr. Shep, Big Shep." He takes a sip from the flask, coughs, and takes another sip before handing it to me. "It's pretty strong, Shep."

"Burns, does it?" Chuckling, I take a taste. It's rough, smoky, fiery, much like the flames warming our toes. "Uhhf. Nice. Recalls me to the flavor of peach moonshine back home."

We sit in silence for a while, passing the flask, listening to the fire's hissing as resin drips from twig ends and to the wind's clamor around the cabin. I open the door once to see how high the snow's getting. Nearly a foot's gathered outside, whipped into blue-white serpentines by the restless winds.

"Ooof, I can feel this brew in my head already." Brendan rubs his temples. "When will we fight again?" he says, pulling the blanket more tightly around his neck. I can hear the liquor in his consonants' blurred edges. The firelight on his hair and beard edges both with pale gold. I want to stroke that gold. I want to kiss his cheek, lift him in my arms, ease him belly-down on my bed, and then…

I shake my head and scratch my chin. How rarely do queer desires of mine ever leave the realm of dream and enter the realm of fact. "Not soon, I hope. Maybe not till spring thaw. With luck, Milroy and his Yanks have settled into winter quarters like us. On Cheat Mountain, we hear, way across the valley. Our armies are like two painter-cats glaring at one another from opposing heights. Have you been in a battle yet, son?"

"No, sir. Not yet. I'm fairly afeard, I don't mind admitting, for this applejack's loosened my tongue and lowered my pride, and I think I can trust you, I think you're a man to be honest with. And you? Big and fierce-looking as you are, well, I suspect you're a fine soldier. If I saw you heading toward me, if you were my foe, well"—Brendan gives a soft laugh—"I don't mind telling you—those big shoulders and that broad chest, those thick arms, and all that long black hair and a black beard so long and bushy—you look like some of the half-wild mountain men up the holler from my folks' farm—well, I'd—sorry to be crude—either piss myself or run. Most likely both."

I laugh out loud. So he's aware of my looks, at least. A promising sign. I take the liberty of slapping his back, and then, even bolder, giving him a quick hug. "Thanks, son," I say, positioning another dry stick of pine onto the flames. "I've done some damage. Fought at Rich Mountain and Cheat Mountain before ending up at Camp Bartow."

"And have you killed a man yet, sir?" Brendan looks up at me, blue eyes wide and moist.

"Yes." I take a deep breath, then a big gulp of applejack. "At the battle by the Greenbrier. Early last month. Three Yanks. All three as young as you. They…interfere with my sleep still. I tell myself that it was my duty, for my country's good, that they were invaders—and so they were, and would have killed me, had they the chance, and if God had willed differently—but they were mere boys too, and…enough, son! I'm weary. Have you books? I have some Emerson. Folks think, as big as I am, I'm good for nothing but brawn and brawn's many uses, but my daddy brought me up on literature. Have you read Emerson? 'Self-reliance,' that essay's my favorite."

"I have heard of Mr. Emerson. I did like some poetry in school, and Shakespeare's plays, so I have these"—he pulls two thin volumes from his haversack—"a collection of English poems—I'm fond of Mr. Wordsworth, how he writes about the countryside—and here's Shakespeare's sonnets. I also brought the Bible, sir, uh, Shep." Brendan brandishes a tattered copy. "I do love Proverbs, and the Song of Songs, and the Psalms, though—forgive the blasphemy—some of the rest of it seems…cruel."

I laugh. "Cruel? Well, I agree. Christ seems to have been a great, great man, and perhaps indeed the son of God, but those Hebrews being directed to slaughter the Canaanites, even the women and children… Your questioning of the Bible I'd keep to myself, if I were you. Nothing surlier than piety offended."

Brendan smiles and nods. "Yes, I know. My late father—he was very devout, though sometimes I think—not to seem disrespectful—sometimes I think his piety made him backward…anyway, he said the Bible's the only book you need, and any time I expressed doubts he waxed surly indeed."

Brendan stares into the fire, his good-looking face gone melancholy. "We used to argue about that. He and I used to argue about religion. I regret that now he's gone, but…My cousin Irene, she…grew large with child…out of wedlock…and our minister denounced her, and she hanged herself the week before she was due. I left the church then—it was guilt the church inspired in her, and it was guilt that killed her. I left the church, and my father, he never forgave me."

"I'm sorry, lad." Shyly, I give his shoulder a consolatory pat. "Well, perhaps, in the long months we're liable to perch up here, we could contribute a bit to one another's education. How about I read to you?"

Such is how we end our first evening together, Brendan and I, lying in our separate beds while I read a few favored passages of "Self-

Reliance" to him. "Whoso would be a man must be a nonconformist." "I suppose no man can violate his nature." "What I must do, is all that concerns me, not what the people think." Mr. Emerson, Yankee that he is, seems to be speaking to me, even exhorting me, but the independent life he describes is one I doubt I possess the courage to pursue. I can run across a battlefield howling the Rebel yell and dodging grapeshot and musket balls, but acting on my desire for this adorable, auburn-headed, bearded boy is a far larger matter. Things of great consequence can paralyze a man.

When the candle's nearly a stub and the firelight too dim to read by, Brendan returns my blanket and we say our good nights. We sleep fully clothed, the coverings being too few and too thin to provide sufficient warmth in and of themselves.

It's very dark when I wake. Wind's howling around the cabin, and there's a nasty draft around the door, dusting the hut floor with snow. I rise long enough to nudge another log onto the embers, stoking the fire up a bit, and to piss in the can we've set in a corner to spare us from having to step outside. I'm back in bed, booted toes numb and fingers throbbing with cold, when an odd clicking across the room catches my ear, followed by a series of hoarse coughs.

"Lad," I whisper, rising on one elbow. "You awake?"

Brendan's curled into a ball on his bed. The dim fire-glow illuminates his face. "Yes, sir. I'm sorry. It's my teeth a'chattering. And this cough that won't go away. I'm just so, so cold."

"I figured you Virginia mountain boys could take this chill better than us Georgia flatlanders."

"One might assume so, sir. It's just that, my family, we, we don't own much aside from land and livestock, and this is the only coat I have, the army has yet to issue me better clothes, and I lost my best blanket, and this one a friend lent me, it's not very thick, and…"

"Get over here, then, boy. I'll spoon you."

"Spoon, sir?"

"Lots of soldiers sleep together for warmth," I say, trying to conceal my eagerness. "You have brothers?"

"Yes, sir. Three. I'm the oldest. They're still at home, thank God."

"And do you share a bed?

"Yes, sir. It's necessary, seeing as, finances being what they are, we—"

"Think of me as your big brother, then. Get over here, and bring that paltry blanket. While Big Shep's around, you'll not catch your death of cold."

"I...uh."

I count the seconds. Five elapse, during which, I assume, Brendan's craving for warmth and his sense of propriety wrestle. Then he jolts up, lunges across the frigid space, I lift the blankets, and he's in my bed. As narrow as it is, I have no choice but to wrap one arm around him and slip the other beneath his head. He nestles back against me, his wool-clad back against my wool-clad chest; I arrange the blankets tightly atop us.

"How's this?" Oh, God, how long has it been since I've had a man in my bed? How long since I held a boy I wanted so deeply? If only we were naked. His aroma fills my nostrils. I take advantage of the enforced closeness to press my face, ever so gently, into his shaggy hair.

"So much warmer! You put off a lot of heat, Mr. Shep."

"A lot of bulk, a lot of heat." I chuckle. "I'm lending you a little Georgia summer. You should have seen me before army rations pared me down."

"My father used to hold me like this when I was a child and we took naps after gathering in hay," Brendan mumbles. "I miss him." In half a minute he's snoring. Good he's asleep, since otherwise he'd no doubt feel this stiff pole in my trousers wedged against his rear. I want to push my hands beneath his clothing, feel his bare skin, roll him onto his belly and take him hard from behind, but, hell, the poor boy is frightened enough. He needs tenderness, not violent lust. So I pull him closer, here in our tiny high haven, small heat curled around small heat in a sea of winter wind and snow, and when I'm sure he's fast asleep, I stroke his hair and his beard, very softly, till sleep takes me as well.

❖

When I wake, Brendan and I are lying face-to-face, beards pressed together, his arms wrapped around my neck. I only get a few minutes to savor his sleeping countenance—so sweet, so innocent—before damned reveille starts up, that bugle we've all come to hate. Brendan's eyes snap open; we roll awkwardly out of bed, straighten ourselves up, seize our firearms, and dash out the door.

The inspection's hurried, perfunctory, everyone eager to get back inside, that damned camp-cough leapfrogging up and down the ranks. The snow's stopped for the nonce, but it blankets the camp, lying heavily on sagging boughs and wind-flagged spruce. Colonel Johnson strides about, brow furrowed. He cuts an odd figure, with his high forehead and wild wisp of beard, rough looks to match rough manners, but he's likeable, forceful, a leader we believe in. One eye winks nervously, result of a wound he received during the Mexican War, no doubt a cause of consternation to ladies' sensibilities.

This morning, after muster, as I'd promised my own mess-cook John, I take my breakfast with Brendan's mess. They all look like less handsome versions of Brendan, a scruffy crew of starved hill-boys, with dirty uniforms, patchy beards, and hair long and lanky—greasy really, but my formerly-well-kept curly locks are much the same, for who of us in God's name wants to bathe in this weather?

"This is Rick. He's from Head Waters like me. And this is Samuel, my cousin, from Monterey. And this is Joseph, from Hightown. We're all Highland County boys." Soon after I'm introduced to them, I've confused their names. All except the cook, a smooth-faced, sharp-featured boy named Bobby who thanks me for looking after Brendan, pours me out coffee, and fills my plate with some stringy bacon and old bread fried in the grease. Brendan and I sit by the fire on logs and eat greedily, glad to have avoided picket duty. We spend our first full day in camp alternating between wood gathering and warming our hands by the skinny Virginians' campfire, with a meager lunch of the soup beans I've been craving, albeit only one cup apiece. On the other end of camp, some of the boys indulge in a snowball fight, with a great deal of cheering and hurrahs. Colonel Johnson holes up in his tent with Captain Anderson, our artillery commander, no doubt to plan strategy.

The winter-short day ends in a renewal of wet weather, this time sleet, which taps angrily on our hut's roof and door, as if the Yanks were attacking us with volleys of pebbles. For supper, messmate John provides us with short rations of beef roasted on sticks over the fire, with some hardtack we harvested from the Yanks when they fled for

Cheat Mountain after October's battle by the Greenbrier. Evening muster over, Brendan and I are once again blanket-swaddled shoulder to shoulder before our cabin fire, writing letters home, taking swallows from the applejack flask that big-bearded Jason has replenished from his unknown but thrice-blessed source.

"And are you writing to a wife or sweetheart who's waiting for you back home? A handsome, stalwart soldier like you has to have a bevy of admirers," Brendan says. He coughs, clears his throat, and gives me the white gleam of his grin.

"A wife? Lord, no!" I say, too fast, I fear. "I do, uh, love the ladies, but, well, I never was very good at courtship. I prefer the company of men."

"I think I understand, Mr. Shep," Brendan says. This time he's the one doing the shoulder-nudging. "I love my ma, and, though I have no sisters, I have a passel of female cousins I'm mighty fond of, and Ma, she did teach me how to behave in the presence of ladies, for I may be a farm boy, but my manners can be polished when the situation requires—one little girl in Monterey always seemed ever so pleased to see me when Pa and I would come to town to sell vegetables, not that I mean to boast, but she said my beard was handsome, that it was a lodestone for ladies, that—"

My turn to grin. "Are you feeling those spirits, son? What are you attempting to say?"

Brendan snickers, nudging me again. "I *am* feeling these spirituous liquors, sir. If I may say so, sir. I meant to say, sir, that I too prefer the company of men, sir. Strong men, strong men, sir. I do admire a strong man, sir. And, sir, I am stronger than I look, if I may say. I won many a wrestling match back in Head Waters. Well, I'll have you know that none of the fellows in my present mess have been known to beat me, sir. Though, burly as you are, I'm likely to plummet into the abyss of defeat, still, sir, shall we wrestle, sir, Mr. Shep, sir? Feel here, sir!" Brendan cocks his arm and flexes it.

"You're drunk as a lord, as my mother would say." I squeeze Brendan's arm; beneath the wool I can indeed make out sinewy lumps of muscle.

"I *am* drunk, sir. Lord Applejack has conquered me anew." Brendan giggles; I guffaw. "My ma used to warn me, she said that liquor hits a small man harder than a broad-shouldered bear such as yourself." He punches my shoulder softly; I return the favor. "*But*, I reiterate, though I am small, I am strong indeed."

Suddenly his arms are around me, we're grappling and he's tipping me, and now we're on the plank floor rolling around, laughing like mooncalves. He is indeed much stronger than he looks, but I must be twice his weight, and pretty soon I have him pinned on his back beneath me, straining and giggling, his wrists clasped in my grasp and forced above his head. His uniform jacket's come half open in the struggle, exposing a stained undershirt, over the top of which curl thick plumes of red-brown chest hair. God, he's just a boy. A beautiful, beautiful boy. What is he doing here, on this windy mountaintop, in the midst of war?

I lie on top of him, our faces only inches apart. He squirms beneath me, smiling around gritted teeth, arms straining, wrists twisting futilely inside my grasp. His eyes are wide, as blue as that wide Georgia sky I've been denied for so many months, but now the simple laughter I see in them dims, shifting into a look of complicated question. Now I realize the truth, and that realization makes me blush: my damned traitor of a cock is hard again, pressed against his thigh. To my amazement, my hardness is matched by his own, a stiffness fairly prodigious for a boy of his size, pressing against my belly. Our eyes lock; I bump his bearded chin with mine. I'm contemplating that courage that Mr. Emerson spoke of, trying to gather that courage to kiss him, when the moment's shattered, for good or bad, by Brendan's cough, which violently starts up again.

"So sorry," he wheezes. "Began this two days after I joined up, damn it." I roll off him and help him up. He sits on his bed and coughs till the fit subsides.

"Come on to bed, lad." I pat the blanket beside me. "Get warm over here. The cold won't help that hacking of yours."

"Perhaps I should sleep in my own bed. I don't want to disturb your sleep more than…"

"Get over here, son. Weren't you raised to obey your elders? Do what you're told, or I'll take you over my knee."

"That's what my pa used to say," Brendan grouses, but soon he's in my arms and we're spooning again beneath the blankets. I'm half-hard and hoping he doesn't notice. I'm a little drunk too, so really it's Mr. Applejack and not Mr. Emerson that allows me to slip my hand inside Brendan's jacket and pluck at the curls of hair in the pit of his neck.

"Pretty hairy for a boy so young," I say, undoing the top two buttons of his undershirt. "Manly, the fur on a fellow's breast. Reminds us of the animals we are." I take a soft curl between my fingers and rub it. Is he so drunk, or so young, inexperienced, and innocent that he doesn't recognize my desire for what it is?

Sleet splatters the roof; wind whistles around the door. "Thish grew in when I was sixteen," he slurs, patting his chest. "Runs in my father's family." Brendan rolls over, resting an arm across my hip. "I like the way you hold me, sir. It's a comfort; it's a kind of home. And are you hairy, sir?"

Smiling, I unbutton my wool jacket, then my undershirt. "Pretty chain," says Brendan, tugging at the silver necklace my father left me, the only thing of any real value I possess. "Oh Lord, you're a mosshy forest." Drunkenly, he runs a finger over the black thicket coating my chest. Then he presses his face into it, coughs once, sighs, and starts a raspy snoring. I slip a furtive hand inside his undershirt, stroke his torso, loving the contrast of soft hair and soft skin over hard muscle, and know the boy in my arms as one of the few good things war can bring.

❖

"I'm tired of my stink," Brendan snarls.

We've stoked the hut fire as high as we can—this damned pine burns so fast we're almost out of wood—and set a bowl of snow up close to the coals. When it's entirely melted, Brendan does what I've been waiting days for. Shivering, he pulls his jacket and undershirt off. He dips a rag in the water and scrubs his armpits. "Oh, Lord, it's cold!" Then he drops his trousers down to his knees and does the same to his cock, his balls, and finally his ass-crack. "Agghh! Ohh!"

I sit on the bed, a book in my lap. It's Brendan's book of English poetry. Wordsworth's saying to me, "One impulse from a vernal wood / May teach you more of man, / Of moral evil and of good, / Than all the sages can." The words are telling me not to look at the words, to look at Brendan's body instead, and so I do, with feigned casualness, in between polite glances at the page. I look up and smile, as if I were admiring a pleasant sunset or woodland scene rather than the most beautiful sight I've ever seen.

Brendan's shoulders are narrow but his arms are lithe with muscle, as to be expected on a mountain farm boy. His chest's dark with that delicious chestnut fur I've already glimpsed and doted on. His breast's broad and strong, composed of twin curves, firm, full curves, and very small pink nipples barely visible in the thick hair. His belly's equally hairy, but very flat, nearly concave. The rib bones protrude—true of all us Rebel soldiers, I'd imagine, since the rations have always been meager and are getting more so—as do the hipbones, sharp angles that grade down to his sex in its cloud of wiry hair. It was limp when he stripped, but now, to my surprise, it's stiffening.

I drop my eyes. Wordsworth whispers, "Sweet is the lore which Nature brings…" I look up. Brendan's very hard and very well endowed. I drag my glance from his swelling spear of flesh—which, here in the heart of this dead season, seems to distill all of summer's ripeness and spring's youth—resisting the urge to lick my lips, and look into his wide blue eyes. His face is as red as an autumn windfall apple.

"S-sorry, sir, the scrubbing must…"

Inane excuse. Stuttering, he turns away, which only allows me a slow study of the buttocks I've been aching to see bared. They're prominent, chunky, coated with dark brown fur that grows thicker in the cleft. Now that he's not looking, I can lap my lips with abandon. I want to fall on my knees and kiss each hairy ass cheek. I'd give half my days left on earth to be inside him, to feel him wrap those thin, hairy thighs around my waist.

Instead, heart hammering, I veil my nervous reverence with vulgar humor. "Cold makes most men dwindle, yet it stiffens you? Odd creatures, you Virginians. God has blessed you with a significant manhood, lad. Small as the rest of you is, you're even bigger than me down there," I note with envy and a sharp laugh. "No wonder those Monterey girls were enamored of you. Surely you pleasured them, one or two, with that lengthy tool?"

Brendan bends, giving me a last glimpse of his ass, the dark forest of his crack, before jerking his trousers up.

"Why, certainly!" he blusters. He's shaking violently now. "T-they couldn't get enough of my charms!" Then, blushing even deeper, he shakes his head. "No, sir, Shep, I wasn't brought up to…I…I flirt with the girls, but…"

"You haven't indulged in carnal love, I'm guessing, young as you are?"

"N-no, sir." Brendan tosses me a fresh cloth before tugging on his undershirt and jacket. "D-do you want to bathe?"

"Yes indeed. I'm tired of reeking too." I follow his lead, pulling off my upper garments, dropping my trousers around my ankles. The cold air goose-pimples me instantly; a violent shaking seizes my limbs. "Oh, hell," I groan, swabbing myself with the wet cloth. "A snow-bath. Ahhk!"

Brendan sits on his bed, face still flushed, watching me. His attention causes me to show off: I arch my chest, flex my arms, cock my ass. Cold as I am, my balls drawn uncomfortably up, my cock's stiffening too. "Same disease as you," I mutter. My grin must resemble an idiot's. "Contagious…"

"You have your own gifts, sir. And your chest, it's a bear pelt," Brendon mutters. "You are finely built. I've never seen such a form. You're magnificent. A Goliath."

Now I'm blushing. Shaking with cold, I turn away to fetch my undershirt. Behind me, Brendan takes another coughing fit. By the time I'm dressed, the coughs have subsided and he's heading for the door. He looks back at me, red-faced, red-eyed. "I'm going to the woodpile. I need to chop some wood. We need wood." Then he's disappeared into another afternoon of snow, leaving in his wake flakes on the floor that linger long before finally melting.

❖

A few frigid weeks pass; Brendan and I grow more and more inseparable. We spend our days like our fellow soldiers: gathering wood, engaging in snowball fights (in which Brendan proves to have a much more accurate aim than I), gobbling our fireside meals, constructing and manning breastworks, attending musters, shivering in our huts at night, reading by firelight, exchanging stories of home, writing letters while winds whip the flimsy structure and snows alternate with sleet. The routine would be monotonous if it weren't for this handsome boy to spend my time with. The only changes are skimpier rations, a worrying increase in Brendan's cough, and, to my pleasure, the hour that we retire to bed. Each evening it's earlier. Brendan looks up at me, blinks his blue, long-lashed eyes, closes his book, and says—God, so ingenuous—"Big Shep, I'm mighty cold. I think it's spoon-time," and something held back in my heart snaps and floods, like a logjam, and I say, "Yep, lad. C'mon," and Brendan's in my bed, his trembling body pressed against mine, warmth building slowly between us. We lie there, shivers subsiding, telling tales about our homes, watching the fire crumble and flicker.

Night after night, as Brendan snuggles in my arms, I contemplate bold action, for I ache to confess my longing and to make love to him. But night after night, I'm simply not brave enough to initiate more than the friendly touch and the sharing of body warmth our frigid context makes necessary for survival. The boy admires me, I know that. His sex has grown hard several times now. But he's so young; it takes nothing to harden a cock so young: an errant thought, the brush of woolen fabric. He holds me so tightly at night, but that might simply be because he's cold, he's lonely, he's starved for affection and touch, as are we all on this bitter mountaintop, in this bitter war, all of us far from home.

So, despite Emerson and Wordsworth muttering in my mind, night after night I hold my boy close to me, but I do not caress him, taste him, kiss him, ravish him as I would want. His fondness for me is innocent, I think. And to see fear or contempt in his eyes, that would be the end of me. If he repulsed my advances and then reported my perversion, as such desires are so commonly known, I would be banished from the army in complete disgrace. And how could I go home then, knowing I had betrayed my little friend and my country too?

I mull these doubts over every night as we huddle together beneath our shared but still insufficient blankets. And as lustful as I feel, wanting so to strip the boy and take him, there's a greater and a deeper feeling, something warm and loving alongside the violence of those suppressed flames. This must be what most men feel for their sons and wives, all melded into another form, a new form. To hold Brendan as he sleeps, to stroke his hair and kiss his forehead while the snows heap up outside and the wind growls about the hut and rattles the fragile boards, that's a blessing I could never have imagined being bestowed on a rough old fool like me. To be honest about my desires would most likely be to lose the gift of that grace, and that's a risk I shan't take.

Jason slams open the door. Brendan and I both jolt up, startled; for the first time, we've taken an afternoon nap together in my bed. Brendan rolls off the side, looking frightened. "Uh, Mr. J-Jason, what is it?" he stammers. "Is there anything w-w-wrong?" Surely Jason's seen two men spooning in winter weather; it's not at all uncommon, and my guess is that he, Rastus, and John do the same to keep from freezing to death. Still, Brendan's looking like he's been caught at something, and I'm feeling much the same.

Jason has no time to analyze the situation or read the signs of guilt. "The Yanks are on the move!" he gasps. His beard is crusted with ice. "They've moved down from Cheat Mountain! They're on their way to Camp Bartow and likely to get here tomorrow!"

We have no time to digest this information, for the bugle's sounding. Reluctantly I toss off the blankets, still toasty from the shared heat my little lad and I produce, button up, shoulder on my greatcoat, pull on my cap, grab my musket, and follow Brendan and Jason out to muster.

It's as Jason said. Grim-faced, Colonel Johnson, pacing before our coughing and shivering rows of tatterdemalion gray, explains the situation. The Yanks will be at the bottom of the mountain by dusk. They're likely to attack us by morning. Brendan and I are among those men assigned to picket duty.

Jason slams open the door. Brendan and I both jolt up, startled; for the first time, we've taken an afternoon nap together in my bed. Brendan rolls off the side, looking frightened.

I chew fear like moldy bread as Brendan and I shiver side by side behind our makeshift breastworks of stones and fallen tree limbs. Our muskets are loaded, our cartridge boxes full. We're positioned on an outcrop overlooking the turnpike a couple of miles from camp. The sky's clear, brimming with sharp stars. Around us stretch the woods, snowy and silent.

I'm not afraid for myself as much as I am for him. I fear for his young life, his beautiful but so-fragile body—I'm already so fond of him I can't imagine losing him. If he falls, he wouldn't be the first comrade to die in my arms, but he would certainly be the one I would grieve the most. Again, I think of the insanity of it, that a boy so youthful, tender, and handsome is here, a rifle in his hands, in this winter-white wilderness, rather than home by his family's fire. I wonder how he will face battle for the first time. The boy's so sweet and sheltered, and a man never, never knows how he will perform in the heat of battle till he's there, amid the musket smoke and shouting, the screams and the whistling of balls, the screeches and booms of artillery. If he proves a coward, how will he live with that? What is bitterest is that, as big, strong, and seasoned as I am, I can protect him from very little. Every fiber of my being snarls at that hated fact.

"Shep? I can't feel my toes."

I turn my eyes from the turnpike—still blessedly free of foes—to my lad. He looks up at me in the dark, and I can make out his pale brow beneath his cap, the dark bush of his beard, thicker than when we first met, and ice forming in his mustache and the fur beneath his lower lip.

"Keep your voice down, boy," I whisper. Gently I pat his shoulder. "The water in my canteen's half-frozen, and my feet are in the same condition. You look like a Laplander with that ice around your mouth."

Brendan grins nervously—white flash of teeth in the dark. He brushes his frozen beard with the back of his hand, then reaches up and brushes mine. "And you the same, big bear. Bewhiskered with ice. God, I hate this waiting. I wish they'd just come. Are you afraid?"

"Yes, I am."

"I've shot many a deer and squirrel, but never…where do you get the strength? To hold your ground? I fear I'll break and run, and if I do, the shame will surely choke me."

"Ah, boy, the strength comes, the Lord knows from whence. My hands and knees shake, but I load and aim. Just think this. These mountains are your home, not theirs, those invaders coming up the turnpike. And what will happen to your mother, your brothers, if the Feds make it past us?"

Brendan chokes back a cough and gives a curt nod. "Yes. Yes, sir. That's helpful. I—"

That's when we hear it, a horse's distant clopping. "Shhh!" I say, laying a hand on his shoulder. "This is it, boy. They're coming."

We duck behind the breastworks and wait. The dim light preceding dawn creeps through the forest, and by that light, we see them moving up the mountain, over the half-frozen mud of the turnpike.

Brendan hisses, a deep intake of breath. He raises his rifle and takes aim.

I grab his arm. "Not yet, little one. Wait till they're within range." Beneath my grasp, his muscles are taut, quivering.

Brendan nods. I too take aim. More clopping of hooves. The low voices of men. Where are they from? Indiana, Ohio, that's what's been suppositioned about the campfires. No matter. Wherever they hail from, they should have stayed there. They should not be here.

From the picket station a few yards down the hill, where Brendan's buddies Rick and Samuel are positioned, there's a sudden crack, a flash of fire, a plume of smoke. At my elbow, Brendan gasps and starts. The Yankees shout and return fire. A ball embeds itself in a tree trunk above our heads.

"Now, Shep?"

"Yes, boy! Now!"

Brendan's gun roars, spitting light and smoke, and mine a second after. My ears ache. The smoke's foul, acrid, filling my nose, stinging my eyes. Already Brendan's tearing another cartridge open with his teeth, ramming it in the barrel, taking aim. The boy's twice as fast as I am.

I tear open my own cartridge. Brendan's gun flashes a second round of fire. "Goddamn you! Go home!" Brendan shouts in a shaking voice. Balls shred a branch above us, showering us with twigs and splintered wood. Brendan growls, brushes the refuse off his thin shoulders, and begins loading again.

I want to kiss him; I'm so proud of him I'm ready to split open like a ripe seedpod. Instead I take aim—there's a line of Yanks just down the hill, too goddamned foolhardy to take shelter yet. Easy pickings. I'm aiming at one man, when Brendan's gun roars again, and my target falls.

"Christ, boy!" I tousle his hair and, grinning, aim at another man. By my side, Brendan's growling beneath his breath, "Goddamn them. Goddamn them," and tearing another cartridge open between his teeth.

"I do believe I'm witnessing a beautiful, terrible thing," I say, following his lead.

"And what's that, Big Shep?" Brendan pants, tamping his ramrod into the barrel. "Fuck, my knees are shaking." He looks up at me; his lips are black with powder.

I chuckle. "Such language. Mine are too. I'm seeing a tender farm boy becoming a man. I'm seeing the birth of a fine and deadly soldier."

"Forgot to tell you I'm the best shot in Head Waters," Brendan says. "You watch me now. I'll send them all to hell."

❖

We pull back when the main column of the enemy appears. There are too many of them now, and we need to get up the mountain to warn the camp. Brendan and I move as fast as we can through dead leaves, crusty snow, and slippery mud, falling often. Our knees are mud-caked by the time we stumble into camp. We find Colonel Johnson pacing before his tent and we gasp out the news. He grasps a musket in one hand, a club in another, winks at us in that spastic manner of his, and smiles. "Time for the long roll, boys."

The drummers begin it, that dreaded rhythm, the call to arms. In the chaos of preparation, I track down Lieutenant Colonel Conner, my regimental officer, to beg leave to fight with Brendan's unit. "He's just a boy, sir, and I think I might serve as an example to him, and, well, I've grown fond of him, he's like a son to me, and—"

"Stop gushing, Private Sumter," he says, waving me away. "I'll make an exception. Yes, off with you. Go fight with the boy's unit. I have more pressing matters to deal with now."

The Yanks attack at sunrise, pouring up the wooded hill from the right. Our overeager lines return their fire too soon, while the foe's still too far away. Their rifles are better, with longer range. When they return the fire, it's a deadly hailstorm, men falling all around us. Brendan's buddy Rick goes down with a scream, gripping his thigh. Brendan snarls, aims for the Yankee culprit, brings him down in turn, then helps Rick limp away. I fell three men myself, missing twice that many, wishing I were as fine a shot as my little lad. A ball pierces my hat; another tears my greatcoat. Brendan returns to my side, slaps my back, drops onto one knee, and fires again.

The Yanks' numbers are too great, and our lines pull back to the camp. Above us the sky's clear, the sun bright, but the wind's as sharp as ever, freezing our faces as we take shelter in trenches and behind our cabins. We attack, are driven back by concentrated fire, retreat into camp and, past that, into the woods. Our artillery comes into play and we rally once more, driving the Yanks out of the camp, then we're forced back once more. Brendan's a crack shot, almost never missing. He fells another Yank, then another, then another.

Near noon the opposing lines meet in hand-to-hand combat right in the middle of Camp Allegheny. A Yank's Minié ball misses me by inches; I grapple with him, pull my Bowie knife, stab him in the gut, and leave him screaming, face-down in the earth. When I turn, Brendan's wrestling with a big blond Yank in mud-streaked blue. Before I can interfere, the man's struck Brendan in the head with his musket butt. My little lad falls, blood gushing from his temple.

"Get away from him, you fuck!" Lunging, I try to stab the Yank; he dodges, punching me in the gut, but I keep coming, tackling him into a snow bank. We grapple only briefly; not many men on this field, blue or gray, are as big as me. I sink my Bowie into his side and he's still. I turn, retrieve my gun, and look for Brendan. My boy's unconscious, on his back in an icy puddle, blood smearing his handsome face. I lift him up, throw him over my shoulder, and jog back through clouds of musket smoke, darting behind the nearest set of breastworks as Yankee guns pop behind me and balls whizz around me like a riled-up hive of bees.

Farther back in the woods I find the doctors. "Take him," I say, lowering Brendan gently to the ground. I stroke the boy's brow and then sprint back to the fray. All through the camp, bodies lie everywhere, both our boys and the foe. Here are my buddies, mess-cook John and big-bearded Jason, kneeling behind my little cabin, loading their muskets and cussing a blue streak. I drop beside them to tamp another ball in.

"Rastus is down," Jason says, grinding his teeth. "Pretty bad wounded. And Captain Anderson's dead as a doornail. But lookee! Look at the colonel!"

Through the smoke, I can see Colonel Johnson leading a tight row of advancing gray. He's pointing a musket in one hand and swinging a hefty club in the other. "Affix bayonets!" he shouts.

"Let's go!" Jason shouts.

Loping out, we three join the line. My heart's pounding, my strong and able friends are beside me, my bayonet's in place, we have a country to defend, and there's a crazy lightness in my chest. The white world's shrinking to a red tunnel with the faces of foes at the far end. We sound the Rebel yell, high and fierce, loose a deafening volley of gunshot, and break their line. Blue forms fall right and left; we tear into the line's remainder, swinging rifle butts and stabbing with our bayonets. Within a minute, the bluecoats take to their heels, receding down the hill.

"They won't be back today," says the colonel. With a bitter smile, he tosses his club into tramped snow. "Gone! They're gone!" Jason snarls. Around us, boys are jumping and shouting with glee. "Run, damn ye, run!" Jason yells. We load up and release a final volley at their backs.

The noise of the guns fades. My head's ringing; tremors course down my legs. Suddenly my knees give out. I sink down in the mud, cough out smoke, and lean against a log. The big blond Yank who hurt Brendan lies at my elbow, eyes wide, blue as my little man's. I close his eyes, take his cartridge box, then rise shakily and head for the doctors' tent.

Just as I'm approaching, Brendan staggers through the tent flaps. There's a bloodstained bandage wrapped around his head. He smiles at me. "Thank God. Thank God," he says. Then he cups his brow in his hands and slumps to his knees.

"Brendan!" I shout, running over to him. "What are doing out here? You should lie down. Here, let me—"

"Doctor said it was just…It's nothing, Shep. Where's my musket, Shep? I need to fight. The Yanks…"

A shout rings on the far side of the camp. "More Yanks! On the left!"

Brendan tries to rise; I force him down. He sits heavily in the mud.

"Boy! Don't! Stay here with the doctors, or I'll take you over my knee right here. Promise you'll stay here!"

Brendan sighs. On the left, a clamor of shouting; guns start popping. "I need to fight, Shep. I'm no coward. I'm not. Don't think I'm a coward." There's something pitiable in his voice.

"Coward? You're no coward! How many men did you bring down today?" I help him to his feet and lead him back toward the hospital tent.

"I lost count, sir."

"You've done enough, son. Now get in there."

"Please be careful, sir." Brendan squeezes my hand.

"Git!" I give his butt a light slap—the firm plumpness excites me even in the midst of this bloody chaos—then push him through the tent flaps.

❖

A different Federal force, from the Green Bank Road. They meant to get here earlier, perhaps, so that we Rebs might be attacked simultaneously from left and right, but, praise God, their timing was off. These men are slow, no doubt weary from the march up the mountain. I pick off two, one a redheaded boy about Brendan's age—poor child, he should have stayed in the Midwest cornfields—and one a gray-bearded man almost as husky as I. By midafternoon, the new batch of blue-bellies is in full retreat, dragging their dead into the woods and down the slope. A few stray shots echo in the mountain air, and then there's silence save for the groans of our wounded and the whistle of the wind, its lonely music unconcerned with the human loss this day has seen.

I find Brendan passed out on a cot in the hospital tent. "Lucky boy," says the doctor. "Make him rest for a few days, clean his wound regularly, and he'll be fine, though he'll bear a fine scar on his forehead. He can boast of it to the ladies hereafter." I gather the lad into my arms and pick my way through corpses back to the cabin. There, I tuck Brendan in my bed, start a fire to keep him warm, and leave him to sleep while I join my regiment in burying our dead.

Pale sunset over the Alleghenies, the evening star twinkling; now nightfall, and the Milky Way's white arch coursing over our camp like God's benediction. I find John cooking; he's got a pot of beans going. Hands and back aching from hours heaving shovelfuls of half-frozen earth, I sit by our mess's fire, holding out my palms to warm them.

Jason joins me, sitting down with a groan. "Got something for you. Hand me your flask." When I do so, he fills it from another flask, larger and fancily ornamented. "I found me this one on a dead Yank. Whiskey in there. Try it. Smoother than that popskull applejack."

I take a long swallow. "Rastus?"

"Fixing to die," says Jason, staring into the fire. "And your little friend, one of his mates was slain. Buried him myself. Not much more than an urchin. He'd written his name on a piece of paper inside his jacket. Guess he expected he might fall. Samuel, it was."

By the time I get to the hospital tent and ask for Rastus, he's gone, nothing more than a form beneath a blanket, the boy with whom I used to pick peaches and hunt crawdads. I sit on a stump in the forest for a little while, out in a grove of pines where I can be alone, where no one will see me cry. Overhead, in the evergreen boughs, the wind soughs and sighs, ceaseless as a river. Then I wipe my eyes, return to the fire, and fetch some dinner for Brendan and me.

My lad's still asleep when I enter our cabin. The fire's almost out, so I stoke it up. When he wakes, I wrap an arm around him and I tell him, about Rastus, about his cousin Samuel. He cries some. Then he dries his face with his sleeve, and we eat our beans, cold by now.

Brendan scrapes up the last bean, then grabs my hand. "Shep? My head hurts, and I'm real cold," Brendan whispers. "I'd like—"

He breaks off, seized by another coughing jag, then resumes. "Let's us get beneath the blankets now? Please? I can't ever seem to get warm unless I'm…with you, unless you're, uh, holding on me." He looks up at me, blue eyes wet. "I'm just so sad. My heart's overfull and fit to split. Will you hold on me? I'm in mighty need of comfort." He bites his full lower lip and hangs his head.

I nod. Pushing another piece of wood onto the fire, I blow out the candle, take Brendan's hand in mine, and lead him to bed.

For a time we lie unspeaking. Brendan's curled in my arms, his back against my chest, his hands clasped together beneath his chin, as if he were a shaggily bewhiskered and prayerful cherub. The wind continues its complaint; somewhere in camp I can make out more fiddle music, a mournful voice singing "Home, Sweet Home."

"You fought well today, son. I was proud of you."

"Thanks, Shep. And thanks for taking care of me. I was so afraid before the battle, but then something woke in me. Something savage…

something necessary, considering the times we find ourselves in. I knew you were there beside me, and you're so brave…I would rather have died with a Minié ball in my head before showing myself a coward before you."

"Far from a coward." I hug him. "Just the opposite. You were quite the little hero. What a fine shot you are."

Brendan takes a long breath and rests his head on my arm. "The Proverbs say, 'As iron sharpeneth iron, so one man sharpeneth another.'" When he starts snoring, I'm glad. That means he's not thinking, not mourning his fallen cousin. I fall asleep thanking God that I have this warm, furry boy to hold and wondering why Rastus had to die, why this damned war started to begin with.

❖

A jagged noise rouses me. The fire's died down to embers, and the room's freezing. My face is numb, and more wind is coursing around the poorly fitted cabin door.

Brendan's sobbing. That's what woke me.

"Boy, boy," I whisper, pulling him closer. "Boy, there now, boy, poor boy. Rastus and Samuel, they were brave, they had brave deaths. That's the last gift of a good life, a brave death."

Brendan rolls over, wraps his arms around my neck, presses his bandaged head to mine, and cries harder. His sobs are savage and deep, shaking him. "He was my cousin, my favorite cousin! And those men, those bluecoats, I killed them. They pray to the same God we do, Shep. One boy I shot, he cried for his mother. Another one, he was calling to Jesus. Some madness seized me, something in the musket, in the woods, in the snow. There was a fire in my bones. I didn't even know them, but I shot them down like dogs! Just like they shot Samuel and Rastus. It's mad. It's all God's madness."

I'm on the verge of tears myself, but it wouldn't do for both of us to break down, so I take a deep breath and hold him harder. I stroke his hair. I wipe tears from his cheek. I kiss his cheek. I kiss his cheek. I kiss his cheek. He tastes like healing springs, salt springs.

Slowly Brendan's weeping tapers off. He sniffles, pulls back, and looks me in the eyes. He strokes my long hair, tugs at my bushy beard. "I'm so glad I'm here with you, Shep. Thank God. Thank God. What would I do here in this terrible place, cold as the lower depths of hell, without you?" Then he cups my face in my hands and he kisses me on the lips.

"My God," I mutter.

Brendan jerks back, eyes wide. "Oh, sir, I, I, I'm so sorry. Did I give offense? Did I—?"

"Offense!" I bark a laugh. "Lord, no! Come here, foolish boy," I whisper. "I've been wanting this since we first met." I take his sweet face in my hands and kiss him back, gently once, gently twice, the third time harder.

Brendan starts snuffling again. "I've wanted it too. To...lie with you. Folks say it's sin, but—"

"It's no sin, boy. Emerson says—"

"Emerson means little to me, Mr. Shep. What this says"—he pats his chest—"I listen to that. My heart, it says that...that sin's a concept that...well, sin's meanness and cruelty and faithlessness and cowardice...sin doesn't have anything to do with this...with loving."

With that, he wraps his arms around my neck and kisses me again. "I, I love how much bigger you are than I. It makes me feel safe with you. And, and I love how strong and hairy you are. And so handsome. And so, so kind. May I...touch you, Shep?"

I'm so stunned I'm speechless. Without words, I can only lick my lips and nod. Brendan slowly unbuttons my coat and undershirt. He runs his fingers over my chest, kisses the fur over my breastbone, and fondles a nipple. "Lord God, you smell so good." He straddles my thigh and rubs his hard crotch against me.

"I don't really know how to...pleasure a man, sir," he mumbles. "Please tell me if do something you find objectionable."

I give another deep laugh. "Objectionable? Boy, you just brought paradise to the mountaintop. Do what you please, take your time, and later, I'll teach you what I know."

"So you've lain with a man this way, sir? I've only...my cousin Samuel and I once..." He sniffles again, wiping impatiently at his face. "Poor Samuel. I can't believe those bastards shot him. Well, we...he caressed me down there and then he took me in his mouth, and it was truly a wonder, but it never happened again, we never spoke of it, and he avoided me for months after."

"That's the harvest of dogma for you, boy, that venom guilt.

Religion like that's meant to control, not lift up. It's meant to drive a wedge between men, and I have no use for it."

"This is a fine belt, sir. It reminds me of my father's." Brendan unbuckles it, begins kneading the lump of my sex through the wool. "How many men have you known in such a manner?"

"Only two. A surveyor from Atlanta. When I was your age. I fancied him mightily. He taught me things. He ravished me like a woman in my family's barn one day when we were caught there by the rain. Bent me over a bale, took me from behind. It hurt, and then it felt wondersome. Down there, there's a spot deep inside a man, that—I call it the honey-spot—well, he found it, and I've never felt anything half so good since."

Brendan, with a fumbling of fingers, is unbuttoning my trousers, rubbing my underpants. It's hard to focus on speech, but I continue. "And, and five years ago, when I was in—uhh!—Atlanta on business, there was a boy your age, a, a, a catamite, a male Cyprian. He was a mollycoddle, not a manly little fellow like you—uhh, that feels so good!—but he, he was very good-looking. I...paid. I was so hungry, so lonely. I thank God he was honest when he claimed to be free of love-pox."

Brendan pulls my stiff sex out, then wraps his hand around it and strokes it. "I may not know much, but I do know this feels good, because, well, I have one, and I know..." He falls silent, humping my thigh, squeezing my shaft. I sigh, thrusting into his fist. Somewhere, in the far distance, the hut's creaking beneath the punch and jab of mountain winds.

"Mr. Shep, I so want you naked, but..." Brendan gives my sex a parting squeeze, then slips up my body and gives me a soft kiss on the lips.

"And I want you naked too, boy. I want to taste your every nook and curve and angle, but yes, it's just too cold, so there's another reason to endure this hellish winter and survive till spring."

"Shep? May I taste you?" Brendan says, playing with the silver chain around my neck. "It would be a blessing long withheld and long dreamed of to taste you."

I chuckle. "Boy, you're blessing embodied. Yes, lad, Brendan boy, taste me. Please."

Brendan buries his face in my armpits. He licks and nibbles with a frantic hunger. Then he finds my nipples, and he sucks them long, and the feel of his pretty mouth, the brush of his beard, the nip of his teeth on those tender teat-points, it's an ecstasy I would never have imagined. Now he slides down my body, embracing my hips. I groan as his tongue flicks over my sex. He bathes the head with wet assiduity, then takes me into his mouth. He bobs gently, pulls off to lick the shaft, then takes the head between his tight lips again.

"I've never had a man in my mouth before," he mumbles around the flesh. "I've wanted it so badly." Then he leaves off words for a time, sucking me, a soft pressure, then a hard suction, vacillating between the two.

I grip his head, running my fingers through his unwashed hair, careful not to dislodge his bandage. He chokes and coughs, wipes drool off his chin, and dives in again, as if his poor, thin, half-starved body might somehow be nourished by the taste of mine.

Oh no. Too soon. "Boy!" I growl. "Get off! I'm close to...I'm going to spend!"

Brendan chuckles, tightening his grip around my waist, and sucks harder. I feel the edge approaching, inescapable now. I grip the back of his head, shove into his throat, and finish—one, two, three shuddering spurts. Brendan swallows it all, then pulls off, laughing. I fall back onto the hard bed with a groan. Brendan laps at the dripping head, licks seed from my belly hair, then slides up to wrap his arms around my chest. I rise on one elbow, long enough to tug the blankets back over us.

A fit of coughing seizes him. He curses and gasps; I hold him to me. At last it subsides.

"Your seed's sweet," Brendan murmurs against my neck. "Now at last I know what a man tastes like, what a man's seed tastes like. What your seed tastes like, Shep. It's sweet like kindness, salty like my ma's salt-rising bread, and musky-rich as the forest. And I'll want more of it, more of you, on the morrow."

❖

Reveille, followed by a breakfast of flapjacks, thanks to some flour found in a cart abandoned by the Yanks. Coffee beans are gone, so John's parched and ground corn as a substitute. It's foul but it's hot.

Brendan wolfs down his food, giving me a grin—his teeth so white framed by that auburn beard, a bush grown bushier after weeks without trimming—and a sidelong glance. "Word is a blizzard's coming. Might be snowed into our cabins for days."

I snatch up an extra flapjack, avoiding John's fork-jab of mock outrage, and drop it onto Brendan's plate. "Growing boy," I say in excuse. John rolls his eyes and pours more batter into the sizzling pan. Rising, I gulp down the last bit of vile counterfeit coffee. "Blizzard? Better get to wood-gathering, then."

Despite his fresh wound, the doctor's suggestion that he rest, and my chiding, Brendan insists on accompanying me. We spend the morning alone in the woods swinging axes. "Not long till Christmas," I say, wiping my brow, half-expecting the sweat to have crystallized into a glaze of ice. "What will you be wanting for a gift? Or for Christmas dinner?"

"I have what I want," says Brendan, setting a wedge into a chunk of oak and bringing down the maul. The wood parts with a satisfying creak. "I've been given a gift so great it leaves room for little else. Though a chicken pie might be a pleasant addition. Otherwise, sir, I think I'll have all the food I need. On Christmas, I plan to have my fill of fine meat."

Guffawing, I swing my axe. The sky's an arch of iron above us. A few flakes drift down. The hard wind's redolent with the scent of coming snow. I stop chopping to watch Brendan's slender body, his nimble movements, as he splits wood with the same accuracy with which he brought down the foe. He looks up, blinks his blue eyes, gives me a seductive wink, then returns to his labors. I sharpen my axe and do the same—we'll need lots of wood if a blizzard's indeed approaching—but in my head, I'm trying to tally all the kind things I've done in my life, trying to figure out what I've done to deserve so much of God's grace.

❖

"This should work. Spooning's one thing to be caught in the midst of, but sodomy's another." Brendan shoves his bed up against the door. "That should slow down Jason, or any other visitor." He tosses a log on the fire, then drops to his knees and jerks open my trousers. "I'm ready for some lunch, and I want none other than your fat prick." He chews gently on my cockhead for a minute, then gulps my sex down his throat and commences to bob fervently. I lean against the mantelpiece, the fire warming my back and my boy warming my man-parts. "I want your seed, Shep," he mumbles around my cock. He lifts his head, giving me a blue, lust-glazed gaze. "You make me thirsty as a sand dune, as a sun-parched cornfield. Fuck my mouth, Shep, for I shan't cease this till I have your seed," he mutters before taking me in again.

The Highland County farm boy who at first seemed so timid, so innocent, has—now that our desires have been admitted and found so happily mutual—become overnight a clever and wildly eager lover. I never would have imagined that such a passionate and hungry man slept inside that sweet boyish façade, and I never would have imagined that luck would lead such a boy-man to me.

I thrust and groan, caressing his bandaged head. Lifting Brendan up, I push him onto the bed, straddle his face, and fuck the tight hole of his mouth. Loving him in broad daylight makes me anxious, though I must admit the bed-blocked door's indeed a fine mechanism to insure our privacy. What with the blizzard encroaching and Colonel Johnson's announcement that, till the storm's done, we're all to keep to our cabins save for meals, wood detail, and picket duties, Brendan and I are not likely to be disturbed. The god of the snows has fine timing, for I'm ready for days of lovemaking, and my boy appears to be too. "Here, lad," I say, feeling the great crest and spume creeping closer. "Here, Brendan boy, drink me," I whisper, stuffing his throat with flesh, filling him brimful of thick juice.

"A bellyful, a bellyful indeed." Brendan smiles sleepily in our cuddlesome aftermath. Soon he's dozing, then snoring. Good. The doctor said he should get as much rest as possible. I wipe a pearly drop of my sap from his beard, tuck him in tight, and return to the wood lot. Alone there, I lean against a spruce trunk and cry, for the boys we lost, and then with sheer joy, to have found Brendan. By dusk I've amassed quite a pile of logs, and I'm wondering how I could continue living if war's vicissitudes robbed me of my boy.

The storm hits at nightfall, the worst we've seen yet, with winds so savage and snow so thick I can hardly make my way to the campfire. Tonight, I fetch us plates of skillet cornbread and cups of beef stew stretched with white beans, all made from ingredients the inadvertently generous Yankees left behind. The cabin's walls shake and groan about us as we eat. After supper, we scrub our nether parts with more uncomfortably cold water, preparing for the night of lovemaking bound to come. After that, we block the door and relish a quiet evening together by the fire, sharing the Yankee whiskey Jason gave me. Brendan reads some Byron and Tennyson I select. "Behold, I dream a dream of good,/And mingle all the world with thee" and "I watched thee when the fever glazed thine eyes,/Yielding my couch, and stretched me on the ground/When overworn with watching, ne'er to rise/From thence, if thou an early grave hadst found."

"These are love poems, written by one man to another," I say. "I don't know if the love they shared was bodily, but..."

"They do sound like they understand," Brendan says, closing the book. "If men like you and me feel as we do now..."

"Yep. Those things I've read about the Greeks, the mythology about Zeus and Ganymede, and Plato's *Symposium*, and *peccatum illud horribile, inter Christianos non nominandum.* That's Latin for—"

"You know Latin?"

"I know some. I had a good education as a boy, and I learned a great deal more as a teacher. At any rate, it means 'that horrible sin not to be named among Christians.'"

Brendan sniggers. "I'm perfectly happy not to name it among them. As long as they leave us alone. I've met Christians who are mean, and I've met those who are loving, and I intend to be the latter and to love the latter. And why can't I be a Christian and love you too?"

I look up, startled. Brendan's blue gaze is steady and earnest.

"This is love, is it not?" he says, his anxiety audible. "What we've found together? Not just lust? Or am I just a...catamite? A catamite like that Atlanta boy? I'm sorry, sir," he says, looking away now, "for I don't mean to be so blunt, but I am a bit drunk again. The whiskey's very strong. And I need to know how you feel, for who knows when or whether this awful war will part us?"

I close my eyes. *If thou an early grave hadst found.* I take my lad's hands in mine and sigh. "We've known one another only a few weeks, and I've never fallen in love before, but when I think of the Yanks across the valley, and the battles sure to come in the spring, and how easily a ball might pierce your body and end you forever"—I pluck at the hair curling over the collar of his rumpled jacket and kiss his forehead—"yes, this is more than lust. Most certainly. No, I've never fallen in love before, but the way you make me ache here"—I tap my breast—"yes, this is love."

Brendan leans his head on my shoulder. "I feel the same, Mr. Shep. Feelings, it's said, grow fast and vivid in times of war, like flowers in summer's heat. Only weeks, it's true, yet I've come to cherish you. As soon as you sat down beside me on our march up the mountain and shared your lunch with me, and I saw your face and knew your kindness…and now that I've felt you and tasted you, I want to be with you always. Maybe after the war, if, Lord willing, we get through…" Brendan coughs hard, rubs his bandaged head, and groans.

"Lord willing, yes, we might share many a year together. Time for bed," I say. "I can tell you're hurting. Come on."

Beneath the blankets, I curl my bulk around his small frame. "My family and friends," Brendan murmurs, "I hate to think what they'd say or think or do if they knew. Do you think that one day…men who feel what we feel might not be so despised?"

"I can't imagine that coming to pass. Perhaps far in the future, another century, long after we're gone."

"Ah," says Brendan. "I'd rather think about tonight than any far future. Will you lie on top of me, Shep?"

"I'll crush you, boy! Aren't you beat up enough? Isn't your head hurting?"

"Please? The other day, when we wrestled, I…loved it when… when you won, when you held me down and I felt your great weight upon me and no matter how hard I struggled, I knew that I'd be bested by your strength. It made my sex throb. Please?"

"Bossy boy. And I loved besting you. I loved the way you fought me. It stoked me, the fire inside me, knowing I had you, that you were within my power. There's been a bonfire in my innards since the day I first saw your plump rump marching down the turnpike."

"Ohhh," Brendan moans as I lower myself onto him. His erection tents his trousers.

"Give me a little fight," I say. Grinning, I grab his wrists and force them above his head. Brendan obliges, writhing and panting beneath me. When he starts kicking, I wrap my legs around his. He may be thin and starved, but he's a little wildcat. He struggles for a long while, with pauses to catch his breath before thrashing beneath me again.

"Going to be a good boy now?" I say, licking my lips.

"Not now," he hisses between gritted teeth. "Not quite yet."

To my surprise, he gives a great heave, shoving me off him and over the side of the narrow bed. I retain my grip on his wrists, so he has no choice but to accompany onto the floor. There we roll around, laughing like fools. Finally, he's belly-down, and I'm on top of him, using my far greater strength to pin his arms behind his back.

"Now you're caught. Now you're going to be good," I say firmly.

"No," Brendan growls, continuing to squirm. His ass bucks back, bumping against my stiff loins. I've never been harder. We lie there panting for a minute, his compact body straining against me, my erection pressed against his rear. Then I see it, only a foot away: my open haversack, at eye-level beneath my bed, and, inside it, coils of rope I use to pitch my shelter tent in warmer weather.

"It arouses you to be mastered, boy. Am I right? It seems to excite you beyond surpass to submit to a strength greater than yours. Am I right?"

Brendan presses his face to the floor. Then he turns his head, eyes wild and bright, musters a wide grin, and nods.

"Then, my little hero—praise God for mutual desires—I'm the man to master you." Holding his wrists together with one hand, I pull a coil of rope from my haversack. Brendan, giggling, starts struggling again, but within a couple of minutes I've tied the boy's hands tightly behind his back.

"By God, you'll behave now." Climbing off him, I stand above him. He grins up at me, then gives me a hard kick in the shin. "Damn it," I growl. "All right, that's enough." Bending, I fetch another coil of rope, sit on his wriggling legs, and bind his feet together. Done, I sit heavily on the edge of the bed. He lies at my feet, catching his breath, smiling up at me, blue eyes gleaming.

"*Now* you're caught," I say, wiping my brow. "My furry little imp."

"We'll see." Brendan flexes his limbs. He rolls back and forth on the floor, trying to writhe free. He ends up curled around my feet, working his wrists around in the rope.

"Stop struggling, boy, or you'll chafe yourself raw," I order, resting a boot on his chest.

"Yes, sir." He exhales, a long, deep breath, and falls still.

"Caught, yep. I guess I am. I guess I'm your prisoner of war," he says, kissing my wool-coated calf.

"And I'm guessing you're cold as hell on that wood floor." Standing, I drag his helpless form onto the bed.

"My pa used to take his belt to me when I misbehaved." Brendan leans against me, then bites my chin, staring up into my eyes. There's intense need in that blue gaze.

"Really? You want…?"

Brendan nips my chin again. Hard.

"Ouch! Stop that! You want me to…take a belt to your rear?" I can't believe he's asking for such a thing, but the request has my sex so hard I'm suffering.

Brendan hangs his head. He nods.

"Well, I *have* been threatening to put you over my knee lately…"

I need no further invitation. I pull off my belt, double it over, and bend Brendan over my lap. I strike him once, softly, then twice. Brendan groans. He nods. His bound feet give a little kick. His erection grinds into my thighs. "Bare skin?" he whispers.

I drop the belt on the bed, help him stand, unbutton his trousers, jerk them down to his ankles, and do the same to his undergarment. His cock pops free, a thick, bobbing length, absurdly large for such a small, war-emaciated boy. "Christ," I murmur in admiration before bending him over my knee again.

For seconds I can only stare at the plump ass-cheeks Brendan wants me to punish. So beautiful, both curves coated with curly auburn hair. As I'd hungrily noticed that day we bathed in the snowmelt, the hair in his crack is denser, a darker brown. I caress his ass, my heart hammering, thoroughly besotted. This is wonder; this is religion that makes sense.

Then Brendan wriggles on my lap and emits an impatient groan. I bring the belt down, and it makes a sharp whack against the firm curves of my little lad's flesh.

"Harder?" he whispers.

"You're so innocent you're shameless." I chuckle. "It's a lovely and God-sent blending; it's a marvel. But, son, I don't want to hurt you. You're still recovering—"

"Hurt makes me hard. I don't know why." As if in proof, he shoves his stiff sex against me. "Please?"

I oblige, striking him harder. He cocks his butt's hirsute splendor to receive the blows, then rubs his stiff sex against my lap, then lifts his butt again, a sweet rhythm I'd like to savor for hours.

I strike him again and again. But soon he's moaning too loudly in his arousal, emitting stifled shouts and half-choked-back yelps, losing sense of where we are and who in the nearby huts might hear. "That noise won't do," I say. "Far too much ruckus. Keep quiet."

"I'm sorry," he gasps. "I'll try." The next couple of blows he answers with strained grunts, but after that he's yelping again.

I cease beating him. "I think I should stop. I fear I'm truly hurting you."

"No! Oh, no. I'm sorry. I'm sorry. Please, more? Please? I need more. Please."

"All right, lad. But I'll have to shut you up." Holding him on my lap with one arm, I relinquish the belt long enough to pull my haversack up onto the bed. Here, my cap box, no…here, tent canvas, no…here, yes, the handkerchiefs from home. "I need to keep you quiet, boy. Open your mouth."

Brendan does what he's told. I cram balled-up cloth between his full lips, stuffing his mouth till his furry cheeks protrude. I reinforce that with another cloth pulled horizontally between his teeth and knotted behind his head.

"All right? Can you breathe? Is this all right?"

Brendan turns his head sideways, stares up at me with red, moist eyes, and nods.

"Are you crying, lad? Am I hurting you? Are you sure you don't want me to stop?"

Brendan shakes his head. He gives me a wet wink. A fat tear slides down his cheek. He humps my thigh.

"You want me to continue?"

Brendan nods frantically. I pick up the belt and bring it down again. Brendan groans into his gag, keeps nodding, and humps my lap with even greater vigor.

I beat Brendan for a good while, hoping that the ongoing roar of the blizzard will conceal the regular thwacking of leather on bare buttocks. I stop only when his furry ass is fairly scarlet and showing bruises, when his answer to my frequently asked query, "Have you had enough?" is at long last a muffled yes. We're both shivering by now, so, after adding more wood to the fire, I pull him with me under the blankets.

"Should I free you?" I whisper, spooning him. He shrugs his shoulders.

"Are you comfortable like this?"

"Mmm-mmm," he mumbles, nodding, scooting even closer.

"Good answer," I say, pulling my little captive to me. "I'd take that gag out of your mouth, but pretty soon I suspect you'll be making a lot more noise. Once we get warm, it's my turn to taste you."

❖

I can't stop making love to his torso, even when he begins whimpering with discomfort. I've unbuttoned his upper garments and tugged them down over his shoulders to bunch around his bound arms, baring his chest and belly. His armpits' thick scent, musky and unwashed, fills my head, maddening me. Keeping the blankets over us as much as possible, I lie on top of my lad, licking his chest hair, sucking his hard nipples; I roughly knead his pectorals, pinching his teat-nubs till he's whining. Something wild in me, long held back, is loose now, something violent. "Is this too rough? Let me know if it's too rough," I growl, rolling us onto our sides, wrapping my arms around him, lapping a nipple before worrying it with my teeth. Brendan winces, then arches his torso and pushes his nipple deeper into my mouth. I feast on his chest for a long time.

"Now it's time to taste your sex." I give his breast a last nip before tearing open his trousers and pulling out his cock. It's full, quivering, already dripping preliminary sap. When I thumb the sticky head and stroke the shaft, Brendan trembles and moans. I lick the head—it's shaped like a meaty valentine heart—savoring his salty juice.

"Wonderful, Brendan boy," I sigh. "You taste wonderful. Well worth the wait." I take the satiny bulb between my lips, hollowing my cheeks, creating a tight, wet suction. Brendan gives a stifled sob. I suck hard, chew his sex-head gently, then take him entirely in. He's so long and thick I can barely breathe. I pull off, chew the head again, run my tongue up and down the shaft, then swallow him to the hilt. Brendan bucks against me and begins humping my face hard and fast. I take tiny sips of air through the sides of my overfull mouth, his thick pubes tickling my nose, his thighs locked around my head.

Brendan's growling now, a long, low, ragged sound. "Are you close, boy?" I relinquish him long enough to ask. I look up at him; he looks down at me. His cheeks are flushed; his white teeth grit the cloth gag. He nods.

"Wait," I say. "I don't want you to spend yet. I want to love you more. May I…pleasure your…may I…your ass, may I? Just a finger this time."

"Mmm-hmm!" He manages a muffled affirmative and another eager nod. I unbind his feet, pull off his lower garments, and roll him onto his belly. I stroke his ass cheeks, twin curves illuminated by the low glow of the hearth, then kiss each. They're well bruised after the beating I gave him, still flushed and warm.

"You make me burn, son," I whisper. "I want to hurt you, and I want to cherish you too, protect you from all the dangers that surround us. There's a tenderness here, in my heart"—I thump my breastbone with my fist—"I've never known before. I feel it might kill me, or eat me alive, save for the fact that you welcome my touch."

Tears are gathering in my eyes, in the back of my throat, but I choke them down. Bending, I lick his buttocks. His scent's strong here despite the recent bathing, a musky, earthy aroma, warm and rich, like a barn in July. I run my beard along his crack, then the tip of my tongue; dense fur in the ripe, odorous cleft brushes my nose. Spreading his legs, I wet a finger in my mouth and find his tiny pucker amid the fur, a cavern's narrow entrance half-concealed by underbrush. I moisten him, probe, push, add more spit, and push again, gently, then a little harder.

Brendan whimpers once, and the tip of my finger slides in. His channel's very, very tight and very, very hot, the greatest warmth I've known for weeks and weeks of winter. "Does that feel good?" I work my finger around some. Brendan groans, "Uhhhh-mm!" and pushes himself onto me. My finger slides farther in between the furry rounds of his rear. I pull out, add more spit, and penetrate him again. Brendan bucks back, grunts, and my finger slides entirely inside. I fuck him, very slowly. Now I pull out, roll him onto his back, lift his legs, and enter him again. He wraps his calves around my shoulders; I fuck him faster, capturing his dripping penis in my mouth. He squeals into his gag, pumping my face, and suddenly my throat's full of his spurting seed. I gulp it down only to be filled up again and then again.

We lie panting for a while, before I unbind Brendan and remove his gag. As soon as he's free, he's on me with an animal's snarl, slurping down my sex's stiff ache. As aroused as I am and as eager as is his mouth, I reach my crest within a minute, gushing into him while he sighs and swallows.

"I'd say we're both as full of sweet sap as a sugar maple tree," Brendan says. "Here's a drop of it now. Mistletoe berry." He licks his spilt semen from my mustache and kisses me.

Shivering, we pull on our clothes, relieve ourselves in the piss-can, heap wood on the fire, and return to bed. I wrap an arm around Brendan's shoulder; he rests his head on my chest. His damned cough starts up again, racking him for long minutes.

"Easy, boy, easy," I say, rocking him. He sits up, stands, and leans against the mantelpiece, gasping. The coughing subsides; he spits into the fire, then crawls back into bed.

"Sorry," he says wearily, snuggling into my arms. Slipping a hand beneath my half-buttoned coat and shirt, he strokes the hair on my chest. "My God, I love this," he sighs. "My great furry bear. And I loved your finger up inside me, fucking my hole. I want more of that tomorrow. I've never felt such a thing, but I've been wanting it ever since we met."

"And did you mind the rope and the gag, lad? You did say you wanted to be mastered, and you did fight me so vigorously that—"

Brendan giggles. "Yes, sir, I fought so hard and I made so much noise that you had no choice but to bind me and silence my cries. True indeed. It was...thrilling, like a grand adventure. It was as if you'd kidnapped me and were holding me captive here high on this mountaintop. As if I were the hero of a novel, imprisoned, ravished, and cruelly used by a great, dark, handsome villain. As if you were forcing me. It made my balls throb. It made me very happy."

"Brat. You're shameless indeed." I slap his flank with mock outrage. "And perverse. Deliciously so. The way your pain and powerlessness excite both of us…it thrilled me too, to have you so completely at my mercy, to have you so helpless, so sweetly vulnerable. I found a book once, in the back room of an Atlanta bookstore, a coverless thing, by a Frenchman…"

"You understand French too? A polymath indeed!"

"I can make out a good bit. At any rate, it was by a marquis, it was pornographic, and I must admit to being titillated at how his characters delighted in the perverse, things I would never have imagined, and powerlessness and pain aroused them too, so it's good to know we're not alone, not the first in this."

"The rope felt good, Shep, as did the cloth in my mouth. It was heady to know that I couldn't escape, couldn't speak, had no choice but to endure what you chose to dole out."

"And yet you were completely in control." I guffaw. "You made me do exactly what you wanted me to do. Well done. Very clever, little monster. Well, the Lord has certainly filled us with complementary desires. They'd be a terrible curse unshared, but shared they're rich rapture indeed. At some point," I say, "do you think, if we can find some grease to make the process easier, that…I can mount you? I want that very badly. *Very* badly."

Brendan reaches down to squeeze my prick. "Oh, yes. I want that too! I want you to fuck my ass. You're not the only one to have thought of that. I want you to ride me hard, Shep." Emptied as it is, my limp flesh stirs at his frank language, his touch, the thought of being pushed inside him. "Perhaps, if you take your time over a few weeks, and use your fingers every night to open my hole, I'll grow more accustomed. As big as you are, though, we'll be needing a lot of grease."

We both laugh softly. He grips my arm, rolls us onto our sides, and nestles his rear against my crotch. More coughing spasms him. "I love you, Shep," he gasps. "I thank the Lord for this war, not only because it will free the South but most especially because it's brought us together."

The fit subsides, and he's soon asleep. Slumber resists me. I lie in the firelit dimness, worrying about my lad's health. His breathing's as hoarse and ragged as an invalid's.

❖

We have a rough night. Brendan's cough is worsening.

Morning, the piss-can's frozen over, but the blizzard's lessened to a light snow. When my lad's chosen for picket duty the next day, I beg for leave to take his place and receive it. Despite his protests, I make him stay in bed. When I drop by the hospital tent to ask for medicine, hoping some elixir might clear my little lad's lungs, the doctors have next to no medicines left, between the damned Yankee blockade and the weeks we've spent isolated in this high place.

The rest of the afternoon I spend behind breastworks overlooking the turnpike. Far across the snow-swirling valley, the Yanks are waiting. With spyglasses, I can make out smoke from their campfires rising from the crest of Cheat Mountain. Goddamn them. If they'd only leave, head home, then we could do the same. I wouldn't be out here with numb nose, fingers, and toes, and Brendan wouldn't be hacking back in that freezing cabin.

"Shep!" It's Brendan stumbling through the snowy woods.

"Damn you, son!" I shout. "I'm out here to spare you this fucking cold. Go back!"

"I feel bad that you're out here, Shep." Brendan's face is flushed. He coughs, spits phlegm into the snow, and proffers me a cup of coffee. "It's half cold by now, I fear, but it's better than nothing. And here's some cornbread and a piece of fatback." He pushes a bundle into my trouser pocket.

"Thanks, lad. Now go back." I take the cup and sip from it. The slightest bit of heat still lingers.

Brendan coughs again, then grins at me. "Cold as it is out here, I'd still like to drop to my knees and suck your cock right now."

"Lordamercy! You've come to savor the profane, haven't you?" I say, grinning back. After the bodily awakening we've shared, Brendan's language has grown noticeably coarser, though somehow that seems only to arouse me more. "Such an innocent boy once, now corrupted entirely by the army, by bad companions like me. Drinking, swearing, cocksucking. No prick for you here, son. Now git!"

Brendan squeezes my arm, giving me one of those winks that he surely knows by now is the fastest way to melt any resolve I might have. He looks around, checking for witnesses. Then he gives my crotch a quick squeeze before loping back to camp.

❖

By necessity it's a stag dance, there being no ladies handy, and thus a perfect excuse. Here we are, my lad and I, on Christmas Eve, waltzing about the campfire with other male couples. John's playing the fiddle, "Gal on a Log," then "Leather Breeches." Brendan smiles at me, amazingly agile; I do my clumsy best to follow along, my boots ending up atop his once or twice. He leans his head against my chest; snowflakes ride the breeze; constellations shift over the mountains; smoke drifts off the fire. I want to take my boy's curvaceous rear in my hands but think better of it. As it is, dancing in public allows me to pretend for a few minutes that our love is open, honest, and approved. It's a false happiness, but it feels sweet nonetheless. This is a freedom men and women together must feel all the time.

"Tonight, will you open me yet again, Shep?" Brendan whispers beneath the notes of the fiddle. "My hole's aching to be filled; I need it bad. Tonight, I think, I can take three fingers. If you oblige me, I promise you a grand Christmas surprise tomorrow, one you won't soon forget."

I grin with expectation, relishing the frankness of his desire. The last week of camp routine has grown grimmer, as illness, especially pneumonia, has carried off several men, requiring burials in earth so frozen it's almost impossible to dig a grave. But my nights have been enriched considerably by a sweeter routine: Brendan unbuttoning his clothes, then mine, despite the cold; Brendan nuzzling my neck, kissing me deeply; Brendan whispering, "Tie me, sir. Fuck my mouth. Finger my hole." It makes me hard, just remembering. The boy's youth, plus years of repressed desires without outlet, have made him nigh insatiable.

"You've become an obscene and ravenous little demon, lad, and, God help me, I've come entirely to adore you," I whisper back. "I think I know what that Christmas surprise is. I hope so."

"You'll have to wait and see."

With that, we change partners, and suddenly big-bearded Jason's in my arms. We look at one another uncomfortably. "How's your chicken?" Jason asks, stumbling. "That's a bad cough he has."

Chicken. The boys use the term to indicate a younger companion. They'd likely use harsher language if they knew the truth. I've heard the phrases back home: "improper, indecent, a crime unfit to be named, a violation of nature," etc. I wonder if Jason would still be my friend if he knew. We've known one another since we were children, but...

"His cough's gotten bad over the last few days. I asked for medicine. The doctors don't have any."

"Fucking Yanks, blockading our harbors, letting sick men die. That hospital tent's full of men with the flux and men with lungs all et up with pneumonia, and my bed's full of goddamn lice and I got the camp itch. And them damn doctors, they ain't worth a shit." Jason always uses profanity when he's drinking, just as Brendan does when he's amorous. "And your dancing's piss-poor! Who's leading here?"

Jason stops swaying and gives my chest a soft punch. "C'mon. It's Christmas Eve, and we're stuck in hell. I got some whiskey left."

❖

Christmas dinner's good, thanks to victuals some local farmers have risked the frozen roads and foul weather to provide us. My mess has a stewed chicken John's prepared, as well as broiled beef and turnips in bacon grease; Brendan's has, unbelievably, a ham, some fried potatoes, some peaches canned in syrup, and even a few bottles of homemade wine. My lad and I each heap up a plate, then sit on a log by my mess-fire and share them. Dessert's a slice of whiskey-scented fruitcake we gulp down like pigs, accompanied by real coffee, not one of those damned substitutes. Virginia does indeed take care of us.

Yesterday, I again insisted on taking Brendan's turn at picket, but tonight I'm scheduled to take my own turn for my regiment, so after dinner I reluctantly shoulder my musket and leave the circle of firelight, the sound of drunken laughter, the holiday sounds of fiddle and banjo. As I head out into the frosty dark, Brendan grabs my arm. "Take good care, Shep. I'll be waiting for you. I'll have your surprise. Be sure to knock first before you enter tonight." A quick wink, and he's returned to the warmth of the fire.

❖

Colder than ever. No clouds, no snow, just stars and wind, bitter air that gets inside my bones and makes me fear summer will never return. All I can think of as I guard the turnpike is that warm, sweet, hairy boy back in our hut, waiting for me in our bed. Again and again, hard wind off the valley slams me in the face; my breath freezes on my beard. I shift my musket from hand to hand, wishing desperately that I had gloves.

"Howdy." It's mess-cook John trudging up. "My turn. Merry Christmas."

I slap his back. "Even merrier soon, with any luck. That chicken stew was wonderful! Many thanks!" I leave him, no doubt confused at the intensity of my holiday spirit, and jog through the heaped snow back to camp.

❖

I knock as requested. "Come in," Brendan shouts.

I step inside. The little space is almost toasty; there's a bright fire crackling on the hearth, wood heaped in the corner, and a candle lit on the mantelpiece. But it's what I see on the bed that holds my gaze.

Brendan's lying atop the blankets, and he's naked, except for a pair of tattered socks. His cock is hard, standing up, and he's stroking it. Candlelight gleams on the sticky head. On the bed beside him are my handkerchiefs, my coil of tent-rope, and a small vial. He looks down his fur-pelted body at me and gives me one of his brilliant grins. "Merry Christmas, Mr. Shep. Block the door, please."

I do so. I turn, entranced, my eyes ranging over his nakedness, my crotch growing stiff. The hut's small space is redolent of split wood and his body's robust scent.

Brendan leaves off his sex-stroking to tie the rope around his right wrist. He gestures toward the hearth. "I borrowed all that wood from my mess-mates, 'cause we need this room to be real warm if we're to be naked. I told them it was 'cause of this damned cough I can't shake. In return, I promised them I'd cut their wood for a few days."

He lifts the vial. "This is bacon grease. I've been saving it. I told my mess cook I'd clean the dishes for the next week if I could have it."

Brendan chuckles. "I think he thinks I have an unnatural hankering for pork fat. I want you to use it to fuck me, Shep."

"I, uh, boy," I croak. My sex is ramrod-rigid.

"With your fingers first, Shep. As I'm used to. But then with your greased prick. Just go slowly, please. I want you tie me, Shep"— Brendan wraps another loop of rope around his wrist—"and make me your captive as before, and fuck me with that great prick of yours. Fuck me till you spend inside me. Spend your seed inside me, Shep."

I lick my lips. My head pounds. I feel ever so slightly faint.

Brendan rolls over onto his belly. Reaching back with both hands, he spreads his ass cheeks to display his cleft like the gift it is. Thick as is the surrounding hair there, I can see the wrinkled opening that's become such a focus of my ardor.

"Fuck me, Shep. I'm begging you." Retrieving the bandanas, Brendan gags himself in the same manner I had before, then crosses his wrists behind his back and lies still.

I stand there for long, stunned seconds. Then I position another log on the fire, and I strip. Sitting on the bed, I stroke my lad's buttocks. "A wonder of nature," I whisper. "A wonder, a wonder." How few days or nights of our lives allow such marvels or permit such joys, I muse briefly, bending to kiss his shoulders. Then I bind Brendan's wrists firmly together, kneel between his legs, spread his thighs wider, and begin.

❖

We take our time. Despite several nights of preparation, of easing him open with my fingers, his rear is very tight. My tongue ranges over his buttocks—as curved, cleft, and fuzzy as Georgia peaches back home—then I ravage those mounds with my teeth, inspiring in him muted cries. I lick his crevice again, but this time the strong scent of his ass is too tempting and I can't resist trying what I've never tried before: I must taste that tiny entrance. And so I bury my face between his cheeks and lap at his aromatic hole. His moans urge me on, and soon I have my tongue burrowing deep inside him. I take him that way for long minutes, savoring his pungent taste and smell: a bitterness, like mortality, but a sweetness as well, like hard cider, and, oddly, the taste of groundnuts too.

Bacon-greased fingers next: one, then two, then three. Brendan rears like a colt and whimpers like a puppy. His body's straining, tense with lingering resistance.

At last I have my grease-moistened prick lodged between his nether cheeks, nudging the virgin opening there. "Ready?" I whisper, stretched atop him, my arms wrapped around his bound arms and torso, my legs spreading his wide. Brendan nods; I edge in an inch. Brendan whines; I stop. I begin anew; Brendan sobs, nods, pushes back…and of a sudden the head of my sex slides past the ring of his inner resistance. Brendan winces and gasps. Bliss washes over me, greater than any I've ever known.

I stroke his face, finding tears there. "You're weeping! Am I hurting you, boy? I'll stop if you want. I'll pull out if I'm hurting you."

"Mmm-mmm!" Brendan shakes his head; his bound hands grip my belly hair; his ass pucker gives me a tiny, thrilling squeeze, like a tentative gesture of welcome.

Eager as I am to pound him, I keep still for long minutes, allowing his body to accustom itself somewhat to my penetration. I kiss his wet cheek, cup the mounds of his chest, finger his nipple-nubs, and knead his ass.

"Dear God, I love your body, Brendan. Hairy hard curves up front—this sweet chest—and hairy hard curves in back—this sculpted miracle of an ass. It's such a blessing, to be inside you like this."

Brendan emits a deep sigh, spreads his thighs wider still, and wriggles his hips. Turning his head, he looks back at me. His eyes are wide, moist, full of a savage happiness. He gnashes his teeth on cloth and growls like a bear cub.

"More now?" I kiss his cheek.

"Mmm-hmm." Brendan nods, mumbling into his mouthful of cloth. He buries his face in the blanket. Beneath me, the last tension leaves his body. Now his submission's complete.

Inch by inch, I slide farther within him. His channel is fiery and tight, his young flesh pulsing around mine.

"Uhh," I grunt. "Oh, my God. Uhhh. I'm almost all in, wild one. You want the rest?"

In answer, Brendan bucks his hips, pushing back onto me, impaling himself completely.

"Uhhhhmmmm!" he groans, fingers quivering against my belly.

"Uhh-hhfff!" I gasp, hugging him more tightly still. "Good? Feel good?"

Brendan nods sharply and releases another long, loud groan.

"Quiet, lad. Shush." Clamping my hand over his mouth, I pull partly out and push in again. Brendan gasps and shudders.

"Is that it, lad? Is that the sweet place I spoke of? Did I find it? Your honey-spot?"

Brendan trembles. He breathes hard through his nose. He nods again, tightening his body's gateway around me. He rocks forward, then back onto me, then forward, then back, again, again, again, a wild and desperate rhythm.

"Want me to ride you now, lad?" I say, removing my hand from his mouth. Pulling his head back by his lank hair, I press my bearded cheek against his and look him in the eye. "Easy at first, I think, then hard? I'm so, so eager to pound you."

Brendan blinks at me and mumbles. I can make out his beseeching syllables despite the tight interference of cloth. "Yes. Please, yes. Please, yes."

❖

I wake before light to a frigid cabin and a low glow of embers. I feast on Brendan's ass again, suck his cock to fruition, straddle his chest, and finish myself in his beard. Then it's the damned reveille bugle, and we're dressing and dashing across camp to line up. "I won't need much breakfast today," I say before we part to meet our respective regiments. "Your hole tasted better than the best bacon in the Southland." Brendan giggles, coughs, hacks up phlegm, and jogs over to his fellow Virginians.

It sleets all day. I beg Brendan to stay inside, but he swears his cough is better and heads out to chop wood to repay his fuel debt. I insist on helping. He seems more easily winded than normal, but then so am I, for we got very little sleep last night. By noon, the sleet's turned to cold rain, and by midafternoon, we're both soaked, though we've managed to chop a great pile of logs.

That evening, we spend hours by the cabin fire, trying to dry out, but we still end up having to sleep in damp clothes. After midnight, Brendan wakes me with his nudging butt and whispered pleadings. He shucks down his trousers, reaches back to fondle my stiffness. "Fuck me, Shep. Fuck me rough." I take him as requested, brutally—first on his side, then on his belly, tugging on his shaggy hair as if it were a horse's reins, pinching his nipples, covering his cries with my hand. He spurts on the bed as I pump his innards full of seed.

Brendan's ragged coughing wakes me before dawn. When I press my hand to his forehead and neck, his skin's burning. By dawn, his breaths are shallow and his coughing nigh continuous. He's clearly feverish and too dizzy to stand up. "Chest hurts," he says, "my head too." I lift his lean form into my arms and carry him to the hospital tent.

"Pneumonia," says the grizzled doctor, smelling of whiskey. "Bad case. He'll have to stay here." He waves a hand at the lines of beds. "Running through the camp. I already have ten men here. It's killed ten more. We have an empty cot over here."

I lower Brendan onto the makeshift bed and pull woolen blankets to his chin. "I'll be fine, Shep," Brendan says hoarsely, eyes shiny with fever-glaze. I sit by him till he falls into a fitful sleep. He tosses, turns, and mutters.

Another doctor appears, this one young, blond, and ramrod-straight. "The fever's got him, and we have no medicine. But he's very young, and that might make a difference. Come back later, soldier."

I want to cover Brendan's flushed face with kisses but settle for gripping his hand. My lad wakes, squeezes my palm, then, groaning and twitching, falls into unconsciousness.

"Are there no medicines anywhere?" I ask, straightening Brendan's blankets and fighting back terror.

The doctor shakes his head. "We ran out weeks ago."

❖

I spend breakfast in a daze. Jason's absent. "Sick too," says John. "Got the flux and the pneumonia. Very bad." Shaking his head, he hands me a stale slice of bread smeared with bacon grease and fried onions. When I bite into it, the taste of bacon absurdly reminds me of Brendan's ass, the grease I used to enter him. To my surprise and embarrassment, I burst into tears.

John's beside me in two seconds. "Shep! What's wrong? Your chicken?"

Chicken. My devotion must be more obvious than I'd thought. "My little lad, he's very, very sick," I say between sobs. "I should have taken him to the medical tent sooner. I never should have let him chop wood in the rain. The damned doctors, they have no medicine. Oh, I'm so sorry, John. It's shameful to weep like this, like a woman."

"No shame, you big fool. What shame is there in sorrow? And you should know that there's medicine in Monterey. Or at least there was. I have a friend there. In the last letter—brought on Christmas by those fine folks who brought us food—he said they have some medicine yet."

"Then I need to fetch it!" I jolt to my feet.

"Monterey's a day's ride from here, and the road's nigh impassable."

"Thank you, John! Bless you!" I run to the hospital tent. There I find Brendan tossing with delirium. "I'll be back, lad," I say, wiping my eyes, "and you'd damn well better hang on for me," but the boy's too deep in fever-fit to know I'm near. Jason's on a cot nearby, in the same condition, his face covered with sweat. Hurried confabulation with doctors, hurried explanation to my leading officer, permission to depart, and I'm astraddle one of the stove-up carthorses and on my way down the turnpike.

My ride's a rushing, fragmented dream. The road's terrible, a mash of mud and ice. The trip to Monterey takes a day, over steep and wooded mountains. Rain, sleet, and snow take their turns making me miserable. I stop in a Hightown farmhouse to beg lunch, and the family's hospitality is warm and gracious. I'm queried about the progress of the war, served cups of coffee and slices of a golden-brown chicken pie I know my poor sick boy would covet. They invite me to take my rest on a cozy couch, but having no time to waste, I saddle up again. After dark, I gallop—dizzy with cold and exhaustion—into Monterey. I requisition the medicines, then, feeling guilty, give the doctor the silver chain I inherited from my father. "Use this to buy more medicine if you can," I say, gathering my bottled treasure. "Is there lodging for a soldier nearby?"

The next morning, I wake early, my throat ominously scratchy, my joints aching. After a hurried breakfast of sausage and eggs at the inn, I head back along the turnpike toward Allegheny Mountain. Around noon, I enjoy another farmhouse's patriotic generosity: buttermilk, fried chicken, fried cabbage, and butter-rich spoonbread. The weather holds—bitterly cold and gray, but thankfully dry—till dusk, when sleet returns. By the time my half-dead horse begins climbing the eastern slope of Allegheny Mountain, sleet's turned into another thick, wet snow, my head's swimming, and my brow's burning.

"Your chicken's still alive," says the older doctor, taking the precious stash of bottles I pull from my saddlebags before leading me into the tent. Here's Brendan, very pale, insensible beneath an oilcloth blanket.

"Thank God," I pant. Forgetting myself in my relief, I fall to my knees by my little lad and kiss his brow.

"You look feverish. Lie down here, Private," the doctor says, pointing to an empty cot beside Brendan. I collapse onto it, reach over to squeeze my lad's hand, and fall instantly asleep.

❖

I'm too weak to rise, and I can barely breathe. Some fool's forgotten to open the flue; the room's full of smoke. It burns my eyes and lungs. I need to get up. I need to use the sinks. I'm too big to lift, always knew my bulk would be disadvantageous someday. Look now, the damned flux, and I've soiled myself. Here's Brendan stretched out next to me. Silly boy's crying, pretty lips quivering, brow creased up like an old man's. Worry not, chicken. I love you, chicken. Kiss me, chicken. Go back to summer, chicken. I'll fetch you a peach pie, a chicken pie, whatever you crave. There's swamp in my lungs. I didn't mean to cry. Swamp and snot, and the fire's eaten all my air. Yes, I'll drink it, yes, sawbones, here now, it's gone. Foul-tasting, essence of ragweed! Yes, Lord, water, please, yes, that's good. But where's my lad now? He should be sleeping by my side, but, look, his cot's empty. God, where's the boy gone? Oh, God, then I must bury him? No, no, no, no. Brendan, little god, tight colt, come back, boy, let me ride you again.

❖

I wake to a cloth brushing my face. It's wet and warm. When I open my eyes, there's Brendan, looking down at me. His face is gray and thin. There's one white hair on his chin. I reach up and pluck at it. "Gittin' old," I say. "Where's that giggling Head Waters boy I met a few days back?"

"About gone, I guess," says Brendan. "Welcome back, big bear. Welcome to eighteen sixty-two. Here, drink."

"Eighteen sixty-two? What day is it?"

Holding up my head, he lifts a tin cup to my lips. Cold water. Tastes wonderful, like the well back home.

"It's January eleventh. The boys—what's left of us—we all made some noise on New Year's Eve, but you slept through it. You've missed a few more blizzards. It's been so cold that some of the horses have frozen to death standing up."

I look around. It's the hospital tent. There's a strong odor of smoke and feces, the sounds of coughing and moaning, men babbling with delirium.

"Nasty place. Take me home," I say. My face is numb. I wipe my brow only to find I'm dripping with sweat.

"You almost died, Shep. Terrible pneumonia. I almost died of it too. That medicine you fetched saved us both. But Jason's gone, and so are my messmates Rick and Joseph. They all died before you got back. Now the medicine's gone again. But you saved a goodly number of us."

"I want to go back to our cabin." My lips are dry and cracked; my elbow-joints throb. "I want to hold you."

"Shhh." Brendan looks nervously around. "You, uh, said some things in your fever that have folks talking. Anyway, in a few days, I think, the doctors will let you loose. You're in pretty good shape compared to most of these boys, and I think the doctors need your bed for worse cases."

My belly cramps; something shifts inside. "Brendan, can you help me up? I need…"

"The latrine ditch? Better by far than the bed! You had the flux for days. That combined with lung sickness about carried you off.

"Hey! You there!" Brendan shouts down the tent. "I need some help with this man! He's too big for me! He needs the sinks!"

"Lord. Where did that shy child go? You're downright ferocious." I grip the sides of the cot and with great difficulty roll off the side onto my knees. They ache as badly as my elbows. Shakily, with Brendan's help, I rise; a stocky assistant appears; the three of us, swaying, stumbling, leave the tent.

❖

As Brendan had predicted, in three days the doctors release me, and, leaning on my lad, I weave weakly back to our hut. I'm not as young as I once was; it'll take me a long time to feel strong again. But, thank God, within a few weeks, despite the continuing foul weather, Brendan's back to normal save for increasingly infrequent coughing fits. He takes my picket duty, insists I stay in bed, fetches wood for our hut, brings me meals, washes me, helps me stagger to the sinks. At night he reads to me and holds me while we mourn our lost comrades.

The morning of Valentine's Day, I wake to find Brendan tying my wrists together before me. "Easy, easy," he says, when I offer a counterfeit struggle. "My turn, ain't it?" he whispers, kissing me. "Got me more grease. I want to ride you, Shep. I want you on your elbows and knees. Come on now, Shep. Come on now, Shep. Please?"

It's been a long time since I was fucked—in fact, it's only been that one time in the barn so long ago—and Brendan's prick is even bigger than mine. He's young, eager, and inexperienced; he takes me too fast, nudging my hole only a little before plunging in; it hurts considerably. When I start whimpering, Brendan strokes my shoulders, soothing me. "Ah, I'm sorry, I'm so sorry I'm paining you. Easy now. Open up, Shep. Relax. Let me in. I love you, Shep. Surrender, soldier. There now, big man. Easy."

He slows down, giving me a break, then, when my pained grunts have subsided, he grips my hips and starts a vigorous pounding. The bed creaks and shakes, and then the bed's bouncing against the wall, and the cabin's shaking as well. When my moans mount, he stuffs one of his smelly socks in my mouth. "Bite down on this and shut up," he says, his body's weight atop mine, his fingernails sunk into the flesh of my breast.

"Time you got the very treatment you've doled out, big brute. There, yes. Open for your lad. That's it," Brendan growls, seizing my cock in his hand and commencing to pump it. "You're full now, aren't you, Big Shep? Your hole's stuffed full, and you love it, don't you, Shep? Beg me for more, Shep. Want me to ride you harder?"

I nod and moan. Inside me, the burning pangs are gone, and my boy's thrusting has found rapture's seat. The pleasure opens in me like an apple blossom in April.

"Squeeze me, yes, like that!" he growls. "Ah, God. Yes. Yes, yes, yes. Is that your honey-spot, big man? Yes? Yes! Ah. Ah. I'm arriving, I'm here, ah!"

I leave for picket ten minutes after we're done. Standing in a grove of spruce overlooking the valley, musket on my shoulder, I listen to the minute sounds of new snow falling onto the icy crusts of old snow, Brendan's seed trickling out of me, moistening my underclothes. At supper, over a meal of hardtack fried in bacon grease, Brendan slips me a paper before heading off to his own time on the picket line. When I unfold it later, in our hut, I find, drawn with wood-char, the smudged black outline of a lopsided heart.

The calendar claims that spring's come, but, high as we are, the snows continue, the gray's rarely broken. Here and there are a few buds, a few patches of wild onion, a few glimpses of blue sky, the only proof that warmth and green are on their way. A few days after April's arrival, Colonel Johnson gives the order to break camp. We're moving east, to another bastion atop Shenandoah Mountain.

The night before we leave Camp Allegheny my lad and I spend making love. I take Brendan; we doze; we rouse; Brendan takes me. As frigid a hell as this camp has been, as close to death as cold and sickness brought us, still I regret the move, if only because we'll be leaving behind the relative privacy of our hut. Soon, it's likely, we'll be in tents, perhaps even different tents, with different companions; our lovemaking will become rushed at best, at worst impossible.

Reveille, hurried coffee and more fried hardtack—the food supply's almost gone. Then we fall into line, Brendan with his depleted Virginians, I with my depleted Georgians. I look back once, toward the fields and woods where our companions are buried beneath wooden markers not long to last, and toward the cabins. Soon, in our wake, the damned bluecoats across the valley will occupy those huts. Soon the mountain weather will erode them; soon they'll crumble and fall. Someday, with luck, after the war Brendan and I will return together, to remember our time here. Someday, perhaps, centuries hence, men who love like us will pass by, see the pitted chimney stones, and try to imagine our lives.

We reach Monterey, on the first sunny day in weeks, and fall out on the courthouse lawn. It seems like a lifetime ago that I galloped into this town, desperate for medicines. As promised, Brendan leads me to his aunt's house. We gratefully gulp down a big meal of buckwheat cakes, maple syrup, and bacon in her cozy kitchen before dashing back to our regiments and marching out again.

We build Fort Edward Johnson on the high ridge of Shenandoah Mountain: wooden walls, trenches, earthen defenses, rows of cannon. On duty, we huddle behind long lines of breastworks, knees sunk in heaped snow and ice-speckled drifts of dead leaves. We cut down trees on the western slope to allow us a better view and unobstructed aim. Off duty, we descend the eastern slope, huddle about campfires in Georgia Flats, a tent colony four miles distant. As I'd feared, Brendan's assigned to the Virginians' tents, and so our nights together are over. We spend some time together by campfires; we manage a waltz every now and then—my lad's small hands squeezing mine—when the fiddles are brought out and the boys get to dancing. Every night, I lie beside John, the last of my former messmates, think of Brendan—his nakedness, the auburn hair on his breast and around his sex, the smell of his ass-cleft and of his seed—and stroke myself to climax beneath my damp blanket once John's fallen asleep.

On one afternoon I'm commissioned to visit the Mountain House, a nearby inn, to requisition provisions, and Brendan manages to get leave to accompany me. "My cousin works in the kitchen," he says, leading me at a rapid pace up the turnpike, speed bespeaking eagerness. There, he convinces her to lend two weary soldiers an empty bed for a quick nap.

It's a little room beneath a gable in the apex of the inn, with flowery wallpaper and a small canopied bed. We lock the door and pull back the blankets. We strip and fall upon one another like ravening beasts, our mouths slamming together, hands roughly kneading chests, ass cheeks, and hard cocks. I bend Brendan over the bed, moisten him with spit, and take him hard. Impaled, he chews the sheets. Rough as is our lovemaking, it's cautious, silent save for deep breaths and stifled sighs. When we spend, we're careful to catch the seed in our handkerchiefs so as not to besmirch the bedclothes. I drowse, eyes on the mantelpiece clock, while Brendan snores in my arms. After an hour, I rouse him. In the kitchen, his cousin serves us cold milk, fried grits, and salty ham, then pieces of apple pie we loudly proclaim paradisal.

On the way back to camp, loaded down with baskets of food, Brendan stops long enough to hand me his handkerchief. It's still moist with his seed. "Keep this to remember me by," he says, eyes downcast. "Just in case, in case…God sees fit to part us. And I want yours."

Throat tight, I pass him my seed-stained handkerchief. He lifts it to his face, licks it, and buries his nose in it. Then we pick up our burdens and continue our journey back to camp.

❖

A few alarms throughout April, scurrying up the slope of Shenandoah Mountain when we hear the sound of the signal gun. Gasping for breath, sides heaving, legs aching with effort, we man the breastworks and fire at scattered Yankee pickets moving against us from the west. It continues to snow and sleet during the month's first weeks, making tent life miserable, then grows warm, making our woolen uniforms prickly and uncomfortable.

Brendan and I take walks in the woods whenever we can, desperate for time alone. One day we find a small cave in the hillside, near a stream lined with leafing willows. I pull him inside, tear open his uniform, suck on his nipples and cock. I bend him over, tongue and finger his asshole while he finishes himself, shooting seed over stone. I tug my prick out and he sucks me to completion. We've barely buttoned up and left the cave when we bump into some of his Virginians. Nearly caught, but the risk was worth it.

By late April it's greening. A week into May, word comes that Stonewall Jackson's left the Valley, that Yanks are trying to flank us from the west, that we're needed to protect Staunton, so we leave Fort Johnson and the Georgia Flats and move east. The turnpike's a hideous rut of mud, clambering narrowly up wooded hills; the night's black as pitch; the rain won't stop. At Buffalo Gap, we huddle and curse beside campfires hissing and smoking in the drizzle. In West View, seven miles west of Staunton, we pitch camp. To our surprise, Jackson's force appears, and soon, after a short night's sleep, we're all heading west again, a big army now that we're conjoined. We pass the Mountain House, driving off stray Yanks, rushing up Shenandoah Mountain only to find that the occupying Feds have fled Fort Johnson.

Near nightfall, the seventh of May, we camp along a creek called Shaw's Fork. I range about after evening muster, looking for Brendan. I find him wandering around, looking for me, eyes full of worry. We sit by his campfire, each chewing a fatty piece of salt pork. It's a beautiful night, full of stars, gentle breezes, the scent of greening pastures, the purling of creek water, roses blooming along a nearby farmhouse fence. "Pretty sure we'll be in battle tomorrow," I say. "Word is the Yanks have a big force, including those bastards from Cheat Mountain. Let's take a walk."

We stroll along the flower-perfumed fence, then along the stream, looking for a private place to be together. We're in luck: here's a dark barn. I look around, then pull Brendan inside, leading him into an empty stall.

"I need some battle-luck, boy. Give Big Shep a kiss." Cupping his ass in my hands, I draw him to me. We're kissing hard when I hear someone call my name. We jolt apart just as my messmate John appears in a low glow of lantern-light.

"Shep, that *is* you. I thought I saw you come in here."

"John, I, I..." I splutter, but before I can continue, he lifts the lantern and grins. "Ah. Brendan. Shep, you're fonder of that chicken than I thought. I'd heard some of the things you said in your delirium, but I figured...well, tomorrow we're off to battle, boys. Gather you rosebuds how you may. Just don't let the farmer catch you."

He's half-turned before he hesitates. "I'm on picket duty tonight, Shep. So if you and your chicken would like a little time in the tent, you're welcome to it."

With that unbelievable statement, he strolls off. We stand there astounded, stiff as scarecrows for half a minute before I whisper, "It's providence, boy. It's God's grace." We dart back to our bivouac and into the tent John and I share. Within minutes, Brendan and I have torn off our upper garments, pulled our pants around our ankles, and, bony rib cages bumping, are very quietly making love for what could be the last time.

❖

The little village below is called McDowell, and it's lousy with Yankees. This knoll we Georgians are massed atop is called Sitlington's Hill, and, from what I can tell of the shouts and booming of artillery, the bluecoats are moving up the slope, determined to take it, despite our best efforts.

Brendan's with his Virginians, on the right. I catch his eye and smile; his grin is strained but his wink warms me. Then we return to the business of war. I tear open a cartridge, load my musket, and wait.

Thanks to John's unexpected kindness, my lad and I had our night together. We kissed and kissed. I lay on my back, Brendan wet himself with spit and, with wincing determination, sat on my cock. I spent inside him, and soon thereafter he spent in my chest hair and beard. We slept in one another's arms till near dawn, when John returned from picket duty, tapped on the tent flaps, and gave us time to make ourselves presentable.

The Yanks are nearer. I can hear them getting closer, crashing through that greening grove of trees just down the hill. I run my fingers through my beard, lift them to my nose, and grin. I smell of Brendan still. Dying will be a bitter thing if it comes, but at least I've had my love, my little lad, and I'll die with his rich scent still on me.

There's the first line of them, breaking from the shelter of the trees. My name's on a card pinned inside my jacket—in case, God forbid, Brendan and all my friends fall and no one's left to identify my body—and with it a note asking that I be buried with Brendan Botkin, if both of us are slain.

"Ready!"

I drop onto one knee.

"Remember to aim low!"

I lift my musket to my shoulder.

"Wait till you can see their eyes!"

I set my sights on a Yank.

"Now! Fire!"

I pull the trigger. My musket explodes and kicks. All about me, Georgian guns are firing.

I cough, smoke clawing my eyes. Why have so few bluecoats fallen? Goddamn it. I'm in the midst of tearing open another cartridge when flame flashes along their line.

There's a chunking sound, like that an axe makes biting into bark, and pain blinds me. I spin and fall onto my side, clutching my left arm. Blood spurts from the hole in my jacket.

Around me, balls embed themselves in the grass, men are screaming. Roaring fills my ears, then dies to a purling like that stream my boy and I strolled along last night. I look around to find my fellows fallen all around me, our line broken, bluecoats everywhere.

I grit my teeth and spit. Here's one now, looming over me, an ugly thing with a bald pate and a gray-stubbled face. I glare up at him. "Goddamn you to hell," I say. He takes his rifle by the barrel and swings the butt at my head. Praying for Brendan and for the South, I close my eyes.

❖

My lad exists for only a minute; that's about the length of time I can keep my eyes open. A minute here and there.

First, bending over me in the field, blue May sky framing his face and matching his eyes.

Then walking beside the litter, every shift of which causes me to grit my teeth with agony.

Now, here in the vestibule of a church, clutching my hand, giving me the blessing of his wide white smile, whispering, "We won, Shep, we won."

"Hurrah," I rasp, reaching up to stroke his beard, so relieved to see him unharmed, and then a gray veil's drawn across my sight, and I'm gone again.

❖

The floor's cold beneath me, hard as a headstone. I open my eyes. It's dim. Men moan around me. Pain's a low, throbbing ember. I feel of my head and arm, only to find both swathed in bandages.

"Mr. Sumter, you're awake."

"Water," I grunt. I've never felt such a parching thirst.

"Here you go," she says. "I'm Julia. I've been watching over you."

She lifts my head to a cup. I take deep gulps, then gasp, "My lad? Where's Brendan?" When I peer about me, I see the same church vestibule, littered with injured men.

"You must mean that boy who was here before. He refused to leave your side till our army left. Many of your fellows were killed, sir. It's said that the Yankee guns had a longer range, and you Georgians made good targets, silhouetted against the sky. Even your Colonel Johnson was wounded, but General Jackson's pursuing the foe west."

"My lad was unharmed?"

"Yes, sir. His face was blood-smeared, as were his clothes, but he seemed without wounds. Was he your son?"

"No, he was…my companion. And he's gone?"

"Yes, sir. Marched out this morning. He had to leave when the army did. But he gave me this."

She hands me a sealed envelope. My name's scrawled across it. "And he said you should look at the wall. There."

She points to the bricks at my elbow. I roll over with a groan. The letters—SHPSMTRBDNBTKN—are scratched on the wall.

"It took him some time. He used a nail. He did it while he waited for you to wake. He said you'd know what it meant. When he left, I could tell he deeply regretted not being able to say good-bye. The poor boy wept a little. That's when he gave me the letter."

The girl adjusts the blanket over me and says, "I'll fetch you some dinner soon." She rises, moves away, then turns as if in afterthought.

"He saved your arm, sir. If you see him again, you should thank him for that."

"What? Saved my arm? What do you mean?"

"The surgeon was going to amputate it. Said you'd die of gangrene otherwise. The boy wouldn't have it. He argued and argued, swore it wasn't necessary. When the surgeon insisted, coming at you with his bone saw"—the girl smiles softly—"the boy pulled a knife on the man and called him a damned drunk, if you'll forgive my language, and swore to stab him if he persisted. So the surgeon cursed him, called him a fool, and left. But the boy was right. That surgeon did smell of spirits, and there's no sign of gangrene. Your head wound is superficial, and the wound in your arm is clean. The ball, praise the Lord, passed through. Another doctor came by later and said you were liable to heal nicely."

She turns and opens the church door. I rise on my good elbow to catch a glimpse: a road, and, across that, heaps of earth and freshly dug graves. "Well, I have other duties," she says. "I'll come back soon." She steps out into the sun, the door swings slowly shut, and I fall back into darkness.

I lick my lips, try to move my bandaged arm, wince, swear, and fall still, gathering what little strength I still possess. I run my fingers over the wall's etched brick and then I open the letter and con the childish scrawl.

> *Dear Shep,*
>
> *Forgive me for leaving you. I know you will understand. My country needs me. The Southland needs me. But I leave knowing that you will recover. I thank God for that. He gave us leave to meet and to love, and perhaps He will give us leave to meet again. If not on earth, then in heaven. I would much prefer the former and will pray for that possibility every day.*
>
> *We have suffered so much. It broke my heart to see blood on your handsome face. It hurt me to see you weak, but, mighty as a man can be, we are all frail in the end. Our bodies are animate dust. But our souls are another matter, and ours have intertwined like the rose and thorn the old songs speak of. Have they not?*
>
> *I must confess to stealing a lock of your hair while you slept. The lady, Miss Julia, who gave you this letter, lent me a locket, and so I can wear that curl of your hair, my big bear, next to my heart. Lovers must have their tokens.*
>
> *I have another confession, for I have stolen something else. I cut off a short length of your tent-rope, which you used to so sweetly master me. I bear it around my wrist, so as to remember you and our nights at Camp Allegheny. I ache so to know such nights again. To lie with you. To be taken and to take. God willing, we will know such times again, once this terrible war is over.*
>
> *I miss your body against mine, Shep. Your scent, your taste, your great hairy breast. Your manhood. Loving you, dear friend, has made me a man.*

If you hear of my death, know that I fell for honor and that I left this world with your name on my lips.

But I will not fall, I think, I pray. And _you_ must not either. I think God has other plans for us. I want you to heal fast, sweet friend. Heal, grow fit and strong again, and find me in future among General Jackson's men. I need you so badly. Perhaps, after we drive the foe into sorry defeat, you and I can find a farm, here in the hills of Highland—if you are willing. If you must return to Georgia, perhaps I could accompany you. As long as we are together.

Till we meet again,
I am yours,
Brendan

I wipe my streaming face with the back of my hand. Somewhere in the mountains west of here, my little lad is marching with our army, into who knows what sort of peril, while I lie here like a cripple beneath a blanket. I pull out Brendan's handkerchief and press it to my nose, breathing deep the faint scent of him. Then I fold the letter, return it to its envelope, wrap the envelope in the seed-stained cloth, and slip both into my jacket pocket.

Rolling onto my side, I curl around the bunched blanket as if it were my little lad and pull its welcome warmth against my chest. I mumble a prayer of my own—for Brendan's safety and our reunion—pat the letter-etched brick, and close my eyes. All about me, maimed men are moaning, babbling, moving restlessly, but still I must sleep. Slumber, it's said, knits together wounds, brings balm and recovery to torn flesh, and so I must sleep and regain my strength, for strength is everything in times like these. Those holes of red earth across the road, none are yet allotted to me. The grave can wait. I have an army to follow and a beautiful boy to find. Together, God willing, we have battles to fight and a war to win, with a new home at the end of it.

(Thanks to Michael and Carrie Nobel Kline, whose CD, Holding Rugged Ground: The Civil War Along the Staunton-Parkersburg Turnpike, *proved invaluable.)*

HEAVEN ON EARTH
SIMON SHEPPARD

"The few own the many because they possess the means of livelihood of all...The country is governed for the richest, for the corporations, the bankers, the land speculators, and for the exploiters of labor. The majority of mankind are working people. So long as their fair demands—the ownership and control of their livelihoods—are set at naught, we can have neither men's rights nor women's rights. The majority of mankind is ground down by industrial oppression in order that the small remnant may live in ease."

—Helen Keller

Right before he'd robbed his first victim, Eli Berg had gone to the movies.

He'd driven the secondhand Studebaker, the car his father had given him for high school graduation, into downtown Wichita to take in the matinee at the Orpheum, walking into the dark theater during *The March of Time*. Up on the screen, the usual maniac with the little mustache was screaming in German like a fucking idiot, riling up an enormous crowd of Krauts. Then FDR came on, saying something or other about the New Deal. Then shots of Gable on a ski slope. Eli went out to buy some popcorn and a root beer, coming back just in time for the Heckle and Jeckle cartoon. He sat himself down in the next-to-last row—where nobody else was sitting—threw his legs over the seat in front, and got ready for the feature. The Columbia lady, carrying her torch, appeared on the screen and the movie began.

It was a gangster film set during Prohibition, and a pretty darn good one. There were tommy guns blazing away like fiery flowers, car tires squealing madly around corners, none of the stupid boy-meets-girl stuff that ruined too many flicks.

And when the biggest, toughest mobster of them all yelled out, "You'll never get me alive, copper!" Eli couldn't help but hope that the man with blood on his hands would indeed get away scot-free. Because, after all, well…

Sure, Eli was relatively well off. His family's dry goods stores had weathered the Depression more or less comfortably, at least so far, doing well enough to send Eli to school back East. But his father's real money, stashed away someplace Eli didn't know about and couldn't touch, had come from wet goods, illegally purveyed back when booze was banned. That had happened when Eli was a young boy; he'd known about it all along, but up to the present day, he and his father had never actually talked about it. And now his family was the picture of respectability, his parents both rock-ribbed Republicans who couldn't bring themselves to say Franklin D. Roosevelt's name out loud, not without adding a genteel curse.

Eli was intelligent, too, headed back to college in the fall. He was, to all appearances, a model young man. Nonetheless, he knew where his sympathies lay. Or rather, his inclinations. *Fuck the law. Fuck what's right.* Just like whatsisname—Nietzsche—said.

He would be free.

The gang boss and his henchmen had just hijacked a bootlegger's shipment of Scotch when a stranger came into the movie theater, tweed jacket flung over one arm, and sat down right next to Eli; odd, since the weekday matinee was sparsely attended and, indeed, the rest of Eli's row had been empty…until the stranger came along. Eli could smell the man's breath: Sen-sen with a distinct undertone of cheap gin. The stranger looked at Eli, slyly at first, out of the corner of his eye, but that was awkward, they being so close, so he turned his head and they were face-to-face, illuminated by the flickering, watery white light. The man, middle-aged, nondescript—a bit toadlike, really—glanced downward.

"Listen here, sister…"

"And whaddya gonna do about it, huh?"

Eli looked back at the screen. Some brazen, stupid cunt with a grating voice and a marcelled hairdo was half flirting, half razzing the villain, or the hero, or whatever. The ruthless gangster. The hoodlum. The man Eli dreamed of being.

Eli held his breath, waiting. He figured he knew what was coming. And sure enough, the stranger's hand brushed up against his thigh, maybe accidentally at first, then unmistakably. Staccato gunfire erupted onscreen. Eli knew the drill from the weekends he'd spent in New York City while he was going to college upstate. He leaned over and whispered in the stranger's ear, "Slip me a fin, buddy, and I'll let you cop a feel of it."

The man hesitated, his Sen-sen breath growing deeper, more agitated. He reached into his pocket. "How about three bucks?" he asked softly, desperately. "It's all I have."

"Nah," Eli said. But after a few seconds, he put out his hand. Anyway. The man put three crumpled bills in it, and Eli stuffed them into his pocket, then leaned back, spread his legs, and closed his eyes. He felt the man's jacket being thrown over his lap, the stranger's hand returning to his leg. Eli would have bet good money that there was usually a wedding ring on it, though not now.

"You'll never get me alive, coppers!" someone was yelling. Then there was more gunfire, light flashing from the silver screen. Meanwhile, Eli felt the old, familiar darkness descending on him.

The hand was creeping up his thigh, now, approaching Eli's dick, which was, not very surprisingly, getting very hard. There was nothing better than being desired, and the mayhem onscreen, rather than being a distraction, was, to Eli, an aphrodisiac. He decided to help out, reaching down with his right hand and unbuttoning his fly. The stranger's hand hesitated a moment, then slipped inside, cradling Eli's erection through the thin cotton of his underpants. The man's scented breath was hot on Eli's neck.

Most likely the man would be a good mark. Eli could whisperingly suggest they leave the theater, find a cheap hotel room where he could get sucked off, someplace where he could separate the guy from his billfold. It would be not just potentially profitable, but safe; the poor sucker would never dare go to the cops. And Eli would, as he had in similar situations in the past, give value, shooting a big hot load into the man's mouth. A not-bad bargain, all things considered.

The man had drawn his hand away, spat into it, then, with unerring accuracy, guided it back below the concealing jacket, straight into the fly of Eli's underpants. The fellow might not have been a matinee idol, but he knew his way around cock.

These sorts of public encounters excited Eli anyway, but in the man's skilled grip, he was suddenly feeling very close to losing control. It was now or never. "I've got an idea," he said in a hoarse whisper, just loudly enough to be heard over the mayhem unspooling onscreen. "Maybe we should blow this joint, find a hotel room…"

Which was when the uniformed usher came up the aisle and shone his flashlight toward them.

The man with the Sen-sen breath froze like the proverbial deer in the proverbial headlights, then yanked his hand away. He pulled his jacket off Eli's lap and hurried off, fairly running out the theater door.

The teenaged usher hesitated—he was maybe too startled to know what to do, maybe not—long enough for Eli to rush away from him, down the empty row, and leave through the far door, buttoning his pants as he fled.

He still had most of a hard-on when he hit the street, so he quickly bought a paper from a newsboy—who took avid note of what was going on—and used it to not-too-discreetly cover his swollen crotch.

Back out on the streets of Wichita, it seemed for all the world like just another normal day, late-afternoon sunlight still shining down. A little girl was walking hand in hand with her mother, a ragman was guiding his horse-drawn cart up the street, a down-and-outer was hawking apples on the corner. But Mr. Sen-sen was nowhere to be seen. Eli glanced up at the theater's marquee. *Outside the Law.*

He was heading back to the Studebaker, fading erection awkwardly concealed, when he heard, rather than saw, him: "Hey!"

Eli turned. It was the man from the theater, fedora pulled way down over his eyes.

"I was thinking about that offer."

"The hotel?"

"Yeah. I know a place near here."

Eli was certain he did. "Yeah, okay. Only I haven't got any dough for the room. Just the three bucks you gave me." He had to confess: even here in broad daylight, his cock was growing harder again.

"Don't worry about that," the man said, popping another Sen-sen in his mouth. "Follow me."

❖

"Good Lord! What happened to you?"

"Just a, um, a fight, Ma."

Eli's mother looked like she was going to cry; he never could stand that. "Its all right, Ma. Really it is."

"A fight? What happened to the other boy?"

"Really, forget it." He dared not tell her, of course, not now, not ever, what had really taken place. How he'd gone with Mr. Sen-sen to a cheap hotel near the theater, with every intention of making off with the man's money. How they'd checked into a cheesy room. How the client had tossed his hat onto the bed and gotten down on his knees as Eli unbuttoned his fly. And how the man had expertly sucked Eli's already-stiff cock dry, then clambered to his knees, looked deep in Eli's eyes, spat out the single word "Queer!" and punched him in the face. Eli's first thought was to flee the room, but the man, cum still on his lips, stood between him and the door.

"You fucking fairy!" The man reached for Eli's throat. Desperate, Eli flailed out, shoving his assailant as hard as he could. The stranger fell backward, hitting his head hard against the foot of the bed as he crumpled. Backing out of the room, Eli thought he could see a trickle of blood on the unswept floor. As he drew the door closed, he remembered the man's wallet.

He'd looked around the hallway, and, seeing no one, went back in the room. The mark was still lying there, unmoving but breathing heavily. Eli cautiously walked over and kneeled down. Nothing in the man's jacket, or in his front trouser pockets. With some difficulty, Eli turned the man's hulk on its side. There was indeed blood on the carpet; he found that exciting, even exhilarating. But someone might have heard the ruckus, so he had no time to waste. He extracted the billfold from the man's hip pocket and headed for the door. At the last minute, he turned and swiftly kicked the man in the guts. The man moaned. Eli, gasping for breath, his dick again hard as a rock, hurried out of the hotel.

It wasn't until he was safely back in his father's car that he opened up the wallet. There wasn't much in it, really. Seven bucks, hardly worth the trouble…except the trouble had been so damn thrilling, had made the darkness lift, at least for a while. There was an Oklahoma driver's license in there from a couple years back; the man was probably a refugee from the worst of the Dust Bowl. A more recently issued union card from the Wobblies. A membership card for the Communist Party. And there was a photo, a picture of him years ago, with a woman who was presumably his wife and two little girls, no doubt his daughters, standing in front of a farmhouse. Figured. Eli would have bet that if he'd looked, he would have seen a pale band on the finger where his wedding ring usually was…

"Lord, Eli! What will we tell your father when he gets home?"

What, indeed?

He caressed the seven dollars that he'd stuffed into his pocket before tossing the man's wallet in the gutter.

❖

A Studebaker pulled into the Mobilgas station. Jake looked up from the old, tattered copy of *Black Mask*, wishing he hadn't been torn away from "Fall Guy." He slowly stood and made his way over to the car.

"Can I help you?"

"Fill it up and check the oil and water." The guy behind the wheel looked no older than Jake, but he was dark rather than blond, handsome, in fact, in a kind of exotic way.

"Sure, mister." He started up the gas pump, then went around and opened the hood. "Must be swell to own a car."

"Yeah, it is." He didn't bother to mention that after the blow-up he and his father had the night before, his father had threatened to take back the Studebaker. "Over my dead body," Eli had yelled, and run out of the house, gotten in the car, and driven into town, where he'd rented a hotel room and entertained a drunken sailor with stupid tattoos and a remarkably large cock.

"That'll be fifty-five cents."

Eli looked at the boy, as if for the first time. The pump jockey was one of the sexiest things he'd ever seen, or at least seen in the last couple of weeks. Blond, with pale blue eyes, yes, but messed up, and even more attractive for that. His thick lips were more than a bit slack, his pug nose scarred, and his eyes looked puffy, as though he'd been in a fight a couple of days back, or had been crying, or had stayed up all night beating off beneath the covers. He handed the kind-of-scrawny young man in stained overalls a crumpled dollar. It was probably one of the bills he'd taken from the Sen-sen guy. "Keep the change."

"Gee, thanks." A look passed between them, quick and charged as summer lightning. Finally, the boy spoke. "Want to something to drink? A Yoo-hoo?"

Well, it wasn't exactly a martini, but that wasn't what counted. "Sure." He got out of the car, his cock already hard and throbbing beneath his gabardines; he didn't care if the blond boy noticed…and the kid did, his eyes glancing shamelessly downward.

The boy led the way, going into the gas station, grabbing two chocolate drinks from the banged-up cooler, handing one to Eli, flipping the sign on the door to "Closed," and walking into a shed at the rear of the station. Eli followed him and closed the door. It was hot and dusty inside, shafts of light from chinks in the roof illuminating the floating motes. It smelled like grease in there. Grease and lust.

"So you from town?"

"Yeah, Witchita. I'm Eli."

"Jake." He extended a damp hand. Sitting on a packing box, he took a swig of the Yoo-hoo. It was silent, except for the occasional sound of a car passing on the road. Jake looked awkward, as though he were waiting for Eli to take the lead.

Finally, Eli did. "You ever done this before?"

"Done what?"

Innocent? Or just playing that way? Eli decided to play tough, call his bluff. "Sat around in a shed drinking Yoo-hoo with a stranger, whaddya think?"

Even in the gloom, it was easy to see that Jake had been taken aback. "Well, if you want to go…" he began.

Eli realized he'd gone too far. He put down the Yoo-hoo and walked over to Jake, his erection prominent, and laid a hand on the kid's shoulder. Jake looked up, his pale blue eyes soft, even scared. Eli began kneading his shoulder. Jake hung his head, looking down at his lap, where, Eli noted, the boy's dirty, tattered overalls were tented out.

"What?" Eli asked. Jake had mumbled something.

"I want it. I do." He looked back up at Eli. The boy still seemed uncertain, as though part of him wanted to run away. There was an undeniable innocence about him, a sweetness that begged to be despoiled. Eli bent down and gave him a kiss. Jake's mouth tasted like chocolate, like a chocolate malted. His mouth still on the blond boy's generous lips, Eli slipped his fingers between the buttons of the overalls' fly. It was a cinch to get inside the boy's gapped underpants; Eli's fingertips made contact with hot, hard, slightly sticky naked flesh.

At that inconvenient moment, Eli heard the sound of a car pulling into the gas station, its tires crunching on the gravel. There was the sound of Cab Calloway, too, singing about Minnie the Moocher. *Must be one of those car radios*, Eli thought. *Wish the Studebaker had one.* "Ignore it," Eli said, but he drew his fingers out of Jake's fly.

They both sat in the hot semidarkness, waiting for the car to drive away. But it didn't. Instead, the music was switched off, the car door opened, and the sound of footsteps on gravel headed their way. "Anybody there?" a woman's strident voice called. "I need to get my tank filled."

"I've gotta go take care of that," Jake said. "Stay here and don't say anything." Now he sounded miserable. He stood, reaching down to rearrange his crotch, then walked out the door. Eli sat there, sweat rolling down his flanks, waiting for the woman to drive off. When she did, Glenn Miller trailing away with her, Eli walked out into the July sunlight.

Jake looked frightened and confused. "You've gotta go away now," he said. "Gotta get out of here."

"How late will you be working today?"

"What does that matter?"

"How late?"

"Six."

"Okay, you see that corner up the road? I'll be waiting there at six. Waiting for *you*."

It was such a dramatic line that Eli felt, for one giddy moment, like he was in a movie himself.

❖

At first, pulling up nearly fifteen minutes late, Eli figured the boy had chickened out. He sat for a few minutes, revving the Studebaker, feeling like a sucker, a horny sucker. He was about to pull away when he spotted the boy in the rearview mirror, half-running up the road.

Eli threw open the passenger side door, and the boy slid in, smelling of motor oil and sweat.

"I shouldn't be doing this," the blond boy said, sounding desperate.

Eli didn't say anything. He just gunned the motor till they were a couple of miles down the road. He turned off on a dirt side road through the fields, then pulled to a halt, engine still at idle.

Eli turned and looked hard at the boy beside him. The kid seemed genuinely scared, almost in a panic. "If my grampa…"

"Relax, kiddo. Your granddad won't know a thing. Nobody will. Not unless you spill." He paused meaningfully, even threateningly, and laid his hand on the boy's overall-clad thigh. "And you won't."

"No, no…of course I ain't gonna…"

Eli slid his hand all the way up to Jake's crotch. The blond boy's crotch was, as expected, very hard. But when Eli started to unbutton the fly, Jake reached for his hand and pushed it away.

"I really don't know…I mean, I shouldn't be…"

"You're here. You came and met me. So shut the fuck up, you fucking hayseed. You want it. You know it. We both do." He overpowered Jake's grip and grabbed onto the pump jockey's crotch. It was as if all the will had suddenly drained out of Jake's body. He shut his mouth, leaned back, and let Eli unbutton his greasy overalls and fish out his hard cock.

Eli stared at the boy's dick, with its plentiful foreskin. He figured it was none too clean, but that was okay. He leaned down and inhaled; yeah, the boy smelled. He opened his mouth and gulped down the kid's dirty cock.

Jake's voice sounded both strangled with fear and full of desire, a winning combination. "Not here. Please, not here."

Eli half-lifted his head from Jake's lap. "Where, then?"

"There's a place up the road…"

Eli abruptly sat upward, released the hand brake, and gunned the motor as Jake rearranged himself, wrestling his hard-on into his pants. Sure enough, maybe a quarter mile on, there was a tumbledown shack standing off the side of the road, amid fields that had once no doubt borne crops, now fallowed and disheveled. Eli pulled over into the ditch.

Jake just sat like he was waiting for Eli to take the lead. And Eli did. "Get out," he said, "you cocktease."

The messed-up blond boy's eyes looked more injured than ever. He scooted out of the car, looked around furtively, then headed for the shack, followed closely by Eli, who didn't see any reason to conceal his swollen crotch.

Close up, the broken-down building was a mess, a hovel that had, obviously, once been someone's home but now was little more than a rotting pile of lumber and burnt-out hopes.

"Go on in," Eli said.

"Aren't you scared of leaving your car out there?"

"Go on."

The door was off its hinges, and someone had obviously been sleeping, more or less recently, on the broken-down mattress in the middle of the rubbish-strewn floor: there was a raggedy quilt, and a few empty cans that had once held beans and stew were lying around, their labels not yet faded. What was faded was the picture of Jesus someone had glued to one wall; the putative Savior's face was pale and mottled, and only one improbably blue eye kept wary watch over the desolation.

"Take your overalls off."

Jake hesitated, staring out through the ruins of the door.

"Off."

The boy undid the straps of his overalls, unbuttoned them, and gracelessly let them fall to his boots. His shirt was relatively clean, his undershorts less so. Eli walked over and pulled at the waistband of Jake's underwear, pulling it down past the boy's bony hips, exposing a flurry of blond pubic hair and just the tip of his dick. Eli started unbuttoning Jake's shirt, then, impatient, ripped it open, a few buttons clattering to the floor. The boy's chest was scrawny, almost hairless. Eli roughly pulled Jake's BVDs down to mid-thigh. The boy's cock was—maybe surprisingly, maybe not—still soft, its pale flesh looking velvety in the filtered afternoon light, its foreskin long and wrinkled at the tip, and the not-very-big shaft hung down over a big set of furry nuts.

Jake looked confused, then, suddenly, unexpectedly, he threw his arms around Eli, squeezing him tight, as though he were drowning and Eli was his one last chance at life.

There was something almost stifling about the boy's grasp. "Let go," Eli said, but the boy didn't. It took an effort of will to break free, but he noticed that his cock was still rock hard. Jake's, however, was still disappointingly soft, though looking pretty luscious. Was the kid scared? Or, even, straight?

Well, whatever he was, he was going to make Eli feel good. "Get on your knees," he said. Jake did, awkwardly, despite his overalls being down around his ankles. Eli unzipped his gabardine trousers and, not without difficulty, fished out his big, hard dick. Jake's puffy eyes opened wider. In surprise? Because the dick was big? Cut? Hovering right in front of his almost-pretty face? Well, it wasn't worth figuring out.

"Suck it," Eli said.

Jake closed his eyes and opened his mouth, and Eli, standing above him, slid in his dickhead. The boy from the gas station was, obviously, not the most skilled cocksucker in Central Kansas. He was not just reluctant, but technically inept. Not that Eli himself had been sucked off all that often, but the drooling and gagging were pretty damn disappointing. After a few minutes of it, Eli had had enough. He withdrew his cock and stepped back.

Jake's prick was now thoroughly erect, its shiny head half peeking out from foreskin.

"Take your overalls all the way off."

At first, Jake struggled to pull his overalls off over his worn workboots. He finally gave up and pulled off his shoes, and Eli could see why he'd been reluctant; he hadn't been wearing socks, and even in the musky air of the decrepit shack, his bare feet stank. Finally naked from the waist down, his hard cock curving up from his blond bush, Jake, breathing heavy, waited for what came next.

What came next was Eli, dick standing straight up, grabbing Jake's shoulders and forcing him back down to his knees, then shoving him onto the mattress till he was lying on his back.

"Don't fucking move," Eli said. He stripped down, folding his clothes up carefully and laying them on the seat of a broken-down chair, the cleanest spot he could find. He kneeled down between Jake's legs and spat in his hand, using the gob to lube up his hard-on. He grabbed Jake's ankles and hoisted the boy's thin, hairy legs in the air. He could smell that Jake's hole was none too clean, but at that point he couldn't care at all. He lowered himself down, positioned his dickhead over the hole, and pushed his way inside, past resistance, despite Jake's grimace, regardless of the boy's pain.

Jake began whimpering.

Eli fucked him harder, the springs of the filthy mattress objecting. The boy's ass felt good, so damn good. Better than anything.

Jake's chest was slim, ribs sticking out, just a small patch of blond hair in the middle, his nipples small. His cock was still totally hard, its stiffness leaking pre-cum onto his lean belly.

Looking down at the boy he was fucking, Eli thought he'd never seen anything more beautiful. He turned his head and rubbed his face against Jake's dirty right foot. He inhaled deeply, and that was all that it took. He hadn't planned to, in fact had planned to fuck ass until Jake begged him to stop, but he'd suddenly gone too far. He howled, pumped a few more times, and shot off deep in Jake's skinny butt.

When the spasms subsided, he started to pull out. But Jake reached up and pulled Eli down on top of him. Jake tried for a kiss, but Eli turned his head away. So Jake settled for wrapping his arms around Eli and humping against his belly until, in just a few seconds, he came.

Eli looked around: at the flurries of dust in the shafts of sunlight coming through the holes in the roof; at the bleached-out picture of Jesus and—he hadn't noticed it before—at a picture of FDR someone had torn from a newspaper and tacked to the wall nearby; at the beautiful blond boy with cum on his pale belly, his blue eyes looking like he might cry. All at once, Eli wanted to get the fuck out of there.

His cock stank of dirty ass, though, and there was nothing around that was clean enough to wipe off on. "Gimme your shirt," he told Jake. The blond boy quickly sat up and peeled off his ripped-open shirt, handing it to Eli, who used it to clean off his belly and dick, then threw it back to Jake.

There was the sound of a horse and wagon going down the road. The sun was sinking low in the sky. While Eli carefully dressed himself, Jake, cum drying on his belly, pulled on his overalls and stuck his bare feet back into his scuffed boots.

It wasn't till they were back in Eli's father's Studebaker, driving down the road, headed for the sunset, that either of them spoke.

They'd just driven past a hobo jungle by the railroad tracks.

"I love you," Jake said, his voice cracking.

That was stupid, of course, but Eli didn't know what to say.

He settled on "Shut the fuck up."

❖

Over the next couple of weeks, Eli paid a couple more visits to Jake. He would pull up to the gas station in his Studebaker, his cock already hard, around six o'clock, just when Jake was locking up.

"Your grandpa won't care if you're late for dinner?" he asked once.

"He drinks his dinner," Jake said.

"And your parents?"

"They both died in the influenza epidemic. I don't even remember them."

Eli knew he should say "Sorry," but Jake's tone implied that no sympathy was necessary.

That time, they'd gone back to the tumbledown shack, where Jake had wordlessly disrobed and, not even waiting for Eli to pull his cock out, gotten down on all fours on the filthy mattress, his ass in the air, waiting to be fucked.

The time after that, though, they'd driven further on and gotten out at the edge of a big cornfield. As they made their way through the rustling green stalks, Eli impulsively reached out and grabbed onto Jake; it was the very first time they'd held hands. Nevertheless, it was still Jake who got down on his knees, who unbuttoned Eli's fly and pulled out his swelling cock, enveloping it with his lips. But as Eli looked up into the hot late-afternoon sky, crows whirling overhead, hearing just a rumor of a distant thunderstorm as Jake near-obsessively sucked his cock, he felt for a moment as though everything was all right, as though he could turn his life into something other people would recognize as good. As though there were actually a god after all, and that god was a beneficent being who was smiling down on him. On him and the blond boy on his knees, sucking him off in the middle of a ripening cornfield.

But when Eli came down Jake's throat, all he could think of was heading back to the car; he'd left his Luckies on the seat.

Partway back to the auto, Jake said, "I've really got to pee."

"Well, go."

Jake turned his back to Eli and began to unbutton his fly, but Eli said, "Turn around."

Facing his friend, Jake took his cock out and let his piss flow. Eli stood spellbound, watching the stream arcing from Jake's foreskin, gleaming in the late-afternoon sun. When the flow had subsided, Eli reached over and wiped the last few drops, bringing his fingers to his mouth and licking them clean.

Jake expected Eli to drive him back to the Mobilgas station after that, but once Eli had cranked up the Studebaker, he drove it in the opposite direction, out toward the main road, taking the curves too fast. As the two of them sped along the highway toward heaven-knows-where, Jake felt an odd mixture of dread and glee. A series of red and white signs flashed past the car window:

> WITHIN THIS VALE
> OF TOIL
> AND SIN
> YOUR HEAD GROWS BALD
> BUT NOT YOUR CHIN...USE
> BURMA-SHAVE.

It was several more miles before either of them spoke.

"I hope you don't have to get back," Eli said.

"Why?"

"You'll find out."

The sun was setting by the time Eli pulled off the road and into the gravel parking lot of a roadhouse. An unlit neon sign over the door identified it as "The Queen Bee."

"We're here," Eli said, and opened his door.

The inside of the single-story place was smoky and underlit. The burly, sweaty men at the bar didn't bother to look up, but the blowsy woman sitting in one of the place's three booths cast a speculative eye at Eli and Jake before turning all her attention back to her beer.

Eli strode up to the skinny, cockeyed man slouching behind the bar, Jake following hesitantly behind.

"Two bourbons," Eli said, not bothering to ask Jake what he wanted.

"You boys of age, then?"

Eli threw two silver dollars onto the bar. "We are now."

As the cockeyed bartender poured cheap liquor into two dirty glasses, Eli asked, "You have a room for the night?"

"Yeah. Three bucks. But it's only got one bed."

Eli knocked back the booze, the fumes blending with the masculine stench of the bruisers at the bar. "One bed is just fine."

The barkeep grimaced. "Five bucks, then."

"Okay, but throw in another round." He looked over to Jake, who had, with some difficulty, gulped down the rotgut.

The man reluctantly poured out two more drinks.

"Here's your fin," Eli said. "The key, if you don't mind."

"Give the fairies their key, Leroy," the broad at the table slurred out.

"Shut up, Myrna." Then to Eli: "I think you should maybe give me some more dough, kid. So there's no trouble with the cops."

"Bastard," Eli muttered under his breath, but he peeled a few more dollars off a roll of bills.

❖

By the time Eli and Jake entered their room, night had fallen and the red neon glare of the roadhouse sign blinked on and off and on against the half-lowered, yellowed window shade. They were both more than a little drunk.

"So how'd you get all that money?" Jake asked as Eli locked the door behind them. He didn't bother turning on the lights.

"Tell you later," Eli said. He shoved the blond boy across the room, onto the bed. The well-used bedsprings creaked in protest.

Eli strode across the room and stood above Jake, a nimbus of flashing red light surrounding him. "Strip," he commanded, "down to your skivvies."

Jake was wearing dungarees and a blue chambray work shirt instead of his usual overalls. He reached down and undid his boots, then squirmed around until he was wearing only his shorts and a ragged undershirt. He lay back on the bed, the neon blinking luridly on his flesh.

Eli launched himself onto the boy's supine body, his legs driving apart Jake's thighs, the bed groaning beneath them. Eli looked down into Jake's dimly lit eyes, then impulsively kissed him on his thick lips.

Improbably, at that instant the skies opened, disgorging melodramatic flashes of lightning and peals of thunder. Eli pulled himself up, then drew back his hand and slapped Jake's face. Jake looked astonished for a moment, tears welling up in his puffy blue eyes. Then he reached up, throwing his arms around Eli's neck, drawing him back down toward him, and he threw his legs up, wrapping them around Eli's torso.

Eli avoided any more contact with the kid's mouth. Instead, he reared up, pinned Jake's hands to the bed, and began dry-humping the blond boy. The rising stench of Jake's hairy armpits was intoxicating, the look of unalloyed desire on his face even more so. He released Jake from his grasp and got shakily on his knees. Wobbling around on the cheap mattress, he unbuckled his belt and tugged his pants and underwear down to midthigh, his swollen cock leaping free. Then he grabbed Jake's undershorts. It was too dark to see, but he knew they'd be old and stained; all of the boy's underwear was. It was something of a struggle, but he managed to rip apart Jake's undershorts, the boy's smallish cock as hard as his own.

Sliding off the edge of the sagging bed, he grabbed Jake's ankles and folded his legs back, exposing the boy's hole. It was none too clean, but that wasn't a problem. In fact, it was something of an aphrodisiac. He put his face in Jake's furry crotch, licking at the boy's loose balls, sliding his tongue down the raunchy ridge, down to Jake's musky hole. He dove in, slurping devotedly as lightning flashed and thunder rolled, just like in some smutty melodrama. At first, the hole resisted, like Jake was ashamed of it or something. But all at once, it loosened up and Eli's tongue went deep, the scrawny blond's insistent moans loud enough to be heard over the rumble of summer thunder.

Eli wanted to destroy that ass. He wanted that more than anything in the whole fucking world. He took his mouth off the wet pucker, reared back, and brutally launched his hard cock into Jake.

Jake screamed. Not that Myrna could hear him, or that she'd give a fuck if she could. Eli shoved in harder, all the way. It hurt. Eli knew it hurt. He didn't mind that. In fact, he liked that.

And Jake liked it, too. His pale eyes filled with tears, and with an expression of desire, even love.

Like Mussolini thrusting deep into Africa, Eli thought, stupidly, and then tried to stop thinking altogether, just fucking and fucking and fucking, the smell of shit rising to his nostrils, kind of disgusting, yes, but he didn't care. There was nothing left of him now but dick and will, and he plowed into Jake, spitting down for more lube, then spitting on the boy's chest, in his face, the flashes of lightning turning the abandoned smile on Jake's face into something more, something wild, and then Eli came.

"Jesus," Jake said, as though the Savior was going to answer him, as though they were not already in Heaven. As though Eli hadn't dragged him, not at all unwilling, down to Hell.

Eli slept fitfully through the storm. When he awoke, Jake, still naked, was already up, going through the pockets of Eli's pants.

"What the…"

Jake looked up, startled. "I just was looking for some money so I could go get us coffee." He had a big roll of bills in his hand. "Where'd you get all this money?"

"Come back to bed and I'll tell you."

Jake hesitated, as though afraid.

"I'll even let you keep some of it," Eli added.

Jake cautiously put the bills down on the broken-down nightstand and got back into the bed.

There was a long, awkward silence. "I've never been this happy before," Jake finally said.

"I rob guys."

"I kind of figured."

"And sometimes I shoot them."

"Really?" Jake looked up at Eli, who didn't say a word.

"You really shoot people?" Jake repeated.

"Yes, I really shoot them," Eli sneered. He realized later that he hadn't been at all sure what Jake's reaction would be, but hadn't been at all surprised when the thin blond boy threw his arms around Eli and snuggled into his chest.

"And kill them?" Jake asked, with what sounded for all the world like boyish admiration.

❖

Several nights later, Eli was driving back to Jake, someone else's cash still warm in his pocket, his heart light, when his Studebaker began to cough and sputter. He'd managed to coax it into limping to the edge of the hobo jungle outside of town when it gave a final anguished wheeze and came to a stop. With a sigh, he reached under the seat and pulled out his gun, tucking it into his jacket pocket, hid the money down where the gun had been, grabbed what was left of a bottle of gin, exited the car, and started walking toward the glow of fires of the trackside encampment. Halfway there, he reached down for a handful of dirt and messed up his clothes a little. Even in the semidarkness, the denizens of the camp would be able to figure out he wasn't one of them; looking too well-off might be asking for trouble.

As he approached, he heard the sound of a mournful harmonica playing a gospel tune. There was a bigger crowd than he'd expected, maybe thirty or forty men. He knew that when morning came, he might be able to get back to town under his own steam, leaving the broken-down car sitting beside the road, but that was risky. It would be better to try to get the Studebaker fixed and then drive back. With the money. And the gun.

As casually as he could, he approached a cluster of half a dozen men sitting around a campfire. A few of them looked up and nodded, but the mouth harp player just kept on with his tune. Eli held out the gin. "Mind if I join you?" he asked. There were no objections. He found a space on a log next to a tall, rail-thin young man, then proffered the bottle. The kid looked up shyly, then took the bottle and downed a swig, passing it on to an older man a few feet away. The young fellow looked back at Eli; in the firelight, he looked suddenly, crushingly handsome, though he was missing a few teeth.

"So what brings you out here?" *You don't belong here* went unspoken.

"My car broke down. It's sitting on the highway back there." Maybe that was too much to have said, maybe not.

"Hey, I can probably help you," the beautiful young man said. "I was a mechanic back in the army. In fact, I have a few tools here with me, 'cause I do odd jobs for people when I can."

"You were a doughboy?" The guy seemed pretty young to be a veteran.

The smile faded. "Yeah, but I had to…leave."

There was a long moment of silence. Finally, a ragged man sitting on the other side of the campfire spoke. "Fuckin' cars. Fuck everything," he spat out.

"Don't pay no attention to Nate," the young man said. "He's just pissed off 'cause he lost his meal ticket."

"Oh yeah?" Eli was just making conversation, but what he heard next made him take notice.

"See, I was working for this Reverend fella at his tent show," Nate said, taking a long second pull from Eli's bottle. "Rich bastard, too, though he only paid me a few bucks out of that big bankroll he had."

"What'd you do for him?" Eli asked.

"Pretended to be a cripple, then got healed. Every fuckin' night. Always brought in lots of green from the rubes, and it was easy work for me. But I caught him one too many times screwin' around with young boys, and I threatened to go to the cops, so that was that. He fuckin' ran me off with a shotgun."

"Big bankroll? Being a tent show preacher can't be that profitable these days."

"Story is that he's mistrusted banks ever since the Crash. I heard he keeps hundreds, maybe thousands of dollars in his mattress. Never had the courage to do anything about it myself, though."

"And where is he now?" Eli tried to sound as casual as he could.

"Somewhere near here, I guess. He don't tend to move around too much, just enough not to get caught. If you look around, I bet you can find his handbills. Reverend Ray Cobey."

The gin bottle, nearly empty, had made its way back to Eli. He handed it to the thin young man to his left, who tilted it to his lips and finished it off. "Thanks for the drink," he said. "Listen, if you want me to get an early start looking at your car, maybe we should turn in."

Just then a freight train approached, whistle blowing, slowing down as it approached town. Eli spotted a few hobos jumping off before the train made it to the station and they risked getting caught by the bulls. When the racket had died down, Eli said, "I'm afraid that I don't have bedding, so I guess I'll stay awake till I'm able to fall asleep sitting up."

"Aw, that's no problem. I got enough of a bedroll so's I can share."

The harmonica player ceased his song, but when Eli looked around, no one else seemed to have reacted to the offer. "Sure," he said. "I appreciate the generosity, friend."

"Name's Bernie, brother."

"Bernie, then."

"C'mon. Let's get set up and turn in." The young man's face looked friendlier than ever. Handsomer, too. He stood, hauling his army-regulation duffel bag up from the ground, and led Eli away from the fire, out to the darkened edge of the encampment.

"Listen," he said, as he got his blankets and bedroll out of the duffel, "I don't want you to get the wrong idea. I'm not…" The sentence went unfinished.

"Don't worry. I just want to get to sleep, and you do, too, right?"

"Right." Bernie grinned a crooked grin.

Eli left his clothes on, just taking off his shoes, but Bernie stripped down to a soiled union suit that was, Eli couldn't help but notice, distinctly well filled at the crotch. When they crawled inside the makeshift bed together, it was a close fit but manageable. Eli had carefully taken off his jacket, gun still in the pocket, and folded it up to use as a pillow. Now he lay down with his back toward Bernie, taking care not to provoke the stranger by making untoward contact. Even though he had a gun, he knew, there were enough men out there—some of them desperate men with nothing to lose—that causing a ruckus could be bad for his health.

He lay awaiting sleep. The buzz of distant conversations dwindled. Another train rumbled by, this one not even slowing down. He could smell his bedmate, who clearly hadn't bathed for a while; surprisingly, the scent was anything but unpleasant.

Then Bernie spoke, softly. "It's pretty lonely out here, ain't it?"

Eli grunted in agreement. There was a long moment when neither said a word, made a move. The stranger's breath was hot against his neck. Then Eli felt Bernie's hand softly touch his waist, pausing there a moment before gradually snaking around toward his crotch. Eli's cock swelled in response. Bernie hesitated again, then placed his hand directly on the hard bulge in his bedmate's pants. He pressed down.

It felt great, that contact. Eli lay unmoving as his bedmate awkwardly unzipped Eli's fly and fished his hard-on out of his underwear. The hand went away for a moment, then came back wet with spit. Bernie's touch was unexpectedly skilled, better, in fact, than Jake's. He'd obviously been practicing on himself…or on somebody else.

Eli moaned and began to thrust his hips, feeling close to coming. Immediately, Bernie took his hand away. He unbuttoned Eli's trousers, then tugged the pants and underwear down.

Eli felt the skinny young man's hot, rigid cock rubbing against the crack of his ass, not making any effort to get in, just sliding up and down, its hard head pushing against Eli's hole. Bernie's hand found its way back to Eli's dripping dick and resumed stroking.

Feeling the stranger's hard cock humping his ass was too much for Eli; with a muffled gasp, he let loose, his cum soaking into the inside of the bedroll. Then Bernie, his hand still grasping Eli's cock, whispered, "Thanks, buddy," and spurted out a wet load, jism flowing freely into Eli's hairy asscrack.

"That was great," a stranger's voice said.

Eli, startled, looked up. Maybe ten feet away stood a man, his face hidden in shadow, his hand on his cock. Scared for what might happen, Eli shut his eyes. When he opened them, the man was gone, walking away into the heart of the encampment.

"I wouldn't pay him no mind," Bernie said. "He just does that sometimes." Then he sighed heavily and rolled over. Within five minutes he was snoring loudly.

❖

Eli wondered for a long second where the fuck he was. Then he remembered: out in the middle of nowhere, carless. Bernie was already awake, sitting a little way off, watching him. Eli dragged himself out of the bedroll.

"Good morning, buddy," Bernie said. Eli still hadn't told him his name.

In the morning, the smoke of open fires was rising into the hard morning light. The camp looked even shabbier in the daytime, the men more worn down by life. Some of them were washing up from buckets, others boiling coffee, a few starting the morning with a taste of rotgut. One young man, not more than a boy, really, was sitting reading his Bible. Society's losers, castoffs, men who'd left their homes and families and hopes behind.

Nobody gave a sign of caring about what had happened last night, if any of them—except for the one who'd watched, whoever that was—even suspected. Maybe out here it happened all the time. Eli didn't really care. He just wanted to get home. And to Jake.

Bernie, too, gave no sign of remembering what he'd done. But he was as good as his word. With his tools in hand, he followed Eli to the Studebaker. He raised the hood as Eli unlocked the door and got into the car.

"Try starting 'er up."

Eli pressed the starter. Nothing but a grinding noise. As Bernie tinkered with the engine, Eli slipped the stolen Colt back under the seat. To his relief, the money was still there, too.

"Try now."

Still nothing.

Five minutes more, then Bernie said, "That should do it."

Sure enough, the Studebaker roared to life.

Bernie slammed down the hood, then walked over to the driver-side window. "Well," he drawled, "looks like you're on your way."

"How much do I owe you?"

"Oh, nothin'."

"Look, you seem like you could use some money."

"You already returned the favor, buddy." He smiled that charming smile with the missing teeth. "Last night."

"C'mon." Eli proffered a bill. "Five dollars?"

"Well…all right." Bernie jammed the bill into his pocket. "Thanks. Think of me kindly, okay?" He held out his hand.

Eli shook it. "Always."

As Bernie shambled away, Eli took off down the highway.

The flat countryside with its ruined farms rolled past. Just yesterday, doing the deed, he'd felt so powerful, so free. And then he'd been a victim of his own machine, and fear had made him weak, like a little boy. He'd let an inferior being touch his cock, shoot sperm on his ass. The darkness had returned. He slammed his foot down on the accelerator. The Studebaker sputtered, then shot to sixty.

He'd have to figure out where the miracle-working Reverend Cobey was preaching the gospel. And then pay him a visit.

❖

"Where the hell were you?" Jake sounded peevish. "I thought you were coming for me last night."

"My fucking car broke down outside town. I had to spend the night at the hobo jungle."

A look of doubt passed over Jake's pale blue eyes.

"Honest." Why the hell was Eli acting apologetic? He should be slapping Jake around instead.

He glanced around the crummy Mobilgas station, the stack of oil cans with the flying-horse labels, the broken-down furniture, the sun-bleached pin-up calendar on the wall that was two months out of date. How far was it, really, from the tramps' encampment? How different was Jake from Bernie, from the other young, desperate men that the times had wounded, and wounded so badly?

"How about you close up the station and we go for a drive?"

"Really can't do that. Grampa would pitch a fit."

"I'm so fucking horny, Jake."

"I'm *sorry*."

"Then lock up for a few minutes. We can go in the back room. You can blow me."

Jake sat, saying nothing. Eli hauled off and hit him in the face.

"Fuck, Eli…" He sounded pissed, but he reached down and grabbed at his own crotch.

"You're not fucking around with anyone else, are you? Because if you are…"

"No, Eli. Nobody."

"…I'll kill you, I swear I will."

"Want me to suck your dick? I will…"

Eli walked over to the gas station door, shut and locked it, bolting it from within, then pulled down the shade.

"Someone could still see in the window," Jake said.

"Suck my dick. Now."

"But you said the back room."

Eli was already getting his hardening cock out of his pants. Jake hesitated, looked around furtively, then dropped to his knees and opened his mouth. Eli grabbed a handful of his shaggy yellow hair and fucked his mouth, hard, until he was about to come, then pulled out and shot a load of sperm all over Jake's scarred face. Jake wiped the cum from his eyes, then licked his full lips clean.

"Aw, fuck, I didn't mean nothing, Eli. It's just that I missed you."

Just don't say, "I love you."

"See, Eli, it's just that I…I…"

There was a loud banging at the door.

"Jake? You in there, boy?"

"Oh Christ," Jake whispered, "it's Grampa. Don't move."

The knocking grew more furious. "Boy, I know you're in there. Lemme in."

Neither of the young men moved a muscle.

"When I get my hands on you…"

But when the old man peered in the dirty window, he couldn't see the two boys huddled in the corner. And he seemed to already be losing interest; it was probably drowning in liquor. As he walked off, his voice grew faint, fading into an angry mutter. "goddamn…goddamn… ungrateful…"

"I should go," Eli said, not wanting to be on the receiving end of a shotgun blast.

"Nah, don't worry. Won't be long till he's passed out again."

"Well, if you think so."

"Christ, I wish the old bastard would just up and die."

That can be arranged, thought Eli.

"I want to get out of here. I want it so bad I can taste it."

At that moment, Jake seemed so deeply, permanently unhappy that Eli for some damn reason wanted to make him cheerful, or at least less sad. "Go where?" he asked.

"Mexico."

Mexico? Where had he gotten that idea? Probably from one of those pulp magazines he was always reading.

"That takes money."

"We can get money. You can take me out with you on your jobs. We can be a team."

"Like Leopold and Loeb?"

"Who's that?"

"Never mind."

"So you'll take me with you? We'll stick up people together?"

A car pulled up to the service station, its tires crunching on the gravel, and honked its horn.

"I should get out of here. I'll be back tonight at nine, okay?"

Jake nodded, suddenly happy as a puppy. "Oh, Eli, it's going to be so great."

Great.

❖

It wasn't till he was driving back that night that Eli had fully made up his mind.

Jake was there as arranged, standing by the side of the road. Eli pulled the Studebaker off on the shoulder and leaned open to unlatch the passenger door. "Get in," he said. "We're going for a ride."

"Where to?" Jake had, Eli noticed, cleaned himself up and was wearing slacks and a button-up shirt, neither of them in visibly bad shape.

"Chisolm Creek Park. I'll explain before we get there."

As they drove along, Eli detailing his plan, Jake put his hand on Eli's knee, then let it slip down his leg, down to his crotch. Eli didn't object, though he was so intent on driving and talking that it took a while for him to get hard.

"Any questions?" Eli asked at last.

"Nope."

"And you're up for it?"

"Fuck yeah." That sort of bravado sounded a little forced to Eli, but he was not about to argue.

They drove in silence for a while, passed some boarded-up stores and the Boeing plant, then pulled up at the edge of the park. Eli killed the engine and they got out of the car and walked toward the wooded park. Clouds scudded across the full moon, turning the trees black, then silver, then black again. At first the place seemed deserted, but as his eyes adjusted to the darkness, Eli began to spot the shadowy forms of men, some walking back and forth, one or two lounging in the shelter of trees. As they'd agreed, Jake led the way while Eli hung back.

As he stood watching Jake's form grow smaller, Eli was approached by a middle-aged man wearing, fairly improbably, a business suit and a fedora. Standing directly in front of Eli, the stocky man groped his own crotch. Eli turned away, and the man wordlessly moved on.

Eli stood there so long he was beginning to get worried. He was afraid that Jake wasn't up to it, that something had happened to him. That the darkness would come over him again. Then he heard Jake's signal, dim in the distance: "Yeah, mister, feels good." It wasn't much, but in the general silence, it was enough.

Eli headed cautiously for the woods and soon spotted Jake leaning against a tree, a man in a white undershirt kneeling in front of him. Step by step, Eli headed for the two, taking care to position himself behind the kneeling man. Jake had his head tilted back and his eyes closed; he seemed to be enjoying himself. Eli almost hated to interrupt. Almost.

He tiptoed up to the cocksucker and stuck the barrel of his revolver right up against the back of the man's neck. The man in the undershirt stopped sucking.

"Don't move," Eli said in a hoarse whisper. "Just let me grab your wallet and nobody gets hurt."

The man backed off Jake's dick, wet and erect in the moonlight.

Eli kept the gun pointed at the stranger's neck while he slid his other hand down the man's muscular back until he made contact with his belt, then his wallet, which the man had foolishly left tucked in his back pocket. Eli withdrew the billfold.

Jake was standing still, a foolish grin on his face, his pants around his thighs.

"Get dressed, you idiot," Eli snapped.

Jake flinched as though he'd been hit, then wordlessly pulled his pants up.

"Don't move," Eli said to the kneeling man. "Don't look back, and nobody gets hurt."

But the idiot didn't listen. He began to turn his head, to say, "Listen, you…"

Eli brought the butt of the gun down hard on the back of the man's head. The poor sap hovered for a second, then fell backward. That's when Eli noticed two things he hadn't seen before. First, the man had a set of dogtags hanging over his shirt. He was—oh, shit—military. And second, he was really handsome, much better-looking than Jake, if it came to that.

Three things, really: The jerk was wearing a wedding band. "Grab his ring," Eli ordered, "and we'll get the hell out of here."

Jake bent over and, with some difficulty, pulled the ring from the unconscious man's hand, which had fallen just beside the long, pale cock that was hanging out of his open fly. "Eli, I think he's bleeding," Jake said. "Are you sure he's still breathing?"

"Let's go."

Jake didn't move.

"Let's go!"

Jake gave the soldier a swift kick in the ribs. The man didn't move.

"Yeah," Jake said. "I'm comin'."

They were just a few steps into the clearing when a voice called out across the clearing. "Stop where you are! Police!"

It was the man in the fedora. Undercover cop.

They made a run for the car and piled inside. Eli grappled for the key, then cranked up the Studebaker and burned rubber on his way out of there. He figured that, given the angles, the flatfoot wouldn't have been able to read the license plate, and it was unlikely the army boy would tell either his superiors or the missus what had really happened.

The car's headlights raked across the landscape as they sped onward. Eli, feeling like he was the star of his own movie, yelled out, "You'll never get me alive, copper!"

At last, when they'd reached the river and it was certain they weren't being followed anymore, Eli swung the car to the side of the road and killed the engine. When they'd gotten out of the Studebaker, Eli asked, "You okay?"

"I feel totally swell," Jake said, a broad grin breaking out across his almost-pretty face. "Lookee, blood!" He held his hand out. In the palm lay the man's gold ring and, next to it, a little shiny smear of what probably was in fact blood. Standing on the riverbank, Jake did a little dance.

"Fuck, I'm hungry," Eli said. "Let's go to White Castle."

"Don't think that's such a good idea," Jake said. "I got so excited back there I pissed my pants."

❖

Up till now, Jake hadn't asked Eli much about himself, certainly not where he lived, so Eli hadn't had to choose between lying and telling him the truth: that he'd been staying at the Wichita Y.

The arrangement did have its advantages, notably the always-horny college-age kids, husky off-duty soldiers, straying missionaries who'd swapped blow jobs with him in the steam room, and the older businessmen who'd traded a buck for a fuck. One traveling salesman, a handsome, hairy married man with a yen to get spanked, was even more generous than that, taking "his nephew" Eli out to dinner a few times before adjourning back to the Y for some corporal punishment; it had been a minor miracle that the racket they'd made hadn't gotten them found out. And afterward, when the man was pulling his pants up over his tender butt, he always turned to Eli and said, "You're not going to tell anyone about this, are you?" Which is when Eli always agreed, for a suitable sum, to keep his mouth shut. The first time, Eli thought he was taking advantage; subsequently, he wondered whether the whole exchange didn't provide an additional thrill for the guy.

Then there was the well-built young artist who'd been working for the WPA. They'd first met in the shower room. When Eli walked in late one night, the guy was there lathering up with his back to him, taking extra care to clean his hole, penetrating it with one soapy finger, then two. The stranger looked over his shoulder at Eli, his hawkish face impassive, then, fingers still in his ass, turned back.

Eli, cock swelling rapidly, walked up to the next shower nozzle and turned on the water, hot as he could stand. He looked over at the wet, naked man. The man stared back, took his hands from behind himself, and began soaping up his long, uncut cock. He was not yet hard, but he was clearly interested.

Eli looked around. Nobody there except the two of them. He furtively grabbed for the man's soaped-up cock. The man took his hands away, clasping them behind his head, and turned toward Eli. As the shower pounded down on them, Eli gave the slick, uncut dick a few tugs.

"It's not really safe here," the man said, hands still behind his head. "You have a room?"

"Yeah. Come upstairs with me?"

A few minutes later, having dried off and dressed, Eli was sneaking the swarthy man into his room. Wordlessly, they stripped down and got into the narrow bed. Despite having played with his ass, the stranger made it clear that he was in no mood to get fucked, and neither was Eli. So they settled for a bit of mutual masturbation, lying side by side, moving after a while into sixty-nining, each one's dick in the other's mouth. The stranger's cock was fully hard now, long enough to make it tough for Eli to get it—with its curve, its big swollen head—all the way into his mouth. After a while, his jaws starting to ache, he pushed the young man away. The fellow looked puzzled, then pulled his body around on the bed, wrapped Eli in his arms, and kissed him on the lips. At first, Eli felt uneasy, resistant. But then he opened his mouth, let the man's tongue in, and that was how they came, kissing, the man lying on top of Eli, rubbing his long cock against Eli's belly, Eli thrusting upward. After they'd both shot off, the man reached down between their bellies, swirled his fingertips in their commingled cum, and brought his wet fingers to his lips, licking off the jism.

As they lay in bed catching their breath, Eli noticed a scar running down the man's side. He ran his fingers gently over the pale ridge.

"Spain," said the man.

"You were fighting in the Civil War?"

"Yeah, but I did something stupid, got wounded, and was shipped back here."

"Gee." It sounded dumb, but Eli couldn't figure out what else to say.

"Since then I've been doing sculptures for the WPA. I was in New York for a while, working on Rockefeller Center. But then…" His dark eyes clouded over. "And you…what do you do for money?"

"I'm, um, unemployed."

There was a long moment of silence. Then the man slid off the bed and slipped into his clothes.

On the way out of the door, he said. "Oh, by the way, I'm Pablo. I'm staying down the hall."

"Eli." Immediately, he wished he hadn't given his real name.

"Good to meet you. Maybe you want to come to a Party meeting with me tomorrow night?"

"Maybe."

But Eli didn't see Pablo till the next week, when there was a knock on his door. They had sex that night, then a third time. That time, Pablo told Eli that he'd be leaving the next day; he didn't say for where, and Eli didn't ask.

After that, the Y seemed even lonelier, somehow. Still, though it was a roof over his head, it was hardly the place to impress Jake, and the no-outside-guests policy made that off-limits in any case.

One time, when he was driving past the hobo jungle, he'd stopped, on a whim, and went looking for Bernie. But he was nowhere to be found, and when he asked around, nobody who'd known him had seen him for weeks. "He gone off somewhere with all his things, don't know where," said one man, the one who, Eli seemed to recall, had been the one playing the harmonica that first night.

There was, though, a photographer hanging around the camp, a young Jewish-looking fellow who, he said, was taking pictures for *Life* magazine, but who, once he and Eli were hidden in some bushes, was only too happy, camera still around his neck, to trade documenting the Depression for getting his thick cock sucked.

And then came the day when Eli spotted the handbill on the YMCA's bulletin board.

COME TO CHRIST! it read, the words surrounded by sunbeams and flying doves. But it was what followed that excited Eli:

REVEREND COBEY'S TRAVELING CRUSADE
WILL HEAL THE LAME,
RESTORE THE FORTUNES OF THE NEEDY,
AND BRING THE LIGHT OF THE LORD TO ALL.

And underneath was handwritten a list of upcoming dates and nearby towns.

Eli smiled to himself, looked around to make sure no one was watching, ripped the handbill off the board, and stuffed it in his pocket. Then he headed upstairs to his rented cubicle, to smoke the rest of a reefer he'd bought on a street corner and afterward beat off.

❖

"So you're in, then?"

Eli and Jake were lying naked in bed, in a motel room that Eli had rented with the money provided by the traveling salesman who liked to get spanked. The smell of drying jism hung in the dim and dusty air.

"Sure am. Especially if it means we can go away together." Mexico, again. "But you were saying something about a third person being involved?"

Eli had suggested that, reluctantly. He hated the idea of someone else getting a cut, but the way he had it planned out, he figured there should be a third man to stand guard. Better a reduction in his take than a stretch in the pen.

"Yeah, I guess. See…"

"Because I have an idea," Jake said. "There's this older man I know, Duane Hollings. He was a friend of my pa's, actually, but he's tough and trustworthy. He was in the service and he used to be a trucker but he doesn't have a job now and I bet he'd help us out."

"He's not…"

Jake seemed confused for a moment. "Oh, no," he finally said, "he's married. I mean, he doesn't know about you and me, anyway."

Eli was more dubious than he wanted to indicate. After all, he hadn't even met the fellow, but he didn't himself have anyone in mind for the job, and given Cobey's schedule, plans would have to be finalized soon.

After a minute of Eli's silence, Jake reached over and grabbed his cock, which, rather amazingly, began to get stiff for a third time. "Please," Jake cajoled, giving the blossoming hard-on a firm squeeze. "Just talk to him about it."

"Okay…I'll meet up with him and we'll see." There was a lot, Eli realized to his chagrin, that he would do for the sake of getting in Jake's ass.

"It's a girl, isn't it, Eli? Some girl?"

"Oh, leave the boy alone, Karl."

"Edna, our son borrows money from me and runs off, and we don't see him for weeks at a time, he's probably with some hussy, and all you can say is 'Leave him alone'?"

"I'm just saying…" A part of her, she secretly knew, would be relieved if it *was* a girl, and not something worse. But that was just a mother, worrying.

"The two of you!" Karl said, exasperated. "What a pair!"

Eli wanted to escape. From his parents, from the living room, from this life. All he'd intended to do was sneak home and pack up his things. Instead, he had to go through *this*. Everything was going dark. Everything was going dark. Without a word, he turned and headed upstairs to his room.

"You come back here, young man!"

"Oh, Karl, don't be so upset. Your ulcers. He'll be going back to college soon and he'll forget her, whoever she is."

Eli hated it, hated the house, hated his parents. Hated his lousy little life. Everything was going dark.

That night, after he'd finished packing his bags, he set the alarm for five in the morning, then fell asleep.

He sank into a dream, a dream that looked like a dance number from one of those stupid *Gold Diggers* movies. He was hovering above a giant swimming pool, and down below was not one, but a dozen Jakes—all buck naked, their slim, wet bodies shining—swimming with geometrical precision. Floating on their backs, they fanned out into a circular shape, like the petals of a flower. Gesturing as one, they smilingly reached up to him, inviting him to join them. Their floating dicks grew hard, then huge, and started jetting streams of piss far over their heads, piss that turned into cum. For a moment, Eli felt warm, so warm and wonderful, but the oceanic feeling of bliss turned suddenly to alarm, and then he was falling, plunging into the wet darkness at the center of the circle of Jakes, and he knew he could not stop himself, did not even want to, that he would surely drown in the inky blackness, and the Jakes all began laughing, screaming with shrill laughter.

The alarm clock was ringing. Eli struggled to wakefulness and turned off the Big Ben. There was a rapidly cooling wet spot in the middle of his bed.

It was time.

❖

The last night before the revival meeting, Jake and Eli checked into in a hotel room that Eli had rented.

Once the door was locked, their suitcases thrown in a corner, they tore off their clothes. They were both already hard. When they kissed, Eli slipped his hands around Jake's throat and squeezed hard. Eli had never known Jake to become so instantly, overwhelmingly excited: pressed up against Eli's bare belly, the young blond came almost instantaneously.

"I'm sorry," Jake said when the spasms had subsided.

"It's okay, really."

But Jake had already dropped to his knees and, face buried in dark, wiry pubic hair, begun sucking Eli's cock like it was the only thing in the universe, the one thing that mattered. The only thing that mattered.

Eli looked down at the nimbus of yellowish hair, the boy's skinny shoulders, and pumped a load into his friend Jake's perfect, perfect mouth.

Once they were cuddled up in bed, Jake, lying in Eli's arms, murmured, "It's going to be so good…It's going to be great," and drifted quickly off to sleep.

Looking at Jake, his face soft in the dim light, Eli felt like he had that first day in the cornfield. Jake was an angel. Okay, he could never say that out loud, not even to himself. But an angel he was. And he was still, despite everything, oddly innocent. He gently drew Jake's hand up from under the covers and kissed the bitten-down fingertips one by one.

It was, indeed, all going to be good. Great.

It was going to be great.

❖

Duane Hollings had clearly been very handsome, once. But time and the Depression had not been kind to him. His face was lined with wrinkles, and when he smiled, there were a few missing teeth.

He wasn't the most articulate of men, either, but when Eli had met with him, he'd managed to say all the right things. No, he wouldn't mind getting a smaller cut of the take, and yes, he would take Eli's orders without asking too many questions, and no, he had never done anything like this before, but yes, he was ready for anything. So Eli, somewhat reluctant to trust him, but even more reluctant to shop around for someone else in the limited time they had left, had agreed that Duane would be the third man.

Now Duane was silently huddled in the backseat of the Studebaker as Eli drove him and Jake through the fading twilight on the road to Mount Hope, headlights swerving across sunflower fields. They were still a couple miles from town, stopped at a railroad crossing, when Eli noticed a frail old woman limping up the side of the road, an apparition in the middle of nowhere.

"Maybe we should give her a ride," Duane Hollings said, the first words he'd spoken during the entire ride.

But Eli didn't respond, and once the freight train had roared past and the gates had lifted, he put his foot down on the gas pedal and roared off.

"Aww," Hollings said, "what if the poor lady was your mother?" Which was sentimental, all right, but the wrong thing to say to Eli.

Then Eli felt Jake's hand on his thigh. "C'mon, let's give the old gal a ride," Jake chimed in. "We ain't in that much of a hurry."

Eli didn't want to cause a rift over such a minor matter, not now. And his cohort's hand reminded him of how, just that morning, Jake had, for the very first time, stuck his tongue into Eli's ass until Eli was squirming in uncontrollable delight. He stopped the car and backed up.

"I'll get in back with Duane," Jake said, opening the passenger door.

Close up, the woman was even frailer than she'd first appeared. Clutching a cane in one hand, she climbed into the car. Her face was a cliché of old-woman sweetness, and her smile was shy but genuine. She was wearing too much cheap cologne, and the car began to stink of gardenias. "I want to thank you fellers for picking me up. I don't know what I would have done if you hadn't. It's such a long way…"

"Where are you headed, ma'am?" Duane asked from the backseat.

"There's a revival meeting up the road a ways."

Eli had been afraid of that.

"Why, we're headed that way ourselves." Duane sounded like butter wouldn't melt in his mouth. Why couldn't he just have stayed silent? Eli starting doubting his suitability, after all. He felt like he could cheerfully strangle him.

The woman rearranged her awful flower-print dress and smiled. "Why, isn't that something, that you boys are in search of salvation? What a blessed coincidence."

Duane, thank God, said nothing to that, but the woman kept right on, her feeble voice tinged with honey. "Dear Reverend Cobey's been such a comfort to me. I'm all alone, you see, my husband having passed in the Great War."

Eli mumbled condolences, hoping to shut her up.

No dice. "And times right now are hard, they surely are, especially for an old Christian woman alone." She lowered her voice to a near whisper. "Most especially with that nigger-loving commie Roosevelt in the White House, him and his kike advisers. Why, they're going to ruin whatever's left of our country!"

None of the three men knew what to say to that, so they all sat in awkward silence until, as sundown faded into darkness, they reached the edge of town.

"It's over that way," the old lady said. Eli turned right, soon coming upon a tent set up in a field, a panel truck parked alongside, and a Ford-drawn house-trailer parked a little ways off, a "Come to Christ" banner hung on its side. The place wasn't crowded, but some congregants were already there, having arrived in the horse-drawn wagons, old sedans, and broken-down farm trucks parked helter-skelter on an open patch of dirt.

"Well, thank you kindly for the ride," the old woman said when Eli had switched off the engine. "You boys coming in with me?"

"Thanks," Eli said, anxious to be rid of her, "but I think we'll walk around for a bit beforehand." He watched the old woman get out of the car and totter into the revival tent. Then he got out of the car, followed by Jake and Duane. "Let's go for a walk," he said.

They made their way to the edge of the field. Fireflies dotted the humid darkness, a chorus of frogs echoed through the night. In the distance, there were lights from the town; closer in, a hum of conversation coming from the tent.

"What the fuck were you trying to do, Duane?" Eli said. "That's what we really fucking need: a witness."

"I'm sorry, Eli. I guess she just reminded me of my grandma."

"Yeah, fuck, sure. What, were you trying to sabotage this operation?"

"No, I swear it."

"And you can be trusted?"

"Yeah, I swear…boss."

Eli looked over at Jake; his expression was unreadable. But they'd come this far… "Okay, Duane, we're going ahead with this. Ready, Jake?"

The blond boy nodded. He got right next to Eli and whispered. "We go away after this, together, right? To Mexico? It'll be so beautiful down there. We'll get a little house, one of those little tiny dogs, live on the fruits we pick from the trees…"

Eli was silent.

Jake walked off in the direction of the tent, followed at some distance by Duane and Eli. As they approached the glowing canvas, a chorus of voices began singing a hymn. Jake entered the meeting as Eli and Duane hung back before walking in the door. On a platform facing a dozen rows of folding chairs stood a middle-aged woman and two young girls, leading the assembly in singing "The Old Rugged Cross." Jake was already taking his seat in the front row. Eli led Duane to seats way in the back, as far from the old-lady hitchhiker as they could get.

Eli turned to Duane and hissed, "Just don't mess up again."

…To that old rugged cross I will ever be true, its shame and reproach gladly bear…

"I won't. Eli. I promise."

…Then He'll call me some day to my home far away, Where His glory forever I'll share.

"Because if you do…" Eli paused for dramatic emphasis.

So I'll cherish the old rugged cross, Till my trophies at last I lay down…

"…I swear I'll kill you."

I will cling to the old rugged cross, And exchange it some day for a crown.

The Reverend Ray Cobey was a large, florid man whose considerable girth pointed to success in this life, if not necessarily the next. A large, glittering crucifix hung from a chain around his neck; it looked like it was real gold.

"Beloved brothers and sisters," he said, when he strode to the middle of the stage, "thank you for coming to this blessed, blessed night of our Kansas crusade." He lifted his big hands into the air; he looked like he might be a tough man to overpower. Eli was glad, after all, that he'd brought Duane along. He looked around the torch-lit tent. People were still straggling in; the rickety seats were beginning to fill up.

"I can promise you," Cobey continued, "that tonight will be a moment you'll never forget, a night full of healings and miracles and the Holy Spirit descending on us all!"

"Amen!" shouted several in the crowd.

The Reverend went on for a while longer about the Savior and his bleeding hands and the freedom that could only be found by surrendering to Him, then turned the proceedings back over to the trio of singers, who gave forth with a spirited rendition of "I'll Fly Away."

Eli glanced over at Duane, to see how he was taking things. Hollings, it turned out, was staring straight at Eli's crotch. That was not only, given the surroundings, incredibly stupid. It was also, given the excitement of the moment, stimulating enough to make Eli's dick instantly swell. Duane smiled. Eli looked away. Duane's thigh began pressing against his own. Then Duane's hand began creeping over, touching Eli's thigh, brushing against his hardness before slipping away. For a married man, Duane Hollings was behaving pretty fucking unexpectedly. Maybe it was something he'd learned in the Army or somewhere, or maybe on the road. Eli looked around; it seemed that no one was paying any attention. Still, he dragged his chair away from Duane's and whispered, "Stop that!" The darkness was beginning—Eli had to keep his mind on the goal.

The singing ended and the preaching recommenced. Cobey worked himself into quite a dramatic lather, the torchlight making his eyes glitter almost crazily, throwing strange shadows on his face. On and on he went about sin and redemption, evil and sacrifice, and the Light of the World. Eli, thinking about Duane's unexpected attentions and what was to come, found it hard to keep track. But the rest of the crowd grew in enthusiasm, the "Amens" growing louder, some standing up to wave their hands spastically and speak in tongues. Credulous idiots.

Eli fucking hated these people, hated them all. The darkness had descended over him for real now, almost pitch black.

"And now," the Reverend Cobey shouted out, beads of sweat dripping down his porcine face, "it's time for the Holy Spirit to come down and do the divine work of healing. Who needs to be made whole?"

One old man yelled, "I have the rheumatism real bad!"

"Come up then, sir, and let Jesus wash away your pain."

The man hobbled to the stage, where Cobey laid hands on him. "I'm healed!" the man yelled, then hobbled back to his seat, no more mobile, as far as Eli could tell, than he'd been pre-miracle.

The old lady from the roadside was next. As the crowd halellujah'ed itself into a frenzy, Cobey hollered, "I command you, Satan, to leave this poor woman's body!" The preacher leapt down from the stage and grabbed hold of the old lady's frail body, pressing one hand forcefully on the top of her head. She cried out, her eyes rolled back, and she crumpled onto the ground, her cane clattering beside her. But instead of squirming around in ecstasy, she just lay on the ground, hardly breathing. The hymn-singing woman, who'd been standing at the back of the stage alongside the two horrid little girls, looked alarmed. She leapt off the platform and bent over the supine old woman. The crowd had grown silent, but now, led by Cobey, they joined in prayer. A couple of minutes later, the hymn-lady, helped by Cobey, managed to get the old lady onto her feet. She was led away, pale as death, by two men from the congregation, out the door of the tent.

So far, the healing didn't seem to be going so well.

Then a man in a wheelchair rolled himself up the aisle, up to Cobey, who bent down to talk to the cripple.

"This poor man," Cobey then announced, "was injured in a farming accident at the age of ten, and has been lame ever since. But now"—he laid his hands on the man's head—"I command you in the name of Jee-sus to rise up and walk!"

The man slowly, slowly raised himself from the wheelchair, using his hands at first, then standing fully up. "Praise the Lord!" he cried, as the crowd went wild. The hymn woman—Cobey's wife, perhaps?—screamed out unintelligible syllables so shrilly that it hurt Eli's ears. And the newly healed man steeped away from his wheelchair, turned, and walked unsteadily from the altar. Eli stared at the man's face.

It was Bernie, the man who had humped him that night in the hobo jungle. Their eyes locked, then Bernie half smiled and turned away.

Apparently, that was the climax of the performance. Cobey interspersed his praise for the Lord with pleas for free-will offerings.

"Please, beloved, give as much as you can and you shall surely be repaid tenfold," Cobey said as Hymn Lady began circulating through the crowd, carrying a locked wooden box with a money slot in the cover. "Yes, I know that times are hard, my brothers and sisters. But tough times do not last. Tough people do, tough people who give generously to the Lord's work."

The two homely little girls, still on the platform, began trilling "What a Friend We Have in Jesus." The crowd, some of them thoroughly fleeced, began filing out of the tent. Oddly, many of the suckers had expressions of peace, even joy, on their worn faces.

Eli and Duane hung back, watching Jake go up to the platform. Reverend Cobey leaned over and the two spoke for a few moments. Then Jake turned, nodded at Eli, and walked out into the night.

The three met up in a secluded spot at the very edge of the clearing, far as possible from Cobey's house-trailer.

"So everything went according to plan?" Eli asked Jake, his voice low.

"Yeah, it was a cinch. I just said that I wanted to meet up with him in private, maybe in his trailer."

"That was all you said?"

"Yeah, but it worked like a charm. He said he'd be there in fifteen minutes, after he got some things squared away. And that he'd make sure his wife and kids weren't around."

"We're on, then. I'll bring the car around. Duane, you'll be standing guard outside the trailer, to make sure there are no interruptions. If anything looks like it's going wrong, you'll whistle like this." He demonstrated.

Duane repeated the whistle. "Right, boss."

"And after it's over, we'll all jump in the car and get the hell out of here. Then we'll split the loot." Actually, Eli still wasn't sure what he was going to do about Duane. The man was, pretty clearly, something of a loose cannon, a loose end that had to be tied up. Maybe a loose end that shouldn't just be left lying around. Eli absentmindedly patted the bulge beneath his jacket. The decision could wait till afterward, after it was done. For now, the darkness was throbbing in his head.

Duane went to take his assigned place, watching the door of Cobey's house-trailer from a safe distance, half-hidden in a copse of trees.

Jake turned to Eli. "It'll be good," he said. "And soon we'll be in Mexico." He reached down and gave Eli's crotch a squeeze.

"Mexico," Eli said. He could never tell Jake, or at least not now, but Jake's Mexican obsession bored him; it was the kind of stupid dream that his own boring, hopelessly bourgeois parents might have. Eli didn't want to retire somewhere with burros and cactus. He wanted to be rich, really rich. And famous. And rich. And famous.

Or at the very least, notorious.

He walked around to the far side of the trailer, the one opposite the door. The windows were too high for him to look through. With some difficulty, he dragged over a log and stood on that. He was able to see through the window now, and luckily, the curtain at the screened window was only partly closed. Meanwhile, Jake had headed off to meet the Reverend Cobey.

Long minutes ticked by. Though he was far from the tent, Eli could hear the good-byes of the last stragglers, the sounds of wagons and trucks leaving the encampment.

"Hey." The whispered voice was right behind him. It was Bernie. "I figured that this was what you were here for, you not being one for the succor of the Lord or nothin'." He sniggered softly.

Fuck, Eli thought with alarm, *this could ruin everything. He knows me, and if he wants in, it'll be a four-way split.* He was pretty well sure that Duane, the wild card, wouldn't like that. Come to think of it, neither would he. He smiled at Bernie. "Good to see you," he whispered. "Let's go over there."

Eli stepped off the log and headed into a nearby thicket of trees, followed by the skinny young veteran. Once they were shrouded by darkness, Eli turned and made a grab at Bernie's crotch. Bernie gasped, but didn't object; in fact, his cock almost instantly swelled up.

"So you're not queer, huh?"

"No, I ain't, but..."

"And you're here because?"

"Because I want to help you rob old man Cobey."

"I figured. But your dick is still hard as fuck, isn't it?"

Bernie seemed nonplused by Eli's tone. "I guess it is..." he finally murmured.

"So go on, show me how not-queer you are."

"Huh?"

"Suck my cock."

"I…"

"If you want in on this, suck me. Now."

After a moment's hesitation, Bernie fell to his knees and started fumbling with Eli's fly. He'd just started licking awkwardly, reluctantly, at the head of the still-soft prick when Eli growled, "Faggot!" and brought the butt of his gun down on the back of Bernie's skull. The young man tottered, then fell over, leaving Eli's dangling cock exposed to the cool night air.

Eli looked down at Bernie; he just, for some goddamn reason, couldn't bear to hurt the boy any worse. But assuming he'd take a while to come to, by the time he knew what was happening, Eli, Jake, and Duane would be long gone.

At least Eli hoped so. He walked back to the house trailer and resumed his perch on the log.

At last, the low voices of two men approached: Cobey and Jake.

"I've told her to stay away for a while," the Reverend Cobey was saying, "so we'll have some privacy for our chat."

"Good," Jake said, "I'm real glad."

The door of the house-trailer opened, then was firmly shut. A minute later, a lantern's light flickered inside. Tottering on the log, Eli backed away from the window; it wouldn't do to be seen by Cobey. He needn't have worried; the preacher remained standing with his back to the window. Jake walked into view. In the dim, flickering light he looked beautiful, so surprisingly beautiful. Eli knew he should be concentrating on the task at hand, on what was happening in the trailer, but he couldn't help himself; all he could think of was Jake. The way his slim body looked when he was sweaty from sex. The expression in his pale eyes when Eli slapped him around. The beauty of his cock when it stood stiff, shiny head peeking from foreskin, shaft arising from a flurry of dark blond hair. The way Jake had eaten his ass, like a starving child. The feeling of fucking him, slight resistance changing to hungry, wet heat, the boy's ass drawing him in, taking him heaven-knows-where. His smell. His taste. The secret flavor of his ass. And always, Jake's glorious cock, swelling up, pissing, spurting cum. Eli had to admit it, even though he could never tell Jake. He had…feelings, unmanageable feelings for the boy. Complicating things, fucking things up, and yet…

He snapped out of his reverie, his cock inconveniently hard. He was the star of his own movie now; it was time to play his part. Jake was saying something. What was it? "I thought you'd want this." The blond boy reached down to his fly, undoing the buttons, reaching inside, taking out his cock, already half-hard. The pale shaft was all that Eli could see. Leaning up against a wall, Jake, eyes half-closed, spat on his hand and began to stroke himself. Eli, too, reached down to his crotch and began squeezing his own cock. The darkness was gathering again, shutting everything out. Everything but his buddy's dick. Only Jake was more than just a buddy. He was...

"How *dare* you?"

Cobey sounded angry. He wasn't supposed to be angry. That wasn't part of the plan.

Jake, hard cock poking out of his pants, seemed confused.

"I'm a man of God," Cobey heatedly said. "A preacher of the Gospel. And you...you're nothing but a *sodomite*." Cobey's bulk drew itself up, casting flickering shadows on the trailer's wall. "Get down on your knees, sinner, or be *damned to hell!*"

Jake did as he'd been told, but instead of sliding his cock into Jake's mouth, as they'd expected, the preacher laid his meaty hands on Jake's head.

"Satan," the Reverend Cobey, intoned, "I cast you out. Unclean demons, I demand you leave this boy in the name of Jesus!"

Clearly, the situation was spiraling out of control. It was time to intervene.

Eli thrust his hands into his pockets, caressing his hard-on, and slid backward off the log. He cautiously made his way around the house-trailer, taking care that no one but Duane noticed him, and went up to the door. As arranged, Jake had made sure it was unlocked. Eli listened at the door for an instant, just to make certain that the situation hadn't taken a turn for the better, but the silly old fool was still going on and on about the sin of Sodom.

Eli opened the door.

Jake was still kneeling on the floor, his now-limp cock hanging out of his open fly. The Reverend Ray Cobey stood over him, his hands buried in the boy's thatch of blond hair. Cobey's head was thrown back, his eyes closed in something approaching ecstasy, and the preacher was making incoherent sounds. He wouldn't have looked much different, Eli thought, if Jake *had* been sucking him off.

It took the slamming of the door to wrench Cobey from his communion with the Divine. He opened his eyes and stared at Eli as though he'd seen a ghost, an unholy one. "What in blazes…" he began.

Eli pulled his gun. "Shut up. Lie down on the floor and keep quiet. One false move and I'll drill you."

The preacher glanced over to one corner of the little room. There was the shotgun Bernie had told Eli about.

"Don't even fucking think about it. I'll kill you before you can reach it. I surely will."

Cobey began to whimper pitifully; a stain spread across the front of his trousers.

"And you," he said to Jake, "put your dick away and get cracking."

Jake stuffed his cock back in his pants and struggled to his feet. It was crowded in that little house-trailer, with him and Eli and Cobey's flabby bulk sprawled out on the floor. The room began to smell like piss.

"There's the bed," Eli said. "Look under the mattress."

Jake awkwardly made his way to the unmade bed and hauled up the lumpy mattress, the fetid bedcovers tumbling to the floor. Underneath was just a broken-down set of springs.

"Nothing, no money. Nothing."

"See what's inside the thing."

Jake reached into his pocket and pulled out a buck knife. He unfolded the blade and slit into the mattress, tearing its stained, stitched-up ticking to shreds.

"Got it," he said, a triumphant note to his voice. Jake held a bulky sack, one end loosely sewn shut, in his hand. He sliced the end open. "Well, lookie what the fuck we have here!" He held out the sack toward Eli.

Inside was money, and lots of it, a jumble of banded-together stacks of bills. Eli grinned with pleasure.

"Take it," Cobey whimpered. "Take it all. Just don't hurt me, please. You'll regret it."

Eli kicked Cobey in the ribs. The preacher groaned loudly. Eli kicked him again. Jake thought he heard a *crack*.

"So let's get rid of him and hit the road," Jake said.

"No, please! I beg you, let me live."

"I thought you *wanted* to see Jesus," Eli snarled. He leaned back to kick Cobey a third time, but lost his balance and started to fall backward. To steady himself, he threw his hand out to the table and tipped over the kerosene lantern. In a fraction of a second, the curtains had caught fire.

"Holy shit!" Jake said, grasping the bag of cash to his chest. "Let's get out of here."

"Don't leave me here, please," Cobey groaned. He tried to raise himself from the floor, but Eli kicked him again—in the head this time—and he collapsed.

The house trailer was filling up with smoke. Jake made his way to the entrance and threw open the door. *"Eli, let's go!"* He jumped to the ground.

Eli had his gun in his hand. He followed Jake, stood in the doorway, and turned to face the preacher's motionless form, luridly illuminated by the leaping flames. "You're a dead man!" he said.

A shot rang out.

❖

Jake loved getting fucked. He loved the moment right before a big dick entered his ass, when he was unsure whether he'd be able to take it. After that came the point when the wet cockhead made contact with his sensitive hole, when he felt himself relax, felt the hard flesh sliding inside him. There was initial discomfort, sure, no matter how much he wanted it, no matter how much liquor he had in him. But that pain soon became pleasure, the pleasure of surrender, of having his secret parts raped into submission.

And that's where he was now, lost in that pleasure. He was on his back, legs in the air, his lover above him, dripping with sweat, pounding his hard-on into Jake's young ass. The strokes were deep and firm, reaching far into him, hitting just right. He closed his eyes, floating off into reefer-enhanced sensations. He used his right hand to squeeze and stroke his nipple, his left to jack his still-hard cock.

"Sorry."

Jake opened his eyes. "Huh?"

"I thought maybe I was hurting you."

"No, you ain't at all. My legs are getting kinda tired, though."

"Want to get on top?"

"Sure." The dick slid out of his ass, leaving a gaping void. The two men switched themselves around until Jake was straddling the other's body, squatting down until the big, stiff prick was once more firmly inside his ass. Leaning forward, he slid himself up and down on the hard-on, sweat dripping copiously from his face. He shut his eyes again, thinking about exactly nothing, then opened them and looked down at Duane, at his friend's handsome face, his still-muscular body with its hula girl tattoo on one biceps, blurry blue crucifix inked on the other.

"I really want to come," Jake said, stroking himself.

"Not yet." Firmly. "Not till I do."

Jake didn't argue. He took his hand away and kept on riding his pal's cock, squeezing with his ass muscles, hoping to get Duane to shoot. But Duane just kept plowing greedily. A couple of times he reached over and fetched an almost-done beer from the bedside table, pouring the brew carelessly into his own mouth, stray rivulets running down his chin and cheeks.

Minutes later, Jake asked, "Now?"

"Shut up."

Jake's ass was beginning to get sore. He reached over and grabbed the bottle, draining it into his mouth, then bending down and spitting the beer into Duane's mouth. As he did so, he reached behind himself and gave Duane's big balls a ferocious tug. "You're going to come inside me," Jake said, "now."

"All right, all right," Duane said from between gritted teeth, as Jake increased the pressure on his nuts. "Ow! Not so rough."

Jake relented, letting go of the now-aching balls, sliding his fingers further down between Duane's hairy cheeks until he was able to shove the tip of one finger into Duane's tight, maybe even virgin, hole.

That was all that it took. Duane groaned loudly, then began frantically thrusting upward. With a tortured animal cry, he let loose inside Jake's asshole.

At that, Jake took his hand from Duane's ass and brought the fingers up to his nose, sniffing the dark scent. His other hand worked his own dick, hard and fast, until he, too, came, spraying long, hot ropes all over Duane's chest, one gob hitting him in the face.

"Baby," Jake said, as Duane's softening cock slid out of his ass, "I love you."

When there was no response, he repeated himself.

"Yeah, yeah, I heard you," Duane said, shuffling off to wash his dick in the sink in the corner of the room. His ass, Jake noticed, was starting to sag.

The room smelled like Jake's shit now, but that was almost an improvement.

"So what I did back there at the trailer..." Duane began, getting back into the rumpled bed, pulling the stained sheet over them both. They hadn't talked about it since they'd arrived in Tijuana.

"You mean shooting Eli?"

"Yeah," Duane said, looking improbably sheepish.

"I'm okay with it. It had to be done. Eli was always the one who didn't want to leave any loose ends."

"Yeah, but maybe..."

"No maybes about it," Jake said. "Anyway, nobody'll ever know nothing. The evidence is all burned up. Along with Eli."

"And now we're rich."

"Now we're rich."

There was a knocking at the door.

"*¿Sí?*" Duane called out.

It was a boy's voice. *"Dos cervezas, señores."*

Duane rose from the bed and wrapped a threadbare towel around his middle. He grabbed a few pesos and went to the doorway.

Outside, the light was fading, the smoke from cooking fires beginning to rise. A dark-eyed boy, no older than ten, stood there holding two bottles of beer.

"Gracias," Duane said, pretty much exhausting what Spanish he knew. The boy skittered off, leaving Duane to look around the parking lot of the crummy motor court. Some pathetic old man leading a donkey looked up and smiled. In the distance, wheezy music played. They had real money now, they'd have to do better than this. They could move to a new place *mañana*. Or the *mañana* after that. He gave the Studebaker

the once-over to make sure none of the beaners had messed with it, then shut and locked the door.

He set the beers down on the bedside table, next to the morning paper that Jake had insisted grabbing as they'd headed out of Kansas. Wichita Businessman and Wife Brutally Slain, the headline read. There was nothing in the news about a fire at a flyblown revival tent, but if there had been, it probably wouldn't have rated anywhere more important than page three.

Duane lay back down in bed, and Jake skittered over and cuddled up, his head on Duane's chest.

Jake murmured, "We're really here, aren't we?"

"Yeah, sweet boy. It took some doing, but we're finally here. You happy?"

"Oh yeah." He gave Duane's prominent nipple a kiss.

The next day, while Jake was in the shower, Duane disappeared with the Studebaker. In something of a panic, Jake checked for the bag of money. It was still where they'd left it, under the mattress. Jake was too bored to want to stay holed up at the motor court, but he had to; he was not about to leave the money there, nor to haul a big sack of dough around with him, through the dangerous streets of a shitty Mexican town. So he was stuck, fed up. He wanted to send the kid out for more reefer, but he settled for another few beers, instead. The last thing he needed was the cops dropping by.

When Duane finally reappeared that evening, merely grunting to Jake, he was drunk off his ass, dragging along a whore, a homely woman with big tits and a vacant expression. Jake sat in the chair in the corner of the room while Duane pushed the floozy down onto the bed. Duane hiked her dress up, pulled down her panties, and started fingering her cunt. Jake had a good view of the action; in the beginning, he was interested in looking at Duane, if not at the woman. He took his dick out and began to play with himself, getting semi-hard. But after a couple of minutes, he couldn't have cared less. Duane pulled his cock out, but he was too stewed to get it up. He crouched over the woman and shoved his dick into her mouth, but that didn't get him hard, either.

"You fucking *bitch*," Duane spat out, hauling off and slapping the whore across the face. There was a tremor of shock, even rebellion, in her expression, but she didn't move. Jake guessed that Duane had agreed to spend quite a few pesos for her company.

At the third slap, Jake bestirred himself. "If you want to hit somebody," he said, "hit me." This was probably less an expression of concern for the woman's safety than a plea to get treated real rough. That was, he had to admit, something about Eli that he was going to miss.

Duane turned away from the now-cowering woman, looking like he was about to say something. But at the last minute, he leaned over the side of the bed and puked onto the already-filthy floor.

The whore looked disgusted. Assuming some sort of mostly long-gone dignity, she stood up, straightened her clothes, then reached down into her bosom, pulled out a roll of dollar bills, and counted them, twice. And without so much as an *adios*, she headed out the door.

Jake would have liked to call the kid in to clean up the mess, but that would have been a lot of trouble. He hauled himself off the chair, sighed heavily, and used the ratty towel that had been hanging by the sink to wipe up the puke. Gagging, he went to the door and chucked out the filthy towel. Then he went over to the bed and hauled around Duane's passed-out body until it was in something like a normal sleeping position. He turned out the light. The room was illuminated solely by the lurid red blink of the neon sign outside.

He went back to the chair in the corner, thinking idly about just how much dough was hidden in that bag. How much further it would take one of them than two.

He watched Duane sleeping, his chest rising and falling. His snoring filled the room. Eyes closed, Duane could not see Jake, of course. But if he'd been able to, he might well have noticed an equivocal expression on Jake's battered, almost-pretty face.

TENDER MERCIES
DALE CHASE

W e need to build you a proper cabin," says Virgil Haupt as he fastens his pants.

I lie naked in my recently acquired bed but do not respond to his comment as I hear such things from most of the men who come to my tent. I know Virgil means well, and sure enough his next words are what I have come to call the prospector's promise.

"When I strike it rich, I'll build you the best place in town, two, maybe three rooms, and we'll do it up fine."

His words are tinged with a longing I find in all the men, whether or not declared, and it makes me both sad and hopeful because maybe one day the promise will be made good. Until then, it's gold dust, which is not unwelcome.

When Virgil is gone I wash up and put on the blue robe I had sent from Sacramento. It's surprising what can be acquired in such a place as Beeler Gulch, but gold lies in this bend of the American River's south fork and it's enough to keep miners afloat even as few gain true riches. As the men crave sex as much as gold, it has fallen to me to satisfy them and take their dust in return. I do not indulge in drinking and gambling like most so I am able to acquit myself well amid the rough squalor of the camp. I am also well protected since I provide a valuable service.

I did not come to California with the intent to sell my body. Like everyone else, I listened to stories of gold nuggets lying in riverbeds and sparkling veins lacing the hills to such extent a man had but to work a pan or swing a pick to grow rich. Two thousand miles I journeyed from St. Louis to California only to find there was more men than gold. Still, I partnered with two men in Auburn, set up a rocker box on the

American River which yielded barely enough to keep us alive. Then came news of a fresh strike along the south fork so we packed up and staked a claim in Beeler Gulch, where we had some success but it soon petered out and again we were reduced to poor circumstance.

Beeler Gulch is raw like most gold camps. Men crowd against one another with their claims and when not laboring they drink and carouse to such excess that many lose what little they gain. Winter cold, rain, and mud compound the hardship and these things preyed upon my partners until they called it quits. One headed back to the Pennsylvania farm from whence he had come, the other signed on as ranch hand out of Sacramento. Alone, I knew I must find work on another man's claim and in this I ultimately found opportunity.

Gene Bromley was a bear of a man, fine-looking, good-natured, frank in manner, and highly industrious. When he heard of my companions' departure, he sought me out and offered work. Shaking hands on the deal, his big paw lingered and I saw need in his eyes and considered embracing such a fine idea. Up to that time, I had known only my two partners, and with their leaving had but my hand to offer comfort. Thoughts of Gene's dick brought a good stir to my nether region.

The only building in Beeler Gulch is the saloon though a few who prosper are starting to put up cabins. Tents make up most of the camp and I live in one at the western edge and it was there Gene followed me one night after supper. Once inside, Gene declared himself taken with me and I assured him I felt likewise. We then stripped naked and had us a fuck on my cot.

Gene had a pelt to behold, his dark beard running unchecked down his whole self until sprang his big prick. Hair covered his legs as well so it was like welcoming an animal, which I found an improvement as both my partners had been smooth skinned.

What surprised me was Gene didn't just do it and run. Oh, he fucked like a bull the first time, mounting me from behind and roaring when he came, but he then rolled me over and sucked my dick with great care, causing me to spurt into his mouth.

"How old are you?" he asked afterward.

"Nineteen."

"More spunk than a bear," he declared, licking his lips. "I could suck your cock to kingdom come."

He lay with me then which no man had ever done, on his side so he could attend my tits and run his hand down to my crotch. He played until he had himself hard again, then said he'd fuck me proper.

He put me on my back, legs up, and he eased his big thing into me like he savored every inch and when it was all inside he said my butthole was better than all the diggings had to offer. Then he proceeded to fuck at length and I got stiff and worked myself and spurted all up my front, which got him riled and he started to ram it in, growling and carrying on as he unloaded.

His eyes blazed as he came and I could see in them pleasure more raw than anything hereabouts. It took him some time to empty and when he was finally spent he pulled out and collapsed beside me, slept a bit. I liked him near and as he snored I petted his fur, enjoying his considerable warmth.

I worked for Gene five months, assisting him and two others in a long-tom setup, and he paid me extra because I fucked anytime he wanted. He was always forceful yet gentle after, kissing me, which I'd never known before, caressing me, and telling me how good I was for him. Then one day he remarked that a living could be had doing just what I did for him.

"Women do it elsewhere and if a woman ventured here, she'd do well but, you know, most men will put it to one another with no compunction and a good many, like me, prefer it. And you, Luke, are a fair piece."

He saw immediately that he'd wounded me with such talk and hurried to make amends. "I'm not saying you should do it, boy, just making an observation. I am happy with our arrangement and trust you are too. We will continue so long as you'll have me."

I see now he knew something was afoot inside him because he was soon laid low with fever, took to his bed, and spent his last days with me by his side. I nursed him to the end and when it was over, kissed him one last time. We buried him at the forest edge, up where man's footprint fades. For a while I thought I'd die too.

Turned out Gene had bequeathed his claim to Roy Mullin, who came to me, asked me to stay on. "I know you and Gene was close and this is a time of hardship for you," Roy said, "but I also know you are industrious and we need to keep such as you on the job. Gene always spoke highly of you, said you was special."

We were in my tent and I was clad in just the robe, stretched out on my cot, looking up at him. As he said this last about my being special, I took him in from toes up so I could catch sight of what lay between his legs and sure enough, he presented a good bulge. So I knew he was saying more than he was saying and it brought to mind Gene's comment of how I could do well by fucking.

"Gene was a fine man," I said as my gaze traveled on up to take in the rest of Roy Mullin.

He was red-bearded and cut it close, which gave him a clean appearance which was welcome among so many who let themselves go wild. Lean and lanky, Roy stood with hat in hand, revealing a head of copper hair that curled somewhat. I wondered if he had a red patch between his legs.

"The best," he said of Gene and then, after a pause, he ventured to where he had intended all along. "I know you two spent many a night together."

"We had an understanding," I offered, deciding to give Gene's suggestion a try. I slid my hand into my robe and onto my prick, which had stiffened with opportunity.

Roy clutched his hat to his chest. "I need me a fuck, boy," he rasped. "I'll pay to do you."

I didn't think to negotiate. He held out a poke of dust and I took it, then threw off the robe. Roy, who seemed surprised at closing the deal, stood mute before my nakedness. He looked down at my hard cock, which brought his tongue to his lips like a prick looking for a place to go. He then tossed away his hat and undid his pants.

He didn't bother to strip, which was fine with me as I wanted no more than pay for my trouble. He pushed down his pants and his drawers to reveal a thick red patch and a stiff plug of prick. "Get down on all fours," he said and I did as told, then felt him behind me. His calloused hands parted my buttocks and his prick prodded my center, then pushed in with one thrust. He grunted and started to pant like he'd run a mile and he hadn't even set to work. It was like he needed a second to enjoy getting into a butthole though he possibly knew he might not last long once he set to work. But set to work he did and I do think his fat piece of meat blazed a new trail as it hurt to take him, even as I liked him doing it to me.

Moaning and mumbling throughout, he kept a powerful thrust but this is to be expected of a man grown strong from hard labor. As Roy picked up speed his actions got my own juices rising and just before he let go a roar and a load, I began to spurt into the bedding, the first come I'd had since Gene. While in the throes, I enjoyed the release but once spent, I was overcome with grief and by the time Roy pulled out, I was in tears.

"I am sorry," he said, pulling me into his arms as he settled onto the blankets. "I didn't mean to hurt you but my need was great."

"It's not that," I managed. "This is the first since Gene and it brings him to mind so I again suffer his loss."

Roy's tender mercy allowed me a good cry. He stroked my hair, petted and embraced me until my sobbing relented. Then, in an effort to lighten things, he said, "So you don't object to my fat cock?"

A chuckle escaped me. "No, I don't object. You see the spunk there," I said, pointing to the mess in the bedding. "I let go while you went at me and if that doesn't say how much I enjoyed your fat cock, then I don't know what to tell you."

He did not kiss me and for that I was grateful as I liked Roy but did not have the same kind of feeling as I'd had for Gene. And so that day I began to learn about differences in men and in their fucking and how I could, just as Gene said, make a living selling my body. That I have lived as such for eight months serves as testament, but those eight months have also led me to consider that I may not wish to make a life of such ways. I am well attended, highly valued, yet it is for body alone, which leaves the man inside wanting.

Now, rested from Virgil Haupt's early visit, I dress in preparation for a trek to the restaurant for I have not as yet eaten a meal and the sun is well up. Once clothed, I pocket Virgil's dust and venture out into the camp.

I resist calling our much traveled and deeply furrowed passage a street as that word calls St. Louis to mind and to think back whence I came is to invite melancholy. Instead I concentrate not on the much abused ground but on the men who make their way along, most on foot, some toting shovels and picks and headed to their claims, others looking haggard, coming from their played-out stakes hungry and with little in the pockets. Several greet me but others who know me resist acknowledgment of base impulses and hurry past. When Virgil Haupt sees me, he ducks into the assay tent, never mind his spunk drips from my bottom hole.

The restaurant is the biggest tent in camp and is set with long benches and rough-hewn tables that are most often filled. It's a wonder with so many working their claims to all hours that so many can sit idle over a beef steak but I suppose it says much about the number of men seeking their fortune. Too many, some say. I don't disagree even as I welcome more to my tent each day.

Roy Mullin motions me to join him and Ted Brady scoots over to make room. I slip in between them, see their plates near empty. I order ham, eggs, potatoes, and coffee.

"Bob Smathers shot Farley Green this morning," Roy tells me and Ted chimes in to add, "I knew one day it would happen. No two men was worse suited to partner a claim."

"Why'd he do it?" I ask, thinking of Bob, who blushes every time he comes to my tent and never says a word before, during, or after.

"Says Farley was holding out on him, had a nugget big as a turd and never told Bob, which was cheating as they dug that claim together."

"Is Farley dead?" I ask as my food arrives.

"Winged him is all. Doc fixed him up but he can't work and Bob's still hot as fire."

Doc Calder is actually a dentist from Illinois who spends more time drinking and digging than doctoring but he's the only thing we have for medicine. He also does not visit me but I think it's because he's drunk so often, although I'd venture his not seeing me may be reason for his drinking.

Other gossip is passed along the table as I eat my breakfast. When the men rise to return to their diggings, Roy squeezes my shoulder, says he'll see me later. I know that plug of cock is likely stiff in his pants.

With room on my bench, a man I don't know takes a seat beside me. "I hear you're the camp boy," he says. "You do me?"

"Cost you."

"'Course." Here he squirms on the bench and were others not about, I'd venture he'd get his prick out then and there and have me sit upon the thing.

"Let me finish my meal," I tell him. "My tent is last one west. Be there when the sun's high and we can do business."

He issues a sigh and I give him a good look then, find him not much older than me with fine features and scarce any beard. He is clean to such extent he could be called well groomed, which is rare in these parts. "My name is Luke Farrow," I say and he says, "Quinn Lanham."

Where you from, Quinn?"

"Virginia."

"I hear that's nice country."

"Ain't nothing compared to what lies here for the taking."

"High noon," I say and he gets up, adjusts himself so I can see he's got a good bit in his pants. Then he is gone and as I finish my meal, I think on him toting his swollen meat around until I provide relief.

With my belly full, I walk the camp, greeting the men, stopping to talk with some, passing those who avoid me. Most labor down along the stream, working their rocker boxes or long-toms, the newcomers with none but a pan. Beyond these others dig the land, which has all but ravaged the little valley. Nature's tranquility is lost to the rocker boxes' awful rattle and accompanying this are the men's grunts and groans, which I liken to those exhibited when fucking. This gets me to thinking how at least with me there is always a payoff.

Finally I am past the diggings and out to where the land rises. There are but a few claims here, men with picks digging into valley walls in hopes of finding a vein, which has been known to happen. One such claim employs several men and is owned by Dewey Kane who is said to be the richest man in town. Dewey does not employ me as he is known to fuck the men who work for him. He is a handsome devil, clean-shaven, well dressed, and he eyes me at times but it seems more tease than come-on. I cannot define his intent beyond the fact that he exhibits more control than most.

An easy climb takes me beyond the diggings and into land untouched. It is here I regain myself. I have found a low rock beneath an old oak that seems to have been set out as welcome to those aspiring toward more than the greed below. Here the sounds of commerce die away. Birds call to one another, squirrels cavort in the branches above and knock acorns down upon me. I settle onto the rock and draw deep breaths of good mountain air. Summer will soon arrive, heat descending to scorch us all, but for now the bite of cold is welcome.

In moments like these I allow my thoughts to wander back home to St. Louis where my family resides in hopes I will strike it rich and share my bounty. At first I wrote them often with stories of my labors but now that I have forgone prospecting, I have not sent one letter. I do not wish to lie to my loved ones but how can I tell them my current occupation? I thus push them from my mind, think back to Gene and allow how much I miss him even though months have gone since his passing. He alone declared himself to me and for our months together I felt as never before, which makes the present suffer an emptiness I did not foresee. Dare I allow myself to dream of another such man? Dare I acknowledge the yearning that flickers within? As men arrive to seek their fortunes, I cannot help but hope that one day a man might seek more than gold. Can the prospector's promise ever be more than a dream?

The sun is almost overhead when I push myself from my solitude and make my way back to camp. When I am near my tent, I see Quinn Lanham up ahead so I holler to him and he turns, cups his crotch. When I reach him, he pushes me inside.

"Pay first," I say as he undoes his belt. He reaches into his pocket and extracts a gold coin, which he hands to me. I examine it as this type of payment is rare. "Part of my stake," he explains.

"It'll do just fine," I tell him and I begin to undress.

Quinn peels off pants and underdrawers but leaves on his shirt, which don't bother me as few of the men get clear naked. His prick is long and narrow, hard out and flushed pink. He grips it as if it might start up on its own. When I'm naked, I lie on my bed and open my arms.

"I ain't gonna last," he says as he gets on top of me. Amid the shirttail, I feel his rope of dick against me and he starts to hump and swear because at first touch he comes. His stuff wets my front and his shirt and it's a good lot due to his being so ready. When he rolls off he's upset. "Shit, I wanted to put it to you."

"You still can. That coin paid for more than one go. You do all you want."

He relaxes with this, begins to take note of me, and lies on his side to play with my cock. When he reaches for my balls, I spread my legs and he rolls and rubs, then steals a finger toward the back and I raise up to tell him to wet it, which he does. Then he puts it in and begins to prod.

"Gonna get my dick in there," he says. "Ride me one goddamn fuck. I ain't had none since home. Let me suck you."

I say nothing as he is welcome to all of me, and as he continues at my backside, he gets his mouth on my front and sucks so fierce I spurt another bit into his throat. This he swallows amid much noise and when I am spent and soft, he still sucks until at last his own dick is up again. "Now I'll fuck you proper," he says and he rolls me over, pulls my bottom high.

I hear men outside and wonder which are considering a stop. They could do one another and save the expense but most prefer not and I don't ask why. Meanwhile, Quinn is starting to thrust and I am aroused by his long piece of meat snaking into me. And because he's already come once, he is not urgent so I am well used for a fair amount of time.

When Quinn's juices finally start to rise, his fingers dig into my hips and his stroke goes even deeper. I get a hand on my cock because I am stiff and want to come with him inside me. Seconds later he calls out he is there, invokes the names of God, the devil, and somebody's mother while I receive him. I remain silent while spending a few drops by my own hand.

After, Quinn falls over and laughs. "Ain't gotten off so good in a month." He lies splayed, spent cock lolling on a thigh, and I find myself atingle as he is most appealing.

"You can do more if you want," I tell him as I wish him to stay on awhile.

"Well, I still want," he declares. "Just rest a bit first."

The men outside are gone now, either having lost interest or gotten so worked up they are off with their dicks in hand. More likely they don't have money to pay me and know not to ask for credit.

Quinn begins to snore which is fine with me as I like a rest between fucks. I ease out of bed, pour water from the pitcher, take a long drink, then wash up, all the while watching this man slumber. The gold piece has impressed me, I'll admit, but so has the man.

After a while Quinn awakens with a start. "Just you and me here," I say to quiet him. He blows out a breath and lies back, pulls on his cock. "You ready for more of me?" he asks.

He shifts and stretches like he's been asleep a week, then says to get him hard. I crawl down between his legs and start to lick his thing, which draws from him a welcoming moan. I continue to play, hand at the base of him, knob not yet juicy but still tasty. He puts his hands under his head so he can watch me work him and I make a show of my tongue licking and poking at him until he begs me to get on with it. So I slide my mouth over him, down much of his long shaft, and commence to suck until he is good and hard. "Now sit on it," he says and I withdraw, grinning because no man thus far has wanted me astride.

I climb over him and squat until I feel his prong at my hole. He rises up to jab at me, which makes me chuckle and then I drop down, which drives him up into me. For a second I do nothing more than squeeze my ass muscle, which gets another good moan from him. He allows this until he can stand it no longer. "Ride me!" he commands and I begin to do just that, up and down on him until I've got a good motion going.

"Full gallop," I say and he lets out a "yee hah," slaps his thigh. We are at it for some minutes before he bucks and comes. His face scrunches into a familiar grimace as he's lost to the release and I find myself pleased more than usual. When he is finally done, he manages to tell me he is beyond empty. "I doubt I can walk," he adds.

He doesn't hurry to dress for which I am grateful. When he asks about me, I tell him what I left behind in Missouri and even share what I had with Gene and how I suffered his loss and took up my present occupation as a result. Quinn is most attentive and I find a relief of sorts to share my history. When it is completed, we pass a moment of quiet and then I ask if he will work a claim by himself or hire on somewhere.

"I don't intend to work no claim," he says as he sits up. "Guess I forgot to mention I'm a sporting man and these camps are good pickings. Men lose their gold quick as they find it."

After so many men soaked in sweat and filth, it's refreshing to find one who will not descend into the muck and mire. "We're alike in a way," I offer. "Both get our gold secondhand."

"True," he says and I realize he is quickly becoming more to me than the others. Before I can much enjoy the idea, I hear men outside and tell Quinn he must leave as other customers wait. He agrees that business must be attended to and so he dresses but before he departs he asks if I'll be around the camp later. "Saloon?" he adds.

"Business permitting," I reply.

He laughs and leaves and seconds after I don my robe a miner I do not know enters the tent. He is older than most, somewhat grizzled, and though I'd rather not take his cock just yet, it is a business. He presents a small nugget. "Dug her up today," he says. "Ain't she a beauty?"

I take the pea-sized nugget, venture it equivalent to what most pay in dust. Then I drop my robe. The man strips naked, exposing a fleshy middle and gray patch around his hard prick. "On your back," he says, "like a woman."

I do as told, raise my legs, knowing he has a wife somewhere and will close his eyes and think of her as he gets his money's worth. And I am right. He gets into me and does it quickly, grunting out a rough fuck that I'm sure his wife all too often endured with her eyes closed. He cries his woman's name as he comes and when he is done, hurries to dress and leave. I venture he suffers as much guilt as relief.

I don my robe, sit in my chair, and have a drink of water, knowing another customer will be along soon because it is often this way. "You in there?" a voice calls and I reply to the affirmative and in comes Harry Hirst, a skinny drink of water who does me regular, once a week. He tosses me a poke of dust and undoes his pants, gets out his cock. Harry never drops 'em, he just opens up and gets on with it. And he's always quick, which I figure means he don't attend his needs by hand.

He comes at me, dick in the lead, and I stand, throw off the robe, turn and bend over the chair. He grabs me at the waist and shoves in, pumps his dick in quick strokes and comes with a cry, then pulls out, buttons up, and leaves without so much as a how-de-do. Quiet then descends and after I add his gold to my strongbox, I lie on my bed and rest, thinking back to Quinn, who seems to have something to offer.

Two more men visit me before suppertime, both unknowns. As they grunt out rough fucks, I think on how new men keep appearing in camp and wonder how many more the place can accommodate. Claims already pock the little valley and the stream is full of rockers and long-toms while places free of these contraptions occupy panning men. Farther upriver, sluice boxes are now in place, teams of men engaged at each. The camp teems like a city yet remains raw as few think toward improvements. Most are here to make their fortune and move on.

I take supper at the restaurant, then venture to the saloon. A log structure, it is but one large room with a plank bar set atop barrels, the rest tables and chairs. Men linger outside and as I make my way in, Elmo Polk asks if I'm open for business later.

"Always open for you, Elmo," I tell him which, as expected, makes the others snigger and hoot. I am full aware that I am a joke to many and yet the jibes are all good humored and help the men deal with their cravings.

Inside the saloon, I spot Quinn in a card game at a corner table. More striking than most, he gives off a confident air, settled in his chair like he owns the place, and maybe if his playing is good enough he will one day. Until then it belongs to Dewey Kane, him being the only one with enough money to build such an establishment. He manages regular deliveries of liquor and such but has never encouraged women to work for him. As a result, not a one lives in Beeler Gulch. I presently spot him at one end of the bar, engaged in talk with one of his employees, and wonder if he's making plans to fuck later on.

Roy Mullin buys me a whiskey and while I prefer not to drink, I never refuse such offers as they keep me in good standing with the men. I sip the liquor, feel it warm my belly as Roy leans in close to tell me he's got a hard prick and asks what can I do about it.

"You get it out and I'll suck you right here," I tell him, playing along as he expects.

"Goddamnit to hell, I want to do just that. Got stiff soon as you came through the door."

I am leaned back against the bar so I can talk with Roy while watching Quinn, who deals poker with expertise. He catches me looking, nods, then goes back to his game while I tell Roy we've got all night to fuck. "Or suck, whatever's your pleasure."

"You are my pleasure," he drawls, whiskey breath at my ear. He reaches down to adjust himself and nobody takes note as men are all the time getting a hand on themselves.

Jed Spafford comes up, says he wants to buy me a drink, and I tell him he must wait a bit. He looks to Roy, nods, and retreats. "He's after me," Roy says and I agree, recalling Elmo Polk's earlier offer. It is going to be a busy night but then most are.

I take my time with the whiskey while watching Quinn and wondering if he could become special. Then again, a man's a fool to think another will carry him away. Maybe I'll have to keep on with the here and now, take his pleasure and leave it at that. I wish I could sort things out to my liking but that brings me back to the prospector's promise and I must not lean any hope on such a thing. As I keep my eyes on Quinn, I am taken with his quiet strength. He is sure of himself, which is refreshing amid the desperation so many exhibit. How am I to keep myself in check when my heart has already gone over to him?

"I can't wait no longer," Roy says. My whiskey is half-gone but I leave it and go with him, passing a look to Quinn, who raises his head to acknowledge my tending to business. As Roy and me walk along, I think how both Quinn and me are working and how later he will come find me, give me that cock of his, maybe stay the night.

Roy has had too many drinks and is most garrulous as we walk along. He squeezes my bottom and says all manner of nasty things. Soon as we're inside my tent he drops his pants but I put him off. "Pay first," I remind him and he reels back, passes me a look I see on far too many. He thinks he's become special and ought not to have to pay. "Let's do business," I say as I strip, "then have us a fuck."

He hands over a poke of dust smaller than usual. "Claim's drying up," he says and I don't quibble as he is a good man and gold comes and goes. When I've set aside his payment, he grabs me, gives me a rough kiss which I allow as I like him better than most. But his drunkenness renders a stiff dick no more than wishful thinking. Work is ahead for me.

I get him to lie down, which is more fall than descent. He quiets and I crawl down and start to suck his cock, which offers little response. Roy's eyes are closed. Were I not at him, he could be sleeping and his prick is already in slumber, never mind my efforts. After a bit, he says, without opening his eyes, "put a finger in me," and rolls onto his side.

I wet the digit, push into his bottom hole, and begin to prod, which sets him to moaning. He gets a hand onto his cock and starts to pull and with me at his backside and him at the front, he manages enough to get himself off. Once spent, however, he falls asleep.

"Roy," I call to him, prodding his side. I'm in my robe, business concluded, and it's time for him to leave but he does not budge until I sock him in the gut. He then comes up swinging and I have to remind him where he is. "Time to leave, Roy," I say and he looks down at his bare self, staggers to his pants. Reeling, he says he's going to take me away from all this, go to New York soon as he strikes it big. I agree that New York will be wonderful and push him out onto the street. Jed Spafford enters as soon as Roy is cleared out and when Jed has had his way, Elmo Polk hurries inside to give me yet another one.

The men keep at me until time slips to another day. My strongbox enjoys fresh bounty while I feel like a horse run to lather. I reek of sweat and when I stand, the men's accumulated spunk runs down my leg. I take time at my basin to clean myself but there is only so much can be washed away. I then eat a little something, don my robe, and lie down. I have no idea the time when Quinn wakes me.

He lies naked beside me and reaches inside my robe to tug my cock. A poke of gold sits on my chest. "For you," he says and it takes me a second to get back to the present, such is my stupor. As encouragement, Quinn opens the bag to reveal three good-sized nuggets. "The men couldn't wait for me to rid them of their labors," he offers.

I raise a hand to his cheek, feel his stubble. "I've had half the camp tonight," I tell him. "Doubt I can do much more."

"You don't have to do a thing," he replies, hand now under me, prodding my pucker. "Just let me have you for the night."

"You mean the morning. What time is it?"

"Two thirty when I ran out of takers." He adds a second finger and I can't help but squirm, never mind all the pricks before. "I'll do you easy," he whispers. "Gentle like."

My eyes fall shut as I enjoy his efforts at my backside. His thumb plays at my ball sac while his fingers explore my passage and I swim in pleasure, offering little moans as who can remain silent with such attention? When Quinn presses his lips to mine, I open my mouth to welcome his tongue, which mingles as if it too will fuck. And after this, he slides down to my chest and licks my tit nubs until they are hard, at which he sucks the things, never stopping his work at my bottom.

The camp goes quiet as we lie together. In my mind we are elsewhere. I think on a fine hotel room in San Francisco with clean sheets and soft quilts which are turned back to allow what we do. We will walk out together later for all to see, my man and me, knowing we will return to the hotel later to fuck again. All this as the fingers work me.

"Roll over," Quinn says, which brings my eyes open. I allow him to put me onto my stomach and feel him get down between my legs. He pulls me up and parts my buttocks. "There's the treasure," he says, voice raspy. I know that voice. It's the sound of a stiff-dicked man, one who will do most anything to gain release, and I welcome the assault as I need but receive him.

"Man's own gold mine," Quinn says as I feel him moving around. Not sure what he's up to but I don't really care as I remain in the swoon of anticipation. Then he's behind me again, parting me, rubbing my hole. I expect his knob next, poking around like some pig, but instead I feel something push into me.

"Quinn!" I call.

"Quiet down, it won't hurt you."

His finger retreats only to return and push in another something and it is then that I realize I am taking his gold up my bottom. "What are you doing?" I demand, looking back at him.

"Just playing with you. Relax, enjoy it."

I lie back down and he pushes a third nugget not quite into me. It stops at the entrance like some unexpelled turd, which seems to please him. "Now that is a sight," he says. "You stay put," he tells me as I hear the unmistakable sound of a man abusing his prick.

The bed shakes as he pumps himself. "Bottom full of gold," he growls. "All a man wants." He's working himself with a fury now, breathing hard, setting the bed to a shudder and then he lets out a cry as his spunk sprays upon my buttocks.

When he's done he sits back. "Goddamn good one," he declares. "I do wish you could see yourself. Like a seam of gold runs through you and I've but to set my dick to prospecting. A sight to behold. Drove the cum out of me."

What can I say? I remain bottom up but feeling disgusted instead of aroused. I wish he'd free me as I don't know what more he'll get up to. "Quinn," I say, thinking he'll get my drift.

"Lie still," he says. "We ain't done."

I fear he'll push more gold into me but I do not complain because the part of me that cares for him is doing battle with the part suffering humiliation. Then he runs his fingers over my bottom as you might over horseflesh you consider buying. He goes under to tug my soft cock and cradle my ball sac, then comes back to the buttocks. The nugget remains poised at my entrance.

"Now," is all he says before he gets his tongue onto me.

He licks up and down my crack, licks the nugget, then presses against me and with his tongue dislodges the thing. As he says nothing, I take it that he receives it into his mouth. I hear some smacking and suffer a shudder of revulsion.

"Best boy there is." He chuckles. "Ass of gold." Here he brings the recovered nugget around for me to see. It is, of course, wet and clean. "Let's get us another," he says as I feel movement inside me. When things don't happen to Quinn's liking, a finger goes in to pull the nugget to the entrance and once again, his tongue works it out. He repeats this until I am empty and the three nuggets sit on my pillow. He then puts his prick into me. "Gonna dig deeper now," he says as he starts going at me.

I do not stiffen with his attentions as I am truly put off by the gold play. Instead I receive him as I have the others, his appeal now in tatters. When at last he comes, I am near tears.

Rolling off, he notes I'm soft. "You come?" he asks.

"No, but that's okay. Too much for one day."

This seems to satisfy him and he lies beside me, blowing out long breaths of satisfaction while I try not to think of what he has done. Soon he snores and I slip from bed, wash, don my robe, and sit in the chair. The three nuggets remain on the pillow, sight of them raising a repulsion in me that I find born not only of his acts but of what I've become. How far will a man go? How far will I?

The camp awakens before Quinn. I dress, then shake him. "I'm hungry," I tell him. "You want to go get breakfast with me or rest here?"

"Here," he mumbles before turning over and going back to sleep.

Outside the day is fresh and cool. I suck in air like some bear out of hibernation, then start not for the restaurant but for the path to my hillside rock. I wave at the men as they call to me when I pass. Soon they are below and I am above, climbing up from my life. My rock basks in early sun and I settle onto it while trying to empty my mind. I seek only nature's bounty and crows above me oblige with their caws. I also welcome rustling of squirrels and squawks of scrub jays. All make room for one another, all are in harmony, while I suffer an unrest nature fails to ease. Thinking back to my months of selling myself, I cannot understand why Quinn's play with the gold bothers me so. I sell my bottom. It was his to do with as he pleased and I should not complain that he wanted a different game. But what will he do next time? Is he the kind of man who needs to humiliate? I want so badly to hold on to him yet it is he who pushes me away and this brings on a wrenching knowledge that I will never leave this place. I will pass my days in the employ of men who give me only their pricks.

When my stomach begins to growl from hunger, I take it as a sign that I have suffered enough self-abuse and I descend to the restaurant where I eat a meal and attempt to resume my life. News has Jed Spafford gone away, given up working his claim. "Back to Springfield," Roy says. "Had enough."

One less fuck, I think to myself, knowing this matters little because two new men will take his place. Then Elmo is at my elbow. "Looka this," he says, holding up a large nugget. "Found her yesterday, just the one, but ain't she a beaut."

I nod as I suffer thoughts of Quinn's nugget play.

"Worth a month's work," Elmo adds, laughing. I am happy for him as he is a good and hardworking man. "You help me celebrate, Luke?"

"Sure, Elmo. Come by in an hour."

Walking to my tent, I try to allow that Quinn was simply a man excited by winning and sexual need, but I cannot get past what feels a desecration. I become more certain by the minute that he did not need to do what he did to work himself up.

He is awake when I reach my tent, lying naked in the bed. When I step in, he takes hold of his cock and begins to pull. "You filled your gut, now let me fill your bottom. C'mon, get out of those clothes and come sit on me."

The poke resides on the bed beside him, the three nuggets back inside. Quinn reaches over to finger it. "All yours," he says. "You're worth every damn ounce."

Here I engage in battle with myself as I cannot deny he is powerfully handsome. Beard stubbles his chin, his hair is mussed, his eyes bleary, and yet he gives off such a manly air that he is hard to resist. I think back on his desecration of me, feel again the repulsion at such use, and yet his appeal causes me to strip away my clothes and climb onto him. As we fuck, I look into his eyes and see an innocence of sorts or maybe an ignorance, one man taking from another while not knowing what he leaves in his wake.

Once Quinn comes, I tell him Elmo has had a good strike and is

due soon to celebrate with me. "You're going to be a rich man," Quinn
says as he dresses.

I have no reply. Before he leaves, he says he'll be by after his
night's work. I do not tell him otherwise and when Elmo arrives, I allow
him a good long fuck. When he has gone, I gather up my washing and
make my way to the laundry, then stop at the mercantile for canned
goods and other supplies. I am happy to be out and about the camp and
when the men hoot and call, I welcome their attentions as this somehow
gets me back on the ground Quinn had upended.

My night is like most. I receive the men one after another until
one breaks into tears after he comes, telling me he is broke and wants
to go home. It is Daniel Picket of North Carolina, who I know has
wife and children there waiting for him. I take him into my arms and
encourage his tears, after which he apologizes and dresses. Before he
leaves, I return his poke of dust, which I have made heavier than what
he brought to me. He notes this with quivering chin. "You are most
kind, Luke. I will never forget you."

"I wish you a good journey home."

My spirits rise after this and when Elmo visits me again, we share
a laugh. "Still celebrating," he says as he drops his pants and drawers.
He's half-drunk but manages to get it up and in, giving me a quick one.
He then all but collapses. "You'd best get on to your tent," I say and he
agrees. "A fine fuck," he remarks on the way out.

When he's gone and I've cleaned up, I sit in my chair as I wish
to avoid the bed awhile. I think on Quinn coming by later and have no
idea how his appearance will strike me. Will I still be put off by his
desecration or will his general appeal win me back over? I am lost to
such thoughts when two men burst into the tent. Both are unknown to
me.

"Gonna have us a fuck," one slurs and I know they've come from
the saloon, having heard I'll give myself for a price.

"Pay first. Two ounces," I tell them, caution now upon me as some
men become unruly. They eye each other, then approach. "Ain't got us
no gold yet," one says.

Night changes most men. It forgives the day's labor and conceals
both good and evil, prosperity and pain. Things never done in the
light of day start to occur and I see these two have joined up to wreak
havoc. That I have been chosen is not surprising as men often lead

with their dicks. It is not the fucking I fear but what may serve as accompaniment.

"I don't do it for free," I tell them as one gets his pants unbuttoned. He is blond and fair yet crusted with dirt and reeking of sweat and whiskey. The other, darker and heavily bearded, leers but says nothing. I don't back away as showing fear undermines what little control I have and besides, there's no place to back to. "Two ounces of gold," I demand.

"Told you we ain't struck it yet so you'll have to give us credit which we are good for," says the blond. "Now throw off that robe and let me have your bottom."

His cock is free now and I know I am lost yet I refuse him because I cannot let any in for free. "No," I say, arms crossed.

"Get him, Tom," the blond commands and as I scramble toward the tent flap, I am waylaid, stripped of the robe, and thrown onto the bed. The dark one holds me down while the blond shoves his cock into me. As he takes what he wants he whoops and hollers, then goes quiet as he unloads his stuff. When he pulls out he tells me to stay put and I know not to fight. They change places and I take the other's prick. This one, Tom, comes soon as he's into me, swears at not getting enough. When he pulls out I think the ordeal over but I am wrong.

"Turn over, boy," comes the command and I do as told.

"Look at that pink candy," the blond says, eyeing my cock. "Gonna have me some of that." And he crawls onto the bed, down between my legs, and sucks me while pulling on his dick, trying to get it up again.

He's rough with his mouth, fierce with his pull, and when I don't stiffen he draws back. "Ain't much of a dick," he declares to Tom, who stands working his cock. "What's the matter with you, boy?" he demands, slapping me across the face. He then begins to pummel me and throws me to the floor. Tom joins in, kicking me and calling me all manner of nasty things until I lie bruised, one eye swollen near shut. As they finally do up their pants, they begin to speak of my riches. "Must have him a fine stash of gold," Tom declares and with this they open my trunk to find my strongbox. "No need to dig," the blond declares as they depart with my gold.

I crawl to my bed in pain that is not new. Others have done this in months past but those who care for me usually drive off the offenders once the deed is made known. The trick, I have learned, is not to dwell on the incident but to rest and heal. I doze off again reconsidering my occupation and when I wake, Quinn is at my side with a cool cloth he applies to my swollen face.

"Who did this to you?" he asks and before I can speak he adds, "He's a dead man."

Much as I want the return of my gold, I want no bloodshed as enough red has run through the camp. Killing is commonplace and while some deserve it, most do not. "I don't know them," I tell Quinn. "They're new. One black-haired, heavy beard, brown shirt, red scarf. Name of Tom, looked maybe a half-breed. The other was fair but foul, reeking like a muleskinner. They took my strongbox but don't go killing them, Quinn. Ain't worth it."

"Hell it ain't," he says and he departs, not returning until morning when I am slow to meet the day. As he hands me my strongbox, I dread learning what happened as miner's justice is swift and ugly.

"Doubt it's all there," Quinn offers as if he's responsible for any shortage.

"It's fine. Thank you."

Quinn scarcely pauses before he starts the telling and I see he's as stricken with blood lust as are the others. Never mind his caring for me fueled the revenge. He has killed two men and as he eagerly relates horrific details of shotgun justice, I raise a hand to call a halt. He is taken aback, excitement over his accomplishment upended by my failure to fully appreciate his efforts. He becomes awkward then, more like some new customer than one who's had me.

"I appreciate you getting me my gold," I tell him, "but there is too much killing. That you took part on my behalf doesn't make it more palatable."

Here he stands as if he's suffered great insult. His jaw goes rigid, his eyes flare, but he says nothing. After a silent impasse, he leaves. I then lie on my bed, strongbox beside me, and feel myself an outcast. Not because I sell my body but because I value it and those of others, no matter their ways. In my time here I have seen men hanged for cheating at cards, shot for poor choice of words, sliced up because they committed some real or imagined infraction. Punishment is extreme and only now do I see how it piles onto a man like some heavy coat he cannot shed.

When I take breakfast in the restaurant, I endure further news of payment extracted from the two who robbed and beat me. Roy Mullin was in on it, as was Elmo Polk, and as I eat my eggs, I don't try to stop the telling because it's like some river I can't hold back. I hurry my meal and attempt to stay afloat long enough to leave. None comment on my quiet. All are good-intentioned and this I must accept, even as it greatly puts me off.

In my time here I have come to question God's ability to oversee his flock. A minister came to camp once and attempted to preach the Word but soon fell to lust for gold, moving on to Humbug Creek where he'd heard of a strike. Didn't matter much as few attended his services and those who did grew impatient to get to their Sunday drinking and gambling. It is with this in mind that I am amused to hear fiddle music nearby. God may not control lawlessness but he does sometimes provide accompaniment.

Leaving the restaurant, I discover a finely dressed fellow playing fiddle outside the saloon. Men have gathered round and he gives them a sprightly tune, which sets some to tapping their toes and others toward a jig. Those capable of killing one another over a hand of cards suddenly cavort like children and it is soon decided a dance must be held. When I am spotted, Elmo Polk pulls me to the center of things.

"You can dress up like last time," he says and to the newcomers he adds that I have feathers and scarves and doo-dads that make me look right girly.

I allow myself to embrace the moment because I see the need of something to raise me up out of the deep that events of late have pulled me into. I tell them I will play the girly part and am off to my tent to prepare. "I'd best not be disturbed the rest of the day," I announce. "A girl must have time to make herself ready."

The men hoot and holler at this, some bowing deeply as I pass. I make my way home, lash the tent flap, and fall onto my bed. My body complains and I allow myself to fall asleep.

"Luke Farrow," someone is calling in the dream. I think it's Gene but my eyes open and I feel the hurt about my body and know again he's gone. But somebody is outside and night is nearly upon us.

"Who's there?" I ask.

"Dewey Kane."

I sit up. This man has scarcely done more than pass me a look and never has come calling. I stand, straighten my clothes and admit him.

As he surveys my realm, I wonder if he's killed anyone. So handsome and clean, he appears far removed from bloodshed. He could well be the Sunday preacher if he didn't look such a devil. "Right nice," he says of the place.

"I do my best."

"Men seem happy."

"That what you come to tell me?"

He grins and something flutters pleasantly in my chest. I can't help but smile because he offers what most others do not. Features so regular, skin untouched by rough weather, teeth white and straight. And he doesn't smell like most. Bathes regular, which gets me thinking on him naked, soaping his dick. All this to mind before he gets out a reply.

"Nope. I come to ask a favor." He has a package under one arm and offers it. "I want you to dress up for the dance."

"What's this?"

"A dress. I had it sent from Sacramento with the last whiskey shipment because I figured we'd get a fiddler through here again and the men deserve more than feathers."

"A man in a dress."

"Yep."

"And I'm that man."

He cocks his head like this is a given and I cannot much argue as I am slight of build and shorter than most, not to mention younger and, as Gene once said, prettier.

"You'll cut a fine figure," Dewey coaxes, "and I'll pay you for your trouble."

I am impressed by his attentions and wish to tell him how refreshing he is after the crust and stench of so many but all I manage is I'd be happy to dress up and it will cost him nothing. "Maybe a drink after," I add.

He nods, ever the gentleman, and I think how maybe he does notice me and has been holding back. Maybe my dressing up stirs him.

"I'll see you tonight," he says, tipping his hat before he departs.

I don't open the package right away but sit with it for a time as it is such a turn from the morning. Thoughts of Dewey are welcome as he pushes Quinn aside. I also appreciate his trying to bring entertainment to the camp. Nobody will die tonight. Dancing instead of shooting.

The dress is finer than I expect, dark red silk with long sleeves puffed at the shoulder and a plunging neckline. In the package are also chemise and petticoat and I think how Dewey must know women. I set about trying on the ensemble, which is of good length to hide my boots. I fill the chemise bosom with rolled-up socks, which completes the female illusion. I then take off the dress and lie back down to rest. My body aches where the men kicked me, my side deeply discolored and most tender. And my eye remains swollen so I'll be a damaged girl tonight but I doubt the men will care.

The dance will take place in the saloon. They'll push tables and chairs to the wall to clear a spot and I won't be the only one dancing. With the men drinking, they'll discard notions of propriety and dance with one another, some tying a kerchief about their head or a scarf around an arm. It's a touching sight as the ones playing female take to it heartily, sashaying about in an exaggerated manner that no woman would condone. But they please one another and it allows them to resume lost lives for a time, giving way to music and joy and perhaps even happiness, which is scarce in the diggings.

Last time we had a fiddler come through, we near wore him out with demands for his playing and he earned a good amount of gold for his trouble, not to mention whiskey. The men were a sight and I was much attended. I'd fixed myself up with turkey feathers and scarves and played the feminine part with care, the men responding in highly courtly manner. A fine time was had by all but now I am to dress up as a full girl.

It's not a disagreeable situation, even though it goes beyond my wishes. But with Dewey Kane paying court, I'll play-act for them all. He'll be watching and the thought of him giving me the eye and maybe working up to something later on urges me to present myself with care.

I light my lamp, clean up, and begin to dress. I can hear men passing outside, eager for the festivities, and I like the idea that for once they'll be doing more than gambling. Tonight they need not lose an ounce and this brings Quinn to mind as he'll get no business. Will he return to my bed or have events of late done us in?

With socks tucked into the chemise, I have a bosom which I ease into the dress, smoothing the whole ensemble until I am the picture of an almost woman. Problem is my hair. Though well past my ears, it is short of what any girl would wear. I tie it to one side with a ribbon, which will have to do. Then I find the tiny pot of red dust kept from last time and I wet some, smear it onto my lips. This completes me. Miss Luke appears once again.

I wait until it is quiet outside before I venture forth. Fiddle music can be heard up the street so all are engaged. I plan to make an entrance as this pleases the men and so I walk out, lifting my skirts to keep the hem clean. As I go along, I wonder how women put up with being trussed up and cinched in, gathered and pressed until near nothing is allowed where it grows.

Men are gathered outside the saloon and fall quiet as they find a woman in their midst. Then they see she is me and they turn playful.

"Well looka that, Miss Luke got herself all dolled up."

"Purdy gal."

"What's under those skirts?"

"Let her pass, boys," says Elmo Polk, hat in hand. "Miss Luke," he adds with a deep bow.

The fiddler stops his music-making at my entrance and all turn to look upon me. Silence such as I have never heard in all my time here comes over the place and for a few long seconds I enjoy a new importance. Then, to get things moving, I swish my skirts, twirl once around, and move to the center of the room. "Boys," I say in a most come-hither voice.

This undoes them, as expected, and when the fiddler resumes his lively tune I am waylaid by a horde of grasping hands. As I attempt to manage, a voice commands they step back. It is Dewey Kane, proprietor. He steps forward and declares the first dance his. I am then drawn into his arms and whirled about the room. The hoots and hollers I expected are absent as the men stand in awe. I am swept along and see Roy and Elmo, both smiling, and then Quinn, who is not.

There are new faces among the crowd, most haggard and worn from their labors and not bothering to wash up before socializing. I see a white-haired old man, stooped and grizzled yet grinning, and I think of St. Nicholas who, were he not a child's fancy, would surely be here digging his fortune. Near him is a boy so young he must be someone's child and yet he seems on his own and I wonder if he's even fifteen. On and on I whirl, Dewey's strong hand at my waist. He is masterful in his step, obviously well schooled, and I wish the music would slow so we could get up close as I'd like to feel what I'd guess is a cock far from rest.

At last the song is over and Dewey, before he releases me to the others, pulls me close and says, "You're beautiful, Luke." He then lets go but commands the men to be orderly. "Your mamas taught you how to be polite to a lady. Well, it's time to call up your manners and not trample this girl. The night is long."

After some scrambling, the men form a line, Roy Mullin being first. Taking me in his arms, he acts like some schoolboy at a dancing academy. His steps are awkward but he manages a good reel about the room and by the time the song ends he's relaxed enough to gain a good step. Before he hands me off to the next man, he whispers in my ear. "Gonna need a fuck later." I nod, knowing business will be brisk.

They all dance with me, even the stooped old man who seems to straighten a bit. His gait is heavy but his face is lit with joy and I welcome him into my arms. His white hair and beard return the Christmas image to me and I pass a moment of longing for home before banishing such from mind.

It is later, as some men don scarves and kerchiefs, declare themselves girls and partner with the men, that I dance with Tom Brady, who tries to rub his cock at me. Pushing him back to arm's length I remind him we can meet later but he's drunk and persists, which causes Dewey to intervene.

"Mind your manners," Dewey says as he grabs Tom by the shoulder. "Miss Luke must be treated with respect."

"Fuck her," Tom slurs. "Fuck him."

He has no time to say more as he is pulled away and shoved out the door. Dewey then returns to me, apologizes for the incident, and asks me to resume. "The men adore you," he adds and his look gives me cause to wonder if he might too.

Virgil Haupt, who has hung back, now takes me up but he barely looks at me as we dance. His step is large like so many of the men and I know he is pent-up as he hasn't visited my tent in some days. Then Elmo Polk has a turn.

"You make a fine lady," he offers. "But then I always thought you beautiful."

"Thank you, Elmo. You are most kind."

This brings a flush to him and I enjoy an almost courtly dance.

We could be in some St. Louis salon and for a time I allow the streets outside to be paved with stone.

Will Hansen makes a show of bowing deeply before taking me into his arms and I nod to accept his attentions. He twirls me to such excess that I begin to laugh and the men, now mostly drunk, carry on in response. I find myself laughing and smiling more than I have in months, warmed by fun amid such bleak surroundings. I continue to look upon the men as I am swept and spun along and as I do so my eye catches another stranger, this one hanging back yet impressive in his quiet. He isn't worn and dirty like most, wears a buckskin jacket over black shirt, denim pants. Square-jawed, clean-shaven, and ruddy from too much sun, he gives off an energy I can feel even at a distance. He has one foot perched on a chair, which serves to exhibit his crotch, and on the next twirl past, I make a point to look there, as I suspect he intends. And oh my, what I see.

The bulge in his pants is substantial and I consider if he gets it out, it will drop some good inches upon his thigh or if aroused, will stand near a foot out from his fur patch. As I am in contemplation of such, the song ends and Will bows and retreats, after which I beg for respite. When the men persist, Dewey comes to my aid and escorts me to his table.

"Thank you for dressing up, Luke. You've given the men a good night," he says as I am seated.

"And you?" I reply, emboldened by his attentions.

"Most pleased," he says, looking upon me at length yet giving little indication of further interest. I am thus puzzled by his attentions as my prick is stiff beneath my dress. I suspect he knows this as I cannot take my eyes from his face which, even in repose, is most welcoming. I think to invite him to my tent later on, the words at the tip of my tongue, when up saunters Quinn Lanham.

"Miss Luke," he says.

"Mr. Quinn," I reply.

"Join us," Dewey says, pulling out a chair beside him which Quinn settles into. "Fine party," Quinn declares, adding to me, "You dress up right nice."

"Thanks to Dewey here. He got me the duds."

Quinn nudges Dewey and in this small gesture, I see an intimacy from which grows a recognition that all but knocks me off my chair.

Quinn already knows about the duds and his chair is close to Dewey's for a reason. Once I open myself to such consideration, I am all but trampled by recognition that they are joined by more than cards and that I am a fool.

"It's a fine costume," Quinn says. "Makes you wonder what will come next from Sacramento. You gonna order Luke a parasol or some lip rouge?" he asks Dewey. "Maybe some lace underdrawers?" They share a laugh and I see I am mocked which leads me to wonder if Quinn taking up with Dewey is genuine or some kind of getting back at me for my failure to applaud his killing on my behalf. He is laughing now, full of himself. "How do you fit a dick in your lady unmentionables?" he asks. "Likely ain't much room but then you'll drop 'em anyways."

I don't reply and Dewey, attempting to turn the conversation, suggests Quinn get me a drink. Quinn snorts a laugh and goes to the bar. "Ruffians," Dewey says but I note his eye strays toward Quinn's backside.

Men begin to hover and after a few sips of whiskey, I resume dancing. They are louder now, rougher, and some pull and push as much as dance. Then Harry Hirst, who wears a scarf tied to his arm, slugs his dance partner, who likely made a rude proposal. Jud Freeman enters the fray, punching Harry, and the fiddler jumps in with "Turkey In The Straw" to accompany the melee. Others take up sides, Roy Mullin all but throwing a fellow over the bar, and the festivities are soon asunder amid flying fists and broken furniture. Men are run against the bar and come back swinging while others kick and scuffle and punch, all this accompanied by swearing and shouting. When Dewey attempts to quiet the fray and Quinn jumps in with his fists, I am left on my own, rising from the table and hugging the wall as I attempt flight. The men, completely unleashed, crash and fall to block my way. I have no defense but to huddle in a corner.

Tom Brady comes back amid the fighting and sets upon me, pants undone. I look for Dewey or Quinn or Roy but all are engaged in the fight so I am left to resist Tom on my own. He is clawing at my skirts when the fellow in buckskin intervenes and without a word punches Tom in the gut, which causes him to upchuck. As he retches, the new man leads me through the fighting and outside. Once there he asks if he can escort me home.

"Yes, please. You're very kind."

He puts his hand to my waist, as any man would escorting a woman, and I am slightly put off by the gesture because it is made to Miss Luke and thus not to me. Surely he knows I am a man and yet one cannot be sure of men too long in the diggings. This knight who has rescued me may be thinking on a wife back home, touching me as he does her, or am I letting my mind run from reason? Maybe he has a hard cock in his pants, looking to make use of it, and is simply a gentleman in his approach.

By the time we reach my tent, I'm worked up both from the saloon fight and this man's courtly manner. It's been some day and I figure to now close it with his attentions. I am surprised when at my tent he does no more than tip his hat. I look him in the eye and he doesn't turn away so I jump in.

"You know I'm dressed as a woman only to give the men their dance," I say which causes him to grin.

"'Course I know, even if I ain't seen you as a man."

"Would you like to?" I offer, holding open the tent flap.

He nods, steps into my world, and as I light the lamp he remarks on the bed. "Didn't expect such finery. Don't often see a proper bed hereabouts."

"You're welcome to try it," I reply, realizing only then that I am not considering a request for payment.

He sits on the bed, takes off his jacket, and looks around. "Fixed up right nice," he says.

Surely he's heard I'm the camp boy. Surely he's here to partake, but he seems more like a guest come to call, which I find myself liking. I unloose my hair and the buttons on my dress. He watches with such calm that I begin to think he may not want me and while I am not put off by this, it is surprising as I am more acquainted with urgency. I note his hand absently plays over the quilt, as if in appreciation of something soft amid the roughness of camp.

Down to my chemise and petticoat, I remove the socks from my bosom and only then think, socks in hand, to ask the man's name.

"Cullen Markey," he tells me. "From Laredo but that's some time back. And you're Luke."

"Luke Farrow. And I'm pleased to meet you, Cullen, and to have you rescue me from the fight. I'm not often caught in things like that."

"My pleasure."

The chemise falls to the floor and I stand in nothing but underdrawers. "You strip down right nice," Cullen offers without the leer I'm accustomed to and this leads me to think he's courted women in his time as his manners remain uncorrupted.

The moment of truth has arrived as my hard cock pokes forward. He gives it a look, then eyes me to such extent a tingle runs through the whole of me. "You want to show me the rest?" he asks.

"That I do," I tell him and I drop my drawers.

He does not leap upon me like most, nor does he get out his cock and make ready. Instead he seems to enjoy the sight before him and so I slowly turn around a couple times to allow him a good look. As I then face him, I take hold of my stiff prick and work it which draws his eye downward. Now that I have him, I turn again to present my backside and hear him draw a long breath which confirms the urge is upon him, however restrained and mannerly.

I run a hand onto my buttocks and slide a finger up my crack, then spread my legs and push into my hole to prod a bit. When I've given Cullen this for a minute, I relent and turn to find him unbuttoning. Recalling the snake along his thigh, I seize with anticipation and sure enough, he pulls out a rope of hard prick. My eyes widen at the sight and Cullen becomes near apologetic. "Horse cock," he offers. "Too big for some."

"Not for me," I tell him as I approach. He pushes off his boots, gets out of his pants and drawers, opens his shirt and throws it off to reveal a pelt befitting a bear. I am set aquiver at the sight.

"Get on all fours," he instructs and I do as told, feel him get in behind. I hear the smack of spit upon his hand, know he is wetting his cock, and then I feel the knob at my pucker and his steady push as the whole of him goes in. I issue a cry at which he stops but I assure him it is pleasure and so he continues.

The prick is truly a snake crawling into my bowels. Once fully inside, it retreats partway out, then shoves back in which causes me to moan and shudder and when he begins to do it regular, setting up a rhythm, I lose control of myself and declare, "Sweet Jesus, I want it all."

He obliges by driving the entire piece of meat into me, which causes my breath to catch. And when he uses all of himself in his stroke, when he pulls nearly out then shoves back again, I am impaled over and over which causes me to shoot my load into the bedding with not a hand on myself.

It is truly an animal fuck. The horse cock name is apt, I decide as I writhe in the throes. He is more stud than man and my bottom muscle clenches to encourage, even as my passage is filled to capacity. Finally he announces he is coming. He grips my waist and issues a long moan while I envision spurts befitting horse not man. He keeps to his thrusts as he empties and even as he quiets he keeps on, cock in and out until at last it lies spent inside me. By virtue of its length it does not slide out like most. I give it a squeeze and he chuckles, then pulls out.

When he does not hop off the bed or lie beside me, I roll over to see him sitting back on his haunches, the great prick flushed red and hanging spent but still impressive. Sweat makes his fur glisten and I think how I want to get into it, find his tit nubbins, rub them, maybe get a suck. I also see a ragged pink scar not far from where the heart lies. He has been wounded in his past. Is he perhaps a gunfighter? A lawman? He has few prospector characteristics and for a second I question everything about him but then he tugs on his cock, declares the fuck a fine finish to the night, and lies down beside me. I slide a hand onto his chest, find a tit, and as I begin to rub a voice calls from outside.

"Luke, you in there?"

"Not tonight," I call out.

"But you said!"

It's Elmo Polk. "I'm sorry," I call. "Things have changed. Go home, Elmo. Tell the others."

There is some swearing and I hear others nearby, voices rising as he shares the bad news. They linger awhile but as all respect me, they eventually wander away. At this point I feel compelled to speak to Cullen on the situation.

"You know I'm the camp boy."

"I'll pay if you want."

"No, I don't want pay. I just want to make sure you know others have been in this bed."

"I don't care about others," he declares. "I'm interested in Luke Farrow."

Lying together, I ask him about himself.

"Been up on the Feather River since not long after the big strike, then worked my way down the American. Last try was on the north fork, around Auburn, but that played out. Done right well, though, enough to maybe try another line of work. Maybe ranching or such. Digging gold is hellish and I've seen it use up too many men with little reward."

When he asks about me I share my St. Louis roots, the gold fever, Gene. He listens attentively, even as his hand strays to my cock. "Sweet body," he says when I conclude my story. "I can see why you do well." He then crawls down, gets his mouth onto me, and commences a suck.

Having come, I am slow to rise to his ministrations and I think he likes this as there is some slurping and slopping down there, lots of tongue play and licking. He seems almost ready to make a meal of me but when I begin to stiffen he gets serious and before long I am giving him something to swallow. He receives my offering with his mouth on the whole of me, face buried in my hairy patch, and after I am done he continues with my soft prick on his tongue. At last he pulls off, rolls onto his back, closes his eyes.

In the quiet I am given to reflect on how Cullen is both forceful and caring and thus offers great appeal. I also remind myself to use caution as my judgment of late has become suspect where men are concerned. I had thought Quinn to be of good nature but his desecration of my body and his bloodthirsty way have put asunder such feelings, as has his alliance with Dewey Kane. Dare I welcome another man to my innermost places? I look around my tent and find it can become, if I so choose, a private world inhabited by just two. I warn myself not to fall too quickly or too hard yet know I am lost to an outpouring I can little control.

As sleep beckons I douse the lamp and settle into the crook of Cullen's arm. He murmurs and I kiss his cheek, slide my hand onto his chest where the steady rise and fall urges me toward sleep.

Camp noise awakens me shortly after dawn and I find Cullen gone. The tent flap is done up and I look around to see not a trace of him. Save for the spunk he left in me, there remains no evidence of his attentions, which brings on fear of being duped. He's had me for nothing but his courtesy, which renders me a fool. How could I let myself be overpowered by his charm? I should know better and yet I cannot help but lie back to recall him upon me. I tug my dick in fond recollection and despite likely suffering failed judgment, I'm soon bucking and spurting which causes me to forget my dilemma for a time and doze until camp activity awakens me again.

Never mind the men were drunk last night, they are out of bed and working their claims with all the usual clatter. Shouts and calls, the thunk of picks and shovels, the crack of rock, the toss of bucket or spade. All is clamor, the night asunder.

I linger abed to decide if I shall seek Cullen Markey and if I do happen upon him, what will next take place. He's been set apart in not paying and while I allowed it, I now know regret even as I contemplate him upon me again. Unless he's had his fuck and run. I thought I knew men yet find myself at a loss.

I rise and dress, fighting an underlying eagerness to see if he has merely risen early to get a meal or attend to some business. Gazing into my mirror, I see forgiveness all too ready and scold myself for such indulgence. Odds are he's gone but if he's stayed, he's likely smug in having had the camp boy for free.

Setting out to breakfast, I find my step light, as if Cullen Markey's presence has altered things, never mind his motive. I suck in a breath and feel new vigor, which I attempt to embrace as my own, even though I know it born of this man. Making my way along the busy street, I am greatly undone and can only hope it does not show.

The restaurant lies beyond the saloon and before I reach either I see Cullen Markey ahead, engaged in a verbal encounter with Dewey Kane. My heart seizes with relief at his remaining in camp but suffers from the discourse at hand. They stand close up, in front of the saloon. That they took their words to the street seems significant, as does their increasing volume. I slow my progress as something about their way together indicates familiarity. They are most emphatic with one another and speak with mannerisms that lead me to conclude they have a history. Moving closer, I catch a bit of the argument and hear Cullen demanding gold owed him. Eager for more, I continue toward them until Quinn Lanham steps into my path.

"Where you headed, Luke?"

"Breakfast," I tell him, looking past him to the two men who are most heated now.

"Why don't you hold off a bit," Quinn suggests. "No business of yours up ahead."

"My business is breakfast," I counter but when I attempt to pass he again stops me.

"Breakfast can wait."

"You telling me I can't move on?"

"I'm telling you that's a private conversation up ahead."

"A man wants privacy, he don't conduct his business on the street. Now let me pass."

"Leave 'em be, Luke."

"I have no intention to interfere. I just want a meal."

Neither man has given way up ahead and for a second I fear gunplay as Cullen's hand is at his holster. Dewey makes no such motion, as if confident he will prevail. Quinn looks to the men, then steps aside. "Leave 'em be," he says again and I do just that, although on reaching them their argument stops.

Cullen's look is fierce at my approach while Dewey breaks into a grin. Nothing is said until I've gone by, at which Cullen declares to Dewey, "This ain't over," and flees in the other direction.

"Mornin' Luke," Dewey calls as I hurry into the restaurant. Soon as I'm settled with my grub, Quinn slips in beside me.

"Your new man is trouble," he tells me and when I refuse to bite, he goes on. "Says Dewey owes him, which ain't true. Says they shared a claim on the Feather River two years back and Dewey run out with the gold but that's hogwash. Dewey says he weren't never on the Feather River, made his money right here, and you know he's got the biggest strike so there ain't no lie. His men pull out nuggets big as your balls."

I eat without comment until Quinn derides Cullen to ridiculous extent, saying it was him that stole from Dewey and he's likely stole more, maybe horses, maybe shot a man, maybe part of some gang looking to rob us. At this point I tell him I'm not interested in any of this. "Just let me eat in peace."

Quinn swings a leg to straddle the bench and gets his face in close to mine. "The whole camp knows Cullen had you all night," he says. "Took Miss Luke home, got under her skirts, and fucked her till dawn. The boys were there to hear, Elmo and Harry and Will. And Roy Mullin swore up a storm as he was ready to do you when Elmo brought word you was engaged for the night. How much did he pay you, Luke? You get a fat nugget for your time?"

"He paid for the night, that's all."

Quinn slides a hand onto my thigh. "Then you and me can do some business once you've eaten."

"Noon, not before."

He squeezes my leg, says he's carrying a powerful load, and when he rises he stands with his bulge at my cheek. "Noon," I say again.

I don't go back to my tent. Instead I walk up to my hillside rock but as I go I keep a lookout for Cullen, all the while telling myself not to do so but unable to heed my own warning. Going along, I know more of the vigor he brings on, the air fresher, sun warmer. Like something has sparked whether or not welcome.

"Hey, Luke," I hear as I pass the diggings. "Why don't you come over here and drop your drawers? I got me a couple nuggets in my pants." Hoots follow this, which I ignore where usually I'd play some with the men. But today I don't feel party to their ways, wanting only to get up out of the filth. Thus when I reach the rock I am much relieved.

Looking down upon the camp, I wonder where Cullen has gone. His saying his business with Dewey is not finished has given me hope to see him again though I must decide how to receive him. If he is not to be a customer then what does he become? Thinking back to his encounter with Dewey, I add what Quinn told and wonder what is true, recalling that Cullen seems a most genuine man while Dewey, though appealing, still displays much of the devil. He is more the type to cheat a man than Cullen is to make a false claim and why would any man come to town and rely on falsehood to gain his gold?

Viewing the camp from my hillside, I cannot help but see the men working away their lives, shoveling dirt and gravel from the river into their rockers, hopes pinned on what's left in the sediment. I see Virgil Haupt working alongside Tom Brady, one shoving the other as words are exchanged. And not far from them there's Roy Mullin and his men with the long-tom, all but Roy bent sluicing the water through, Roy down at the paying end, sifting, hoping. Over and over the scene is the same, scratching out a living side by side. Piles of gravel and rock litter the land while the river is crowded with equipment. Too many men, too little gold. How long can they go on?

As the sun works its way into the sky, its warmth eases my concerns while the pine-scented air invigorates my person. I forget the camp below and once again embrace life just going about its day. Birds twitter, varmints scurry, and a bit of breeze announces all is well—at least up here. Were the rock larger, I would stretch out upon it and doze but as it is small, I remain upright, the sun's progress my only marker of time passing.

I do not want to fuck Quinn Lanham. This comes to me when the sun is nearly overhead and it's time to go back to camp. He is nothing but business now and I also think he means, by way of his dick, to take what Cullen gave. I doubt there's a genuine need, what with him and Dewey, but I cannot refuse as to do so would allow feelings for Cullen and I cannot, as yet, give them room. I rise from my rock and make my way back down into the valley with little confidence at what is next to take place.

"You open for business today?" Elmo Polk calls as I pass his diggings.

"Sure am," I tell him as I dare not close up shop again. The men often get riled up by their work, as if the promise of gold gets their dicks hard, and some are known to break from digging to come to my tent. A man is said to do better with his prospecting when he's well spent.

When I reach my tent I don't find Quinn out front. I find him inside, lying naked on my bed, hard cock in hand.

"Not right to come inside like this," I tell him. "This is my home and you are trespassing."

"You said noon and the sun is high so my time has begun. I can't rightly free my prick outside. Now strip and get over here."

I don't argue but I do ask for payment.

"There," he says, nodding to my trunk where I see a poke of gold atop the lid. I examine the dust, nod, and take off my clothes.

"Suck my dick," Quinn commands. "I want to come in your throat."

Climbing onto the bed, I wonder how I could have seen promise in him. The man I first knew has disappeared into one akin to the devil. He grins wickedly as I take as much of his long cock as I can manage. I then begin to bob and pull, working him until he cries out and spurts his stuff. I gag as he shoves his cock into my throat but I manage to swallow all he gives me, after which I sit back. Quinn lies with eyes closed, basking in his pleasure.

"Luke, you in there?" It's Elmo Polk.

"I'm with a customer. Come back later."

"Damn it to hell, Luke, I'm hard right now."

"Man paid me, it's his time."

Elmo swears a bit, then all is quiet. Quinn opens his eyes, tells me to straddle him. "Want to suck your dick," he says and so I crawl over his face, drop my soft prick into his mouth.

He seizes me like a sweet and sucks until I'm stiff while his finger finds my bottom hole and begins to prod. Soon he's got me going front and back and I give him a fresh load of spunk, which he gobbles with much noise. Pulling off, he tells me to turn around so I reverse, which gets my bottom onto him and he parts my buttocks to get his tongue in where his finger has just been.

I cannot but return to the nugget desecration as he licks my pucker and yet his attentions send a shudder through me as there is no denying the intimacy of this nasty attention. As Quinn's tongue starts to poke at me, I can't help but grab my cock, which is up again. The nuggets, on their way east with Dan Picket, become ever more distant.

When Quinn pushes his tongue into me, I gasp as the arousal is of great intensity. And then he plasters his mouth onto my bottom and drives in the whole of his appendage, commencing a tongue fuck that sends me to my limits. I start to pull my prick because he is going to bring on a come without my consent. That he smacks noisily as he does me only enhances my arousal and soon I am spurting onto him.

When Quinn's had his fill he pushes me off him, rises up, draws me to him, and plants his mouth onto mine. The tongue just up my bottom is now in my mouth and I recoil from the filth. No man has ever done such a thing. I try to pull back but Quinn's hand is at the back of my head, holding me fast while his tongue runs rampant in my mouth, licking my tongue, my cheeks, even my teeth. I struggle to break free but am overpowered and so I relent, allow him his fill.

When he finally releases me, I fall back and he begins to laugh. "Nothing like eating out a shit hole," he says. "You like the crumbs?"

I say nothing as he gets up and dresses. "Nobody gonna do you like me," he declares as he leaves.

Alone, I wash, rinse my mouth, then slip into my robe, hoping Elmo isn't waiting outside as I want some recovery time but when I hear a voice call out, I admit him to my tent and take his cock, allowing that it will help me forget what Quinn has done. And once Elmo is finished, Roy Mullin arrives.

"You ain't gone sweet on us, have you, Luke?" he asks as he drops his drawers. "That new man is trouble."

"If I'd gone sweet, you wouldn't be getting into me," I say as I get onto all fours like he likes. Roy climbs in behind and when his cock is in me and he's starting to thrust, he warns me again. "Kane says he's trouble."

To this I do not respond.

Nobody comes by after Roy, which is most welcome as I am tired from what Cullen has stirred as well as what the men demand. I allow myself to doze and when I awaken it is with a start, as if some unseen hand insists I regain the day. I can tell by the light it is late afternoon and I think on what I should do next. Venture out to find Cullen? I wonder if he's seen Dewey again. That I've heard no gunshots is some comfort.

I rise and wash, brush my hair, tie up my robe. I should tend to chores that await such as getting dirty clothes down to the laundry tent or buying incidentals. I am just opening my trunk to get at the strongbox when my name is called.

"Luke Farrow, you in there?"

My heart seizes because it is Cullen.

"Luke?"

I draw a long breath and tell him to come in.

He doesn't approach like most but eyes me up and down, as if the sight of me eases him. "Mind if I sit?" he asks and when I gesture to the bed, he instead takes the chair. There he stretches out his long legs and settles in to rest. I pull my robe cord tighter as I am lost as to what goes next.

I begin to think he means to explain what I saw earlier and so I wait. He seems to be gathering toward something and I am hopeful until he blows out a sigh and asks me to drop the robe. "I want to look at you awhile."

My nakedness reveals a stiff prick but he makes no comment. He just sits there, eyeing me up and down, then motioning with one finger for me to turn, which I do, slowly going round. Finally he speaks.

"You are the most beautiful man I have ever seen," he tells me.

"To find you in this hell hole is beyond me but I crave the sight of you, Luke. Oh, I'm gonna give it to you pretty soon but for a while I want the look of you to fill that part of me that's been too long untouched. We men scrape and scrabble our lives together and start to forget about beauty. And we shove our cocks in and get so caught up in our coming that we don't take notice when perfection lies under us."

I have no idea how to respond. A flush turns my face hot and Cullen smiles. "Didn't mean to make you blush," he says, "but you are like some angel come down from heaven."

"You are too kind," I reply, at a loss for more. My cock is drooling with anticipation but he seems not to notice.

"I would like to kiss you," Cullen says, rising. "Would you permit that?"

"Yes," I manage as he takes me into his arms.

"Ain't never kissed no man before," he says. "Ain't never wanted to." And then his lips are upon mine and I am swept away. What little control I had over my feelings is quickly asunder and I return his affections. Allowing his tongue to mingle with mine, his lips to impress upon me until I cannot help but rub my cock against him. We are still kissing when I spurt my stuff but he doesn't seem to care. It's as if he's quenching a long thirst.

At last he relents but still holds me close, looking into my eyes. "You have captured me, Luke Farrow. My heart is no longer my own."

"Likewise," I stammer, giddy with his declaration. "From first sight of you at the dance, I've been taken."

He kisses me again, then pulls back. "This fuck is going to be the best ever." And he proceeds to strip naked.

Through the course of the afternoon and evening, he does me three times, powerful yet caring with each encounter. The first is like most, mounting from behind and ramming deep into my bowels until he spurts his load. The second, after we've rested awhile, has me on my back, legs high. This one is pure pleasure as we are able to look upon one another as we do the deed. He takes his time now, drawing his long cock clear out, then pushing in anew until I am pumping my prick, unable to keep the urge down. When I let go he shoves into me as if to acknowledge my issue, and then he finally gets to serious work, going at me rapidly until he again reaches the summit. We then doze and I am grateful that none of the men come by. I lie tucked into Cullen's arm and find myself happy to be compensated by the man himself, not his gold.

It is dark when we awaken and I light the lamp. "Are you hungry?" Cullen asks and I tell him no as I crawl back onto the bed. He allows my lips on his chest, my tongue on his tit nubbins, and for a time I lick and play and suck at length. He moans softly beneath me and for a few minutes I think of us gone from this camp. We have traveled as a pair to some distant star where we may lie naked forever, needing no sustenance but our bodies together.

I feel Cullen reach a hand down to stroke his cock and after a while he tells me to roll onto my side, which I do, back to him. He then guides his stiff prick into me, pushing it to the hilt while wrapping his arms around me. And there we lie with him in a low undulation that moves him just enough inside me to pleasure us both. Never have I been taken so slowly yet so thoroughly.

Arriving unbidden is the thought that Cullen might take me away from Beeler Gulch and we'll set up a life together. The prospector's promise has never seemed so real and yet I hear no such thing from him. The one man who has admitted feelings for me makes no offer. All this I think as his cock works my passage and it causes me to squeeze my muscle around his prick, which makes him issue a low chuckle. "You want more?" he asks, taking my efforts as overture. When I don't reply he puts me onto my stomach, raises my bottom, and proceeds to give me a rough fuck, after which he collapses and says he's done in.

"Your bottom is likely tired as well," he adds, which is a kindness of sorts.

"It's a happy bottom," I say, rolling over to kiss his cheek. "I adore you," I tell him. "You give me so much."

He issues a sharp laugh and I add that I refer to the man and not just the cock, although it is an appealing part of the whole. We lie a bit more and when I hear men passing outside, it brings reality into the tent that, though unwelcome, cannot be ignored. Based on his declarations, I feel confident to ask him about his morning encounter with Dewey Kane.

"We had a claim on the Feather River a couple years back," he tells me, then pauses as if taking care what to say next. "He ran off with our gold and I mean to get it back. Been looking for him a long time."

"So you were friends?"

"You might say," he replies after a bit and I see I'd best not ask more. We lie quietly for a while before he rises up, says he has business to conduct. "Don't worry yourself about me, Luke. I can handle Dewey Kane. A man with right on his side usually wins."

When he is dressed, he comes back to the bed where I still lie naked. He leans down and licks my spent cock, then slides up to my mouth and offers a most endearing kiss.

"You're welcome to come by later," I tell him.

"Might just do that," he says before he leaves. "Boys," I hear him say as he passes others outside and only then do I realize I love this man. I toy with that powerful word until Virgil Haupt calls to me and I admit him, take his money, and allow him to do me.

It makes no matter how many men I take this night. I am beyond caring about their use of me because I have something more now, a man who truly cares and who might take me from this occupation. Even as Roy Mullin grunts out a rough one, I envision fine rooms in San Francisco and walking out with Cullen as a pair.

When the line of men runs out, I find hunger upon me so I pull together a meal in my tent because I'd just as soon not go out. Bread, canned beans, and peaches are enough. I have lost weight in my time here, as do most in the diggings. Hard work keeps a man lean as does meager return, though if a man falls too far down on his luck he is helped out by others so none ever go hungry. Lean but never hungry. It is these tender mercies that make camp life tolerable, never mind tempers that flare or the occasional gunplay. A company of men brings out both the best and worst, compassion alongside greed, care hidden behind killing. How much longer can I remain in such a place?

As I take my meal I hear the camp turn from productive to loud and boisterous, the men's rising voices replacing the clatter of the rockers. They drink and gamble to excess and spill into the street, most drunk, some happy with a day's earnings, others angry at losing what they'd gained. Mostly it's men letting off steam, and those who don't do this with liquor or cards do it with me.

Gunfire cracks and I cringe as I never know if it's some miner shooting to the stars to celebrate a strike or one man turning on another. My meal is scarcely finished when a man calls, "You the boy who'll fuck?"

I reply that I am and invite him in. The tent flap is thrown open to admit a burly, reeking, buckskin-clad creature who looks more mountain man than prospector. A thick black beard and shaggy hair conceal all but blazing black eyes, large nose, and wide forehead. As he starts to undo his pants I ask for payment. "Two ounces."

He grunts, pulls a poke from his jacket, and extracts two small nuggets. "That do?" he asks as he hands them over.

"It'll do fine," I reply and I get onto the bed, open my robe.

He throws off his buckskins, peels away stained underdrawers, seeming more comfortable in his nakedness, as if his fur is all the cover he's used to. His stink is powerful but I've known it often as many men fail to wash. He gets a hand between his legs to pull his cock from the furry forest and I see it, fat and soft.

"Raise up your legs and show it to me," he commands and I slip out of the robe, lie back until my butthole is in display.

"You fuck 'em all?" he asks.

"Most."

His tongue reaches from his mouth like it can lick my bottom and his hand works his stiffening prick. Soon he's hard and I see it's not a long cock but a thick plug of meat befitting an animal. As it issues juice in anticipation, he smears the stuff down his shaft, then approaches.

On the bed he shoves into me, then takes hold of my legs and pushes them back until he can drive into me with his full weight and as he does this I reel from his stink. With just a few thrusts he comes and he's not quiet. A roar issues forth that can surely be heard through the camp and it continues until he's spent and slips out. He sits back on his haunches and when I start to lower my legs he stops me. "Keep 'em up," he says. "That ain't but one nugget's worth."

He fixes his eyes on where he's just had his cock and I start to hope he's not one to lick me down there. Finally he reaches a big paw to rub my buttock, then slide a finger into me. He prods some, then his thumb starts to play with my balls. My cock is up and primed, which he seems to enjoy. He adds a second finger inside me, begins to work in earnest.

"Want me some cream," he says before he lowers his bushy head and gets his mouth onto my cock. His suck is powerful, tongue expert, and I quickly let go a good load. As he swallows my spunk, he growls like a bear finishing off a deer.

When I soften he still plays his tongue on me, then finally withdraws but a hand takes up where his mouth was. "Sweet little pickle," he says, sounding like a kinder animal now, dog maybe, loyal companion. "Ain't had no cock but my own for months," he offers. "And yours is downright sweet." I don't reply and when voices are heard outside he gets up, dresses, and leaves.

A hand catches the tent flap before it closes and in steps the next man, who I am surprised to see is Dewey Kane.

"Well looka you," he drawls. "All laid out and full of spunk. He give it to you good?"

"Hello, Dewey. Didn't expect you down this way."

"Don't have much need. Got me a man who likes a hot poker day or night."

"Then what do you want?" I am up and into my robe now, tying it tight.

"The new man, Cullen Markey, goes on about how he fucks you regular and don't pay, says you'll do all sort of nasty things, so I thought I'd give you a try, show you what a real man can do."

My body begins to quake as I know Cullen would never say such things. Dewey is likely looking to claim me in revenge for Cullen's demands. I try to remain composed, even as my body trembles.

"You ain't afraid of me, are you, boy?" Dewey says. He is dressed in his usual finery and unbuttons his pants, reaches in to extract a good cock. "Kneel down here," he instructs. "Suck my dick."

I look past him to the tent flap, hear voices not too far off, and wish someone would burst in and spare me, but none do as it is unwritten law not to disturb a man's fucking.

"Take off the robe," Dewey says. "I want you full naked."

I do as told, kneel before him, open my mouth. He guides himself into me and I close my lips onto him, inhale his smell, feel his juice on my tongue. "Suck!" he commands and I begin, head bobbing.

Dewey is well along toward a come when from behind I hear Cullen's voice. "Pull off, Luke," at which I do just that. "Get up and stand over there," he adds and I scramble to cover myself and retreat to the corner he indicates. Dewey, meanwhile, stands with stiff dick as he faces his enemy. To my surprise, Cullen holds no gun upon his prey.

"You took everything I had, Kane, shot me and left me for dead, and now you take my boy? There's no end to your wickedness and it would be good if somebody was to rid the world of you but I'm not going to do that as you ain't worth the trouble. But I will keep you from getting at this boy, who I declare here and now my own. His time of putting out for anyone else is over so you take that dick of yours and put it to the others because you ain't putting it here anymore."

Cullen has a gun in his holster but his hand is not upon it and Dewey, while he wears no rig, is known to always have a weapon upon him. I look him up and down, as if I might see evidence of such, and am surprised to see his prick is still hard, which makes me consider that he is aroused by danger. He makes no move to cover up as he begins to speak.

"Luke, you know who you got here? You got a liar. Somebody maybe shot him and stole his gold but it wasn't me."

Cullen's hand slides onto his gun. "You believe who you want," he says to me. "I can't tell you what to think but I can tell you the truth. We had a claim on the Feather River and struck it big and he shot me and stole it all, took off and left me for dead, and I've been tracking him ever since."

I am afraid to speak. The air in the tent has dried up and my breathing is thin. I'd like to ask these men to settle their differences peaceably but know it futile. Cullen's eyes are ablaze with anger and Dewey's with defiance. His stiff dick is part of that, brazen and hard for Cullen to see.

"Lies," Dewey says. "He tells you lies, Luke, so he can sweet-talk you for a fuck. He's using you but you're too blind to see it. He doesn't care about anything but gold."

"Stop it!" I cry, gaining enough courage to stand my ground. "I don't want to hear it. I want you both out of my tent. This is not my argument and if you're going to kill one another, do it in the street."

Cullen considers this, nods, and turns to go but as he does I see Dewey pull a small pistol from his coat and I cry out "No!" at which Cullen draws his gun and in one swift motion turns, drops down to elude Dewey's shot, and blasts a bullet into Dewey's middle, which sends him flying back onto the bed. I try to scream but cannot make a sound. Cullen wraps an arm around me while still holding his gun on Dewey. Others burst into the tent in time to see Dewey expire, cock still exposed, soft now.

"I am sorry, Luke," Cullen says quietly. "Never meant to bring this upon you."

"I understand," I manage to say as a red stain grows at Dewey's middle.

Roy Mullin takes charge and examines Dewey, then declares him dead. "What happened here?" he demands.

"Dewey drew on him," I say. "It was a fair killing. Dewey was going to shoot Cullen in the back as he left and I called out and Cullen turned, shot him in defense of his life."

"Why's his dick out?" Roy asks at which the others chuckle and snort.

"He was making me suck him when Cullen came in."

Roy considers this. "You interrupt a man getting his dick sucked, you're asking for trouble," he says to Cullen.

"Man getting his dick sucked for the wrong reason is asking for trouble," Cullen counters. Roy then looks to me.

"There's history between them," I tell Roy, "and if you ain't heard it you're the only one in the whole camp who hasn't. Cullen called Dewey out about stolen gold and Dewey refused to pay up and was taking revenge by way of me."

"Sucking his dick."

"Sucking his dick and making it known to Cullen who has declared himself to me."

"That true, Markey?" Roy asks.

Cullen looks at me. "Yes, it's true. I mean to have Luke as my own. His days of trading upon his body are over."

Roy here transforms from layman judge to crestfallen customer, realizing I am lost to him, but he quickly recovers and Cullen proceeds to tell the story of how he and Dewey partnered on a Feather River claim, how Dewey shot him and stole the gold.

"You got any proof of such?" Roy asks and Cullen shakes his head. "He knew," Cullen says, nodding toward the deceased. "He alone knew."

The body is taken away and Cullen and I are left alone. He does not come to me but sits in my chair, the turn of events now upon him.

I see for the first time that in with his strength lies a vulnerability. His quest is over and has not been a success for there is no way he can prove claim to Dewey Kane's gold. He has been forced to kill the source of his renewal and my heart goes out to him for his loss. I kneel before him and lay my head upon his knee. He pets my hair and we are quiet for a time.

"The scar on your chest," I say after a while.

"Dewey's bullet. Nearly died of it."

"How did you know he was here?"

"Word travels."

I want to ask what he had with Dewey besides the claim but don't as it's no business of mine. I do, however, want to know what happens now. He has declared for me but that was before the killing and the loss of his gold. Anguish rises up and I peer into Cullen's eyes, find them red. He is stricken by what he's had to do and I embrace him, kiss his neck. "Much as I dislike bloodshed, you had no choice," I tell him.

"Never took a man's life before. Winged some but that's different. He's killed, dead and gone, and though I was in the right it ain't no less a wrong."

"Come to bed," I say, getting up. I tie the tent flap and lower the lamp until we are in shadow. I throw off the robe, turn back the covers, and crawl in while Cullen strips. When he is bare, he slides in and presses himself to me, nuzzles my cheek. "I meant what I said," he tells me. "I want no other."

"Nor I. Oh, Cullen, can we go away from here?"

"After what's happened I suspect it's best we both move on, although I don't know what we'll do. I'm finished hunting gold."

"Maybe Sacramento or San Francisco. Places where there's opportunity for honest work."

"You don't look to go back to your St. Louis kin?"

"Not now. For a while I want just you and me, and I've got enough gold to stake us somewhere new."

Cullen chuckles. "Stumbled into camp, turned my life upside down. Took one man's life but found another." And with this he begins to kiss me, rolling to poke his stiff cock at my leg. "Gonna have to do you," he says as he eases me onto my stomach and gets on top. When his prick is inside me, pumping easy, he leans forward and tells me, "I got all I want now."

THE VALLEY OF SALT
DAVID HOLLY

The family reclined on our dinner couches, my father, mother, brother, and I, while naked servants brought platters of kid roasted in pomegranate. Grandfather was confined to a chair where servants spoon-fed him millet and goat milk. I turned my face so I would not see Grandfather eat. Across from me, Rhadamanthus, my brother, stuffed a gigantic portion of flat bread in his mouth. I turned away, revolted by his gluttony. I glanced down at the indigo breechclout that barely covered my hips and wished I could scratch the perverse itch. Trying to avoid groping my cock, I turned my attention to my dinner. I forked in a helping of roasted young goat with pomegranate and basil. Issaruutunu, the male servant, filled my bowl with crushed watermelon nectar.

"Zedek," my father barked. I looked up from my kid and herbs, wondering what I had done this time. Rhadamanthus laughed. "Zedek is going to get it," he sneered, jumping to the likely conclusion that I would be receiving the family rod across my buttocks again that night. *Who was that asshole who wrote that sparing the rod would spoil the child? That sadistic prescription was nothing but an invitation for abuse—and not just of children, since I had reached the first year of my adulthood.* I mentally began to number my recent misdeeds.

"The Priests of Baal reckon the moon cycles of every Gomorrahan lad until he achieves viripotence. Today I received this missive." He held up a piece of clay with voices cut into it. "Greetings, Abimelech, and joy unto your family."

We all guessed what was coming next. The only member of the family who did not respond was Grandfather, who continued drooling into his millet. I shifted fretfully while my father brandished the tablet.

Smirking, Rhadamanthus tried to catch my eye. Ignoring my younger brother, I looked at my mother. Her eyes were glowing with satisfaction. "Speak out the voices in the clay, Abimelech."

"As you request, Shahar, I shall talk the voices," my father said. The girl servant, Kullaa, who had been pouring the chunky wine into our bowls, stopped to listen, as did Issaruutunu while he replenished the platters of bread and the bowls of olives.

Lifting the tablet before his eyes, my father read slowly, his lips forming the voices from the clay. "Once a year, the Baal Marduk guides our selection of three Gomorrahan youths to make the holy sacrifice," he intoned. "On the new moon, Zedek shall climb to the top of the ziggurat. He will perform a Holy Dog's sacred duties until the moon is full. From now until the hour Zedek enters the ziggurat, no raiment or adornment shall touch his body. He will walk the streets in the skin of his birth. So say the Priests of Baal."

My asshole tightened at the words, and a cold chill ran down my back. It did not help that my mother was gleaming over the news of my ritual penetration or that my brother was snorting bread out his nose.

"This is wonderful, Abimelech. Our son will offer up his asshole to Baal. Do you hear, Zedek? Do you hear?" Mother began shaking me in her excessive joy. "Many men will take you anally and cast their seed into your ass in honor of Baal Marduk."

When I whimpered, my mother finally noticed that I did not share her enthusiasm and that my brother was hysterical with ribald laughter. "You should welcome this tribute, Zedek," she said. "Only boys from the highest-class families are considered." She turned upon my brother. "What is so funny, Rhadamanthus? Perhaps, when you come of age, you, too, shall be selected."

That prospect quieted my brother, but it did nothing to still my tortured soul. "The Priests of Baal are planning to fuck my ass?" I asked. "And in the meantime I have to walk around naked like a servant?"

"Not the priests. The holy parishioners. Burning with divine lust, a man comes to the temple—whether from his farm or stall in the bazaar, selects a boy to penetrate—you, I hope, and pays the priests the price of your asshole. A circle of priests and acolytes will form around you as the man mounts your ass. When you have received the sacred seed, the man will declare his satisfaction. The more men who select your rear, the greater the honor to the god."

My mother was too fulsome in extolling anal surrender. I shifted fearfully, a movement not lost upon my brother.

"Zedek is going to get butt-fucked," Rhadamanthus chanted with glee.

My father slapped his palm on the table. "Zedek, your mother is repeating common gossip. She has not witnessed the ceremony. You will do as the priests require of you, and thus bring the god's favor upon our family and our business interests."

"Yes, Father."

I looked at the two servants who had been removing our salad bowls. Their bodies had been thoroughly depilated; there was not a hair left upon their smooth naked skins, and they had been deeply oiled until they glistened. I thought of rising from the table and penetrating Kullaa. She was young and good-looking. Her hair had been golden before its removal. Her twat was a bare mound, and if I pushed into it, I would have asserted my masculinity before my family. However, I found my cock shriveling at the thought.

Of course, I could have penetrated Issaruutunu. He, too, was good-looking, with a prominent bubble butt that sang out for entry. I could hoist him over the table before the eyes of my astonished brother and parents. However, as I fantasized, a darker image crossed my mind. *Suppose I pushed my ass against Issaruutunu's cock. Suppose I impaled my rump upon him?* At the thought, my cock stiffened, my heart beat faster, my mouth dried, and my face flushed. I drained my bowl of watermelon nectar, and Issaruutunu hastened to refill it. As he did, he brushed one hip against my arm. I gasped as if I had been speared.

"Whatever is the matter, Zedek?" Mother demanded.

"Zedek is thinking about those cocks stretching his ass," Rhadamanthus hooted. "Hey, Zedek, at least you will not see their faces."

We finally got through the meal. My father's stern glances, my mother's euphoria, and my brother's taunts past, I fled out of the house.

"Zedek, remove your clothing," my mother shrieked.

"Tomorrow," I yelled over my shoulder. "I will go naked tomorrow. Not tonight."

The streets were crowded. Sacred prostitutes were hawking their cunts for Ishtar. Peddlers were selling everything imaginable, while table dwellers touted scrolls, bowls, vessels, baskets, and beads. Sellers of perfumes and cosmetics howled from their stalls. Tightening my breechclout, I rushed to the workroom of Ekron the Gadite.

This was, indeed, the same Ekron who in times past had invented the screw pump that supplied the town's water system, bringing running water into our house and filling the vast pools of the town baths. Sennacherib, King of Assyria, had employed Ekron's inventions for the water systems at the Hanging Gardens of Babylon and Nineveh.

"Zedek! Zedek, see what I have invented," Ekron the Gadite exclaimed as he pulled me into his workroom. He pointed toward the common batteries used by jewelers to electroplate gold onto other types of metal dishes.

"What do these do?" I asked.

Ekron touched two wires to the battery and a strange glass object began to glow. Soon the glass reached a level of brilliance unrivaled by no oil lamp I had ever seen. The yellow light suffused and illuminated the whole room.

"What is this?" I shouted. "Ekron, what hath Baal wrought?"

"Electricity," the inventor said. "With this invention we will cast away the darkness. Houses will be lit with my invention. Lamps along the streets shall light the travelers' way. The whole of Gomorrah shall be a better place, touched by the hand of the creative man. My invention shall light up the sky itself."

As I studied Ekron's invention, my heart raced harder. What magical changes would our future bring? Criminals could not pounce upon benighted citizens. Merchants could see far into the night.

"I discovered a thousand ways that did not work," Ekron related, "and then I finally hit upon this particular element." In his wild enthusiasm, he slapped my ass. "Think of what we will soon be able to do."

I did think upon the marvels he expounded, many quite strange. If we could avoid war and the destructive capacity of religious superstition, could we conquer disease? Could we travel over the land in powerful machines? Could we fly through the air or explore the depths of the sea? Could we travel to the moon? Could we spread our knowledge to other worlds?

❖

The next morning my mother ordered my attendants Abishalom, Maachah, Jeroboam, and Ahaziah to shave me, wash me, and oil me. Thus cleaned and utterly without hair except for that I retained upon my head, I strode out our front door and the through the streets of our beautiful city of Gomorrah.

Striding stark naked through the dusty, hot, shit-strewn streets, I felt that my body was on display. Many looked through their parted linens, woven by a thousand naked maidservants in moonlit sewing circles. Shapash, goddess of the sun, cooked my skin as I hurried through the street. Sun beat off the high yellow clay walls and the cyclopean stone Temple of Kotharat. The Temple of Baal stood near, as did the fire pit of Moloch. The town harlots called to me and lifted their clothes to display their wares.

I stopped once at the pissing wall, joining the robed old men who lifted their robes, the younger men who pulled aside their breechclouts, and the naked servants. Ithiel and Ucal, sons of Gomorrahan nobility, were as blushingly bare as I. We traded mortified glances as we directed our piss streams against the stained stones.

"Are you a Dog now, Zedek?" the flax merchant Lemuel sneered.

"Would I be as bare as a servant otherwise?" I demanded. "I am a servant of Baal, but I will not tolerate insolence."

"Insolence, indeed," Lemuel snorted. "Perhaps I shall come to the temple and plant a tree in your ass."

"Zedek is rounding up customers already," Ithiel called, which made Ucal laugh.

My face flushed hot. "Ithiel. Ucal. Mock me not, for you are both as naked as I," I chided. "Perhaps Lemuel will prefer to plant his tree in your own asses."

"Perhaps I shall, young sir," said Lemuel with a randy laugh. The man was a he-goat and a horseleech.

Leaving the pissing wall, I turned down a long winding lane between hundreds of conical houses built of baked orange mud. Here the commoners lived, ate, shat, and fucked to their hearts' content. Many of the residents of this development worked at my father's brick factory, picked dates and olives in his groves, threshed hay in his stables, or pressed grapes at his winery. I had thought my nakedness would be no oddity here, for the commoners bred like maggots and could hardly afford to clothe their children. Adolescents played rough games in the

DAVID HOLLY

street. My heart smote me because I would have liked to join in the games. But I was under summoning to service to Baal, which set me apart, so people still stared at my naked skin.

"See, the son of Abimelech walks in the raiment of the god," I heard a father explaining to his gaping children. "Come the new moon, rich men will pay to fuck his ass in the Temple of Baal."

Feeling more naked by the second, I rushed to the Bathhouse of Rephaim. Ucal and Ithiel caught up as I approached the bathhouse gate. "You look bathed and oiled already, Zedek," Ucal said. "Why do you come to the baths?"

Ithiel had more of his wits about him. "Think, Ucal. Zedek is as self-conscious as we are. We are neither servants nor children, so going naked is uncomfortable for us. Not to mention that everybody knows that we will be used as temple Dogs in just a few days."

"Since everybody is naked at the baths," Ucal agreed, finally getting it, "we will not stand out."

I wriggled my cock. "I stand out wherever I go."

Laughing uproariously, we passed through the door. Fat Rephaim, the Hivite owner of the bathhouse, oiled about the room with such gelatinous unctuosity that I thought he would melt into a puddle.

"I see youse da boys number what's come up. Come in, come in. No charge for them what's to prostitute their assholes for the Great God Baal."

I had expected good-natured ribbing from the men at the baths, but I was unprepared for their barbarous taunts. Crude jokes dropped like turds from a camel's ass. It got so bad at one point that a bully tried to stick his thumb into my ass crack. Fortunately, that straw brought the dromedary to its knees, so to speak, because Dogs must refrain from sex until they enter the temple. Touching a sacred Dog before he opens his ass in the presence of Baal Marduk is a terrible sacrilege. The men loosed their wrath upon the offender. That ended the taunting.

Ucal, Ithiel, and I were sitting placidly in the cooling pool when I saw Ekron slipping into the hot bath. "Hail, Ekron," I called.

"Zedek, our meeting is fortuitous. A great day. I have found a way of generating electricity from the power of the wind. Soon we will create our own power and send it through wires strung throughout the entire city."

His thick cock was more than half-hard as he described his new invention. As I listened, I felt the strongest urge to reach forth and touch it. As Ekron expounded formula after formula, my lust grew. My hand seemed to stretch forth under its own power. My fingers were coming closer to the scientist's cock when an abrupt shout shattered my almost hypnotic trance.

"Have you heard the news?" Clad in the black breechclout worn by bearers of unwelcome news, the boy was practically dancing in his excitement.

"What news?" Ithiel demanded, tossing a coin.

The boy turned toward our group. "The four kings of the North, Chedorlaomer, Amraphel, Arioch, and Tidal, have formed a coalition. They are demanding tribute from the Pentapolis of the Vale of Siddim." Loud gasps filled the room. Most of the bathers were wealthy merchants who would surely be called upon to relinquish their fortunes in the event the city had to pay.

"Gomorrah is too large to pay tribute to any self-appointed high king. The four kings are not so powerful."

"Youse fellers got nothing to worry about," Fat Rephaim chortled. "What's Chedorlaomer got what we don't got? Nothin'. What's we got what he don't." He pointed toward Ekron. "The Gadite gonna let loose that 'trisity and fry them four kings."

The newsboy tried to regain his lost audience. "King Birsha says the same. He has sent a messenger to Chedorlaomer and his cohort declaring that Gomorrah will war against the kings of the North rather than submit. Messengers are riding with similar warnings from King Bera of Sodom and King Shemeber of Zeboyim."

❖

Staggered along the intricate grid of streets and avenues, massive towers searched the heavens for the cooler air. Cupolas caught sun and rain, sweeping their goodness down the countless lavishly gardened terraces that descended the sides of the towers. Massive temples dedicated to many deities dwarfed the villas of the wealthy, including the house of my father, and hung with forbidding power over the conical homes of the common folk.

Three rows of high walls surrounded the city, with massive bronze doors facing in four directions. Passing the Temple-Tower of Samael, which we called the Seventh Heaven, I heard the guide telling tourists from Ninevah that not only had Samael tempted the Great Mother of the Hebrews, Eve, in the guise of the Serpent, but he also seduced her and caused her to bear the child Cain. Rather than attending to their guide, some of the tourists were casting pop-eyed glances at my naked body. Blushing as the lords and ladies of Nineveh gaped at my cock, I tried to shrug off the gullibility of tourists. Feigning insouciance, I sauntered toward the bazaar—presenting a rear view as I went.

Towering over all else was the great ziggurat of Marduk, Baal of sun-drenched Gomorrah. This House of God sat at the top of the hill. The temple's great base covered the entire hilltop, rising several stories with a long series of steps. Above the base, the ziggurat ascended seven stories, the outer walls of each story painted in a different color of the rainbow. The shining cupola at the top crowned the astronomical observatory.

I would be entering the ziggurat in two days' time, but meanwhile I had a chore in the bazaar. Passing through the stalls and booths, I examined bolts of beautiful fabric, glorious with dye. A women hawked the long lance-shaped leaves of the aloes, the anointing oils made from the sweet-smelling calamus, and the perfumes of the spikenard. Shopkeepers were selling exotic items imported from Arabia, India, Persia, and Egypt. Of course, the merchants of wine and opium were doing brisk business. I stopped to examine a carpet, but the foolish merchant mistook me for a servant.

"Not all who are naked serve fools," I rebuked him. "Some are called to serve Baal. I am a Dog." He cringed as if I had cursed him.

"He is a holy Dog Boy," an awed voice informed her neighbor, and her carrying whisper was met with a suppressing hush. Buyers gathered to stare at me. I waved to them as I sought Kuwari's Fruit and Spice Emporium.

No ignoramus he, Kuwari prostrated himself when I passed through his doorway. The mix of scents within was overwhelming. The scent of apples, dates, figs, grapes, melons, olives, pomegranates, and raisins mingled with the more heady aromas of anise, coriander, cinnamon, cumin, dill, garlic, mint, mustard, and rue. Earthenware vases large enough for me to hide inside, should the need arise, brimmed with the best grains.

"Zedek, honored sir," said he.

"Greetings, Kuwari," I said. "I come to solve a mystery. Yesterday my mother sent our servant Maachah for millet to feed my grandfather, but the fool came home with spelt. What does this mean?"

"A thousand apologies, Zedek," the fruit and spice dealer exclaimed.

"Zedek! I thought that I heard your name spoken." My friend Lillake stood in the doorway, her eyes sparkling over my nakedness. I had been getting used to being naked among the clothed, but seeing my Lillake made me self-conscious all over again. Lillake was wearing a striped dress of thin fabric and her breasts were bare. Laughing, she slapped my ass. "I heard that you had been selected."

I nodded and gave Lillake a half-assed smile. I was expecting more taunts, but she treated my selection casually. "So when do you get butt-fucked for God?"

I pretended a detachment that I did not feel. "I have to report at the ziggurat tomorrow. The moon will be new on the day after."

Meanwhile, Kuwari was bowing and scraping. "It is the fault of your servant, sir. He was drunk, doubtless, and ordered the wrong meal. I will, of course, replace the grain at once—at my own expense." Using a hollowed dry gourd, he dipped out a generous amount of millet into a reed basket. Humming to himself, he prepared three bowls of fragrant tea from his supply of dried spring flower petals and fixed three plates of white cheese, honeyed almonds, raisins, sycamore figs, and dates.

"Thank you, Kuwari," I said, grabbing the snacks and sipping tea.

The louche merchant's eyes ignited with ill-concealed passion. "Perhaps I shall see you in the temple. Perhaps I shall make my offering during your days of holy sacrifice." Then he giggled. "Perhaps I shall see you, though I shall not see your face. Only the other end." *Where had I heard that joke before? It made me uneasy.*

Lillake almost choked on a fig from laughing. Coldness came over me. My hands started shaking so badly that my tea slopped from my bowl. My legs wobbled.

"Whatever is the matter, Zedek?" Lillake exclaimed. Her eyes widened. "Do you fear the days of sacrifice?"

I shook my head. Fearing a holy sacrifice would be the meanest sacrilege. However, Lillake saw through my denial. "Anal penetration is nothing to fear, Zedek. It is quite pleasant, especially for the male."

"How would you know, Lillake?"

"Not from personal experience, I assure you." She touched my arm gently. "Think about it, Zedek. The Holy Dog Priests get fucked in the ass every day, and look how happy they appear."

A commotion resounding from the street rescued me. Venturing out of the shop, we found six men gathered around a royal messenger. Merchants left their booths, shops, stalls, and tents to join the group. Lillake, Kuwari, and I added to the throng. The messenger standing at the center of the circle was out of breath, having been paid to shout the news all over town. When he had recovered his breath sufficiently, he answered the loud cries for him to speak up.

"King Shinab of Admah and…what's-his-name…you know…the king of Bala have joined with our good King Birsha. The Pentapolis of the Vale of Siddim has agreed that we will not pay tribute to the confederate kings. Speaking for the five cities, King Birsha sent a message to Chedorlaomer telling him to slap an egg on his cock and beat it."

Kuwari shook at the news. "They will come with their armies. The king's insult will bring them. This will mean war."

"I hope that you are wrong, Kuwari." Carrying my basket of millet between us, we left the merchant to his woes.

"You don't mind being seen in the street with me?" I asked Lillake.

"We've walked together thousands of times."

"Not with me as naked as a slave."

Lillake laughed. "Your bare ass doesn't bother me, Zedek."

"How about my dangling cock?"

She laughed again. "I've seen cocks that dangle lower than yours." Seeing my crestfallen expression, she promptly offered a pacifier. "You have a gorgeous ass."

"Which is going to get ritually fucked," I contributed.

"To the glory of Baal. Do not forget the glory, Zedek. Everyone seeing you knows that Marduk has selected you. Every step we take reflects glory on me. You must see that every woman we pass is jealous of me because I am walking with a holy Dog Boy. The men, too—those who aren't getting hard from thoughts of your ass, that is."

I decided that it was high time I changed the subject. "Have you visited Ekron's workroom recently?"

"No. Has he invented something new?"

"Electricity."

"That's been around for years, Zedek. It's being used for electroplating and storage and shocking the brains of sleepwalkers."

"Ekron has found another use." I found myself getting excited. "Wait until you see. He has made light."

"Light? Like let there be light, and tra-la-la, there was light?"

"Ekron has invented a generator that can create the electricity, and he has invented a bulb that turns the electricity into brilliance. I have seen the result with my own eyes."

"This I've got to see with *my* eyes," she said.

Ekron was delighted at our arrival, and seeing us presented no difficulties, for I had never witnessed anything so brilliantly lit as his workroom. Ekron lived in a square clay and lath structure, with solid beams forming the floor of his second-story home. His workroom was on the ground floor. Ekron led us around to the glowing bulbs to which attached wires led out his back door.

"I calculate that each bulb puts out the brilliance of a hundred oil lamps," the scientist bragged. He picked up one of the conducting wires in his hand. "I have wrapped these so you may handle them with reasonable safety." He led us through the back door into his courtyard, where skeletal winged towers turned in the constant breeze. "Here is the source of my light. Pazuzu, the god of the wind, creates my electricity. With these, I can light up Gomorrah so we will be a beacon to the entire world."

❖

The next morning, our family servants began my preparation. To complete my humiliation, my mother supervised, and my brother offered snide suggestions. "Instead of giving Zedek water in his enemas, why not shoot oil up his ass," Rhadamanthus asked. "Then the cocks will slide in easier."

"The instructions are to clean him inside and out, young master," Jeroboam said. "The priests said nothing about greasing his innards."

"Use the water as I directed, Jeroboam," my mother ordered. "Rhadamanthus is merely being insufferable."

"Why does he need to be here at all," I yelped as the servant Abishalom sharpened the razor he would use to shave my testicles.

Nearly four hours later, the servants inspected me from head to toe. "I have cleaned his big toenail four times, Mistress Shahar," Maachah protested. "Can I help it if he has been walking barefoot in camel dung?"

Ahaziah winced, and Rhadamanthus hooted with laughter. "Would you like to be beaten with wet reeds now, Maachah?" my mother inquired in her sweetest and most dangerous tone, "or would you prefer to wait until my husband returns from his winepresses?"

Maachah began cleaning under my toenail anew, and the grating sound filled the room. After Maachah had cleaned my toe to my mother's satisfaction, Ahaziah filed the nail until it was as smooth as the rest. Finally, I stood smooth, clean, and golden before the reflecting bronze, and just in time. A resounding gong rang through the city. The Priests of Baal were summoning the Dog Boys to the great ziggurat of Marduk.

My mother hastily organized the household. Our servants formed up our procession: cooks; gardeners; Nutesh, a smelly scraper of camel dung; our table servants, Issaruutunu and Kullaa; and my personal attendants, Abishalom, Maachah, Jeroboam, and Ahaziah. To my surprise, Lillake joined our procession. I suspected that Mother had bribed her to stifle Rhadamanthus, should the necessity arise. Even Grandfather, his mouth and ass wiped for the occasion, was placed in a litter and borne along with the rest of the family. Some servants carried wooden pole fans, brightly painted parasols, or palm fronds, while others beat upon tambourines or played cymbals with their fingers or rang bells. My father Abimelech, hastily returned from supervising the winery, met us at our front door, and led our procession along with my mother and brother. I came next, gloriously naked, and our servants followed with great fanfare.

Crowds of well-wishers and hopeful supplicants turned out to watch us pass. Many people wanted to touch me in hopes that the glory of my sacrifice would reflect upon them or that they could share in the god's bounty, and the multitude of hands slapping, reaching, and clawing at me became somewhat painful before we reached our destination.

The two other processions joined ours at the base of the ziggurat. However, neither Ucal nor Ithiel had so impressive a procession as mine. My father's house was the wealthiest, and we had more servants than the families of my two fellow Dog Boys.

"I'm scared," Ithiel confessed as our processions merged and he and Ucal walked beside me. "I've never done anything like this before. I do not think that I can open my ass for a man's cock."

"We have to take those cocks into our bodies, Ithiel," Ucal said stupidly. "The god demands our sacrifice."

"I know that."

"We're all frightened, Ithiel," I said, comforting him. "But we all know about the others who were Dog Boys before us. Nobody ever died from it. And after it is over, we will be in the city's debt for the rest of our lives. No matter what fortunes or disasters may affect our family businesses, we three will live in luxury."

"Some of the Dog Boys end up as Priests of Baal," Ithiel said. "I wouldn't like that. I want a wife. I want children—a son to carry the memory of me into the future. I do not want to be forgotten in a hundred years. Do you think that anyone will remember the name of even one of these priests in a thousand years?"

"Who cares about their names?" Ucal said, feeling his freshly shaven face. "I think that my family made me look like a woman."

I started to laugh. I tried to stop it, but the laughter came from deep down. It was infectious because Ithiel began laughing, too. "What's so funny?" Ucal demanded. "What are you boys laughing at?"

The beating of the gong continued as we approached the hill of the great ziggurat. Our procession began its ascent by way of the triple stairway. In the rear stood a spiral ramp on which merchants made the deliveries of food, fuel, and temple acolytes.

"Have you ever been inside?" Ucal asked, stupidly because the ziggurat was not the place of public ceremony. It was the house of Marduk, the Baal of our city. Unlike the temple towers of Dagon, Kotharat, Shapash, and Resheph, through the great ziggurat, the Baalim could come close to humanity, but humanity could not grow closer to the gods. Only the Priests of Baal witnessed those religious rituals performed within the ziggurats. Thus, the priests provided for Baalim's needs instead of the needs of the people. We, the inhabitants of Gomorrah, were simply the fodder, or the sex slaves of Marduk as in the case of the three Dogs: me, Ithiel, and Ucal.

Like the houses and shops in our city, our ziggurat had been constructed of mud brick, with a glazed brick façade. The base was square with steps rising to the sanctuary. Here Ucal, Ithiel, and I parted from our families. Naked, cleansed, carrying nothing, we climbed toward the abode of the god. The walls sloped, and horizontal lines were convex to make them less rigid when seen by the human eye and to make room for the gardens of lush trees and blooming shrubs that grew up the inclined walls.

As we neared the top, the doors of the sanctuary opened to grant us admittance. The gong reverberated with a final dong as we passed through the doors. The finishing note seemed almost ominous. Perhaps that final ring had given rise to the rumor among the ignorant desert dwellers that the sons of royal families were sacrificed to the Baalim. As I was to learn, consecration in fire did not involve getting burned in actual flames, but in a different kind of fire altogether.

I expected the interior to be dark, but great pillars of sunlight streamed directly downward with alternating streaks of darkness. The effect was so blinding that we stood blinking like owls while the immense doors closed behind us. Before we could quite recover, three forms stepped from behind tall painted poles. The creatures appeared to have the lower bodies of men, but their upper bodies were dangling strips of fur that reached to their buttocks. Most alarming, they had the heads of dogs or jackals.

Ucal gasped and threw himself onto the floor. He lay blubbering until Ithiel prodded his ass with his toe. "They are wearing masks, Ucal. You are cowering from masked men."

Ucal stood and cast about with suspicion as the three men took us each by the arm. Wordless, the masked man holding my arm urged me to walk with him. The other two gently lured Ucal and Ithiel in other directions.

"I am Zedek," I told the silent man. He said nothing in return.

During the procession, I had forgotten my fear as I marched before the adoring crowds. Walking beside the silent masked man who dragged me along gently but insistently, I felt my buried qualms resurface. "Where are we going?" I asked. "What happens to me now?" Next to my companion's silence, my voice began to sound like the *oop-oop-oop* of a deranged hoopoe bird.

We were walking toward sunlight, through a forest of painted poles. I touched a pole and saw that it was shaped like a human penis. Some were red, some yellow, and some deep purple. At last, we came to a cushioned divan, shaped at one end like the head of a jackal. Three boys clad in yellow thongs that held their genitals and threaded between their buttocks grasped thin poles with wooden paddles attached.

"You have managed your fear well, Zedek," the masked man spoke. His voice was soft, melodious, and strangely familiar. "You may now remove my mask."

Apprehensively, I placed my hands on both sides of his head and lifted. The mask slid off easily, and I was looking into the laughing face of a boy my own age.

"Obededom? Is it really you?"

"Of course." Obededom lifted his robe of strips and tossed it onto the floor. He sat down on the divan and patted the cushion beside him. Boy servants hastened to bring goblets of wine and platters of delicacies. "You remember that I was chosen last year to make the sacrifice to Marduk."

I nodded my head. "I never saw you again after. I didn't know what had happened to you."

"I gave more than was expected," Obededom said with a lewd smile. "Much more."

"What do you mean?"

"Zedek, there are many ways of receiving a man's cock anally. Dog Priests enjoy receptive anal intercourse. A Dog enjoys the penetration, but not all who aspire to the position can endure it. Some must suspend the holy act due to distress, soreness, or fatigue."

"Oh," I moaned.

"However, others of us have the ability to enjoy long sessions of anal penetration. We can take a cock many times from one partner, or multiple cocks from multiple partners, or cocks galore for a long time. Last year the Dog Priests discovered that I could actively encourage fervent thrusting all day without stopping. My enthusiasm for the act, my lack of reticence, and my energetic participation impressed them enormously. After the full moon arose, they offered me the chance to become a Dog Priest myself. Now I am a novice in the Priesthood of Baal."

"What are these boys? Are they also novices?"

"They are the acolytes. They fan the flames, light the incense, and serve the priests. They wear the thong because they must never be touched. Acolytes watch and even assist in the penetration of the Dogs, but they never participate. An acolyte may grow up to be a priest, but most serve the king. They are advisors, scribes, lawyers. Many government officials are former acolytes."

I was glad to hear that the youths were never molested. For some reason, they reminded me of my brother. Still, I was growing more uncomfortable in another direction. The wine must have inflamed my passions, for I found myself growing erect as I sat close beside my former friend Obededom. The fumes from the burning incense seemed to be twisting into my brain. I felt very hot, and I was glad to see that the paddles at the ends of the boys' staffs were fans. They began to fan the air, stirring a perfumed breeze that flowed over Obededom and me.

"What does it feel like?" I asked, thinking of a man's cock pushing into my asshole. "Why do you like it so much?"

"Funny you should ask, Zedek. The time has come for me to perform my holy duty."

A nameless thrill shot through me. "What sacred duty?"

Obededom's chuckle invited titters from the acolytes. "The priests would hardly send you out to service the parishioners with no advance knowledge of how to open your ass for penetration. I am to prepare you for your sacrifice. I will open you slowly and gently, and teach you the ways of anal pleasure. I will stretch you until you can take any cock comfortably. I will be the first to orient you into the pleasure."

"You are supposed to come in my ass, Obededom?"

"Yes, Zedek," he said, beaming as though he were offering the greatest gift ever. "That is precisely what is going to happen."

My heart was beating fast. *Why was I chosen? Who was I to be fucked for Baal? Why did the priests pick me?* My breath seemed hardly to enter my chest; I felt like I could not breathe air in, and when I did

I could not push it back out. Obededom laid his hand gently upon my thigh. "Do not fear," he whispered. His hand moved closer to my cock, but he did not touch it. His cock was rigid. The perfumed air was too thick to suck in. Black spots swam before my eyes.

"Don't try to breathe," Obededom said. Then he touched my face with his hand and brought his lips to mine. His lips pressed. His tongue licked my lips, slid over my lips, pushed between my teeth, and rode along my tongue. Something released within me. I found that my tongue was responding to his, responding against my will, responding with burning lust. Fevers rose within me. I pressed my tongue against his. I probed along it; then I closed my lips around it and sucked it. He did not let me push my tongue into his mouth. It all happened in mine; I was the receiver and he the giver. When he finally pulled his mouth from mine, he smiled at me. Finding that I could breathe again, I smiled back.

"Turn your ass to me and place your weight upon your knees," Obededom suggested. "Grip the ears of the jackal with both hands."

The inevitable moment had arrived. Helpless to disobey, I did as he directed. My body was tense, but my cock was still hard from the kiss. Obededom's hands gripped my buttocks. He stroked them slowly, gently kneading my curves.

"Very nice, Zedek," he said as he caressed me. "Nice indeed."

A strange ripple ran up my spine as Obededom stroked my ass. "Yes, let it happen, Zedek," he urged. "Give in to it. Surrender. Surrender your will, and submit your body to mine. Make your ass a vessel for my lusts."

I shivered. *Would I open my body as if I were a woman? Would I be the pricked and not the pricker? Would I receive the spurted seed from this man, this boy really, a former friend with whom I had played upon the sporting fields?* Obededom's hands still fondled my buttocks, the fingers of one sliding deeper into my cleft, the fingers of the other tracing down my back and over the bump of my tailbone to part my buttocks. One finger traced down my cleft to my balls. Then up again. Time after time, his finger lightly brushed my asshole. Finally, he stopped there.

His finger circled my asshole. Slowly he traced the contours of my opening. One of the acolytes brought a small bowl filled with thick oil.

The acolyte smiled knowingly as Obededom dipped his forefinger into the oil and then touched his finger to my asshole. "Zedek, push your ass toward me," my friend suggested.

Another acolyte brought a tray of carved wooden objects, polished smooth. Obededom selected the narrowest of these, oiled it liberally, pressed it against my asshole, and twisted gently. "That's the way, Zedek," he murmured. "Let it in. You know that you want it. Oh, yes, you're taking it all the way."

The tiny tube did not feel like much of anything. Obededom turned it this way and that, and he pulled it out and pushed it back in. I felt a pleasurable sensation in my anus as he manipulated the object. "You are ready for the next larger size, Zedek," he said. I noticed that his fingers hovered over the object next to the one he had used first; then he skipped that and picked up a larger one.

I felt a pressure in my ass. It was as if he were pressing against it instead of going inside. Pushing with my anus, I suddenly felt fuller. "That was fast," Obededom gasped. "You took the whole thing."

He pulled it almost out and pushed it back in, which made me catch my breath. "Did that hurt?" he asked.

"Not at all," I admitted. I was not yet ready to confess that I had never felt anything so pleasurable. As Obededom slowly drew the plug out and pushed it back in, ecstatic ripples radiated from my asshole. My cock was hard and dripping. One of the acolytes wiped the tip, and the touch of the cloth was nearly enough to unman me.

"Give me the largest one," Obededom asked, handing the plug back to the acolyte with the tray. "This one is larger than my cock, Zedek," he assured me. "I do believe that you are ready to receive me, but first I will pleasure your ass with this object."

For a moment, I thought that he would split me. However, the sensation was more pleasurable than painful. It was more like a deep tickle and a fullness that I had never felt before. A deeper, perhaps darker, pleasure rose with the tickle. Something inside me was being milked. Without realizing I was doing it, I pushed my rump back to impale my ass deeper.

"Oh, yes, Zedek," Obededom purred. "Oh, yes, you feel it. Yield to the sensation. Let it master you. Imagine that you are a hole that only the eternal powers can fill with their everlasting pricks and cum."

Obededom pulled the object out of my ass, and the acolyte took away the tray. Obededom placed his hands upon the swells of my buttocks, and another object pushed between my spread and touched my asshole. "Push your ass onto my cock," Obededom urged, and I did so. I pushed my ass back, willing that I should be filled with hard cock.

"Oh, Zedek," Obededom groaned. "You are taking my cock. You have taken it all the way."

Indeed, Obededom was pressed tight against my ass, and I felt that pleasurable fullness. He pulled back, and raptures of pleasure rippled from my asshole. Pushing forward again, he sent deep tingles radiating up my ass and down my cock. Faster, harder, wilder, he thrust, and I humped my ass back to meet him. My body was a flame of pleasure. Without warning, Obededom reached around and gripped the head of my cock. My foreskin was slippery with the thin cream that had been leaking from it. The slippery skin gave him leave to stroke and twist the head of my cock freely as he thrust.

"Obededom, I'm going to come," I moaned. His only answer was to thrust harder in my ass. His hand jerked me while his breath rasped hot in my ear.

Tingles of pleasure rushed through me. My orgasm was in my cock, but it was also in my ass. I felt a different pleasure than any I had known before, and I wanted it to last forever. Obededom was slamming his body against my buttocks. My ass cheeks were making a smacking sound as he slapped against them. Loud wails issued from his mouth, signaling without words that he was shooting his cum into me. Meanwhile the acolytes were catching my cum in a rag, which they threw into a burning brazier as a semen offering to Baal.

❖

The day after I left the ziggurat, I pretended an important errand in the market. A sheer fabrication. I had to escape my mother's persistent questions and my brother's heckling. When I stopped to adjust my breechclout, someone gripped my arm and swung me around.

"How was it?" Lillake demanded. "Did you like getting fucked in the ass?"

Shopkeepers stared with mouths agape. I walked on, pulling Lillake along with me. "I'll tell you about it another day. Not today."

"You look happy, Zedek. You must have had a good time." Lillake was intensely curious. I smiled with my secret knowledge, which frustrated her further. She tried a different attack. "How did Ithiel and Ucal fare?"

"They fulfilled their sacred duties," I said, not adding that neither valued the experience. "What has been happening since I've been gone? Is war looming? Did King Birsha agree to pay tribute? Last I heard messengers were riding with warnings to Chedorlaomer that Gomorrah will fight rather than pay. Am I about to get drafted into the army? We do not receive news while we are serving Marduk."

"That's all blown over. Even as we speak, Chedorlaomer's entire delegation is here in the city conferring with King Birsha."

I grabbed her arm. "Inside the walls of Gomorrah, Lillake? Is that wise?"

"It's a delegation." She grabbed her arm back and pushed me against the wall of a wine bar. Sometimes I forgot that she was stronger than I.

I pushed her back. "Are they armed? Did they bring guards? Soldiers?"

"For the love of Anat, Zedek. Whatever is the matter?"

"Did the delegates come alone, Lillake?" I wanted to shake her, but I was afraid that she would shake me in return.

"Of course not. They brought their bodyguards."

"An armed force?"

"No more than ten times the fingers on your hands."

My heart smote me as I opened my hands ten times and realized that it was a number only Ekron could contemplate with equanimity. "It's a Trojan horse."

"Did all the cum you took up your ass soften your brain? What in the name of the three-fold goddess is a Trojan horse?"

"It's in a story I heard from that Achaean singer. Never mind that. King Birsha is being deceived."

"To what purpose, Zedek? Chedorlaomer and his allies want their tribute. We do not want to pay tribute. So the king will offer them something to keep them from losing face, but not enough so that Gomorrah looks weak. It is an old story."

Resuming our walk, we passed two carts driven by strangers. The carts carried odd-shaped bundles that kicked and emitted muffled oaths.

"Those are people," I gasped. "People are being kidnapped. We need to warn the authorities."

Lillake stopped arguing with me then, and we ran toward Ekron's workshop. "Ekron has the ear of the king," I assured Lillake. "Also he will believe us. I could run to tell my father, but he would think I was making up a story. He would refuse to do anything until it was too late."

Our plans were foiled in the worst possible way. Flames were shooting out the back of Ekron's workshop and a dark smoke out the front. "His experiments have gone up in flames," Lillake said. "I suspected that playing with such forces was dangerous."

"I hope that Ekron got out okay," I agreed worriedly. We raced around the corner, only to stop at the point of a spear. The spearbearer pressed his tip dangerously close to my stomach.

"These two look like nobility," the spearbearer shouted. Another man inspected Lillake's bare breasts, bright with blue paint, and her golden bangles. Then he lifted my short yellow kilt and saw the design the priests had tattooed upon my buttock. "This one is a Dog, one of the princes. Somebody will pay big to get him back. Snatch them both. If nobody wants to ransom this big girl, we'll whore out her ass to the Avvites."

Lillake promptly kicked the speaker between his legs, but his long kilt prevented a solid strike to the balls. A sharp knife at my throat prevented me from interfering while a sack was thrown over Lillake's head. She kicked and swore, but they soon had her trussed up tight and tossed her into a cart. My turn followed directly.

"Umpf," Lillake huffed as I landed atop her. Trying to roll off, I drove my shoulder into the stomach of another captive. A loud fart followed, which brought more moans of distress.

"Sheol! Lie still, Zedek," Lillake ordered. "Don't raise up any more of those stinkers. This is bad enough without you thrashing around."

"There is nothing to worry about, Lillake," I assured her. "They will never be able to transport us through the gates. Our captors are utter fools, and they will be sitting on pointed stakes before the end of the day."

"Don't be too certain, Dog Boy," another sacked captive moaned. "The Elamites are more successful than we are at the moment. They broke my most beautiful pottery before they set fire to my shop. They are bent on destroying our science and our culture and capturing our most beautiful youths."

"Shut up back there," one of our captors growled. I heard a loud thump followed by a louder howl. The second thump caught me on the side of my head. I felt an exquisite pain, the kind of pain one feels once in a lifetime, and the starry night exploded around me.

❖

"Zedek," Lillake was saying. "Are you all right now, Zedek?"

"I'm really sick," I said, just before I rolled over and vomited. "I want to go back to the ziggurat. I like having Obededom's cock in my ass."

"Zedek, we're in the middle of the desert."

Looking around, I observed that I was in the middle of the group of captives. Men with spears guarded the perimeter and kept us in our place. I sat up and wished I had not. My head pounded.

"What happened? Where are we?" I was aware of a stench, and realized that we were the stench I smelled. Sweating, abused bodies and ripe, unwiped asses did nothing for our sense of self-worth.

"I said, we're in the desert. I thought you were dead. You have been unconscious for two days. That man hit you in the head." She pointed toward one of the spearbearers. "When I get a chance, I'm going to geld him."

"Is that all?"

"Hardly. After I cut off his nuts and hold them before his eyes, I am going to get rough with him."

"What did he do to you?"

"He tried to rape me—in the mouth."

"You discouraged that idea."

"I broke one of his toes. So he kept me tied up while he pissed on my head."

I hoped that she had washed. But where? I looked around and saw nothing but slimy sand covered with dark lichens. "Something really stinks. Besides us."

"We're camped beside a stink pit." She made a rude gesture at the guards. "Camel farts are perfume to these bastards."

Abruptly a thunderous sound rent the air and the ground shook. I leaped to my feet as fire roared out of a hole in the ground not twenty feet away. The flames burned straight up and the roar they made was mightier than the wind.

Four young girls pressed close against me, crying in their terror. I comforted them while trying to move them back to a more comfortable distance, even as something in me revolted against half-naked females pressing against my flesh. Their touch was loathsome.

"Watch out, Zedek," Lillake warned. "Those girls are property."

Ignoring Lillake's inane comment, I stepped back and politely asked the girls' names. Bashfully shuffling forward, they told me that they were Ereshkigal, Nammu, Hannahannah, and Ninanna.

Moving back farther, I introduced myself and asked how they had been captured. As I stepped backward, the four pushed all the closer.

"We live in Sodom," Hannahannah, the eldest, said. "Chedorlaomer's army broke into our house. Our whole family is here."

"Watch out, Zedek," Lillake hissed.

Roaring furiously, a bushy-bearded man stomped toward us. He smacked the girls on the buttocks and sent them toward a depression in the slimy sand. Then he turned on me with a murderous glare—as if I had encouraged his girls, or even wanted them. Violence loomed, but Lillake sprang to my defense.

"Pedophile," Lillake spat at him, stepping between us. "Incestuous pedophile."

"Incest," I gasped. "They are his daughters?"

"Yes, the ghoul is fucking his own children, and him the nephew of the War Chief of the Hebrews, the mighty Al'bram."

"What is his name?" I asked as the furious man stomped off hurling imprecations over his shoulder should I molest his daughters.

"As if you would," Lillake commented. "Of course, if he knew you were a Dog, he would have demanded that you be stoned to death. He is Lhut, the Hebrew of Sodom."

My head was pounding, and my mouth was dry. I rested while I could. After a while, our guards gave us brackish water and horribly stale bread. I gave away my bread but I drank my water ration. Shapash, the solar deity, was beating his waves down, but the divine radiance did not seem as hot as usual. For reasons passing all understanding, the rays did not burn our skin. After we drank, our guards threatened us with their spears until all of the captives were on their feet again.

Fortunately, we were not trussed up in sacks again. Unfortunately, we were not permitted to ride in the carts. We stumbled along behind the carts with the spearbearers following to ascertain that none strayed.

Walking, I had my first chance to survey my fellow captives. We were more than three times the fingers of my hands in number, some Gomorrahan, others from Sodom and Zeboyim, and a couple of luckless shepherds or tribal youths. I scanned the crowd for Ekron, but the scientist was not among the captives. Since they had burned his workshop, would they not have taken him prisoner? But another thought came to wrap a cold fleece around my heart. Slaying Ekron, the inventor, would slay the heart of Gomorrah. And if Ekron was dead, how long would it take before the world rediscovered his inventions? Would another century pass before we discovered how to use electricity to light our streets and homes? A thousand years? What if the marvel was lost forever?

At sundown, we reached a largish lake bordered with white lumps. Later I learned that the lumps were composed largely of salt. Here our guards ordered us to remove our filthy clothing. Several of the captives who had obsessive nudity taboos protested vehemently, but spear points spoke louder than words. Lillake and I shrugged and stripped naked.

Lhut was beside himself. "It is an offense to El Shaddai."

"It's only human skin," I reassured the offended Hebrew.

"El abominates our skin," Lhut repeated. Laughing at Lhut's anger, the guards forced him, his wife R'hab, and his four daughters to disrobe. R'hab and her daughters doffed their clothing submissively, but Lhut protested loudly that nakedness was an offense against their Baal whom he called El Shaddai or simply El. Holding his hands over his mutilated genitals, Lhut glared at me as if I were the author of his misfortunes. He glowered until the guards forced his bare ass into the warm lake water.

Demonstrating his discomfiture, Lhut waved his fist—his other still covered his crotch—and howled that El would smite the laughing guards (I got the impression that El was an almighty smiter of people). When Lhut included me in his imprecations, I turned and gave him a good view of my ass, at the risk of getting smote, of course.

"I hold spirituality as my highest ideal," I whispered to Lillake. "I love all religions. It's only the people who believe in them that I can't stand."

As we waded into the resistant lake water, Lillake asked, "Did you have a spiritual experience as a Dog?"

"It was a tumescent experience," I quipped. "This is strange water. It is hard to walk in."

Lillake dipped a finger and tasted it. "Yuck," she exclaimed. "It's undrinkable. It's pure salt."

"So we're going to come out clean and crusty," I groaned. "I guess having a salty asshole is better than having shitty one."

"At least we need not fear drowning," Lillake said, demonstrating by sitting down. Her trim buttocks sank a little below the surface, enough so she floated in a sitting position. "We could just about walk on water."

I dropped my ass into the water and splashed some over myself. Then we floated side by side for a while as the Shapash disappeared and Shalim, the evening star, came out and Yarikh in his fullness lit the surface of this odd lake. "Are you afraid?" Lillake asked abruptly. I realized that she had been crying softly to herself.

"Not much. I do not like being taken captive, but I do not think we are in danger. Obviously, this is some devious plan Chedorlaomer hatched to force Gomorrah to pay tribute. We are being held for the five cities' ransom."

"I really am terrified, Zedek. That guard whose toe I broke keeps staring at me. I don't want to get gang-raped in the desert."

"I shall not allow that happen, Lillake. I promise." I hardly knew what else to say to comfort her. I, too, had seen the glances the guards had cast upon their female prisoners. And on my ass, too. "How about I tell you about the days I spent as a Dog," I offered. "Want to hear about my holy sacrifice?"

That offer stopped all tears. Lillake glowed in the rays of the moon god Yarikh. She spun around in the water and gave me a direct look. "Tell me all about it, Zedek. Don't spare a single detail, no matter how graphic, no matter how humiliating."

❖

"In my mind I see the scene still. The air hangs thick with the scent of burning incense and perfume. The Priests of Baal wear dangling strips of fur; as they move, the swaying strips reveal their naked asses.

A dog mask covers each priest's face. The worshippers sit on stone benches arranged around the walls—there are many men waiting—more than anyone but Ekron could count—and I gasp to see so many. Proud in their thongs, some acolytes wave fronds to circulate the air, others stand near smoking braziers, and still more hold trays of lotions and sacred phallic objects.

"The worshipers pet their cocks to keep them erect. As I watch, one man plays too hard. His cock erupts, cum flying into the air. When the man finishes ejaculating, the priests lead him from the chamber and he does not return. Near the altar stand three images of Baal: a golden dog, a bronze jackal, and a silver calf. The altar is built around a cone-shaped stone and an ornamented tree.

"You and I both know what we hear from those not of Gomorrah: the stories that we sacrifice the blood of bulls, calves, or dogs to Moloch—grotesque calumnies. There is no such sacrifice in Gomorrah. Libations of wine and beer are poured. Perfumes are sacrificed, as are grains. There is no blood. Those desert tribes accuse us, but they are the ones who make the blood sacrifice. Even one of their sacred stories tells of a son of the first man who was spurned because he made a sacrifice of grain, while his brother performed the blood sacrifice and thus found favor with their Baal.

"It is further rumored that we send children of both sexes down a chute to be burned alive for Moloch—a foul lie. Yes, at one point during the ceremony the acolytes slide down a chute toward a fiery furnace, but the chute twists away and the boys emerge unhurt in the room below.

"Following this symbolic sacrifice, while we three Dog Boys stand naked before the altar, the priests shout prayers to Baal, and the worshippers pray, kneel, and pay homage to the Baalim by kissing the phallic posts, their own hands, and our cocks, which are incredibly hard at that point. The Dog Priests now lead the worshippers in a dance around the altar with Ucal, Ithiel, and me in the center.

"The acolytes are pounding on drums, blowing horns, and shaking rattles. Three priests stand apart from the dancers and chant an invocation to the god. As the dance grows frenzied, the dancers' faces flush. Sweat flies from their bodies. As some of the dancers lose their erections due to their exertions, the priests separate them from the dance and make them return to their seats along the wall.

"At last, the priests select three men whose erections have remained hard as marble. The rest of the men return to their seats, disappointed at not having been chosen, but eager to watch their friends perform the holy act. Acolytes display the sacred vessels of oil. The priests dip their fingers into the oil and slick the three chosen men's hard cocks. The priests stroke lovingly, liberally slicking the tips of the men's cocks, oiling under their foreskins, and kneading the oil into their cock shafts.

"Ucal, Ithiel, and I have been prepared prior to the ritual. Earlier our bowels were filled with warm water repeatedly. After we released the last of the water, we were filled with oil.

"As we stand watching the priests prepare the men, my asshole feels hot and slick. My cock stiffens with anticipation. Ithiel is sporting a semi-erection, but Ucal's cock remains flaccid. It is obvious to all that I am eager to receive a man's cock into my ass, while my fellow Dogs are less thrilled. The masked priests note my erection with appreciation. They whisper among themselves, tittering, and nodding their approval.

"The previous day, Obededom coached me about how to behave. I see him standing behind the priests. Surreptitiously he lifts his mask enough to give me an encouraging smile. Heat rushes through me. My cock stiffens even harder.

"'The Dogs will now assume the sacred position,' a priest commands. The horns blow crazily as the priests enact a homoerotic dance. Ucal, Ithiel, and I go down on our knees, our faces toward the central pole of the sacred temple. Equidistant apart, we remain on our knees, place our forearms on the floor, spread our legs, and push back our rumps.

"'The Dogs offer up the sacrifice,' the priest continues. 'Let the worshipers fill the holy vessels.'

"One of the selected men grips the mounds of my ass. Imri is in his mid thirties, black-bearded, and muscled. He owns a successful furniture factory and employs many men to work at building chairs, beds, and tables in order to increase his profit. Twice Imri, along with his wife and son, dined at our home.

"Imri presses his thick cock against my asshole. A wild chivaree accompanies his action. The priests sing praises to Marduk while acolytes ring bells, shake cymbals, blow horns, and rattle drums. A thrill of fear rushes through me, but the remembered pleasure of the previous day smoothes my qualms. Following Obededom's lessons, I push hard with my asshole. As Imri's cock mounts pressure against me, I do not try to shut it out. I push hard with my ass, push as though I am trying to evacuate my bowels, and draw deep breaths as I do so. The harder I push, the more the pressure increases. I push harder, aware that I am not pushing anything out, but that I am opening my ass for Imri. He slides his cock into me.

"When I open my eyes, I see tears dripping from Ucal's eyes. He is fighting the inevitable. Obededom had mentioned that some Dog Boys find the sacrifice to be a rectalgia, but a select number find it transcendent. Seeing Ithiel's look of determination and Ucal's expression of pain, I grind my rammish ass back to take more of Imri's cock. Despite my earlier trepidations, I welcome the sacrifice.

"'Marduk, oh great Baal,' I whisper as I embrace the fullness of Imri's cock. 'I submit my ass to you, mighty Baal. I am yours, body and soul. Come into me. Make me one with you.'

"When Imri impales me to the fullest extent, a hot guerdon rushes through my body. I feel as though I had touched Ekron's generator. Ucal has stopped crying, but both he and Ithiel are gritting their teeth. I cannot understand their disgust. I feel wonderful. Surges of delight rush up my ass. My cock is so hard it feels liable to burst. Ithiel and Ucal stare at me with amazement. My face is wreathed in glory and a laugh of pure joy escapes from my mouth. Neither Ithiel nor Ucal are moving of their own volition, while I am slamming my ass back to meet Imri's thrusts. I twist and wriggle my ass to give him greater pleasure, but his pleasure can be nothing compared to the wonder I feel.

"Sharp, soul-tripping tingles reverberate up my ass. I feel everything my body feels, but I am not my body. I rise above. I am behind my own head, behind Imri's head; I am looking down on the feverish scene below, and I feel all. I am filled with hard, quivering cock, a cock steadily leaking into me. Imri's cum is a pleasure unto itself. His semen is a powerful drug that takes me higher into euphoria, better than kef from Scythia, better than opium from eastern ports, better than thick beer, better than red wine.

"Lost in the throes of emergent orgasm, Imri thrusts ruthlessly. He does not touch my cock, nor do I, but the tingles rising in my ass throb along its shaft. I ride his cock feistily; I grip it with my asshole as he pulls out and push as he thrusts inward. The tingles ripple through the head of my cock. A deep, intense sensation I cannot describe fills my ass. A farrago of lascivious fictions fills my mind. Now my cock is in full orgasm. Imri huffs and wheezes as he pours his cum into me. My cum splatters onto the floor.

"When Imri pulls out, my asshole makes a popping sound, which brings laughter from the worshippers. Even the priests titter gleefully. An acolyte washes Imri's cock with perfumed water. Now he washes my ass, cleaning deep between my buttocks. The warm wet rag cleans my rather swollen anus. For some reason, the touch of the cloth feels even more intimate than the insertion of Imri's cock."

❖

Yarikh dropped low in the starry sky. His yellow beams cast streaks of light upon the lake. Lhut drove his family toward the shore, but our kidnappers pushed them back. Apparently, they thought they could control us better while we were hampered by the strange water.

"We will be swallowed by a gigantic fish, a leviathan, or a behemoth," Lhut shouted querulously.

"Be silent, you wicked pedophile," Lillake called. "This lake is lifeless."

Most of the captives floated close together, speculating fearfully about our eventual fate. "These Philistine cocksuckers will take us to Gaza and sell us as sex slaves," a woman speculated.

"They aren't Philistines. They are taking us to Assyria, the land of onolatry."

Lillake pricked her ears. "Ass worship?" She laughed at some private speculation. "Zedek will fit in nicely."

"Those women are ignorant, Lillake. She means the worship of donkeys, which the Assyrians do not practice."

"Well, that's the way of the world, so get on with your story, Zedek," Lillake demanded as I pondered upon our captivity. "I want to hear the rest of it. Tell me more about how you enjoyed taking cocks up your ass."

❖

"The remainder of the day is spent in prayer, meditation, and relaxation. We Dogs sun our bodies by a private pool atop the ziggurat, while acolytes serve platters of dates, fruits, nuts, and breads, and offer drinks of crushed watermelon.

"The next day is the same. One man is selected for each of us. Ucal and Ithiel grow more habituated to submitting their asses, but they do not savor the practice—not in the way I do. To me, each day is sheer bliss."

❖

"I want the truth, Zedek," Lillake demanded. "Do you ever think about females sexually? Do you imagine what it would be like to slide your cock into a cunt?"

"Should all men desire cunts?" I sought for the lust within myself, and I could not find it.

Lillake was relentless. "Have you ever felt any desire for me?"

"Desire?" Could I desire Lillake? In some ways, Lillake was more mannish than I, but she did not possess the instrument I craved.

"Don't you ever fantasize about fondling my breasts or stroking my ass? Have you never thought of sliding your cock into my cunt?"

As Astarte threw down her countless spears, a queer frosty sensation came over me. "No," I gasped. "You're my friend. I never thought about you in that way."

"That's what I thought," she murmured with a secret smile. "You are special, Zedek. Appreciate the gift the gods have bestowed upon you. Now tell me what happened every day you were in the ziggurat."

"Every day was the same—until the last. Ucal and Ithiel never found ecstasy, but they sacrificed nonetheless. Each day we performed our rites, swam in the pool, sunned naked, dined on tangy food, and consumed sweet drinks. We slept alone when Yarikh was high, and slept until Shapash was fully risen.

"Obededom never shared your bed?"

I smiled at a secret memory. "If he did, it would have been a minor violation of his vows."

"Only a minor violation?"

"The Priests of Baal appreciate the lust of man for man."

"There is something you are not telling, Zedek."

I laughed. She hardly needed to know that I had discovered where Obededom slept, and one night I crept into his bed. She hardly needed to know that after a day in which I received the cum of Kuwari the merchant, I also received Obededom's cock in my ass. And after I had given him pleasure, he satisfied me with his mouth. It was the first time any man took my cock into his throat. It was the first time I fed another man with my seed.

"Lillake, let me describe the final day. Let me tell you of the great jubilee, the frenzies of penetration and ejaculation that went on far into the night."

"Oh, yes," Lillake said, and bathed in the darkness of the night, she slipped her hand between her thighs.

"Having been fucked daily, I awake on the final morning in a state of high arousal. My cock rises and stands long before partially wilting before it rises to full hardness again. The acolytes laugh at my wanton cock as they bathe, shave, and prepare me for the long ritual. Washed inside and out, oiled and naked, aroused and ripe, fluttery and churned, I enter the sacred chamber.

"As the priests select the three who would penetrate us, my heart sinks. The first chosen is the flax merchant Lemuel who had threatened to plant a tree in my ass. I hold my breath until the priests indicate that Lemuel should fuck Ithiel. The next man chosen is Fat Rephaim from the baths. An overwhelming despair comes over me as Fat Rephaim drools toward my ass. However, the priests turn Fat Rephaim toward Ucal's ass. Ucal's moan nearly brings a blasphemous laugh to my lips, but fear of what man I will get restrains me.

"I did not need to worry. The third chosen is the youngest of the worshippers, hardly more than a youth himself. He is the weaver Buttatum. His face is as well shaved as mine, and his glimmering wheat-colored hair is cut short. Naked, his shape is almost feminine, though feminine with a thick stout cock.

"'Zedek,' Buttatum breathes into my ear. 'Oh, Zedek, I prayed to the Baalim that I would fill you today.' His cock mounts a gargantuan heaviness against my asshole. I push hard, harder than I needed with any previous man's cock. The pressure grows. I stop. I breathe. I force myself to relax while Buttatum whispers wanton declarations into my ear: 'Oh, Zedek, you have a beautiful ass. I have seen no woman to sashay an ass like yours. Your curves are bountiful, golden as the swaying wheat, sweet as honey, delicious as butter. To fill you is my greatest desire. To fill you after today, to be your lover for all time'—here he thrusts forward and his superlative breadth enlarges my rectum—'such would be the fulfillment of my dreams.'

"I am in ecstasy. My asshole is fully dilated with sweet sensations tripping around the rim. Buttatum pushes his cock in deeper. 'Am I hurting you?' he asks in response to my yelp of pleasure.

"A joyous laugh escapes unbidden from my throat. 'It feels good,' I assure him. 'Is this your first time?'

"'With a man? Into an anus? Yes.' With pusillanimous vigor, Buttatum pushes harder against me. I drive back to meet him, smashing his loins against my buttocks.

"'This is the way, Buttatum. Fill me all the way. Pull back and thrust again.' Titillating sensations flood me. My cock drips as I tighten my asshole around Buttatum's cock. I stroke him with my anal muscles. A wild laugh escapes. I hear Fat Rephaim grunting with exertion as he fucks Ucal's ass. Ucal is moaning, but it is closer to a mortified whine than a cry of joy. Ithiel's buttocks make a loud smacking as Lemuel slaps against them.

"'Feel the pleasure,' I urge. 'Accept it. Submit to it. Thrill to it. Let it carry you to bliss.'

"'I feel it,' Lemuel shouts. 'I come in this Dog's ass.' I do not explain to crass Lemuel that I did not mean him. I had spoken to the penetrated, not the penetrators.

"'I feel it, too,' Buttatum bawls. 'Oh, Zedek, your ass is grainy. It is tight. It is hot.'

"Buttatum thrusts faster in my ass. He slams me. He moves from exhilaration to frenzy, and as his passion mounts, he emits a shrill keen. Tingles ripple through my rump. A crinkling in my cock's head signals imminent orgasm. Buttatum spurts his cum into me. I am wet, and still willing. His thrusts grow sloppy as he delivers loads of slick semen.

"My body contracts. My mid-section fires in dark heat. I burn. My orgasm is rich and deep. Thick cum drips onto the floor. Through my fluttering eyelids, I see Ucal and Ithiel staring agog. Living through one of Baal's eternities, I droop forward. Buttatum's cock slides out of my ass. I sprawl exhausted in my pool of semen while the acolytes wipe my ass. My fuck angel falls beside me.

"For a time squeezed out of infinity, Buttatum's eyes meet mine. His face looks stunned, dazed, lost in wonder. I smile, and he responds as if the power of Baal had descended upon him. The acolytes raise him and wipe his cock. He staggers as they lead him to the assembled worshippers.

"On previous days in the ziggurat, our ceremony had ended on this point. Today is different. The priests signal for silence. Ucal, Ithiel, and I face the priests.

"The high priest looks us one by one in the eye for an uncomfortably long moment before he speaks: 'Today's ritual concludes with a special ceremony. You may choose among you. Lots will be drawn among the worshippers, saving only those you have pleasured already, and each of you will satisfy them with your mouths and swallow the holy seed. Or you may select one Dog to represent all three, and he shall choose three worshipers and do as I have said three times.'

"'Ugh,' Ucal says. 'I would throw up.'

"Ithiel looks at me with deep supplication in his eyes. 'Will you suck their cocks, Zedek? For us? Will you?'"

❖

"Did you?" Lillake gasped. "Did you suck cocks?"

"I never took a cock in my mouth before that day," I informed her. "Though Obededom sucked mine." I said that before I remembered that I had concealed that night's work from her. "When Obededom finished, and my cum was residing in his stomach, he advised how to proceed. At the time, I did not realize that I would be called upon to do likewise."

"So you did it. You sucked a cock." Lillake was delighted. "You sucked three cocks." Lillake was obscenely overjoyed.

❖

"'I shall stand for my fellow Dogs,' affirm I. 'I shall suck the seed of men.'

"Ucal and Ithiel sigh with heartfelt relief. The priest demands. 'So be it. Now choose the cocks you will drink from.'"

❖

I went no further with my story because our guards were shouting. Two waded in to round us up. Their job was difficult because they were working by starlight. Eventually all the captives were ashore. We emerged far from where we had left our clothes, and our guards did not permit us to return to that place, but urged us along. Lhut howled the loudest against being herded naked into the desert. A guard clouted him twice with the butt of his spear. "Be silent, you," the guard admonished. "Thank your gods that you still have your skin."

"Our God is one," Lhut muttered, which I thought pathetic. I for one needed as many gods as I could get.

Our guards kept us trotting at a brisk pace, discounting our stumbles and stubbed toes. Auspiciously, the sand was not too rocky for our bare feet, and our guards herded us around the worst obstacles. We were exhausted by the time Shahar, goddess of the dawn, painted the eastern sky.

Still they rushed us along, though Shapash beat down and the terrain grew more fantastic. We passed stinking pools of slime bubbling out of salty sand. Pits of pitch were there as well. As we passed one stygian well, a jet of blue flame shot upward, growing into a ball of fire that dissipated as it fell to the floor of the desert. It was a place which Dagon, god of grain, and Nikkal-wa-Ib, goddess of orchards, had abandoned utterly.

Men had been joining our guards since before dawn. These luckless rascals had run hard themselves, or they had ridden horses or camels into the sand. They carried messages that our guards read with despair. Our group was either running from menace or scurrying toward safety.

Just as we captives were drooping, we saw two clouds of dust arising in the horizon. The nearer cloud met us soonest. Our guards hailed their friends, joyous in the swelling of their numbers. Too little; too late. Turning, the soldiers viewed the other dust cloud with dread. One voice rose among the others: "We must sacrifice a virgin to Anat." Others nodded at this inspiration.

The broke-toed guard pointed toward me: "Fetch your woman to yonder pitch pit."

Mystified, I scanned for "my woman."

Lillake nudged me. "That sheep's dreadlock means me, Zedek."

"They're not going to sacrifice you."

As the cloud took shape into an army of men riding from the horizon, the hobbled guard seized Lillake's arm. "Give me the blade of sacrifice."

"No," I shouted.

Ignoring me, another tossed his knife. "Cut the virgin's throat."

I voiced the finest lie I could think up. "Choose another," I shrieked. "Lillake is no virgin. A false sacrifice is worse than no sacrifice. You will incur the wrath of Anat."

"The Dog lies," Lhut thundered. "Put your fingers into her. She is virginal."

"I have fucked her," I lied. Lillake was struggling, but in vain. Strong men held her, and the knife was too close to her throat.

"She is a whore," I yelped. "I have fucked her, as have many men."

They attempted to examine Lillake, but she did not make close inspection painless. She struggled, wasting their time until she was able to steal a long knife from a slacker.

"Any man thinking to sacrifice me can kiss his balls good-bye."

"The doom is upon us," Chedorlaomer's captains howled. "We either slay the slaves of Al'bram or we perish."

Panicked, the men abandoned the notion of sacrificing Lillake. I pulled her away from the spearbearers. Then I got my first view of Al'bram himself. Wild haired and bushy bearded and riding a pale horse, he swung his bronze blade with reckless abandon. Human blood sprayed. Body parts flew.

"Give me my knife," the desperate guard begged Lillake, but she slashed at his crotch. Backing into the arc of a swinging scimitar, he lost his head. Al'bram's men hacked from horseback, hewing or spearing any man afoot.

"Get down," I urged Lillake. I pushed her into a depression, and she pulled me atop her. As I dropped, a blade cut the air where my neck had been. Lhut's wife and daughters were on the ground, too, though Lhut stood and cheered his uncle on until a spear took a swath of hair from his head. Lhut slumped as if he had been axed, which made his fellow captives laugh.

"You, too, shall be smitten," Lhut vowed darkly. "All evildoers shall fall beneath the wrath of the servants of He whose name cannot be spoken." Lhut glared across his huddled naked daughters toward me. "Dogs and whores shall fall by the sword. The foxes shall devour their corrupted flesh." That was a despicable anathema, especially since Lillake and I were the only captives who had not mocked him.

The end of the battle came faster than expected. The desert was strewn with mutilated corpses, which did nothing to improve its appearance. Al'bram rode to Lhut. "Arise, nephew. Arise and cover thy nakedness." Al'bram pointed toward the corpse of one of our guards. "His robe doth be less bloody. Attire thyself, and make thy daughters and wife to cover their shame."

Lhut's daughters leaped to their feet and began to rob the corpses. All except one daughter. Making no effort to cover herself, Nammu touched Al'bram's robe. "We must sacrifice a he-goat to Asherah," Nammu declared. "The wife of Yahweh has delivered us from bondage. We must make an offering of meat."

Lhut had finished dressing in the guard's clothing. To my shock, he ripped the hem and dumped dirt onto his own head, while Al'bram and his men shrieked and covered their ears.

"Wife of the name that canst not be spoken?" Al'bram shouted, pointing toward the thunderstruck Nammu. "Dost the woman knoweth the extent of her blasphemy? Our God is masculine and our God is one. This is what cometh when the daughters of the chosen people go unto thy sons of the unrighteous. Lhut, thy daughters have gone a-whoring after foreign gods."

"She meant no harm," I protested.

Al'bram looked at me for the first time. I had wrapped a soldier's scarf around my waist, so the War Chief of the Hebrews was able to look upon me. "Who art thou to speak to me?" he demanded.

"Zedek of Gomorrah."

My name must have meant something to Al'bram, for he looked at me with wonder. Later the Hebrew storytellers got the facts completely wrong. They claimed that I was Melchizedek, the King of Salem, and that I brought gifts to Al'bram and blessed him. The stories entered into their mythology, and before long people believed the rash chitchat with religious fervor.

Lhut was not about to let the occasion go quietly. "He is a Dog," Lhut said. "We must stone him to death. And the whore with him."

"We dost not have time for stoning," Al'bram said, glancing at the sky and then looking me over. "Bring him with us." He sneered at Lillake. "Leave the foreign woman that the lions and the jackals might devour her."

Lillake gave Al'bram a hard look and held out the knife she was still holding. "The only jackal I see is…"

I clamped my hand over Lillake's mouth. "Where I go, she goes. Her people are my people, and I cannot depart from her."

"You hear? You hear?" Lhut jabbered.

"Is the woman a whore?" Al'bram demanded.

"Of course not," I assured him. "I lied to prevent Chedorlaomer's soldiers sacrificing her. Lillake is more pure than the apple blossom falling chastely in the orchard. She is as gentle as the young hart and sweeter than honey in the honeycomb." Nammu, who had pulled a man's garment around her, regarded Lillake speculatively.

Ignoring everyone else, Al'bram questioned Lhut. "Nephew, will thou now return to thy people, even unto their tents, and my God shalt be thy God?"

"I must sojourn yet a while in Sodom," Lhut said. "My heart is there."

"Thy cock is there, nephew," Al'bram muttered. "No matter. Our god will deliver thee in His own time. We shall convey thee hence."

"Our families in Gomorrah must be frantic," I said. "Lillake and I come from prominent households." Getting only blank stares, I added, "Set us as a seal upon thy heart, and return us to whence we were stolen."

"Enough," Al'bram shouted. "Thou art turning my stomach. Bring Zedek and his woman. We will deliver them unto Sodom, and let the Sodomites determine their fate." He lifted Lhut up behind him on his horse. Other men lifted up R'hab and her daughters. A servant of Al'bram seized Lillake's arm and tossed her over the horse behind him. My own turn came next. I threw my arms around the middle of the Hebrew rider and pressed my cock hard against his swelling buttocks.

Leaving the remnant of our fellow captives weeping in the desert, we pounded away. The horses' hooves flew over the hot salty sand.

Tiny whirlwinds rose around us as we rode. The sun shimmered off the sand, creating bizarre shapes before our eyes.

In the afternoon of that day, we stopped at an oasis. Tall date palms provided shade and sweet food while the Hebrew men and their beasts drank deeply from the chill spring. Lhut's family, Lillake, and I were permitted to quench our thirst after the men and the horses were satisfied. Pomegranates grew there, as did yellow melons. We ate the sweet fruits and sucked the seeds. But all too soon, Al'bram ordered that we ride again.

The desert faded behind us as the land grew more fertile. We passed terraced slopes of grapes and olives. Wineries and olive presses were abundant. Men and women were working in fields of barley, corn, millet, and wheat. The planters waved merrily as we approached, greeted us with glad cries, and offered us refreshment. I was impressed with the general mood of joy. Even the hardest workers were reveling in their labors, as if work were a celebration rather than a drudge. Small shrines to the deities of crop fertility and the dying and reviving divinities of the underworld dotted the land: Dagon, the fertility god Hammon, Hadad of the storms, Nikkal-wa-Ib, and Melqart, god of the underworld.

As Shapash dropped to the horizon, we passed the ponds of the fish farmers. Cattle, sheep, and goats grazed in lush pastures. Even in the failing light, we could smell the produce grown in the farms: beans, cucumbers, gourds, leeks, lentils, and onions.

A long, shallow pool stretched beside us. Darkness had fallen, but by the light of Yarikh's orb, I saw the hideous shape rising from the center of the pool. It had the body of a lion and the head of a man, but it was greater than any animal or man. "What is it?" I gasped.

The men shunned my query, but Lhut's daughter Ereshkigal spoke up. "We are passing the Great Sphinx of Sodom."

A little way on, we came to twin rows of enormous pyramids. I could not say their height, but they rent the sky. Near the pyramids, Al'bram dismounted. Lhut had fallen asleep, but Al'bram pushed him off easily. Lhut hit the sand with a wild cry.

"We camp in this spot," Al'bram ordered. "After the sun rises, we wilst approach the gates of Sodom. Lhut, I will see that thou art treated as an honored citizen and not as a ghul out of the desert winds. These others may enter the city with thee, should'st the Sodomites accept them. Nor I nor my men shalt enter into this city, but we shall return from whence we cometh."

"Dost thou enjoy living in a tent, Uncle?" Lhut asked.

"It is the will of our God. Now rest thee."

The sand remained hot for a while, but the air chilled rapidly. Lillake and I huddled together and covered ourselves with the bloody scarves we had stolen from the dead. From the desert came the roaring of frightful beasts and the trampling of terrible feet and the glowing of hungry eyes and the whispering of malicious demons. From over the walls of Sodom came the laughing of reveling men and the crying of orgasmic masses and the moaning of the joyously penetrated and the grunting of ejaculating males.

As Yarikh dropped below the horizon and Shamayim spread his countless winking lights above us, I whispered to Lillake, "Tomorrow we shall see Sodom, city of wonders."

❖

Shapash was riding high before the great bronze doors of Sodom swung open. The six guards wore short kilts and pectoral covers. They were shaved completely, even their heads. They bore short spears with wicked points, and each had a curved knife belted around his middle. They wore makeup on their eyes and lips, and a couple appeared hungover. Still they were utterly gorgeous, to a man.

"Greetings, strangers," their captain said. "What business have you in Sodom?"

"I live here," Lhut said. "I was captured by Chedorlaomer's men while you stood around with your cocks in your hands."

The guards there did not appear to be overjoyed at Lhut's return. "Oh, so *you're* back," they said, as Lhut rudely brushed past them. His wife and his daughters followed him. The guards looked after them with undisguised disdain.

I waited politely until the guards turned back to Lillake and me. "I am Zedek of Gomorrah, also captured by these same unlamented minions of Chedorlaomer. This young woman, Lillake, and I are seeking hospitality until we can be returned to our families in Gomorrah."

The guards looked us up and down, and a sight we must have been. Encrusted with salt and filth, dressed in bloodstained wraps, and burnished by the hot beams of Shapash, we could not have presented a worse spectacle. Yet the guards at the gate of Sodom were gracious.

"Welcome, young sir," they said to me. One patted my ass in a friendly fashion. Lillake giggled, and I smiled at the guard.

The captain addressed the guard whose hand lingered on the curve of my rump. "Mordecai, you convey Zedek and Lillake to the palace of King Bera." He turned to Lillake and me. "You shall be honored guests, and the Sodomites shall provide food, raiment, shelter, and entertainment for you until such time that you may be escorted safely back to your own city."

As we passed through the bronze doors, I was stunned to realize that the walls of Sodom were not only six times the height of my body, but that they were doubled. After passing the gates, we entered a space wider than the height of a man, with walls of cyclopean block tightly fitted on either side. We turned three sharp corners before we passed through a smaller door and were inside the city proper. Mordecai kept talking about the graciousness of his city while Lillake and I gawked like a pair of sheep dippers just in from the desert. Three enormous ziggurats towered above us, their terraces lush with growth as sprays of water cast rainbows on their way to nourishing the blooming fruit trees. Smaller sphinxes and statues of various gods and goddesses stood in profusion. Words painted on walls declared that Sodom was the City of Love.

We passed down a tree-lined street of brilliantly painted houses with outsized windows and arched doorways. Many houses boasted outside wall murals depicting love in its more deliciously carnal aspects. Scenes of men sucking men's cocks and women licking women's crotches greeted us profusely. Lillake stared at the scenes of sexual pleasure between women with her mouth agape.

"These must be wealthy citizens," I suggested, which made Mordecai laugh.

"What is funny?"

"This is the poorest section of Sodom. But here, even the most impoverished people live above the level of wealthy people in other cities. We are greatly favored by the eternal Baalim."

"I should say so," I agreed, gazing at a fountain of spraying streams surrounded by a circle of statues. The life-sized marbles depicted a circle of men, each with his cock plugged into the ass of the man before him, and each in his turn plugged from behind. "Is this erotic statuary intended to honor some particular Baal?"

"It is intended to celebrate the pleasure of man with man," Mordecai advised. "Have you ever experienced the joy of a man's cock in your ass?"

"Many times," I assured him. "I was a Dog in the great Ziggurat of Gomorrah."

"Zedek loves anal sex," Lillake contributed. "He takes cum up the ass with greater enthusiasm than any other boy in Gomorrah."

"This is wonderful," Mordecai gushed, practically drooling on me. "Tomorrow is the Festival of Qadeshtu. I hope that you can join us."

"I would be honored." Then I confessed, "I am not familiar with Qadeshtu."

"She is a local deity, a goddess of love. We celebrate her by giving our bodies in acts of pleasure."

We passed a shrine erected to the god of craftsmanship, Kothar-wa-Khasis, before we came to the bazaar of the craftsmen. Weavers, tailors, potters, smiths, and wheelwrights were working industriously, with many a jest and ribald shout to lighten the day. A potter's boy, naked and burnished, tittered with laughter as he carried a long tray of vessels to the kiln.

I judged the boy to be my own age, and I was wondering whether he would attend the Festival of Qadeshtu, when Lillake gasped with astonishment. A pair of women sculptors took a break from their labors and began to kiss each other lasciviously. The sight of two women kissing did not interest me, not so much as the sight of the potter's boy, but Lillake was clearly flushed with interest. As we watched, one of the women dropped to her knees and pushed her face between the other's legs.

Mordecai appeared to be puzzled. "Women do not love each other in Gomorrah?"

"Oh, they do," Lillake said. "But never so publicly."

"Here in Sodom," Mordecai lectured, "we celebrate love and pleasure. We bask in the spiritual aspects of the love that is pure and we revel in the physical aspects of pleasure. We do not think that the two are the same. Some acts of love are made to engender children. It is good and proper. However, those acts beget lifetimes, and we approach them with caution and planning. The act of physical love between men or between women cannot result in lifetimes. Those acts are freely given and freely taken, and we celebrate them. They are divine pleasure, untainted with disastrous consequences. No female in Sodom has been filled with a child she did not want, or for which she was not prepared."

"I'm going to love this city," Lillake said, gazing at a painted marble statue of three women locked in carnal endeavors.

❖

At first glance, I thought that the king was a woman. King Bera was delightfully effeminate; he spoke in mincing tones, and his every movement hinted at seduction. Not seduction of Lillake, of course. Seduction of me. Delighted to meet us and eager to hear about our capture, treatment, and rescue, King Bera gripped my thigh and caressed me in a charmingly lewd manner during our entire conversation.

I apologized for our appearance, arriving filthy, smelly, and wearing nothing but hip scarves, but the king waved away my apologies with a flowery gesture. Gorgeous laughing attendants brought crushed watermelon and wine mixed with pomegranate juice to refresh us while we talked. King Bera registered dismay several times, but most especially when he learned that Lhut had returned to Sodom.

"We have had no end of trouble with that man," the king said mournfully. "I cannot imagine why he sojourns here, for he disapproves of our ways. Also, we have reason to believe that he might be violating our strongest taboos. We practice sexual freedom, but one must be a proper age to participate. The local gossips assure us that Lhut has violated his own daughters from an early age.

"You may have heard of the abuses perpetrated by the people of Salem, though I do not say that the Hebrews endorse such monstrosities. Their own traditions decry economic crimes, blasphemy, and bloodshed. If only they *followed* their own sacred teachings. Wealthy landowners were stamping out gold strips that bore their own names, paying their sheepherders and field workers with this coin, and then refusing to accept the money back when the unfortunate workers attempted to buy food. Then when their workers and their families starved to death, the landowners would reclaim the money that bore their names."

"Lhut did something like that?"

"He attempted to do so," the king said, "until the merchants in the bazaar conspired to accept the scrip Lhut forged.

"Lhut says that he simply believes that what is his is his, and what is yours is yours. In truth, he means that what is yours is his also. After the city merchants accepted his gold scrip, giving good value, Lhut started a false rumor, which he borrowed from another tradition, and Mot only knows where he got it."

Lillake and I exchanged a shocked look when the king used the name of Mot. King Bera obviously had strong feelings about Lhut's behavior, or he would not have evoked the name of the God of Death.

"Anyway," the king continued, "Lhut claimed that we had a rack in the bazaar, and that strangers coming to buy wares would be measured on it. Those too short would be stretched until their bones broke, and those too tall would have their heads and feet sawed off. It was a vile fabrication but effective, for business suffered for a time.

"After we traced the source of the rumor to Lhut, we ordered him to leave Sodom. However, Al'bram sent one of his henchmen, Eliezer, to arrange Lhut's passage back to his people. Eliezer promptly fell into a quarrel with a cloth merchant over the price. The Hebrew attacked the Sodomite with his knife, so the Sodomite defended himself with a stone. During the ensuing struggle, Eliezer was hit in the forehead with a stone, making him bleed. The case went before a judge, and in the end, the whole matter dropped, and Lhut remained in Sodom.

"Of course, Lhut later claimed that the Sodomite merchant had demanded Eliezer pay him for the service of bloodletting. When the Sodomite judge sided with his townsman, Eliezer took a stone and struck the judge in the forehead. Then Eliezer told the judge to pay the Sodomite."

"None of that last part was true?"

"Hardly. It shows Lhut's true character, though. He was able to twist a true story into something vile."

"Lillake and I have also seen something of Lhut's character."

Lillake spoke up: "He told a story while you were still unconscious, Zedek. I did not believe it when he said it, but he claimed that his first daughter Paltith and another girl had their naked bodies smeared with honey and hung from the city walls until they were eaten by bees.

According to Lhut, the Sodomites did this to the girls because they gave some bread to a poor beggar."

"No one goes begging in Sodom. We take care of our people," said the king. "And Lhut has four daughters, all of whom are still alive. That man despises this city and everyone in it. He does not join the revels. He abominates the pleasures of male with male and female with female, even though those acts of erotic love are the glory of Sodom. Yet here he continues to sojourn."

"Because he thinks that here he is safe to fuck his daughters with impunity," Lillake observed.

King Bera shuddered at the image. "We will talk further," he promised. "But you are exhausted and hungry. My cooks are roasting a pig with many fine side dishes. While you are waiting for the pig to cook fully, the young men and women of Sodom are eager to assist you in cleansing and refreshing your bodies after your ordeal."

The king daintily rang a golden bell, and a crowd of young men and women entered the chamber. They hurried Lillake and me to the baths, where we were given cool water with lemon juice while the youths purged us with warm, scented water, scraped our teeth, flushed our noses, scrubbed our bodies, cleaned our ears, and washed, trimmed, and combed our hair. They shaved my body, except for my head, and both of us received the traditional Sodomite hairstyle worn by males and females. Lillake ran her hand over the hair remaining on her head, which was no longer than her forefinger to the first joint.

"I like it," she said. "For a moment I thought that they would shave us bald, like the heads of the guards at the gates."

After we dined on roast pig and accessories, we spent the afternoon dozing naked under the sun by the enormous swimming pool in the courtyard of the palace. A young man served us with mugs of cool pomegranate juice before removing his loincloth and stretching out beside me. He rolled onto his back and shifted his cock to catch the sun.

"You never had a chance to tell about your cocksucking experience," Lillake murmured, her eyes flickering over the young man's cock. "I would love to hear how you liked it."

The young women who had attended to Lillake looked bored, and I guessed that most had no interest in men's cocks. However, the young males pricked up their ears as I took up my tale, continuing where I had been interrupted.

❖

"'I shall stand in for my fellow Dogs,' say I. 'I shall suck the seed of men.'

"Ucal and Ithiel sigh with heartfelt relief. The priest demands, 'So be it. Now choose the cocks you will drink from.'

"A strange feeling sweeps over me. The worshipers stand as I approach. I walk along the ranked men, inspecting them. I squeeze the harder dicks until I find one that feels just right for my mouth. He is a younger man who has sat through every day of our celebrations without being selected. With a start, I realize that he is Enoch, who works at my father's winery. I have seen him laboring naked in past times, but I did not notice that his cock was so thick before. Now I feel its plump swelling and the tiny bead of cum at the tip.

"'Enoch shall be first,' I proclaim.

"'It is well chosen. Now choose your second.'

"Continuing my inspection, I come upon the Egyptian-born carpenter Seth. His cock is as thick as the cock of Enoch. 'Him. The carpenter.'

"'He does bypass the long thin cocks and settles upon the plump ones,' one priest whispered audibly.

"Shapash rides her chariot toward the islands of the west. Shalim girds his loins for his nightly toil. Shafts of light move slowly across the great chamber as I search for the third cock I would suck. I begin to fear I will have to settle for one inferior to the cocks of Seth and Enoch. Then I spy a form darker than the shadows lingering. A single beam of light shines upon the tip of his risen cock. It is black and comely. The rays of hotter climes have burnished it into gorgeous darkness.

"'Who are you?' I ask.

"'I am Aphilas of the Kingdom of Kush, born at the confluence of the Nile and the Atbara. I am a visitor in this city, and your king and priests invited me to participate in your holy rites. I like all that I have seen. I hope that you will choose my cock for your sucking.'

"'I shall, Aphilas. You shall be my third choice.'

"'Thus Zedek chooses the king's honored guest.'

"Ithiel lets loose a sharp gasp, and Ucal snorts. I hope his snort is not derisive, but I do not really care. I look to the priests for guidance.

"'Let the three stand forth,' the priests proclaim. 'All others have fulfilled their obligations to Marduk. Leave if you must: stay if you will.'

"Naked, erect, and trembling, Aphilas, Seth, and Enoch stand before me. I look at their faces, so full of anticipation and trepidation. Men are milling about as some of the crowd must depart to their duties. A few stay for the nightlong revels. They are the men who desire a cock's invasion into their own bodies, and hope to join the holy procession of the penetrated.

"I stand hesitantly until a priest guides me. 'Zedek, slide to your knees.'

"On my knees, I see the three cocks thrusting toward my mouth. 'Remember that Enoch is your first. Touch your lips to his cock.'"

❖

"You really did it?" Lillake asked. The boys lying around the pool are staring at me with obvious interest. Several were rubbing their own cocks or the cocks of the boys next to them as they listened.

"I can't tell this if you keep interrupting," I told Lillake. She laughed, but further interruptions arrived immediately. A group of young females arrived, stripped off their loin skirts, and formed a group on Lillake's far side. I was surprised to see that one was Lhut's daughter Nammu.

"You? Here?" Lillake said to her.

Nammu placed her hand on the thigh of the girl next to her. "The ways of my father are not my ways," she said. "Not when I can escape them." She placed her mouth on the other girl's breast and began sucking it while her hands caressed the girl's ass.

Lillake watched with obvious shock and interest. "Want to join them?" I asked her.

"I want to hear the rest of the story."

"I sucked all three cocks. The three men ejaculated into my mouth. I swallowed. That's the essence of it—to make a long story short."

Boys around me were nodding in agreement, and I was thinking that it would be far more fun to dally with them than to satisfy Lillake's salacious interest.

"I don't want the short version," Lillake protested. "I want to hear all…" She caught her breath sharply. Nammu had just touched the curve of her bare ass.

"What are you doing?" Lillake gasped.

Nammu brought her mouth close to Lillake's. "This is Sodom, Lillake," Nammu breathed. "All acts of pleasure are this city's rituals. Surrender to your lust. Let it happen." Then Nammu was kissing Lillake.

Grinning as I saw Lillake begin to respond, I turned to the boy next to me. He beckoned, and I saw that the other boys had moved to the far side of the pool. I followed him, leaving that side to the girls.

The sun beat down upon me, and sweat burst from my brow. The boys, all about my age and some a little older—more experienced, I wondered, thinking of Obededom—were rubbing against each other and kissing lustily. The boy who had beckoned to me pressed his lips to mine. I squiggled my lips against his and let his tongue push into my mouth. I met his tongue with my tongue. My cock swelled, but I grabbed for his. His sweat had made his shaft slick, so I stroked it.

He pulled back. "Not too hard," he insisted.

"No? I like it hard."

"As do I. But you are new to the ways of Sodom. I will coach you. Our revels start after Shapash rides into the all-encircling sea and Ishat lights our streets. Today we will excite each other, but we will not consummate. In darkness and lurid light, we will go burning into the streets of men."

"What about them?" I hooked my thumb toward the girls. Out of the corner of my eye, I noticed that Lillake was discovering pleasures more personal than my secondhand stories.

"They have their own nightly games," the boy said. "Enough questions now. Before this night is over, you shall know so much more."

"I am hardly ignorant of the pleasure of man with man. After all, I was a Dog in the great ziggurat of Gomorrah, and my enthusiasm for the act so impressed the Dog Priests of Baal that they wanted me to join them. I could have been a Holy Dog Priest. I could have had a life of leisure and pleasure, but I refused. I wanted to experience more of life than delirious ritual sex, which however wonderful, confines the priests within a mind-forged barrier in space and time."

He kissed me hard then and gripped my cock with a fist of bronze, kissing me with such passion and clamping my cock so hard that I almost unmanned myself. A jolt of pleasure ripped through me, but I did not quite ejaculate. I think that I must have experienced a moment's rush of orgasm, but it passed so quickly that my seed did not shoot forth.

The sweat was running from me and forming a puddle around my feet. The boy laughed at my surprise. He released my cock and taunted me. "Did you ever feel such eternal bliss in the Gomorrahan ziggurat?"

In answer, I kissed him hard, pushed my tongue into his mouth, and grabbed his cock.

❖

The gods had shifted their places by the time I emerged naked and lustful from my guest quarters. Tripping down the Street of Desire, I picked my steps by the lights of androgynous Ishtar. Painted brick houses and the cyclopean stones of the city's walls formed my twisting path. I emerged into the Street of Surrender, where blazing torches lighted the scene.

Men were pouring from doorways, alleys, side streets. All were naked, cocks stiff, and burning with anticipation. A strange ululation rendered the night more eerie. Looking up, I saw women watching from balconies performed the festive tongue-trilling that signaled their approval of the men's orgies. A group tongue-trilled directly at me. As I looked, they mimed male-on-male anal and oral sex before they fell upon each other, groping and kissing.

Two men met me then, a native Sodomite and a traveler from Admah, the ford of Jordan. "Gomorrahan, welcome to our festivities. Come join the lusty devotions."

In answer, I grabbed the Sodomite's thick cock. Delighted, he thrust in my fist while he circled my waist with his arm and stroked my protruding buttocks. More tongue-trilling followed, and I glanced up in time to see Lillake turn to suck the breasts of a Moon Priestess.

Gradually Lillake slipped down until her face pressed the woman's groin.

The Sodomite pulled my face to his. His lips crushed mine as his tongue drove deep into my mouth. I sucked his tongue hard and thumbed his heavy foreskin. My cock was nearly bursting with desire to spew my seed. I ran my tongue down the Sodomite's chin. Biting the skin, I kissed his throat, which brought a sharp gasp. His companion, the Admahite, stood behind me, groping me with wanton joy. I pushed my ass back as my mouth settled upon the Sodomite's nipples. The Admahite dropped to his knees and kissed my rear. I licked the Sodomite from his nipples to his cock as I slid to all fours and stuck out my rump.

The Admahite's lips caressed my ass and pushed into my crack. His tongue played around my asshole. I touched my mouth to the Sodomite's cock. It looked impossibly thick in its extreme hardness, so I opened my mouth wide.

"Bide your suckling hunger, Gomorrahan," the Sodomite gasped. "Let us join the others. More men than you can number are commingling in the Cul-de-sac of the Cupbearers. Our orgasms are more intense when we co-arise. The larger the quantity of men, the more intense is the pleasure that all feel."

"I know your words to be true," I said. "I debauched in the holy orgy at the Gomorrahan ziggurat when the Dog Priests fuck in wanton frenzy at the rising of the Dog Star."

"Then surrender your individual lasciviousness to the mass lasciviousness. Behold!" We had turned the corner, and my legs wobbled at the vision of the naked man flesh freelovingly devoted to incontinent deflowerment, despoilment, and ravishment.

Women ululated wildly from the balconies, their trills echoing the cries of the beasts of the surrounding desert. Far beyond the irrigated groves and fields, the lions, ostriches, wild goats, and jackals echoed the shrieks of pleasure rising from the city of Sodom. Goat-hoofed demons danced under the starlight, taking each other's cocks in mouth and ass, while dragons of the lascivious star-shadow frolicked atop the cooling salt sands.

I lost the Admahite when a boy my age took him, throwing the older Admahite face down in the dusty street and driving a thick cock into his ass. The Admahite wailed with joy as his cock spurted. Hanging on to the Sodomite's solid cock, I felt the crowd of men suck us in and thrust us toward its cynosure. A whirlwind of desire swept around me. Still gripping my first Sodomite, I kissed his nipples again, slid down his muscled abdomen, and thrust my tongue into his navel. To my taste, his navel was a golden bowl of masculine ambrosia, but I craved his nectar. I sank lower, kissing his crinkly hairs. The brownish pubic hair tickled my face, wreathing me in smiles as I kissed around the base of his jutting shaft. I kissed his balls, tight and ready.

Drawing my face back even as he cupped the back of my head with both of his crafty hands, I opened my eyes to spy his thick, swollen cock tip peeping from beneath its hood. I opened my mouth and closed my lips around it. It slid along my tongue, driving deeper into my mouth as the beset Sodomite pulled my head forward onto his cock.

He moaned, too far gone in lust to stop his coming. I pulled my head back. I pushed forward, and as I did, I tasted his nectar. His thick cock trembled as his cum pulsed into my throat. I swallowed as the Dog Priests in the great ziggurat of Gomorrah had instructed me. His semen tasted of rich spices, and strangely enough, of grape pudding. I savored the rich texture and tangy sweetness upon my tongue before I swallowed. The Sodomite provided a second dessert after my supper of olives, flat bread, roasted partridge stuffed with leeks, lentils, and onions, drinks of crushed cucumber, wine, beer, goat cheese, and a dessert of honeyed curds mixed with spring flower petals.

After he came, the Sodomite turned to other pursuits, which suited my tastes as well. I became part of the orgiastic ring of men, shouting their lustful thoughts to the ringing sky. A man took me from behind, and I thrust my ass back to meet his cock. I did not even see his face, but his cock was slick already. It slid between my buttocks and pressed wetly against my asshole. I pushed hard, opening my asshole for him. He grunted with surprise as I impaled my rump upon his cock.

My cock was swollen. It brushed along the ass of another man, dimly seen in the lurid glare of the torches. I glided along his ass as I rode the stranger's cock up to its hooded tip. I drove back again as he thrust forward and impaled me. He slammed hard against my buttocks. Feeling intensely full, I relished the sensation before we pulled away from each other again.

He came in me after a few strokes. After he pulled out, I turned to see his face, but he was already lost in the swirling crowd. My thigh was suddenly wet as another man's cum splattered upon it. Moaning, wailing, bucking, thrusting, and squirting, the great mob of men merged their voices with the bestial cries of the wild things. Somebody grabbed my cock with his cum-slicked hand and pounded hard. Another began to ride my butt crack with his cock, not going inside, but sliding his cock up my crevice. He delivered his cum shot to the small of my back. Hot and wet, it dribbled between my cheeks. More cum splattered upon me. Some hit my face just as my own orgasm approached.

Deep throbbing tingles rushed though the head of my cock. My lips curled back and my nostrils flared, as the deep pleasure that was almost painful in its intensity claimed me. My throbbing cock bucked in the fellow's hand and a great squirt of my hot seed painted his soft-haired chest. When I had finished spurting, I leaned into him. His lips puckered and his eyes closed in rapture. I licked his salty lips, and kissed him deeply. He responded with his tongue. He kissed me, probed with his tongue, and licked along my lips. He was licking the wet cum still running down my face.

As he licked, his erection poked my lower abdomen. His hands reached around me to caress my ass. Then he cupped my rounded buttocks, squeezing them like melons. Slowly I turned, but he had another idea. He stretched out upon the street, as men beyond counting were doing around us, and his cock jutted toward the starry sky. It glimmered bronze in the flickering torches. Above us the sound of the tongue trilling continued, subdued because the women were finding their own pleasure with each other. Briefly thinking of Lillake and hoping that she had found her bliss, I sat down upon the eager body.

"What is your name?" I asked as I arose and slid my slick butt crack along the tip of his cock.

"Enkidu."

"Enkidu, I, Zedek, shall ride your cock. Your seed shall be a part of my flesh."

Pushing hard with my asshole, I let my weight slide me downward. My asshole stretched, and a great heaviness filled me. As Mighty Horon, god of the tow of the underworld, pulled me down toward his hot core, the fullness within me grew. My cock erected rakish, trembling for a second release. With my asshole, I felt the meaty cock entering me as I dropped toward Enkidu's crotch. My buttocks touched his hips, flattening as my body demanded I go down all the way, and my ass filled with the entire length and breadth of the shaft of flesh.

Letting my full weight rest upon Enkidu, I savored the twin sensations of penetration and fullness. Rising exuberantly, I lifted to the height of his cock and carefully dropped again. Again I rose, gripping with my asshole, and plunged faster downward. Enkidu, moaning, stroked my thighs as I fucked his ample cock with my ass. My powerful thigh muscles carried me upward toward the stars and Mighty Horon brought me down to the satiety of man's flesh.

Enkidu closed his eyes in rapture. Spasms rushed through his body. Pleasure burned within me as well; a deep burning tickle thrilled up my ass. I was locked in orgasm, but not an orgasm of the cock. Enkidu shuddered, his face brazen with orgasmic twitches. Gripping his cock harder with my asshole, I rode my turbulent ecstasy. My cum dribbled as lather, foaming onto Enkidu's belly.

When Enkidu had come his all, he begged me to climb off him. "You have milked me, Zedek. You have milked me dry."

I lifted off and sprawled beside him. My asshole was sticky with cum, and I savored the sensation. I had hardly caught my breath when a muscled arm caught mine and lifted me to my feet. "No time for napping, stranger," he urged.

"I may be too exhausted," I whimpered. "I think that I drained my balls."

"There's always more to come, boy," he laughed. "But what I shall do to you will tire you no further." So saying, he pressed me against the wall and pulled my ass toward him. I thought that he meant to fuck my sore asshole, but he dropped to his knees and buried his face in my butt crack.

I gasped as his tongue licked my anal crevice. The sensation was wonderful, intoxicating, and enchanting. He was worshiping my asshole, and he was in no hurry. Slowly and luxuriously he licked, and after a long time during which I found myself growing aroused again, he settled upon my orifice. He probed my asshole, dilating my sphincter with his tongue. He pushed further, driving deeper inside. I surrendered myself to him utterly. Just as I bordered the state of rapture, wondering whether after a while I might practice the same craft upon him, three men distinguished by red ribbons called us to order.

"Serve the god," they shouted. "The hour has come. The moon is rising. Now we offer homage to Ur-Baal."

The men organized us. An old fellow had been placed upon my right hand. He was so ancient that he must have been around since the great flood. Still, his cock was thick and hard, and he bestowed a rakish grin upon me. "Squeeze it hard, boy. I am old and need firm strokes to bring me off."

A younger man to my left took hold of my cock. I had dallied with him beside the pool a few hours earlier. "Now I will make you come, Zedek."

"I have come twice already tonight," I informed him.

"You will come once more tonight," he informed me back. "We will coach you."

The old man addressed me again. "Listen, Zedek. Repeat after me, and do as I do."

"I shall," I promised as a strange rush fired me.

Standing in concentric circles, all facing toward the center, each man's right hand fastened upon the next cock, we intoned our boisterous fidelity to the Baalim.

The chant began softly. "Ur-Baal, Ur-Baal." I listened to the men, letting the simple but potent words wash over me. The chant grew more unison, louder. "Ur-Baal, Ur-Baal." I began chanting with the others, raising my voice to the quintessence of our gender. Surges rushed through me. I joined my voice to that of the other men. "Ur-Baal, Ur-Baal, Ur-Baal, Ur-Baal." Our voices rose and fell together, our cries more urgent. "Ur-Baal, Ur-Baal." Throbbing spasms rushed through me. The world seemed to unmake itself as great Sodom rang with the name of the god. "Ur-Baal, Ur-Baal."

The great mountains trembled as Baal rent cloud scud. Baal thundered. Baal flashed. Baal rained upon the city. "I alone give to mortal men the pleasures of the gods. I alone bring satisfaction to the world of men and women born unto flesh, surrender unto pleasure, and perish unto dust."

My body was in orgasm. Crinkles of pleasure tweaked me, yet the chant kept coming rhythmically from my mouth. My asshole was contracting and dilating as if I were being fucked by the god. My cock was in full orgasm. "Ur-Baal, Ur-Baal." I was caught up in orgasm, and yet I did not ejaculate. I did not until I came at one with all of the men of Sodom. "Ur-Baal, Ur-Baal." Our cum flew, drenching all.

❖

One morning after we had passed four phases of the moon in Sodom, King Bera summoned Lillake and me to his private chamber. Sitting around a table as equals, we drank a mug of strong black beer before the king would say why he called for us. Finally, he beckoned a servant to present some flat strips, which the king laid out on the table. Seeing our puzzlement, the king said, "It's the latest thing. Papyrus from Egypt. A scribe may write messages upon it. It is far more useful than impressing words in clay. I believe that this papyrus will revolutionize our communications system. A messenger can carry many messages written upon this reed paper."

"I see my name and Lillake's upon this papyrus."

"Ah, you read writing."

"I do."

"Well, I don't," Lillake snorted with significant vexation. "What does it mean?"

The king's eyes swelled with tears, and I thought that Lillake had hurt his feelings. But empathy rather than affront had made King Bera weep. "There is some good here," he said, "and more that will bring you pain."

Trying to read more than a few symbols upside down was worse than useless. "Tell us."

"I sent an epistle to Gomorrah to assure your loved ones that you are out of harm's way. Your parents send their greetings and bid you bide here in Sodom until it is safe to travel. Roving bands of marauders still think to please the renegade kings. Even travel by camel caravan can be hazardous."

"I, for one, am delighted to accept your hospitality for as long as it pleases you to keep us, King Bera."

"That would be forever," said the king. "However, I know that you yearn for your own people."

"True," Lillake said. "I often long for home, even though Sodom has become a second home to me. I shall happily sojourn here as long as necessary. Nammu and the other girls have been teaching me the ways of Sodom, and I find them most pleasing."

Gossip told that Lillake had developed a lickerish taste for the real estate between girlish thighs. Al'bram and Lhut had referred to that essential female organ as "the hair of her feet," a euphemism that made me chortle.

"You said there was also bad news," I urged, hoping to have the worst over and done. I was looking forward to a swimming date with a group of the local boys.

"Yes, Zedek." The king paused. "Your grandfather died the night you were taken captive."

Tears sprang into my eyes, but I felt a sense of relief as well. Mot had claimed Grandfather at last. A gifted thief and liar in his day, my grandfather had risen from a rude olive picker to a wealthy merchant. He had made our family prosperous, but he had hardly been of any use to himself during his final years.

"Your family arranged a grand funeral procession, and the multitudes from the surrounding neighborhoods turned out. During the procession, the people made great lamentation with mournful gestures and doleful moans. Your grandfather was buried in the family tomb with tin pins, bronze bracelets on both wrists, pottery vessels containing milk, wine, and millet, and a bronze spear with two knives."

I could picture the elaborate procession dominated by my wailing mother. Doubtless, she threw herself upon Grandfather's body while the neighbors looked on. Out of the public's sight, she would not personally enter the tomb. Our family tomb consisted of a deep underground corridor with rectangular rooms regularly spaced and sealed with stone slabs. Grandfather would have been placed in the third room beside the three wives he had outlived. The family reached the tomb by means of an elaborate square shaft that led down to the subterranean chambers.

"I am sorry, Zedek," Lillake commiserated. Then she asked, "Is everyone alive in my family? My mother must have been beside herself."

"Your families are well," King Bera continued. "But they report another death that touches both of you and, indeed, the entire city of Gomorrah."

"Ekron?" His words confirmed what I had known in my blood.

"Yes, Ekron, the inventor, was murdered by agents of the four kings of the North. He was killed and his workshop burned."

"Ekron's death is a tragic loss to all humanity."

"I liked the old fellow," Lillake said.

"Gone, gone, so much knowledge gone," I moaned.

The king left us to our grief. After a decent interval, somber servants escorted us back to our quarters.

An hour later, I was sprawled face-down beside the swimming pool. My body had grown evenly dark during my time in Sodom, a hue that attracted even more men. I received so many offers for extended stays at villas, dinner invitations, and propositions for hasty fucks that I could only accept the most tempting. Therefore, when a man chose the lounge next to me, I expected more of the same. He surprised me, however, for he did not propose a trip to view his olive press or a quick suck.

"I am Tursha, the Sodomite ambassador. King Bera has told me of your tragic loss, and I am heartily sorry to hear it. I hope that I can brighten your day somewhat."

Here it comes, I thought. *He shall offer to brighten my day be sticking his cock up my ass.* I was, nevertheless, wrong again.

"Your opportunity to return to Gomorrah, if you so desire, may not lie too far into the future. In perhaps two cycles of the moon god, the threat will have passed."

"What is King Bera going to do?"

The ambassador hesitated before explaining: "I met your grandfather," Tursha said. "Your father Abimelech has negotiated with me. I know that Gomorrahans are wise people. So anything I tell you, Zedek, must remain between us."

"I do assure you, Tursha."

"The Kings of the Five Cities of the Plain have agreed that we cannot, at present, match the might of the four kings of the north. Therefore, the Pentapolis of the Vale of Siddim will pay the tribute Chedorlaomer demands."

"Appeasement," I spat.

"Yes, such propitiation is unpleasant to us all."

"Appeasement only provokes the appeased to further aggression."

"True, but appeasing Chedorlaomer, Amraphel, Arioch, and

Tidal will give us time to prepare. Admah, Bala, Gomorrah, Sodom, and Zeboyim will pay tribute while we secretly prepare our rebellion. Eventually we will control and spread our ways of love, peace, and freedom through not only the Vale of Siddim, but the entire Fertile Crescent."

"Then you foresee a prosperous future for the Cities of the Plain. You think that those with wit in trade will prosper mightily?"

"To be sure. Our future is bright."

I smiled at him. "Why have I not met you before today, Tursha?" I asked, suddenly stirred.

In answer, Tursha laid his hand upon my naked rump. "You have met me, Zedek. You became well acquainted with me one night during the street revels, although you did not see my face." *Where had I heard that joke before?* "I was close behind you for a considerable period. Very close behind you indeed."

In my asshole, my flesh remembered one outstanding cock that had stretched me deliciously, burrowed deeply, stroked blissfully, and pumped extravagantly. Yes, I had met Tursha.

❖

Seven guards accompanied our group across the plains. Lillake and I rode upon carts laden with papyrus from Egypt, a wonderful cloth from lands beyond the encircling ocean, and other gifts from King Bera to King Birsha. We were small group, but I was imagining vast caravans trading from city to city. The arrival of peacetime inspired grandiose visions.

"I cannot wait to see my home again," Lillake said. "But I am sorry to leave the girls in Sodom. Nammu knew how to use her tongue."

"Where did she put her tongue?" a man asked.

"Everywhere."

I did not need any more information, but my fellow Gomorrahan seemed eager to hear more. "Did she lick your asshole?"

"Enough!" I cried. Unlike Lillake, who had been so eager to hear the details of my same-sex follies, I did not want to know about hers. Fortunately, after she had discovered the Sapphic delights, she had become less curious about male-to-male thrills.

I spent the remainder of our trip planning my great scheme. If

I sprang my ideas upon my father suddenly, he would reject them out of hand. However, I could seduce him into it—seduce him in the metaphorical sense, of course.

It seemed the entire city of Gomorrah turned out for our homecoming. My father stood just behind my mother and brother. My family was waving the fronds of date palms, as was most of the crowd. To my surprise, both Ucal and Ithiel were there in front, along with their new wives. That they had acquired wives did not surprise me. Often lads who did not fully relish the experience of being Dogs in the ziggurat married soon after their holy sacrifice. I assumed that the two felt the need to reestablish their masculinity—or what they thought to be masculinity. For my part, I considered the way I took cock was more masculine than planting my stem in any woman. The flax merchant Lemuel greeted me as if he were an old lover, which he was not unless in his dreams. Kuwari of the Fruit and Spice Emporium was there, as was Fat Rephaim, taking a morning's leave from his bathhouse.

Lillake and I were wearing golden breechclouts, among the gifts King Bera had bestowed upon us at our ceremonial departure from Sodom. It was not customary for females to wear only breechclouts in Gomorrah, so the average Gomorrahan woman sneered at Lillake's scandalous attire, all the while twisting with envy. Lillake was a style setter that day. Even my own mother was exchanging green glances with others of her sex. The tailors winked among themselves and counted their profits before they had threaded a needle.

That night the House of Abimelech celebrated with a grand feast. We started with pigeon pie before the main courses of roasted mutton, venison, and goat. Corn, millet, and wheat had been baked into flat breads or honeyed treats. Eating and drinking, our family, our friends, and our neighbors consumed beer, crushed melon, wine spiced with poppy juice, seasoned beans, creamed cucumbers, goat cheese, cow butter, quail eggs, grapes in honey, dates, and fluffed pastries.

I drank too much wine and beer, as did my young brother Rhadamanthus. Issaruutunu carried him to his bed just before my father and my mother invited our servants to eat with the family. Naked Kullaa was seated beside me by design. I supposed that I was expected to penetrate her, but the desire was not there. Of course, I had penetrated men in Sodom, and I had been myself penetrated as I did so. Nonetheless, I could hardly bring myself to slide my cock into a woman—even if she offered her ass in the way of a man.

I did not venture from the house until late the next afternoon. The city was abuzz with the news. Gomorrah was going to pay heavy tribute to the unscrupulous kings of the North; Chedorlaomer, Amraphel, Arioch, and Tidal, and many citizens were questioning King Birsha's decision, even though all knew that he had agreed with the will of the Pentapolis of the Vale of Siddim. Some even argued that the town elders should send messengers to Mamre, where Al'bram resided, beseeching the Hebrew War Chief's intervention. With an effort, I held my silence, though I told anyone who would listen that our king was wise, and that I supported his decisions in all ways.

Finally, I ended my day at the bathhouse of Fat Rephaim. Naked in the foaming hot water, I looked up at the proprietor, who droned on in his ignorant manner: "Youse welcome, Zedek, youse welcome always. Never a clam will I take from youse."

"I appreciate your generosity, Rephaim," I said.

"Did you meet the king of Sodom, Zedek?" a young man asked.

"Meet him, Onan? I stuck my cock into King Bera's ass. I fucked the king and shot him full of cum."

"Do tell, Zedek. Do tell."

And thus I told of the night I screwed the King of Sodom while taking for the second time the thick cock of Tursha, the Sodomite ambassador:

"It was nearly morning. The men of Sodom had spent the night in revel. No women were left upon the balconies to haunt us with their tongue trilling. They had gone to form their own human chain. Shahar was shining above and a faint glow appeared in the east. A rooster crowed. King Bera stood erect before the men of the city, and commanded that all men should link together."

"And all did?" Onan asked.

"All save Lhut, an unpleasant fellow who showed his face only to curse the king's command."

"You claim that every man in Sodom plugged his cock into the man in front, and they formed a chain behind the king? So who stuck his cock into the king?"

"I was behind the king. Tursha pushed me into position. I had never pushed my cock into a man's ass, but Tursha held me in place. As my cock touched the king's asshole, King Bera bent, and Tursha gripped my waist. 'Shove it into me, Zedek,' the monarch commanded. Giving me not a chance to respond, he drove his butt back and impaled himself. Tursha's hands held my buttocks in place so my cock slid easily into the king's grainy hole.

"I had never felt anything like it. Like any boy from time out of mind, I had stroked my cock, but I had never felt the tight grasping friction of the human ass. I shoved back, impaling my ass upon Tursha's thickness. I thrust forward, going to the hilt in King Bera.

"'Oh,' I gasped. 'Ah, ah.' Not the most intellectual of ejaculations, but I was too sexually inflamed to invoke my intellect's higher powers. I thrust forward, and thrust back. I fucked the king's ass with the first half stroke, and fucked my ass with the second.

"Behind King Bera, me, and Tursha stretched a line of men as long as the male population of Sodom. I thrust my cock into the king's ass, impaling him to the hilt of my cock. I pushed back, taking the ambassador Tursha's cock all the way. He filled me as no man had ever dilated my ass.

"Ripples of pleasure rushed up my cock, while gigantic waves of pleasure broke in my ass. The men chanted 'Ur-Baal, Ur-Baal' as they thrust and lurched together."

"Did you come?"

"I shot my cum into the ass of the king of Sodom. The ambassador came into me." I paused to let the images intrigue them. "Why can we not embrace such freedom in Gomorrah?"

"That stuff's best confined to the ziggurat," Lemuel muttered, shaken to his core.

"Sounds risky," the youth Onan said.

"Risk is the word, indeed, young fellow," said Professor Carmi from the Academy of Resheph. "The ways of Sodom are not our ways."

"Butt-fucking at the right time and right place is pleasing to Marduk," the new husband Ithiel pontificated, "but I would not care to see it practiced in our streets."

"Youse gotta know, Zedek," Fat Rephaim chipped in. "It can't happen here."

Such words merely served to stiffen my resolve to put my grand scheme into motion. That night I began to drop hints to my father. "Father," I said. "With the appeasement, loathsome as it may be, comes opportunities for trade that never existed before now."

The next night I mentioned how trade routes would be opening up for those of an enterprising vein. I described the greater ease of moving goods among the five cities and even farther afield. "Gomorrah could trade with Memphis, with Thebes, and with Ur. We could import goods from Babylon, and Gaza, and Tyre. Not to mention the opportunity to export brick, olive oil, and wine."

My father was nodding in agreement by the time I finished. I let him mull the idea for several days before I popped the question. "It is time that I joined you in prospering this family, Father," I offered.

He smiled, though doubt clouded his eyes. "Our businesses are well managed at the moment, Zedek. Do you mean to start work at the winepress?"

"Father, the frivolity of my youth is passing. We have been discussing the opportunities for trade. The House of Abimelech should dominate the business of shipping goods among the cities of the plain. Since the appeasement is in effect and small merchants are no longer being attacked, vast caravans could transport goods among the cities, buying and selling."

"Caravans?"

"Long caravans. Caravans stretching as far as the eye can see."

"Caravans," Father repeated dreamily. "We could carry our own goods: our wine, our grapes, our dates, our olive oil."

"Of course, Father. And we could buy goods to sell in Gomorrah. Did you feel the strange cloth I brought? Do you know how many women and men in Gomorrah want clothing from that fabric?"

"We could ship the goods of other merchants," my father enthused. "We could charge fees that covered our own costs, and yet gave our merchants margin for profit."

"We would become the wealthiest house in the Valley of Salt," I assured him.

"But who could we trust to drive these caravans?"

"I will drive them. Perhaps, in time, Rhadamanthus. I would trust some of my personal servants; Abishalom, Maachah, Jeroboam, and Ahaziah have the potential to drive caravans—to varying degrees. And our caravans shall be well defended. Our men shall carry swords of bronze and sharp knives and bright spears. To guard against embezzlement, we have the new means of communication. See; I have drawn a plan upon the papyrus."

"Can we convince the other cities to trade with us?"

"Of course. King Bera is my ally. I am a personal friend of the Sodomite ambassador Tursha, who has many acquaintances in all cities, and is even known to the great rulers Hammurabi and Sargon. I have met the Hebrew war chief Al'bram."

My father's face flushed with enthusiasm. Little did he know that I had an ulterior motive. I was looking forward to caravan stopovers in Sodom. However, my scheme would work financially, so my motives were not utterly carnal. I had plotted all upon sheets of the miraculous papyrus. As long as the peace prevailed, I would enrich our family.

"I must think how to proceed in this endeavor," my father said.

"Here is what I have discovered," I offered, showing him the papyrus. "We can purchase the camels at a discount. Howdahs are costly, but necessary. We will not need many, but we may want to charge passengers for safe transport. Equipment, too, I have priced with the merchants, based upon discounts in shipping charges." I showed him the paper. "So when do we start?"

"First thing in the morning, Zedek," my father said, hugging me.

Gazing into the bright future, I predicted frequent visits to the wondrous city of Sodom, where men spent their nights pursuing pleasures more scorching than fire and brimstone.

NOTES

Accuracy: "The Valley of Salt" is a work of fiction, untainted by historical accuracy. The standard interpretations argue that the kings of the north exact tribute from the five cities of the plain for twelve years. After the cities rebel, Chedorlaomer's soldiers capture Lot, which precipitates his rescue by Abraham and his 318 draftees. I have changed that order of events so that the capture comes before the twelve years of appeasement.

Baal: This word literally means owner, and thus does refer to a general god or a specific god of a region, though some sources make him the brother of the Hebrew god Yahweh. The Baal of my fictional Gomorrah is Marduk, and to him the Dog Boys make due obeisance.

Baalim: plural of Baal (the feminine form is Baalat, a goddess of healing)

Anat: virgin goddess of war and strife
Asherah: wife of the Hebrew god Yahweh
Astarte: goddess of sexual love, a star goddess (Astarat, Astoreth)
Dagon: god of crop fertility and grain
Yahweh, El, El Shaddai: the Elohim (plural), the Hebrew God
Hadad: god of storms
Hammon: god of fertility
Horon: god of the pull of the Earth (gravity)
Ishat: goddess of fire
Ishtar: goddess of sexual love, a star goddess (Inanna)
Kotharat: goddesses of marriage and pregnancy
Kothar-wa-Khasis: god of craftsmanship
Melqart: god of the underworld
Moloch: god of fire
Mot: god of death
Nikkal-wa-Ib: goddess of orchards and fruit

Pazuzu: king of the wind demons
Qadeshtu: goddess of love
Resheph: god of plague and of healing
Samael: archangel of accusation, seduction, and destruction
Shahar: goddess of the dawn (the morning star)
Shalim: god of the dusk (the evening star)
Shamayim: god of the heavens
Shapash: goddess of the sun
Yarikh: god of the moon

Dog: An anally passive male homosexual, whether temporarily in religious sacrifice or in lifetime dedication. Also a homosexual prostitute; i.e., Deuteronomy 23:18 refers to "the price of a dog."

Hebrews: I have taken liberties with Hebrew names. The names used by most readers of Genesis, Abraham or Abram, I have changed to Al'bram. Lot or Lut became Lhut. I called Lhut's wife R'hab. I had to decide how many daughters Lhut has. According to some myths, two daughters remained in Sodom to be incinerated along with the rest of the town, while the other two went along with Lhut and supposedly bore their father's children. I called the daughters Ereshkigal, Nammu, Hannahannah, and Ninanna.

Lillake: Another name for Lilith, the mythical first wife of Adam.

Zedek: The Hebrew name for the planet Jupiter, Melchizedek (Adoni-Zedek, Zaduk) is a mysterious figure mentioned in Genesis 14:18-20, Psalm 110:4, and Hebrews 5: 6, 10; 6: 20; 7: 1, 10, 11, 15, 17, 21. Other documents concerning this character include Dead Sea Scroll 11Q13, the Nag Hammadi, the Midrash, the Urantia Book, the Second Book of Enoch, and the Book of Mormon. My Zedek differs from all versions of Melchizedek, yet it is from him that the myths spring.

Ziggurat: A step pyramid with terraces. Each story is smaller than the one below and glazed with a different color. The flat top is reached by way of a long exterior stair.

CONTRIBUTORS

DALE CHASE has written male erotica for thirteen years with nearly one hundred stories in magazines and fifty in anthologies, most recently in *Hot Jocks*, *Hot Daddies*, and *I Like To Watch* from Cleis Press and *Tented: Gay Erotic Tales From Under The Big Top* from Lethe Press. Upcoming stories will appear in *Wings: Subversive Gay Angel Erotica*, *Erotica Exotica: Tales of Sex, Magic, & the Supernatural,* and *Riding The Rails: Locomotive Lust and Carnal Cabooses,* from Bold Strokes Books. Dale has two story collections in print: *The Company He Keeps: Victorian Gentlemen's Erotica* (Bold Strokes Books) and *If The Spirit Moves You: Ghostly Gay Erotica* (Lethe Press). Chase lives near San Francisco and is at work on an erotica western novel. Check her out at dalechasestrokes. com.

DAVID HOLLY lives, moves, and has his being in Portland, Oregon, and environs. He is fascinated by the human penchant for odd mythologies, bizarre rituals, diverse religions, forlorn hopes, and broken dreams. He lives in a garish apartment with multihued walls hung with Haitian paintings and shelved with two thousand books. Sharing the apartment are sundry fur-bearing fellow mortals. He is exceptionally fond of strong coffee, red wine, English bitters, rich stout, inverted roller coasters, nude beaches, and hot-looking guys. He wears bright colors, tight slacks, exotic underwear, and slinky swim briefs. He is joyously pagan and loves making merry in heathen celebrations, marching in pride parades, and frolicking naked on Collins Beach. Find out more about David Holly and his numerous publications at facebook.com/david.holly2 and gaywriter. org.

JEFF MANN'S poetry, fiction, and essays have appeared in many anthologies and literary journals. He has published three award-winning poetry chapbooks: *Bliss*, *Mountain Fireflies*, and *Flint Shards from Sussex*; three full-length books of poetry: *Bones Washed with Wine*, *On the Tongue*, and *Ash: Poems from Norse Mythology*; two collections of personal essays: *Edge: Travels of an Appalachian Leather Bear* and *Binding the God: Ursine Essays from the Mountain South*; a novel, *Fog: A Novel of Desire and Reprisal*; a novella, *Devoured*, included in *Masters of Midnight: Erotic Tales of the Vampire*; a book of poetry and memoir, *Loving Mountains, Loving Men*; and a volume of short fiction, *A History of Barbed Wire*, which won a Lambda Literary Award. He teaches creative writing at Virginia Tech in Blacksburg, Virginia.

SIMON SHEPPARD, acclaimed by *San Francisco* magazine as "our erotica king," is the author of the forthcoming novel *The Dirty Boys Club*, and of three collections of short stories: *Sodomy*; *In Deep*; and *Hotter Than Hell and Other Stories*, winner of the Erotic Authors Association Award. His nonfiction books include *Kinkorama* and *Sex Parties 101*, and an anthology he edited, *Homosex: Sixty Years of Gay Erotica*, won the Lambda Literary Award. He also edited *Leatherman* and co-edited *Rough Stuff* and *Roughed Up*. In addition, his work has been published in more than 300 anthologies, including a record-breaking seventeen editions of the *Best Gay Erotica* series. He lives in San Francisco, watches old noir movies on TCM, and hangs out somewhat disreputably at www.simonsheppard.com.

About the Editor

RICHARD LABONTÉ (tattyhill@gmail.com), when he's not skimming dozens of anthology submissions a month (and relishing a few), or reviewing one hundred or so books a year for Q Syndicate, or turning turgid bureaucratic prose into comprehensible English for the Inter-American Development Bank or the Reeves of Renfrew County, Ontario, or coordinating the judging of the Lambda Literary Awards, or crafting the best croutons ever at his weekend work in a Bowen Island recovery center kitchen, likes to startle deer as he walks terrier/schnauzer Zak, accompanied by his husband, Asa, through the island's temperate rainforest. In season, he fills pails with salmonberries, blackberries, and huckleberries. Yum. Since 1997, he has edited almost forty erotic anthologies, though "pornographer" was not an original career goal.

Books Available From Bold Strokes Books

Sheltering Dunes by Radclyffe. The seventh in the award-winning Provincetown Tales. The pasts, presents, and futures of three women collide in a single moment that will alter all their lives forever. (978-1-60282-573-4)

Holy Rollers by Rob Byrnes. Partners in life and crime Grant Lambert and Chase LaMarca assemble a team of gay and lesbian criminals to steal millions from a right-wing mega-church, but the gang's plans are complicated by an "ex-gay" conference, the FBI, and a corrupt reverend with his own plans for the cash. (978-1-60282-578-9)

History's Passion: Stories of Sex Before Stonewall, edited by Richard Labonté. Four acclaimed erotic authors re-imagine the past...Welcome to the hidden queer history of men loving men not so very long—and centuries—ago. (978-1-60282-576-5)

Lucky Loser by Yolanda Wallace. Top tennis pros Sinjin Smythe and Laure Fortescue reach Wimbledon desperate to claim tennis's crown jewel, but will their feelings for each other get in the way? (978-1-60282-575-8)

Mystery of The Tempest: A Fisher Key Adventure by Sam Cameron. Twin brothers Denny and Steven Anderson love helping people and fighting crime alongside their sheriff dad on sun-drenched Fisher Key, Florida, but Denny doesn't dare tell anyone he's gay, and Steven has secrets of his own to keep. (978-1-60282-579-6)

Better Off Red: Vampire Sorority Sisters Book 1 by Rebekah Weatherspoon. Every sorority has its secrets, and college freshman Ginger Carmichael soon discovers that her pledge is more than a bond of sisterhood—it's a lifelong pact to serve six bloodthirsty demons with a lot more than nutritional needs. (978-1-60282-574-1)

Detours by Jeffrey Ricker. Joel Patterson is heading to Maine for his mother's funeral, and his high school friend Lincoln has invited himself along on the ride—and into Joel's bed—but when the ghost of Joel's mother joins the trip, the route is likely to be anything but straight. (978-1-60282-577-2)

Three Days by L.T. Marie. In a town like Vegas where anything can happen, Shawn and Dakota find that the stakes are love at all costs, and it's a gamble neither can afford to lose. (978-1-60282-569-7)

Swimming to Chicago by David-Matthew Barnes. As the lives of the adults around them unravel, high school students Alex and Robby form an unbreakable bond, vowing to do anything to stay together—even if it means leaving everything behind. (978-1-60282-572-7)

Hostage Moon by AJ Quinn. Hunter Roswell thought she had left her past behind, until a serial killer begins stalking her. Can FBI profiler Sara Wilder help her find her connection to the killer before he strikes on blood moon? (978-1-60282-568-0)

Erotica Exotica: Tales of Sex, Magic, and the Supernatural, edited by Richard Labonté. Today's top gay erotica authors offer sexual thrills and perverse arousal, spooky chills, and magical orgasms in these stories exploring arcane mystery, supernatural seduction, and sex that haunts in a manner both weird and wondrous. (978-1-60282-570-3)

Blue by Russ Gregory. Matt and Thatcher find themselves in the crosshairs of a psychotic killer stalking gay men in the streets of Austin, and only a 103-year-old nursing home resident holds the key to solving the murders—but can she give up her secrets in time to save them? (978-1-60282-571-0)

Balance of Forces: Toujours Ici by Ali Vali. Immortal Kendal Richoux's life began during the reign of Egypt's only female pharaoh, and history has taught her the dangers of getting too close to anyone who hasn't harnessed the power of time, but as she prepares for the most important battle of her long life, can she resist her attraction to Piper Marmande? (978-1-60282-567-3)

Wings: Subversive Gay Angel Erotica, edited by Todd Gregory. A collection of powerfully written tales of passion and desire centered on the aching beauty of angels. (978-1-60282-565-9)

Contemporary Gay Romances by Felice Picano. This collection of short fiction from legendary novelist and memoirist Felice Picano are as different from any standard "romances" as you can get, but they will linger in the mind and memory. (978-1-60282-639-7)

Pirate's Fortune: Supreme Constellations Book Four by Gun Brooke. Set against the backdrop of war, captured mercenary Weiss Kyakh is persuaded to work undercover with bio-android Madisyn Pimm, which foils her plans to escape, but kindles unexpected love. (978-1-60282-563-5)

Sex and Skateboards by Ashley Bartlett. Sex and skateboards and surfing on the California coast. What more could anyone want? Alden McKenna thinks that's all she needs, until she meets Weston Duvall. (978-1-60282-562-8)

Waiting in the Wings by Melissa Brayden. Jenna has spent her whole life training for the stage, but the one thing she didn't prepare for was Adrienne. Is she ready to sacrifice what she's worked so hard for in exchange for a shot at something much deeper? (978-1-60282-561-1)

Suite Nineteen by Mel Bossa. Psychic Ben Lebeau moves into Shilts Manor, where he meets seductive Lennox Van Kemp and his clan of Métis—guardians of a spiritual conspiracy dating back to Christ. But are Ben's psychic abilities strong enough to save him? (978-1-60282-564-2)

Speaking Out: LGBTQ Youth Stand Up, edited by Steve Berman. Inspiring stories written for and about LGBTQ teens of overcoming adversity (against intolerance and homophobia) and experiencing life after "coming out." (978-1-60282-566-6)

Forbidden Passions by MJ Williamz. Passion burns hotter when it's forbidden, and the fire between Katie Prentiss and Corrine Staples in antebellum Louisiana is raging out of control. (978-1-60282-641-0)

Harmony by Karis Walsh. When Brook Stanton meets a beautiful musician who threatens the security of her conventional, predetermined future, will she take a chance on finding the harmony only love creates? (978-1-60282-237-5)

nightrise by Nell Stark and Trinity Tam. In the third book in the everafter series, when Valentine Darrow loses her soul, Alexa must cross continents to find a way to save her. (978-1-60282-238-2)

Men of the Mean Streets, edited by Greg Herren and J.M. Redmann. Dark tales of amorality and criminality by some of the top authors of gay mysteries. (978-1-60282-240-5)

Women of the Mean Streets, edited by J.M. Redmann and Greg Herren. Murder, mayhem, sex, and danger—these are the stories of the women who dare to tackle the mean streets. (978-1-60282-241-2)

Firestorm by Radclyffe. Firefighter paramedic Mallory "Ice" James isn't happy when the undisciplined Jac Russo joins her command, but lust isn't something either can control—and they soon discover ice burns as fiercely as flame. (978-1-60282-232-0)

The Best Defense by Carsen Taite. When socialite Aimee Howard hires former homicide detective Skye Keaton to find her missing niece, she vows not to mix business with pleasure, but she soon finds Skye hard to resist. (978-1-60282-233-7)

After the Fall by Robin Summers. When the plague destroys most of humanity, Taylor Stone thinks there's nothing left to live for, until she meets Kate, a woman who makes her realize love is still alive and makes her dream of a future she thought was no longer possible. (978-1-60282-234-4)

Accidents Never Happen by David-Matthew Barnes. From the moment Albert and Joey meet by chance beneath a train track on a street in Chicago, a domino effect is triggered, setting off a chain reaction of murder and tragedy. (978-1-60282-235-1)

In Plain View, edited by Shane Allison. Best-selling gay erotica authors create the stories of sex and desire modern readers crave. (978-1-60282-236-8)